*For Susan, who watched this book take shape for half a lifetime.*

*And for Kirstin, who never lost faith that Vitya & Co
would see the light of day.*

"Il a été permis de craindre que la Révolution, comme Saturne, dévorât successivement tous ses enfants." Lamartine, *Histoire des Girondins*, 1847.

"Women are, of course, superior organisms to men, so men are likely to take second place to women intellectually once the reign of brute force is over... A woman's body may be weaker, but at the same time it has far greater powers of resistance." Vera Rozalskaya in Chernyshevsky's *What is to be Done?* 1863.

"The conclusion I reached was a direct contradiction of my original idea: starting from unlimited freedom, I arrived at unlimited despotism." Shigalyov in Dostoevsky's *The Possessed*, 1871.

"Of course we won't be alive to enjoy it, but, as far as I'm concerned, the whole purpose of our existence must be to create a beautiful life in the future; we work and we suffer, certainly we must suffer, to create it. Perhaps suffering like that is the only happiness we shall ever achieve." Vershinin in Chekhov's *Three Sisters*, 1900.

# Chapter 1

## I

Anna was surprised. "A gun?" she said. "What sort of gun?"

"A Smith and Wesson. Could you get it past the guard?"

"Probably. Unless they're searching women now," Anna replied.

"Apparently they are."

"That's what I read in the newspaper, but the General has connections. Everybody goes to his receptions – maids of honour even. Who's going to search them?"

"Maids of honour? That hardly applies to you – unless I'm misinformed?"

"I'm on the list," she replied with a tight smile, "though I'll never be chosen."

He nodded with ironic respect.

"As far as the General is concerned," she added, "I'm a relative."

"Then you can get in? With the gun?" he pressed. "A relative and rejected maid of honour won't be searched?"

"I haven't agreed about the gun."

"Not yet. That's what we want you to promise – the gun will go to the ball."

"It's suicide," Anna grimaced.

"We don't think so."

"If I'm caught?"

"That's not the plan."

"I take the gun in, and I don't get caught. You call that a plan?"

"If we thought there was a risk, we wouldn't use you."

For a second she didn't reply. "No risk? Because I'm just a woman? Because I'd tell tales to the Third Section?"

"More or less."

"I might hold out. It's not impossible."

"A life of luxury hardly prepares you," he paused for effect, "for the Sclusselburg."

"You know nothing about my life."

"Even so, no one holds out. No one."

"So a gun – and no risk. What are you after?"

"It intrigues us – the fact that someone like you can walk in on people like the Drentelns. Come and go as you please. And perhaps you can take a friend with you – someone they *will* search."

She took the point immediately. "And pass him the gun? Once we're both inside?"

"You pass him the gun. At the reception," he agreed.

"And who is 'he'? A nobody? Someone they can rip apart and who won't talk because he's got nothing to tell?"

"It would make sense."

"It makes no sense at all. I get him an invitation. We arrive together. He's searched. I'm not. I slip the gun to him so he can – what's the word? – *execute* the General. He gets arrested and they forget about me? Never. It's suicide for both of us."

"No, no, no," he objected. "Don't jump to conclusions. This isn't an execution – it's reconnaissance. Testing their defences. Seeing what might be possible."

"But listen, Alexander Alexandrovich…"

He flung himself back in his chair and threw up his hands in despair. And he was right – she had no patience with his play-acting, but he was right.

"Have you ever asked yourself," he groaned, "why the Committee issues and reissues the rules? To keep us safe. I don't call you Anna Petrovna for a good reason. You have a code-name. And so do I. For heaven's sake be more careful."

It was true. So many people in the Movement knew her name, knew her habits and her friends. He was the *Guardian*.

She was the *Snowman*. No one ever called her that, apart from Alexander Alexandrovich. But why not? The rules made sense. Revolution was impossible without discipline. And they had none – none at all.

"This young man, code-name for the time-being, *Escort*," she remarked sarcastically. "If he arrives with me and anything happens, then I'm suspect. Automatically."

"Nothing will happen. I told you already – this is reconnaissance."

"Since when has the Committee been so cautious?"

"Since August. Since Kravchinski."

Kravchinski. She'd met him half a dozen times – an illiterate hothead.

"He killed his man," the Guardian explained, "in a crowded street. But he had a plan – to escape. And it worked."

"I know. I paid for it."

"You're always generous, Snowman."

She nodded in agreement. "Kravchinski wasn't cautious. He was lucky."

"But he made *us* cautious. Put it this way: a suicide-killing looks like despair. Escape makes us look invincible."

"So no more suicides?"

"The Committee has never ordered suicide, as you know full well. In any case, you're not here to argue policy. You're here to answer a question."

She heard a change in the Guardian's voice – a sudden ring of authority, authority over her. She bridled immediately.

"Can you do what we ask? Get the gun in, find out how the place is guarded and pass the gun to… Escort – the name is fine. And, as I said, plan an escape. For Escort. You won't need to escape. When the time comes to execute the General, you'll get the gun in, but you won't arrive with Escort. And Escort will be somebody else altogether."

Anna glowered at the man opposite her. He had folded his arms and tipped back on his chair, certain that she must agree. "I'll think about it," she said.

"No," he contradicted. "We haven't asked you to do anything like this for years. The Committee has made its decision. You're being…" He paused. "You're being mobilised."

Alexander Alexandrovich Mikhailov, the Guardian. She knew nothing about his history or even where he lived, which was how it was supposed to be. But she knew his type – landowners in a small way, ruined when the emancipation took away their serfs. The emancipation and their own ineptitude. Profligate sons. Unmarriageable daughters. The Movement was rotten with them. And now, for a while, he had her in his grasp, and he intended to squeeze her.

"You find the man," she said curtly. "Leave the rest to me."


# II


Anna took his arm. "Well?" she asked.

"They checked everything. Thoroughly. You?"

"They looked in my bag," she said. "That's all."

"Good."

A magnificently dressed woman and an army officer wearing the Order of Alexander Nevsky joined the line behind them, close enough to hear a careless word. Ahead of them thirty people were standing on the red porphyry staircase, most of the men in military dress. Some wore the dark uniform of the Justice Department, glittering with gold at the neck and cuffs. Only one was dressed like Anna's companion in black evening dress. The women were *en grande toilette*: bare shoulders, tight waist, a heavy ruffled train, and something expensive at the throat. Autumn 1878. Nowhere in the world was the crush more fashionable than in St Petersburg, not even in Paris.

The line wasn't moving. Silence looked awkward – they'd have to improvise. Anna glanced at the young man appraisingly. Presentable – definitely. He was clean-shaven in the new fashion, without even a moustache. It wasn't exactly a gesture of rebellion, like a girl bobbing her hair, but his shaved chin marked him as a 'new man,' the only one in the line as far as she could see. It was three days since she'd first met him. Then he'd been dressed in a shabby student uniform and down-at-heel shoes. A nobody. But she'd looked just as nondescript in her brown dress, like a disagreeable governess. They'd met in one of the safe houses the Movement kept for such meetings, a grubby apartment near the Haymarket. Tonight, though, she needn't blush for her companion. And, as she'd warned him, she'd metamorphosed into the Countess Shestakova, elegant and at home in the glittering line. Except she had a revolver taped to the inside of her leg.

The line moved. They climbed two more porphyry stairs.

"And how's Tobik?" she asked, wondering what he'd say, this Viktor Pavlovich Pelin they'd thrust upon her. Vitya for short, he'd told her. If he was to play-act her cousin, she'd have to make at least that concession to familiarity.

"Tobik?" He thought for a second. "Much better. I've forbidden Aunt Betty to feed him mushrooms."

She laughed, surprised. Anna seldom laughed aloud. When she did, it was a sweet sound, cultivated and attractive. A Gentleman of the Bedchamber turned to look down at her. His wife turned too, studied Anna for a second, and whispered something to her husband. The man bowed to Anna with a hint of obsequiousness. She acknowledged the contact with a nod and turned away.

They moved upward again, several quick steps. At last Anna could see the reception line drawn up in front of the ballroom: two officials from the Ministry, the General's wife, a young girl, probably the General's daughter, and a suffocatingly fat man in the uniform of an admiral. The General was not there.

They reached the top of the stairs, gossiping about lap-dogs in general and Tobik in particular. This Vitya, as he called himself, was amusing, she decided. A tall footman dressed in the style of Catherine II asked their names and announced them in a nasal bellow. Anna went ahead, smiling as she shook the fat, gloved hand of the admiral and then the hand of his nondescript neighbour. Vitya followed. She glanced back to see how he was managing. He had no practiced social smile, but he seemed sufficiently at ease. She saw him shake the admiral's hand and move to the second link in the reception line.

"Welcome," the man said. Like Vitya, he was not in uniform. "I don't think I've seen you at one of His Excellency's receptions before." She saw him retain Vitya's hand and study his face with sharp eyes, trying perhaps to learn it.

"No," Vitya replied. "You couldn't have seen me. This is my first time." He spoke without pertness, quietly intimate. Better than she'd expected.

Anna shook hands now with the General's wife. Anna was a distant cousin of the Drentelns as she'd told the Guardian. The General's wife was faded enough to enjoy the reflected glow of young and beautiful relations. The two women clasped hands in a skilful imitation of delight, the fingers of their white gloves interlocking. The line stopped while the General's wife satisfied herself about Anna's whereabouts for the last year – or was it two? As Anna moved on, the General's wife shook hands with Vitya and told him he was welcome. She eyed him inquisitively but asked no questions.

Anna shook hands silently with the General's sullen daughter and a whiskery collegiate councillor from the Ministry of Justice. She looked back – the girl was plucking up courage to say something to Vitya after the briefest of handshakes. She saw him reply. She heard the girl's suppressed giggle and the word *maybe*. The General's wife smiled gratefully at the young man, and nodded to Anna – it wasn't everyone who earned a giggle from little Tatyana.

One more handshake and he was free. Casually she took his arm, and they moved into the ballroom, her silk train swishing across the floor behind them. A string quartet was playing 'Death and the Maiden' with expensive precision –

General Drenteln and his wife spent a lot of money on their music. A footman offered them champagne, Vitya took a glass, but Anna declined as custom required.

Anna set her face in an impeccable smile though she was anything but happy – the gun was working loose. She'd felt the tape slacken on the stairs. The day before in her dressing room she'd tried it all out – the gun, the tape, walking around. But she'd only walked on the level. Why hadn't she thought of the stairs?

"Viktor Pavlovich," she said. "It's coming loose. Walk with me now. But slowly."

One of Anna's hands rested in the crook of Vitya's arm. In the other she dangled an ivory fan. Friends greeted her; she introduced the young man casually – her cousin studying at the university. The friends were curious. Vitya's cousinship wasn't nearly enough to explain his presence at the General's reception. Anna held her body motionless as she gossiped, not daring to laugh lest she dislodge the gun. It was a heavy gun: a Smith and Wesson 44, the gun bear hunters use for the *coup de grâce*. Anna felt the tape slacken and unravel a fraction more. She imagined the noise the gun would make if it hit the wooden floor of the ballroom. Would it go off? Would it? She didn't know. How could she be so miserably prepared for such a simple job?

They were in the middle of the dance floor. A colonnade of green marble columns bordered the room – it was fifteen yards away. "It's very loose," Anna whispered. "Get me to the dressing room. Over there." She was walking stiffly, her knees together. The gun was between her thighs, tangled somehow in her underclothes.

They reached the colonnade as the quartet intoned the last andante chords of 'Death and the Maiden.' Carpet under her feet. The shelter of the columns.

"I don't think it'll go off," she whispered, trying to keep the panic out of her voice. She'd seen gunshot wounds in Switzerland, when she'd trained there as a doctor. And she'd taped the gun with the barrel pointing upward. "It's carpet here? That'll help."

"It wasn't cocked?" he asked.

She shook her head. "Of course not. And the safety was on. But it's caught up in something…"

"A few more yards and we're there," he said. He repeated the Tobik story, bending his head toward her ear as though confiding an amusing scandal.

A maid in French black and white stood in front of the dressing-room door, watching them approach. Vitya released her arm, made a little bow, and turned his back on her. He sauntered the few steps back to the dance floor, still holding the glass of champagne. The quartet began to play again, something tasteful and melancholy.

*"Vous avez un problème, Madame?"* the maid enquired unsympathetically. Another maid stationed at the dressing room door opened it for her. The room was empty apart from an elderly woman who was having the hem of her train repaired by the sewing girl. The old woman was fussy and stupid. Anna knew her – the wife of a superannuated equerry. Unless Anna spoke to her first, she'd say nothing. The woman watched Anna make for one of the private cubicles. Twenty awkward steps and Anna was alone. With difficulty she pulled up her heavy skirt, unused to handling the rich fabric without a maid to help. She disentangled the gun from her underclothes. A few more tugs and the tiers of her tight skirt sat comfortably again. Round her shoulders was a wrap of ivory sicilienne. She arranged it over her arm and hid the gun beneath its folds. Now to get the gun to Viktor Pavlovich.

She found him leaning casually against one of the green marble columns, sipping champagne. He eyed the difficult bulge under the sicilienne. "Good," he said. "Well done."

Anna frowned. What did he think? That his job was to patronise her? "No one's approached you?" she asked, her face assuming its animated social glaze.

He shook his head.

"Burning with curiosity as they are?"

"Are they?" he asked naively.

"You're probably the only person in the room who doesn't know within a million or two what I'm worth, you rabid fortune-hunter."

"Rabid?" Vitya said. "Then put me out of my misery. Marry me."

She shrugged. "Why not? You'd do as well as anybody else."

"I haven't seen the General," he said, keeping the same easy tone.

General Alexander Romanovich Drenteln was new to the job, and he was breaking tradition. He never showed himself in public, his programme was not announced in the court circular, and when he was in a building, everyone entering it was searched – even women, though not all of them. The Tsar himself was not better protected. Three months before, the Committee had targeted Mezentsev, head of the Third Section of the Imperial Chancellery, with 50,000 political police under his command. Mezentsev the Butcher, they called him. Kravchinski had wanted a job, no matter how desperate, and the Committee had told him to knife the Butcher in the street in broad daylight. Not being a candidate for suicide, Kravchinski had spent a great deal of time and 500 roubles of Anna's money planning an escape. With a sound plan and good luck he'd got away. Mezentsev was dead. General Drenteln was his replacement, the new man, sequestered behind unheard-of security. How could the Committee get at him? The difficulty raised the stakes attractively. Drenteln was the perfect target.

"Let me look at you," Vitya said. That was what they'd practiced. He put his hands on her shoulders. She raised both her hands ready to slip the Smith and Wesson into the breast pocket of his open jacket. The jacket was new – she'd told him to order it with deep inside pockets and with the line a little more relaxed than strictest fashion dictated.

She sensed his excitement. His hands on her naked shoulders trembled. He looked down, so close to her now, his eyes drawn by the fullness of her breast, so provokingly half-exposed. She was used to it. It gave her pleasure. These days even girls in their first season wore the deep evening cut. He looked up. Her thick blonde hair was elaborately dressed and twisted with pearls. She saw his eyes flicker, tracing the line her hairdresser had woven with such cunning. She handled the gun carefully, letting it slip finally from her hand into his waiting pocket.

"Where's the General?" he asked, taking his hands from her shoulders.

"Probably in the Red Room," she took his arm, "Cousin Vitya." He was younger than her, eight years, maybe ten. His excitement was reassuring – if they were to work together, it would help if he liked her. On the other hand, she'd have to make sure he kept his distance. Control – it was something she understood, though she'd learned it the hard way.

They stood together, watching the huge ballroom fill up. Footmen moved with drinks among the guests. There would be dancing later – something new at receptions – but only for the youngsters. Guests greeted guests, uniforms bowed to uniforms, gloved hands were brushed by perfumed whiskers. Cousin Vitya could never have seen anything like it, buried as he'd been in the Ukrainian countryside. Chernigov – she had an estate there too, she remembered. Small. Badly run. While her father was alive, they'd gone there once for the hunting. She remembered the provincial celebrations of their dull Ukrainian neighbours. But here in Petersburg the tone was brilliant: the uniforms glittered with new gold, and the women, some of them anyway, dressed with daring extravagance. She wondered how the scene struck Vitya.

He seemed to sense her question. "Your world," he said.

"It used to be. I haven't been to one of these things for ages. Nothing's changed. Except the fashion. Do you like it?"

"The fashion?"

"Supposed to be a return to nature. The real woman revealed at last after those dreadful crinolines." Anna turned to look down over her shoulder at the blue embroidered silk cascading into a train behind her.

"I've no idea about such things," Vitya said. "I've seen drawings in the papers of course. But the reality…" His eyes sought again the choker of pearls at her neck, her naked shoulders, her white breast. "Perhaps we should walk around," he said ruefully. "In a ballroom there are so many…," he glanced at her again, "so many distractions."

"If you like," she smiled, amused at being called a distraction. "With you looking so eligible, at least we'll generate some gossip." They walked under the colonnade. Tables were set up every few yards, most of them occupied. A voice greeted them: "Anna Petrovna!"

Anna turned quickly. "Vladimir Grigorievich," she said with obvious pleasure. A man of about fifty with a powerful, intelligent face stood up. Anna held out her hand and he touched it politely with his moustache. He straightened up, admiring her, holding her hand and patting it like an affectionate uncle.

"I thought you'd given up Petersburg for farming," he said. "Must be a year since I've seen you."

The old man glanced shrewdly at Vitya, and Anna introduced them. "Viktor Pavlovich is at the university," she explained. "The School of Mines."

"Sit down. Join us," said Vladimir Grigorievich. There was a reticule on the table, a few square inches of glittering rhinestones. "My wife," he explained, "she disappeared to gossip with her friends. So now I can gossip with mine." The old man began to ask Vitya about safety in the mines and the improvements the Ministry was debating. He asked about black-lung disease and if the German ideas for reducing it were being taught in Russia.

"Since when do you know so much about mining?" Anna asked familiarly.

"Not mining actually – more public health. Since July," he said. "Didn't you hear?"

"Hear?"

"They moved me. From Customs to Health."

"Promotion," Anna said. "Let me guess. Deputy Minister. Anything less would be an insult."

"Exactly."

"That's wonderful," Anna said sincerely. "I'm sorry I missed the announcement. I'd have written."

"Too busy on the farm?" the old man smiled.

"I was in Helsinki," she said.

"So what is it now? In Helsinki?"

"The harvester. The big American one. You know – my father's dream."

"I saw an article on it, now I come to remember. The only one in Russia. Owned by Countess Agriculture."

Anna laughed. "I saw that too. And the picture was fun, me in the driving seat."

"It's where you belong, my dear," the old man said. "I've always thought so."

Two gloved and jewelled hands rested lightly on Anna's shoulders. Smiling, she turned to see who it was. She knew how the strong, supple turn would put her face in profile, would change the line of the choker against her white neck. And she knew that Viktor Pavlovich would follow her every movement with his eyes. She wanted him to. For some reason it mattered what this country-boy thought of her. The gun in his pocket, the warm light in his eyes, the quick humour in his voice – it all mattered. Behind her stood Ludmilla Afanasyevna, the General's wife.

"Anna," she said. "If the gentlemen will excuse you, do a round with me. Tatyana has gone off somewhere in a sulk, and Alexander Romanovich is imprisoned in the Red Room. So everything's left to me."

"He wasn't in the line tonight," Anna said.

"No – ever since he's had this frightful job, all we hear about is assassins and revolutionaries. And security, security, security. As if we aren't safe in our own home. People being searched as they came in. Did they search you?"

"They looked in my bag," Anna said. "I think they're more thorough with the men. Much more dangerous animals."

The two women smiled.

"How about you, Vladimir Grigorievich?" Anna pursued. "Did you smuggle in your Smith and Wesson?"

"I don't have one," the old man said, "but they did look in my cigar case." He tapped his pocket.

"Just think of it," Ludmilla Afanasyevna protested, "searching a Deputy Minister. At my reception."

"What times we live in," Anna said.

"Anna, do be a sweetheart and come round with me." It was a big reception, far bigger than Anna remembered from the past. And more mixed. Collegiate councillors – and lower – from the Ministry, diplomats from a dozen legations, and an English duke with his banker. The thought of making the round alone would have intimidated any woman.

Anna stood up quickly and gave the older woman a little kiss on her cheek. "You poor thing," she said, taking her arm. She led her hostess, without seeming to, through the press of guests, greeting those she knew and those who were complete strangers with enchanting indifference. A long delay – another problem they hadn't foreseen.

By the time she found Vitya again, dancing had begun and the reception was thinning out. Anna said a quick goodbye to Vladimir Grigorievich and hurried with Vitya toward the Red Room. They'd been two hours at the reception and not even glimpsed the General – things were not on schedule.

The Guardian's final instructions had been simple: get the gun past the guards and close enough to General Drenteln to kill him. Find out how the land lies and plan an escape route for later. That was all. That *all* left them with many questions. Was there another ring of guards after the first search? Did the General have a bodyguard? Would he stay in one room or move about? Which doors led into which rooms? And in the sleigh, two hours before, Vitya had asked a question of a different kind: "If there is a second check inside the house, they'll find the gun. What should I do then?"

For once Anna had made no reply.

"I'm dead. And so are you," he'd remarked with a young man's bravado.

"I don't think they'll check twice," Anna had surmised. "It's so un-Russian."

"But *if*? Shall I take him with me? If I get the chance? At the last minute?"

"It won't happen," she'd said without conviction.

It was well after midnight as they turned their backs on the dancers and made for the Red Room at the back of the house. As they walked, Anna described the room for him as she remembered it: French windows, a terrace beyond, steps down, then the gardens and a cobbled way from the stables to the street.

"But is he still here?" Vitya asked her. "What did you see on your round?"

"There's a lot of security. But no more searches. Not that I saw."

They neared the Red Room. On the wall opposite the doorway hung a huge landscape: peasants harvesting sunflowers in the Caucasus. Anna turned toward it. "Explain it to me," she said.

Vitya began to talk. Anna turned her back on the picture and studied the Red Room through the open doors. A circle of chairs was drawn up round a low table in the middle of an enormous Shiraz carpet. Only three chairs were occupied. The General sat with his back to the French windows. Two men in uniform sat on either side, colonels, both in the hussars. The nearest of the French windows was open. Beyond, on the gas-lit terrace, a man in the uniform of the Ministry of Justice was smoking a cigar. Then the garden. The old men at the table were deep in conversation.

"Children with no dirt between their toes," Vitya was saying. "What dreamers paint our pictures for us?" Anna turned toward the picture again. "Is he there?" Vitya asked.

"Yes. I'll try to introduce you. Let's go in."

They turned away from the picture, Anna's hand resting weightless in the crook of his elbow. They walked toward the door. Anna talked intelligently, comparing the picture behind them with one that hung in her house in Rostov.

As they passed through the door, Vitya stopped abruptly – the man with the cold eyes from the reception line had laid a hand on his shoulder. "Viktor Pavlovich?" he said. "The General is occupied for the moment." The room was guarded – it was time for a quick retreat.

"We wanted to see the view from the windows," Anna said. "There's a moon. The garden…" She was explaining too much. She should have said *We'll wait* and turned back.

The conversation at the table stopped. "Who's that, Makar Makarievich?" the General demanded.

"Your Excellency," Anna said quickly. "I wanted to introduce a relation to you." It was not what she'd just told Makar Makarievich.

"I'm afraid…" said the General, looking in her direction without recognition. He gestured to Makar Makarievich that he had no interest in talking to the young people.

"Perhaps," Makar Makarievich said mildly, "perhaps you'd come with me, Viktor Pavlovich. For a second. Into the next room."

"Certainly not," Anna said. She hadn't raised her voice, but the General heard her.

"Makar Makarievich, what's the trouble?" he asked in a thick, parade-ground voice. The connecting door into the next room opened. A guard – not uniformed, but unmistakably a guard – had opened it, and behind him, a bright room with cigarette smoke and other men.

Makar Makarievich waved his hand for Anna to disappear – a rough gesture made to an unwanted servant. Anna bridled with anger. Makar Makarievich ignored her. "I'd like a word with this young man, Excellency," he said.

There was a vicious *crack*. Makar Makarievich staggered to the side. Anna had hit him across the face in unfeigned fury.

The General stood up and came across to the little group. He scrutinised Anna closely with a shimmer of recognition.

"You're a friend of my wife, I believe," he said.

"A cousin," she said, controlling herself rapidly. She saw one of the General's cronies whisper her name in his ear. A little crowd had gathered already, attracted by the sound of raised voices. "Alexander Romanovich, everyone understands the need for…" she waved contemptuously at the open door and the faces of the men in the smoky room. "But…"

"Excellency," began Makar Makarievich in the tone of a man accustomed to having his way with his superiors.

The General was three paces from Vitya. He was studying Anna's blazing, ice-blue eyes, a connoisseur of fine women, enjoying a show. Anna knew exactly what was passing through Vitya's mind: in a moment, he'd be searched, and it would all be over. So better act now. Draw, cock, two paces, force the gun against the General's ribs and fire. Anna saw the very spot he'd choose: beside the Order of St Anna on its scarlet sash just below the General's heart. She saw Vitya's arm tense, ready for the draw. Instantly her hand reached out and clasped his wrist, forcing him to hold back.

"Excellency?" Makar Makarievich repeated.

Anna was smiling at the General, anger still glittering in her hard eyes. For a long moment she held the old man's look with brazen persistence, subduing him, piquing his curiosity. Then she lowered her gaze in a subtle gesture of submission – she was placing herself in his hands. Completely.

The General cleared his throat. "Makar Makarievich," he said, "enough."

Vitya's hand relaxed. He turned the movement into a polite bow to the General. "Excellency," he said, as though they'd just been introduced.

The General bowed slightly in return. "Anna Petrovna," he said, turning to her. "I remember now. Of course. My wife even mentioned that you'd be here this evening. And I've been a dreadful host. But we can make up for that, can't we. Let's see if we can find a glass of champagne somewhere."

# Extract 1

Why? Why did we sacrifice everything for the death of one man, Alexander Romanov? What made us believe him the incarnation of evil, when the worst that could be said of him was that he was pompous, ignorant and unremittingly bourgeois? Not virtues in an emperor, certainly, but nothing to deserve dismemberment by dynamite. Where did we find the arrogance and the optimism to think we could change the course of history?

For nearly twenty-five years in the Schlusselburg, I reflected daily on these questions, and I have reached a simple conclusion: we were not heroes – we were simply young. We craved our freedom, and that meant everyone around us must also be free. We trusted philosophers who told us that to act reasonably is to act morally; we knew we acted reasonably, so we took morality for granted. We were young and we believed death could not touch us – mistakenly as it turned out.

I have only one purpose in writing this memoir: to commemorate the facts of history, the story of friends long gone who, as events unfolded, were weak, were wrong and who died, most of them, in ignominy. The recent revolutionary events in Russia *[i.e., in 1905 Trans.]* have shown that even an organised uprising with popular support is easily put down. How little hope there was then for a wretched, improvised rebellion such as ours. But it *was* ours, and into it we poured our souls.

Revolution is, of course, nothing new. In one respect, though, our revolution unveiled a new principle – political terror. Unlike a coup d'état or a popular uprising, we planned to use single acts of violence – of terror – so extreme that society could not survive. After such acts, the institutions we so hated would shatter. On the rubble, a new world would be built – not by us, but by our successors. Our terror was not the terror of a Caligula or a Robespierre; that was terror from above. Terror from below attacks the state, ruthlessly and fearlessly seeking its destruction. We called ourselves *terrorists* – we invented the word. We believed we would change the world. Perhaps we did, though not in the way any of us intended.

Every chapter of history has a human face. The theory of terror has been endlessly debated; the faces of the terrorists have been lost. Some of them I knew: Sofya Perovskaya, Andrey Zhelyabov, and many others. I will write down what I can remember of them, not to glorify terror, but to furnish the human record, however incomplete, of our crushing and appalling failure. (*Memoir of the People's Will*, Preface.)[1]

---

[1] I have decided to add to this story a number of extracts from a memoir published in Paris in 1906 by a certain MF, who is generally taken to be Mikhail Frolenko. Frolenko, if indeed he is the author, is a reliable witness. The details in his narrative seldom contradict those found in more celebrated works; for certain small details of revolutionary practice he is the only authority. Frolenko published a full memoir of his life in 1924 with the blessing of the communist party. It was called *Hard Labour and Exile*. The earlier work offers a fresher, though often disillusioned, account of the extraordinary events on which this story is based. The work was originally published in French; the translation is mine. JRP.

# Chapter 2

## I

Evgenya Antonovna Grishina was eighteen. Though her life was devoid of entertainment, it was not without amusement. Her favourite occupation since the age of thirteen had been to play the piano. The music she most enjoyed was loud, aggressive and usually too difficult for her poorly trained fingers. Her mother, not without reason, called it 'headache music'. Her father took the view that his only daughter had musical talent and that a better teacher would develop it. But good teachers cost money, and the Grishins were almost penniless. Their estates had been sold in the late sixties, ten years before. All that remained was an apartment on the Kurskaya, an unfashionable street in a run-down quarter of St Petersburg, and a small estate, little more than a rambling manor house on the Volga. This house had been left to Evgenya by an aunt and was still, at least in principle, set aside as her dowry. Now, however, there was talk of selling what was left of the property so that the Grishin family could drag on for a few more years in tarnished gentility. Evgenya's agreement was required for the sale and so far she'd been reluctant to give it, not because she wanted the estate or the offers of marriage it might bring, but because it was hers and she saw no reason to give it up. Apart from the violence of her piano-playing and fitful help with the housework, Evgenya's only contribution to the well-being of her family was the hope that one day she would let her father sell the house.

In addition to the piano, Evgenya had two other amusements. One was to visit a friend she'd met at a house-concert given by their mutual teacher. Evgenya, or so she told her mother, visited her friend to play duets on the piano. Evgenya's mother approved of these duets since they took the girl – and her music – out of the apartment sometimes from breakfast till dinner. What Evgenya's mother did not know was that her daughter's friend, Valentina, had five brothers aged between thirteen and twenty-five. She was also unaware that Valentina's father was an army engineer serving with a regiment permanently stationed in Siberia. He'd returned to St Petersburg twice during the previous twelve years and had difficulty telling his sons apart. In Siberia he employed a young housekeeper, or rather a series of young housekeepers, to ensure his comfort and well-being. Meanwhile in Petersburg, Valentina's mother had fallen in with a circle of tractarians who supported a Christian mission to the Yupik Eskimos. Unsurprisingly, the family ran wild. The brothers, three of whom still lived at home, had adopted a style of conversation and behaviour which their sister, Valentina, found radical and amusing. If they said things to shock her, she gratified them by appearing shocked. So did Evgenya. The two girls had begun to enjoy an occasional glass of wine with the young men. On a picnic excursion to Petrodvorets, they'd even discussed – in a progressive, open way – which of the brothers Evgenya would prefer as a lover. Her decision – daring and ambiguous – had become a standing joke: "All or none," she'd said. Of the two choices, she'd stuck so far to *none*. But friendship with Valentina had more to offer than teasing her brothers, rowing boats in summer and sledding St Petersburg's unexciting slopes in winter. Valentina collected radical pamphlets. Though she lacked the scholarship to read Marx or Bakunin, she had old issues of *Kolokol,* dozens of tracts on the woman question, and gleanings from Land and Freedom hidden on top of her wardrobe. In her copy of *What is to be Done?* the more outrageous statements were underlined in red, sometimes twice. She passed on these tracts to Evgenya in whose mind anarchy, the destruction of the bloodsucking classes and free love became three interchangeable expressions of the same idea.

Valentina had another friend, a serious-minded girl who *had* read Marx and Bakunin and who believed that murder and mayhem were the answer to most social problems. She was a 'new woman' with radical views on sexual equality and sexual freedom, though her practice, like Evgenya's, was naively chaste. Her name was Polina. She was short-sighted and, like many New Women, wore blue-tinted glasses. Polina's blunt speech and her readiness to trample on people's feelings amused Evgenya − at least in small doses − but Polina was not a favourite with the brothers. While Evgenya defended herself against their flirtation with giggles and a transparently false "I'm not quite sure what you're talking about," Polina made flirtation impossible by translating cheerful hints into shameless gutter talk. After each translation she added viciously: "That's what you really mean, isn't it?" The brothers expelled her from the group one day after she'd taunted Evgenya: "If you want him to fuck you, why don't you just say so and get on with it?" Evgenya had thumped her vengefully on the back. Polina's expensive blue glasses had flown off and smashed. Polina had said Evgenya should pay for the glasses, Evgenya had refused, and the brothers had sided with her. That was the last Evgenya saw of Polina for several years.

A number of questions preoccupied the brothers. When would Evgenya stop playing games and choose one of them? Which one would it be? Or would it be a good idea to forget her preferences and simply draw lots − winner takes all? Evgenya had nothing against such ribald discussions − she listened with sly amusement but never joined in, perhaps because she was herself confused and unsure of the answers. The source of Evgenya's confusion was something the brothers knew nothing about − her third and final amusement.

To bring in a little money, the Grishins had decided to take a paying guest. There was a spare room which had belonged to Evgenya's brother, Ilya, until he'd joined the army. A paying guest should not be a total stranger, and finding one might have proved a problem. Luckily, however, the solution fell into their laps. Evgenya's mother came from Chernigov in the Ukraine. Her family was large and mostly sisters. There were female cousins too. One of these cousins had married a landowner whose small estate, Pelinskoye, was still profitable though it had seen better days. The couple had only one child, a son, Viktor Pavlovich. At exactly the time when the Grishins were looking for a lodger, Viktor Pavlovich arrived in St Petersburg to begin his studies at the School of Mines. He visited the Grishins and they persuaded him to occupy, and pay for, their son's empty room. Though living with relatives restricted Vitya's freedom, the arrangement suited him. After four years with the Grishins, Vitya was now in his final year of study, a young man of twenty-two, cheerful, unassuming, and ready to help with a few extra roubles when money was tight.

From the beginning, Evgenya had paid close attention to her cousin's affairs. He had a good allowance from his father, and he was clever. He was her second-cousin, a 'kissing cousin' as Valentina called him. At fourteen, Evgenya had decided to marry him. At sixteen she'd tried to coax him into some kind of reaction to her lithe, new-found prettiness. She began to fantasise a life for herself and her kissing cousin in a land where the sun always shone and there was nothing to do all day but amuse each other. At seventeen she'd learned from Valentina, and from an extremely detailed tirade against 'self-gratification' in one of Valentina's pamphlets, how a girl might, to a fair extent, relieve her unrequited longings. Since then Vitya, and Vitya alone, had been enough to keep her imagination racing. And Valentina's brothers? Despite Evgenya's fondness for romps and races, boat rides and polkas, they had no chance whatever.

In her daily study of her cousin, Evgenya had a powerful ally in the family's only servant, Maryanka, a Ukrainian who had once been a house serf on the Pelinskoye estate. When Evgenya had nothing better to do, she helped Maryanka with the housework, in other words she gossiped while Maryanka drudged her way through her chores. When Vitya had first agreed to live with them, he'd often slipped out of the apartment late in the evening. Evgenya had wondered where he went. Maryanka, it seemed, had known – at least roughly. She'd known too when these activities stopped, though not why. She'd known from the absence of medications that he was clean and healthy. And she'd known from his laundry that he was seldom drunk and never ate without a napkin. Over the years the two had giggled together as Maryanka shared her observations with an increasingly curious Evgenya. Maryanka had been with the family long enough to have watched Ilya, Evgenya's brother, pass through adolescence and become a man. She often compared the two young men, and always to the missing Ilya's disadvantage. Maryanka's preference was perhaps influenced by Vitya's habit of tipping her each month for sorting out his laundry – or so Evgenya surmised. In fact the tip was unjustified – the only household task that Evgenya willingly performed was attending to Vitya's clothes. She enjoyed collecting his dirty things and inspecting them when the laundress brought them back, but mostly she liked putting away his clean things in the trunk under his bed. His room was too small for anything but a bed, a desk and a bookshelf, so most of his things were stored in the trunk. In the trunk Evgenya found an ever-changing store of books and pamphlets that intrigued her. Not many were in Russian. She puzzled over the titles in the unfamiliar alphabets of French or English, and sometimes the exotic script of Gothic German. It seemed to her that the books were exactly those so often quoted in Valentina's pamphlets. She tried dropping the names into her conversations with Vitya, but he showed no reaction beyond his usual indulgent smile and a patronising: "Time for that later."

Later! she thought. When I'm grown-up, I suppose. Well, if only he knew... That was a phrase she often used: *if only he knew*. She longed for him to know, though she could find no way to tell him that she shared his concern with forbidden ideas: freedom, revolution and, she supposed, free love. She wanted him to know how often she puzzled over the books in his trunk. She wanted him to guess that it was her and not poor, illiterate Maryanka who folded his shirts with such adoring precision. If he'd given it even a moment's thought, he'd have known. Known and said something. But he made no comment at all, and his silence made her feel rejected and stupid.

Worse – quite apart from refusing to discuss revolution – why wouldn't he look at her? Look at her properly as the brothers did – as they'd done for a long while now. She racked her wits for something to rouse his interest. She tried wearing her long, black hair in different styles. On a hint from Valentina, she went barefoot round the house for almost a week. She even padded her skinny bosom in the hope that he'd look at her. But he didn't. And the padding felt ridiculous. Worse, Maryanka noticed it at once and teased her mercilessly, even though Maryanka was only a servant and Evgenya was the daughter of the house. Things couldn't go on as they were, and indeed a great change was in the making.

One evening in Vitya's trunk Evgenya found a canvas bag containing a revolver and twelve rounds of ammunition. Then, next afternoon, a woman paid Vitya a visit – Anna, Countess Shestakova.

Maryanka showed their exotic visitor into their shabby drawing room. At first there had been no one to greet the great lady. Then, alerted by Maryanka, they'd crowded into the room at the same moment: Vitya, Evgenya and old Elizavetta Ivanovna – Aunt Betty as Vitya called her.

"Elizavetta Ivanovna," said the Countess still standing. "I've come to drag your nephew away, if you can spare him for an hour or two." Evgenya saw at once that Vitya and the Countess were not friends, certainly not lovers. Yet the Countess was beautiful, older than Vitya, with maybe the first hint of crow's feet in the corners of her eyes. But beautiful in the way that rich, inaccessible women are beautiful. Evgenya was painfully impressed. Despite her hatred of the bloodsucking classes, she was already half in love with their exotic visitor.

Now it was Vitya's turn. "Elizavetta Ivanovna," he said to his aunt. "I don't think you've met Anna Petrovna, Countess Shestakova. Anna Petrovna – my Aunt Betty."

"Ah," said the old woman. "Anna Petrovna. Of course. I used to see your picture in the illustrated papers all the time."

Evgenya winced. Somehow she'd always thought her mother would know how to behave in society. The old woman complained endlessly that their poverty isolated her from the world she'd been born to. Now Evgenya saw the truth in a second; her mother was gauche and silly, she put the family to shame.

Vitya tried again: "And this is my cousin, Evgenya Antonovna." Evgenya looked at the Countess, feeling in her turn gauche, silly and close to panic. Her simple house dress, her hair in a tangled, gypsy braid, her fingernails untrimmed and not particularly clean – she was shockingly unprepared. She saw the Countess look her up and down and then smile.

"Viktor Pavlovich told me he had a young cousin, but he said nothing about how pretty she was."

Evgenya coloured and then caught Vitya's eye. She saw a new expression on his face – appraisal. He was looking at her. She straightened her back and set her head with defiant shyness. "You caught us unawares, Anna Petrovna," she said. Sometimes, she knew, her voice had a warmth, a seductive softness to it. Now it sounded tinny and childish.

"If there's one thing I hate," said the Countess ceremoniously, "it's ceremony." Vitya gestured the Countess to sit, and she positioned herself correctly at one end of the Grishin's only sofa. She was still in her street clothes, an elegant autumn coat of dark blue cashmere. Her pretty hat had a veil pulled back over it. Then she touched the seat beside her. "Come and sit next to me for a moment," she said to Evgenya.

Evgenya sat quickly at the other end of the sofa, trying not to look prim. The old woman sat too, ignored, in an armchair.

"I noticed on the piano," the Countess began, "music by Glinka. You have very modern taste."

It was a compliment, Evgenya saw, sensitively paid. How should she reply? "Perhaps," she ventured, "the future of music lies here with us, in Russia."

"In other fields too, maybe," the Countess agreed. "Where Russia leads, others may follow." There was a social finality in her words. Evgenya guessed that the two sentences were as much as politeness required. Vitya was still standing. The Countess smiled up at him. "We must go," she said.

Vitya offered her his hand, as though rising from a sofa would challenge a lady without the help of a squire. Evgenya was pleased – her cousin had manners. It was something she'd never thought about before – drawing-room protocol played little part in their family life. Evgenya stood up too and watched her mother struggle to her feet. The Countess extended two gloved fingers to the old woman as a token hand-shake. With Evgenya, she grasped her hand firmly, almost as one of Valentina's brothers might have done.

"Goodbye, Evgenya Antonovna," she said. "I'm sure we'll meet again."

And they were gone.

## II

Evgenya and her mother sat down together as soon as the outer door of the apartment had closed.

"Well," the old woman began, "Anna Petrovna in my house! How on earth has Vitya got to know *her*?" Evgenya heard speculation in her voice – a match for Vitya, perhaps, with a fashionable and wealthy woman.

"I don't think they're friends, Mama," Evgenya said, hoping her words were true. "I think she needs him for something."

"Then she could send for him. Why come here?"

That was exactly the question Evgenya repeated when Vitya returned at the odd hour of nine o'clock in the evening.

"Why did she come here?" Vitya repeated. "Well, Anna Petrovna isn't one to stand on ceremony. She just wanted to talk over some ideas. Together."

In all her life Evgenya had never seen anyone as ceremonious as the Countess. Had Vitya really been so easily deceived? For Evgenya the question was absorbing and urgent, like so many that had occurred to her during the previous hours of rapid conversation with her mother. The old woman knew a great deal about the Countess – at least a great deal of what had been written about her in the fashionable press. There had been a famous lawsuit that had dragged on for years. An uncle of the young Countess had tried to overturn her father's will, a will that made her heiress of the entire Shestakov fortune. In the end, Anna Petrovna had won. She was a millionaire many times over. After her victory, she'd rejected suitor after suitor – all from the best families, though none of them rich. Then something Elizavetta Ivanovna had never understood – the great heiress had taken up farming. Just imagine! For a while, the newspapers had been full of it. Anna Petrovna had run one of her estates in a totally new way, with a school and a hospital and brick-built houses for her farm workers. Not serfs, not peasants, but farm workers! What did that mean? Workers belonged in factories, not on the land. On the other hand, Elizavetta Ivanovna remembered reading that only one of the Countess's estates was a model – the others were run on more traditional lines. Perhaps it was true. Anyway, during the last year or two, Anna Petrovna had dropped out of fashionable society. Before that, her picture had been in the papers all the time: rich, attractive and so radical that her behaviour was almost a scandal. Still, she was a beautiful woman, Elizavetta Ivanovna had to admit, though not quite as youthful as her pictures suggested. Having exhausted her mother's supply of information, Evgenya was now tackling her cousin.

"You talked over ideas?" she repeated. "Together?"

"Yes."

"What ideas?" Evgenya pressed. "Is she starting a coal mine?"

Again Vitya scrutinised her in the way that had so thrilled her earlier. "Is it too late? Or could we take a walk?" he suggested.

# III

Evgenya greeted the yardkeeper cheerily as they passed his lodge. He edged his door open to see them more clearly. "Ugh!" he grunted, recognising them and retreating. Under the new rules, he had to report to the Third Section any unusual activities in the house, and that meant letting the heat out of his cubby-hole every time he heard footsteps.

The night was clear and frosty. A light wind was clearing the dismal mist that had hung for weeks over the Gulf of Finland. It would snow soon. Snow and then the filthy alternation of snow, frost and thaw that made the onset of winter so gloomy.

She took Vitya's arm. That was how they always walked, her cousinly hand in the crook of his elbow. He'd taken off his handsome new ulster and put on his old coat, she realised – perhaps she'd have disgraced his fine clothes in her untidy wrap and her shawl. She wondered how much Anna Petrovna's coat had cost – so well cut, such beautiful cloth. But her shabbiness didn't depress Evgenya for long. "I was sure Mama would say no!" she exclaimed. "I haven't been out like this, not since I was a little girl. With Papa. Let's walk till morning. Just on and on for ever."

"Walk? All night?"

"Walk and talk," she replied.

Vitya cleared his throat. "If there's something you want to know..." he prompted.

"There's so many things. You've no idea."

"For example?"

She tried to hear from his voice if she'd risen above being his chatterbox cousin, but she couldn't. "For example, where are we going?"

"Now? If we carry on in a straight line, we come to the Haymarket."

"Where the women are? The street women?" She tried to sound casual.

"You know about that? That sort of thing?"

"Of course. For years." It was an exaggeration, but safe enough – Vitya knew so little about her.

"You've been reading?"

"Same as you."

"How do you know what I read?"

"Gerzen. Engels. Villam Murreez. Right?"

"Pronounce it properly," he said. "William Morris."

Carefully she imitated his pronunciation.

"So you've been in my trunk, have you?" He sounded irritated, as though he really hadn't guessed. But anything was better than his usual bored toleration.

"Your shirts don't get in there by magic," she retorted. "Maryanka has a lot of work. I help out where I can."

They walked on for a while without speaking. Then, with something close to concern, he asked: "And when was your last round of laundry?"

In a second he'd know! Know she'd found the gun. She felt a wild surge of energy. She wanted to shout aloud for the sheer pleasure of making noise. "Yesterday," she said, her voice alive with meaning.

"Mmm." He wasn't happy, but at least he couldn't ignore her now, or accuse her of silliness. The gun was serious.

They walked a long way in uncompanionable silence, past bridges, palaces and churches. They reached a street with big houses, gardens and high iron railings. Some of the gates were guarded by sentries in army uniform.

"You can tell me," she said at last, stopping abruptly and

looking up at him. They stood for a moment with grave faces, yellow in the gaslight.

"Move on there." The voice of a sentry startled them from across the street. Vitya took her arm urgently.

"Quickly," he whispered.

"Whose house was that?" she asked, almost running beside him. He had his arm round her now, close and unfamiliar, propelling her forward.

"Drenteln," he replied. "Head of the Third Section."

They turned a corner, and he stopped. "I'm sorry," he said. "We shouldn't have run. We've nothing to be scared of."

His arm was still round her. The warm pressure was exciting. Would he keep his arm round her if she kept silent? Or if she spoke? She decided to speak. "That's where you went with Anna Petrovna? The other night? Isn't it?"

"Yes. What do you know about that?"

"And the gun, Vitya? Is that to do with her too?"

"It's nothing to do with anybody," he said angrily. "Just leave me alone. I don't like being spied on." He took his arm from round her and they walked on, hostile and offended.

"There's a *droshky* stand at the next corner," he said at last. "We ought to get home."

Evgenya stopped. Vitya made for the *droshkies*, leaving her to stand alone. Then he turned back, his eyes, black and glittering in the gaslight, fixed on hers. Ugly shadows crossed his face. She was aware again of her shapeless cape and the old shawl wrapped round her head. What must she look like? A cheap servant girl. She pulled the shawl tighter, shivering with cold.

"Come here," he said, holding out his arms.

She went to him, but not all the way.

"About the gun," he said. "You've probably got the wrong idea – completely wrong. I…" He hesitated.

"Probably I have," she conceded, fearing a real quarrel.

"And my room…"

"I'm sorry, Vitya. I won't do your laundry if you don't want me to."

"You do my laundry?"

"I help Maryanka," she said. "Sometimes."

"The laundry isn't the problem," he replied flatly.

"But at least talk to me," she said, hurt by his coldness. She went to him now, and to her surprise he hugged her as he sometimes did – her cousin. They walked on again, and he put his arm round her waist, something he'd never done. In the summer she'd walked like that with one of Valentina's brothers. Should she put her arm round Vitya now? No, she decided. They walked in silence past the *droshky* stand. The drivers offered their services in voices thick with catarrh.

Evgenya felt his grip tighten on her waist, then relax into an agitated caress. He wasn't angry with her, but everything she said seemed to irritate him. If only she knew what he wanted to hear, she'd do her best to say it.

"Forget the gun," he said at last. "You never saw it."

"No," she agreed. "I never saw it."

He shrugged. "I'm being ridiculous, aren't I?"

"I don't know. Maybe," she replied. Why deny what they both knew? In a way she agreed with him – it was ridiculous.

He stopped again. They were underneath a gas lamp in an empty street. He pulled back her shawl, exposing her face to the yellow light. Then both his arms were around her, one at her shoulders, one at her waist, pressing her body against his. She buried her face in the warmth of his coat. She let her body go soft against him, assuring him that there were no reservations on her side, that she'd agree to anything he wanted.

"You know what I've been planning... all these years," he began uncertainly, not at all in the tones of a lover as she imagined them. Instead, it seemed his inner voice was reaching out to her. "The mine, on the estate. In Chernigov. I know it's a trivial idea – one miserable village might be better off, that's all. And I've sometimes thought that you..." His voice faltered.

She looked up at him wide-eyed. He never spoke of the mine to her, only to her father. And the last, stuttered hint?

Perhaps it added up to what she'd longed for, longed for all her life it seemed – to belong to him. For him to trust her.

Then his spirit seemed to leap. He clutched her shoulders eagerly. "How ready would you be?" he demanded. "If…"

"If what?"

"The gun doesn't shock you?"

"No. Why should it?"

"Perhaps, we might… Perhaps if we stick together…"

At the word *together* she caught her breath but said nothing.

"How much do you know?" he asked.

"What about?"

"The Movement."

She heard an intensity in his voice as he said the word, and it startled her. For her, revolution was a patchwork of half-understood ideas, seductive in its promise of unqualified freedom, unlimited horizons, and an escape from her dreary home. But what did it mean to Vitya? Something quite different, she realised, and completely unknown.

They were in a narrow street, lined with apartment houses. At the crossroads ahead was a small square with a fountain and grass, where nursemaids gossiped in the summer. He steered her to the middle of the square. From the windows of apartment houses, light filtered through leafless branches.

"Let's not go home yet," Vitya said. "Or are you too cold?"

She was cold, her feet were numb in her cheap, flimsy boots. It was a sort of martyrdom, but she welcomed it. A church clock struck twelve, a bell like silver in the freezing air. Then another more distant. Then all the bells of the quarter. "I've never been out so late," she said. "Is it true some parts of the city are still full of people?"

"Not the parts you'd want to see," he replied.

"Yes I would," she contradicted. "Very much." Against her will she shivered and tried to pull her shawl more warmly round her head.

He put his arms round her again. "The wind's getting up," he said. "It could snow tonight."

"And in the morning they'll find our corpses frozen together in the street. Then what will Mama say?"

They were close to the low wall that ran round the fountain. Vitya sat down abruptly, pulling her after him and very close. "So who's been telling you about the wicked city?" he asked. Evgenya frowned – it was a question for a girl of ten. But perhaps he didn't mean it. How could she guess?

"Maryanka," she replied. "When I help her. She knows about... a lot of things. Gossip mostly."

"Not much to gossip about in our apartment, is there?"

"Well, for a start there's you."

He laughed, and she felt encouraged.

"And in the old days when we had lots of servants..."

"Yes. Maryanka's been with Aunt Betty for years. She was with us at one time – when I was very little. And she tells you things?"

"You knew my brother?" Evgenya asked, to her own surprise. Why was she talking about Ilya? A dozen subjects were more urgent.

"I met him once. What did he do? Chase after the maids?"

"Chased after Maryanka – and caught her too. Quite often from what she says." She'd often tried, without success, to picture Ilya and Maryanka together. He'd taken her 'short and sharp' Maryanka sometimes said. What did it mean? Now Evgenya tried to speak of it as though nothing could be more natural.

Vitya tightened his arm round her, drawing her to him. "Is that why they made him join the army?" he asked.

An icy wind swirled through naked branches, showering the fountain with frost. "Can I tell you?" she whispered. "Something only the family knows?"

And she told him. Fräulein Gudrun – her first and only governess. Six months the Fräulein had stayed with them. Then Ilya had got up to his tricks. One night Evgenya had woken up from a bad dream, and she'd gone to the Fräulein. Ilya had been there. In the Fräulein's bed. Not really in the

bed. On it rather. Naked. Both of them. And they'd been…
She wanted to say *fucking* in the same lurid way Polina said it,
but she lacked the courage. The Fräulein had begged her to
be quiet, and Ilya too, but she'd made a scene, screaming
herself into hysterics. The Fräulein had been sent away. And
Ilya had been sent to the army – to an unfashionable regiment
where he could live on his pay. Evgenya had seen nothing of
him since, though she knew he wrote occasionally to ask for
money. "Maryanka says he should have stuck to the girls in
the Haymarket."

"Perhaps she's right,"Vitya agreed. He seemed uneasy.

"Prostitutes," Evgenya said, weighing the word. She'd never
used it before – at least not in the family.

"Yes," he agreed.

"Like Julie and Nastasya in *What is to be Done?*"

"Yes,"Vitya agreed.

"Is it true? What's in the book?"

"Yes. As far as I know."

She paused, weighing the risk in her next words: "Have
you ever been with a prostitute?"

"Yes." She heard reluctance in his voice. She'd expected it,
but she didn't really understand it – Valentina's brothers spoke
openly enough about such things, though in a teasing way.
Soon, they said, it would be time for Timofei, the youngest, to
be *blooded*. It was a strange word. Did boys bleed too when it
was their first time?

"Can we walk? That way?"

"The Haymarket? It's a long way."

"I don't mind," she said, shivering. "Take me."

"Another day."

If he'd taken her, she would have gone. Anywhere.
"Promise?" she asked, risking the childish word. After all, the
subject was not childish – not at all.

"I promise."

She realised suddenly how ignorant she must seem to him.
She'd read nothing, she couldn't speak French let alone

English, she knew nothing of art or history, and her music, her one slight accomplishment, was miserable. She dressed badly, and though she was strong and wiry, her figure had hardly filled out since the age of fourteen. "There's so much to know," she said. "Things Anna Petrovna knew when she was ten."

"You can't forget her."

"No," Evgenya replied. "There's something about her. Who is she really?"

"I hardly know her. She's rich. She's clever. Who she really is, I don't know."

"There are women in the Movement, aren't there? Important women, like Sofya Perovskaya – the one with her picture everywhere. Is Anna one of those? In the newspaper they call them 'The Committee'." Her arms gripped him close and then let him go. "I know you know. Tell me."

He said nothing. Was he still trying to protect her? Or was she too worthless to be told?

"You can trust me," she said seriously. "They could do what they liked to me, I'd never tell them anything."

He took both her hands in his. Her fingertips ached with cold. She tossed her head so that her shawl fell back, exposing her face. He took off one of his gloves and let his fingers play over her cheek. With the back of one finger he brushed her lips. They'd scarcely touched for years, apart from an occasional hug or the ceremonial kisses at Easter. Now, in the raw cold of a December night, he was caressing her face as they talked of dangerous things. Would he kiss her? In the distorting half-light he was staring at her face, his eyes intent with unreadable longings. She wanted more – the touch of his cold lips on hers. There was a barrier between them still, and if he kissed her it would disappear. She saw something soften in the lines of his face and he pressed his lips against hers.

A drunk was weaving his way toward them through the little park, singing quietly.

"We'd better go," Vitya said, half standing.

Evgenya pulled him down again beside her. "No. Let's stay

here," she said, hiding her face against his shoulder.

The drunk came nearer. The singing stopped. Then, a moment later, a wheedling voice very close began a drunken monologue: "You can't fuck her there, mate. Stick her up against a tree, if I was you."

Evgenya held her breath suddenly tight inside her. Could it be true? Did girls do things like that? In this dark, icy world Vitya had brought her to?

"Wouldn't have a few coppers in your pocket, would you?" A pause. "No? Don't freeze to death though. Air's unhealthy this time of night." The voice coughed and spat.

When the drunk had gone, they sat for a long time, holding each other. From the little movements Vitya made, from the tensions and slow softenings of his body, she tried to sense his thoughts, but he was altogether too foreign.

"Vitya," she said at last. "What that man said? Is that what everyone calls it? *Fuck?*" She'd said the word. To him. Surely now he'd guess...

"Some do, some don't. It's not very ladylike – if that worries you."

"Maryanka says that's what everyone calls it... And Polina, she's a friend of mine..."

"Let me kiss you," he said. "Properly."

She was trembling. She knew it was time to be quiet, but her voice prattled on: "Vitya, will you take me to places? Not just the Haymarket. Everywhere. I live in this city, but I only know ten streets of it. And so many other things. I'm so ignorant, it makes me ashamed. Will you? Take me?"

"If I say yes, can I kiss you?"

"Say yes first."

"It's prostitution," he objected.

"I know. Say it."

"Yes," he said.

# IV

Evgenya's first night walk with her cousin had repercussions. The first was a severe attack of chilblains on her frozen feet. Vitya was shocked – why didn't she have proper clothes? The real winter was only weeks away. He offered her a hundred roubles to buy what she needed. She said fifty was enough, but he gave her the hundred anyway.

In all her fantasies, Evgenya never considered that if Vitya began to pay her serious attention, life in their small apartment would become intolerable. She'd amused herself so often with variations on her incessant theme: his coming to her in the night, slipping into her narrow bed and making love to her so that finally she'd know how love actually felt. Or she went to him and gave herself – sometimes bold and shameless, sometimes shy and yielding, but always, always ecstatic. It all seemed so near and so possible. But now she saw it was not. She waited, patiently at first, for him to kiss her, to touch her, to inject flesh and blood into her fantasies. But physically he drew back. A frozen kiss by the fountain, his cold hand fondling her beneath her shawl. And then nothing. Nothing at all. It wasn't lack of desire – she saw desire, or what she thought must be desire, smouldering in his eyes whenever he looked at her. When she could bear it no more, she challenged him: "You don't want me."

"Yes I do."

"Then..."

But Vitya refused. Flat refused. How could he violate the Grishins' home in such a way? Betray their trust? Treat them with such contempt?

Every morning now she went with him to the School of Mines. She met him there again in the evening for the walk home. They began to argue the point obsessively – it wasn't that she wanted to be seduced, but his reasons for not seducing her were, as she saw it, unacceptable. Old-fashioned, ridiculous and unacceptable.

The last lecture of Vitya's week fell on Friday. It ended at six. As always, she waited for him in the great lobby. It was a magic place, glittering with showcases of Siberian gemstones the Tsar had given the school when he'd founded it. She heard doors crash open in a distant corridor. The lecture was over. Cheerful young voices. Footsteps hurrying on marble floors. She could tell his footsteps from any others in the world, or so she told herself. He'd be first at the top of the marble staircase that rose magnificently from the lobby. The steps clattered nearer. At the last second she adjusted the angle of the fur hat she'd borrowed from her mother. It was black, like the collar of her new coat. Not sable of course, but pretty. More than anything she wanted to look pretty for him.

He was there, clattering down the staircase so fast it was a miracle he didn't fall. Joyfully she shook his extended hand – anything more would have been improper for a student in his own school. But seconds later they'd be arm in arm in the street. Nothing mattered. She was with him. There was no school on Saturdays, so they had the whole weekend together. For the first time he'd bought tickets for a Sunday concert, and her mother had said she could go. Outside the building, the streets were dark and cold but still free of snow. He put his arm round her, and the wrangling began.

"But it's none of their business!" she insisted, picking up exactly where they'd left off that morning. "What right have they got over me? It's tyranny. It's unbearable."

"But say they came into the room. Just imagine. You'd be there, like you saw the Fräulein that night, and I'd be like Ilya. Are you going to jump up stark naked and lecture them on the rights of women? And do you think they'd listen?" It thrilled her when he used words like *stark naked*. She hadn't told him, but she was sure he knew.

"So you're scared of being caught. Is that it?" she jeered.

"Aren't you?"

"Not at all," she said nonchalantly. But in fact, Evgenya now realised, if they were caught, there'd be an appalling scene. Her father would throw her into the street without a penny. A modern melodrama with the affronted daughter as heroine. The scene played well, but even so, her *not at all* was mostly bravado. She wondered if Vitya saw through it. Probably he did.

"It's not that I'm scared," Vitya was saying. "But it's simply not right, and I won't do it. I don't know why we keep discussing it. You won't change my mind, Evgenya."

"What if I come to your room anyhow?"

"You can't."

"Why not?"

"The bolt," he said firmly.

"It's covered in paint. It doesn't work."

"It does now."

"To bolt me out? Or them?"

"You."

"Then that means you definitely don't want me. Why don't you just say so and have done with it?" One of the greater certainties of her life was that Vitya wanted her, but it excited her to abuse his indifference.

"Listen. Aunt Betty knows more or less what's going on. She keeps looking at me, expecting me to ask if I can have a talk with your father."

"Vitya! Don't do it. If you ask him, I won't go through with it. Never. I'm not his property. He can't give me away. Not to you. Not to anyone." It was all a game. But it was a modern game, and she played it with exhilaration. "Does he think we're back in the time of Ivan Grozny? Or maybe that's what you think too!" As she finished her tirade, she laughed out loud.

"You read too many books," Vitya laughed with her.

"I think you do actually want to get married," she said with pretended incredulity. "You want me to be your slave." There was one thing everybody knew, she'd read it a hundred times: marriage was slavery. A girl passing from the ownership of her father to the ownership of her husband – it was an outrage as old as the history of the world. And it had to stop. That was what her generation had been born for – to end the servitude of women once and for all. She felt she was putting the argument in exactly the right words, but even so it meant nothing to her – she was far too happy to bewail the lot of women with any hope of being believed.

"Well," he replied, "I agree with you. In principle marriage makes no sense."

"Then…"

"Let me tell you something you don't know."

His tone was suddenly diffident. "What?" she asked, trying to hide her curiosity.

"Ever since you were fifteen I've been thinking – one day, with luck, I'm going to marry my pretty cousin, Evgenya."

She was shocked, genuinely. "Then why didn't you look at me? Ever? I had no idea at all." Was it true? At fifteen she'd been a beanpole, her hair always a mess. And she'd hardly started bleeding. Marry her! What an idea!

"That's what I'm saying. When a man looks at a girl as though he wants to marry her, people notice. And if I'd done it in front of your family – how unfair that would have been. To you. To me. To them as well. How much worse it would be now to… well, you know."

"You beast!" she exclaimed, deeply impressed. "Why didn't you tell me? I thought you were never going to look at me. Never in my whole life. If you knew how you made me suffer! But…" she couldn't let it go. "Really? When I was fifteen?"

"Sixteen then," he laughed.

"Fifteen?" she insisted. "Or sixteen? It's important."

"Whenever you like," he said. "Love at first sight maybe." Then he became serious again. "But now I can't play the game anymore," he said. "I can't keep it to myself. Maybe I should move out. That'd be easiest."

"And then? You'd expect me to visit you? So we could finally…"

"One of us has to say it," he prompted, allowing her the honour.

"… fuck," she said quietly, so quietly he probably hadn't heard her. It was too much. She began to laugh, to laugh uncontrollably in the miserable, icy street.

"Or you could move into my new room," he suggested.

"Like Vera Rozalskaya in *What is to be Done?*" She was still laughing.

"I don't think I'd want Vera," he said. "She's a frightful bore. But you…"

"Moving in with you? How is that different from coming to my room at home?"

"I don't know," he said helplessly. "Maybe it isn't. Maybe it's all impossible."

She felt the game slipping away from her. She'd always imagined a man would dominate her, demand her submission, trample down obstacles. Vitya baffled her. What more could she do? She wanted him, she was ready for him, and he wanted her. What was holding him back? Were men always like that? She had no idea.

"But you love me?" she said, not seeking reassurance but rather firm ground for a new attack.

"God knows how much."

"And I love you, Vitya. I love you. I love you."

All their attempts to resolve their problems ended like this – with a wave of emotion reduced to the trite language of a nursemaid romance. No matter how often they discussed intimate, forbidden subjects, when it came to an outburst of real feeling, their words would not have embarrassed Turgenev's tenderest heroine.

At home, Evgenya watched her mother fall into despair. For years the old woman had cherished a hope that one day Vitya might take an interest in her daughter. Incessantly she'd nagged Evgenya to be less boisterous, stop dressing like a gypsy, improve her mind, always with the implication that it might make her more appealing to her cousin. But now that the trick had worked, she found Evgenya's behaviour scandalous, and she said so. She didn't blame Vitya – he was a man, and he was easily led. As men are. Looked at another way, his money gave him the right to have his own way. Though not of course… But Evgenya was throwing decorum to the winds. Obviously she and Vitya could no longer live under the same roof with the slightest propriety. What had Vitya said to her? Was there an understanding? Had he proposed to her? Evgenya simply shrugged her shoulders and said she had no idea what her mother was talking about. Two or three times a day she came close to telling her mother to mind her own business, but even Evgenya could see that, in a way, it *was* her mother's business. In any case, habits die hard, and, whatever the provocation, Evgenya had never risked a radical confrontation with her mother. Until she was fourteen, her face had been slapped, not often but hard, though she'd never been whipped with a rope or a cane like other girls. And now, if the slapping started again… In any case, what was her mother complaining about? Every morning she walked with Vitya to the School of Mines and home again in the evening. Where was the scandal in that? None – assuming, of course, that her mother had no idea what they discussed or the language in which they discussed it. Vitya had bought her new clothes, but her mother had helped choose them – she'd thanked Vitya even more profusely than Evgenya herself. And the lessons? Surely her mother wasn't upset about the lessons.

Vitya had promised to teach his cousin many things: French and English, the rudiments of mathematics and history. He'd had good tutors, Evgenya no one but the Fräulein and the haphazard efforts of her mother. She'd never gone to school because a good school, though cheaper than a governess, cost money. As to a free school, Evgenya might make undesirable friends in such a place – and nobody wanted that. Vitya kept his promise faithfully. Each evening after Maryanka had cleared the supper table, Evgenya took out the French textbook she'd studied with the Fräulein years before and which her mother had begun with her four or five times since. The first familiar chapters went quickly, but once Evgenya began simple translations into Russian, Vitya was shocked – her spelling was, as he called it, wanton, and her grammar, at best, intuitive. Even so he corrected her mildly – more or less the perfect tutor she'd never had. Where was the scandal in that?

The opportunity for truly scandalous behaviour occurred, of course, after Elizavetta Ivanovna had gone to bed for the night. Vitya would stand behind his pupil, looking over her shoulder as she wrote. Often enough his words of correction were supplemented with an encouraging hand on her shoulder, or a caressing touch of her hair. One evening, not long before Christmas, that changed. Leaning forward to point to a mistake on her page, his hand slipped down from her shoulder and fleetingly touched her breast. Her hand was quickly on his, restraining him perhaps, but at the same time pressing his hand closer to her body. It excited her, not the physical sensation which was meagre, but the fact that he was touching her – touching her intimately. They continued, determined but unproductive, with the irregularities of the *imparfait*. The next morning on their walk to the School of Mines, Evgenya asked him why he'd touched her like that in her parents' house, but still refused to come to her room. Where was the sense in that? It was the kind of wrangle she enjoyed – shameless, lively, and rooted in the subject that was beginning to obsess her: how and when Vitya was finally going to accept that love was free and that he had more or less a duty to relieve her of her virginity.

Evgenya saw that matters at home must be settled soon. Though she steered clear of a crisis, she was no longer afraid of discovery, not by Maryanka, by her mother, not even by her father returning late from the club. The evening after the lively session with the *imparfait*, she decided to go to the dinner table wearing a childish blouse that buttoned down the front. She hadn't worn it for years. The blouse was tight, and with no camisole underneath, it hinted the shape of her nipples, as she noted approvingly in the hall mirror. As she entered the room, her mother looked at her in horror, rose to her feet and blocked her way.

"Go and change into something else this instant," the old woman hissed.

"Everything else is dirty," Evgenya replied, pushing past her mother and sitting down.

Her father glanced at her, trying to guess what the problem might be. All the old man wanted was a quiet life. At every meal his watery eyes pleaded with Evgenya not to annoy her mother. He looked at the blouse. If he'd had the money she'd have gone dressed in satin and velvet – but his days of affluence were long gone, and he was sorry.

Evgenya caught Vitya's glance too. His eyes flickered appreciatively – he understood the blouse perfectly.

Later, when they were alone at their French lesson, she told him brazenly that it was an old blouse, worn out really, and that the buttons were quite loose. He hesitated, her reluctant lover. So she unfastened two of the buttons herself and guided his hand. For a long time he caressed her, arousing her with nervous pressure. On the next evening, Maryanka discovered them exactly so. She was looking for some napkins that had been put away without ironing. She found the napkins and left the room as though it was empty. After this, Maryanka left them alone to their studies. At the end of the week when Vitya's laundry bonus was five times higher than usual, she took the money without comment or thanks. Evgenya felt she was making progress. She began to see the possibility of life as one unbroken, intimate caress. She became quick in nervous response and, as she saw in the mirror, subtly prettier.

Alone at night, Evgenya dissipated the tension of the evenings in the quiet of her unlocked room. One night on a sudden impulse, she left her bed. Vitya had said he locked his room against her, but she wasn't sure it was true. She walked the length of the little hallway, touching herself through her nightdress. She pushed down the latch of his door. She pushed. The door was bolted as he'd said. She knelt on the floorboards and pulled up her nightdress. Passionately whispering his name, she made herself spend. The sensation was so strong she almost cried out in pain.

The next morning on the way to the School of Mines, Evgenya plucked up her courage. "Vitya," she said, "we can talk about anything we like, can't we?"

He hesitated. "Of course," he said without enthusiasm. Perhaps he already knew what she wanted to tell him.

"Last night…"

"Yes?"

"… I was outside your door."

"You tried the latch. I heard you."

"Oh…" Had he heard what followed? She'd made no noise – she was almost sure she'd made no noise. "After…"

"After you tried the latch?"

"I knelt down. On the floor. I…"

*I made myself spend* – that was what she wanted to say, but the words failed her. It was the most secret part of her life, glimpsed perhaps by Valentina, but otherwise unspoken and unspeakable. And now she wanted it exposed. To Vitya.

"Well?" he said, stopping and turning toward her so she could whisper her secret.

She tried again, but it was hopeless. "I… I asked God to make you unbolt the door."

He didn't laugh. They were standing outside a shop. A glove-maker. They turned and stood in silence for a moment, looking at the gloves contorted into extravagant and unlikely gestures. She heard his breath – a little faster than usual, a little deeper.

"I thought…" he said. "I wondered…" At least he didn't believe her nonsense about asking God – that was something. But what he'd thought, what he'd wondered, he couldn't put into words. In half a dozen sentences they could have reached an understanding – tonight, tomorrow night. But the sentences went unsaid.

Of course the subject wouldn't go away. Teasing, indirect, they opened their hearts to each other. Shame, they agreed, was itself shameful and lamentably out-of-date. In any case, lovers should have no secrets. They began to question each other shyly, but with an attention to detail worthy perhaps of a better cause. Vitya surprised her. He was not lacking in experience, she discovered, though all of it had been with prostitutes, some of them quite young. He had knowledge of a certain kind, but it stopped short at his own sensations and the mechanics of what the girls did for him. As to the girl's feelings, her wishes, her sensations, he couldn't enlighten her at all. He knew absolutely nothing. But answering her questions aroused him, just as asking them aroused her. She knew that his door wouldn't stay bolted for ever. On the other hand, their new freedom to talk was satisfying in itself. It allowed them to postpone the crisis for a while, perhaps even till the summer when Vitya finished his studies. Then he'd move south, back to Chernigov. And she knew, without a quaver of doubt, that she would go with him. Meanwhile, the period of postponement had its own pleasures, and she indulged in them without stint but without excess.

As it turned out, Evgenya's dreams of a future with Vitya came to nothing. Within a few weeks of her finding the gun, her life took a different and entirely unexpected turn.

# Extract 2

It might help my non-Russian reader if I describe the political background against which Zhelyabov, Perovskaya and the others played out their lives.

For all the superficial glitter of Petersburg, Russia in my lifetime has been struggling to emerge from feudalism and the dark ages. 1861 was the first step: Alexander Romanov, Russia's new Tsar, abolished serfdom. The Tsar Liberator became, perhaps with good reason, the 'little father of the people', and this aura never quite deserted him until the day he was executed by the People's Will. Today it is hard to imagine the jubilation: after 1000 years of slavery, the folk were free. No longer could they be bought and sold or punished by vicious and arbitrary floggings. In practice the abolition of serfdom had two unexpected effects: the serfs were no longer valuable property so they were left to rot in the darkness of the countryside. At the same time the gentry, hopeless at commercial farming, relapsed into unproductive poverty. Huge new fortunes were made in industry, the rich invested in railways and mines, but politically nothing else changed. For twenty years Russia languished under a hardening autocracy. One man ruled, and his underlings bullied and abused the people as they saw fit.

And our intellectuals? Our philosophers, our writers and professors? They fell into three groups, each with its own programme. The Slavophiles believed in a return to ancient Russian values; the Westernisers wanted to copy Europe; the revolutionaries plotted to smash the old regime and build afresh. Who won? Perhaps it is still too early to decide… *[1906, Trans.]*

A word more about the revolutionaries. Until the late 1870's, the revolutionary movement was fragmented. Each region had its own Section: the Petersburg Section, the Moscow Section and so on. Each Section ran itself according to the political priorities or perhaps the whims of its members. I belonged to Section South. Its programme, insofar as it had one, was terroristic – not terror in the service of a political goal as we now understand it, but rather terror as punishment, terror as an expression of anarchy, terror used to destroy the faith of Russian society in the sanctity of its institutions. And sometimes terror for its own sake. A knife, a pistol, a barrel or two of gunpowder: with these simple instruments we went to work. Successfully. No one was caught, and that made us ambitious.

Just before Christmas 1878, we sentenced Prince Dmitri Kropotkin, Governor of Kharkov, to death because of conditions in the Kharkov city prison: sick prisoners were left to die, punishment by starvation was common. The usual story. Working with Section South at that time was a man called Grigory Goldenberg, who later achieved a place in history by betraying half the Movement to the police. His plan was simple: one evening he waited in a park near Kropotkin's house. When Kropotkin returned home, Goldenberg ran to his carriage and fired a pistol through the window. The Prince died a week later. Goldenberg escaped.

An action like that has a considerable propaganda effect. It lends prestige to the assassins. In reality, of course, we were digging our own graves; it was exactly such actions that persuaded the government to take us seriously, to mobilise its forces against us, and in the end to crush us. Idealism and a conviction of the rightness of our cause did not make up for the two things we so fatally lacked: foresight and organisation. (*Memoir of the People's Will*, Chapter 3.)

# Chapter 3

## I

Sonya was disappointed. So much effort and so little progress. "Coalminer. Tell me what you think," she said. "Truthfully."

Yurovsky opened his mouth to speak, but Sonya silenced him with a quick gesture. "Coalminer?" she repeated.

"Seventy yards," Vitya replied. It still sounded strange when Sonya called him Coalminer. But codenames made sense – the less they knew about each other the better. "Wet sand now," he explained, "and dry sand in a few weeks time, which is worse. 500 square yards of planking, and props every three feet or so. Nearly 200 props. Do you know how much work that is?"

Sonya looked at him shrewdly. "You're saying it's impossible?"

"Yes, Sonya," he agreed. "As you're working now, it's impossible." Sofya Luovna was one of the few who had no codename; they simply called her Sonya, as she'd been called all her life.

"We need more people to dig?" she asked.

"Digging isn't the only problem. The problem is breathing. The problem is water. The problem is the whole damn thing collapsing on you."

"Exactly," Yurovsky agreed. "It's happened twice already. I told you."

"It collapsed on you, because you were working without props. You asked for it."

"We had props."

"Pipe-cleaners, Mister Engineer," Vitya retorted. "And now you're too scared to dig. That's what you said."

"Whether I'm scared or not, that was my last tunnel," Yurovsky retorted. "Lucky for me, my ankles were sticking out."

"You said you could dig a tunnel, Engineer. You said it was easy," Sonya told him quietly.

"I fucked up," the Engineer flared up. "It could happen to anyone? You want me to go out and shoot myself?"

"No," Sonya replied without humour. "That's why the Coalminer's here. He knows what he's doing."

"I still haven't passed the exam," Vitya said modestly.

"Still," she said, "we're lucky to get someone like you. I'm a midwife, Rakhel is a prostitute, the Engineer builds roads, and the rest have disappeared." She paused. "So how many people do you need?"

Sonya was a short, ugly woman. Her forehead was too high and her hazel eyes were hawkish and small. Her voice was small too, ruined by diphtheria. As often as not she wore men's clothes, but whatever she wore, she wore it like a puritan: simply to cover her nakedness. She washed carefully every day, standing in a tub of cold water. She washed her hair every day too, using coarse, hospital soap. It left her short, straight hair bleached and sparse. Yet she spoke with authority and men listened, not only educated men like the Engineer, but rough men too. Yefrem, Danilo and the others cowered from her as farm-dogs cower from the peasant's wife.

"If you want the job done before August, four," Vitya said. "Four to dig?"

"Plus four girls to pull out the dirt and keep the air moving. The Engineer can count as a girl," he added with friendly malice.

"Bastard," the Engineer laughed.

"Four and four," Sonya repeated. She hadn't liked Vitya much at first. He'd seemed too much like the drawing-room fops she despised in Petersburg. And she'd met him on the recommendation of Anna Petrovna – that counted against him too, though not heavily. But now she saw she'd been unfair. There was an intensity about him, almost an anger. In work clothes he looked tough. And he knew what he was talking about. Not many men in the Movement you could say that about. Not many women either.

"And the timber?" Vitya asked practically. He addressed the question to her and she liked that.

"You mentioned it just now," Sonya said simply. "And I had an idea. There's a carriage shed here and a bathhouse, both about to collapse. We could order timber to rebuild them. Would it be enough?"

"It might be," Vitya said appreciatively. "And the air hose? The bellows?"

"No problem," the Engineer interrupted again.

"It *is* a problem," Vitya said. "If you don't keep air pumping to the end of the tunnel, someone's going to die."

"Don't be so morbid, Coalminer. Just remind yourself what's on the other side of that wall. More money than you've seen in your miserable life."

Vitya didn't smile. "And you're sure about the foundation? And the wall of the vault?"

"I watched them build it. Lime mortar. Regular bricks. No steel. Nothing. You do the tunnel. We'll be through the wall in an afternoon."

"In the right place though? Where they keep the money?"

"It's the State Treasury. Every month when they pay the army, this is where they pick up the money. I told you before."

"I know you told me – but that doesn't mean I believe you."

"Rakhel found out exactly which cellar," Sonya said conclusively. "It's true."

# II

Sonya sat on Vitya's bed watching him unpack his books and his few belongings. He'd chosen a room at the top of the house with a large table and a comfortable work chair. He worked systematically and neatly, obviously used to living without servants.

"So," he said at length, "tell me about the people here."

"Who first?"

"Yurkovsky, the Engineer. You said it was all his idea."

"Yes it was. Kherson. Rob the State Treasury. Millions and millions of roubles. We agreed about a year ago, on condition that he found someone to put up the money."

"That's where Alexandra comes in?"

"It's a shame about her. She's a doctor you know. Qualified in Switzerland. Now she just takes morphine and sweats into her mattress waiting for her demon lover."

"The Engineer?"

"Who else?"

"Is she rich?"

"Not as rich as Countess Anna, but she has a pure revolutionary heart. Or so the Engineer says."

"When did she go to Switzerland?" Vitya asked.

"Ten years ago. Zürich let women qualify. In medicine. Only in medicine. A dozen women went from Russia: Vera Figner, Nadezhda Subotina, Anna. But just before they graduated, the Tsar cancelled their passports and ordered them home. Out of pure spite apparently. Alexandra hung on. Married a brutal old man. It got her a Swiss passport and a taste for morphine."

"And the other two? Rakhel? The woman who does the cooking?"

"The cook is Yevdokia. The Engineer found her too. Apparently she has a pure revolutionary heart just like Alexandra, though her idea of revolution seems to be stealing from people's kitchens."

"And Rakhel was a prostitute."

"That's who we get now. So many people joining the Movement. Desperate girls who've read nothing but *What is to be Done?* Exhausted whores. And midwives. Strange mix."

"That's always a joke with us," Vitya said, "opening your Midwifery School right next to our School of Mines. On the same piece of ground."

"I know the jokes, and I don't think they're funny. Maybe I don't have a sense of humour." Men could graduate in Mining, in History, in Music and in countless other subjects. Women could not. They could study midwifery and teaching. Nothing else. Only two women in Russia had an academic degree. And poor, brain-fried Alexandra upstairs was one of them. Where was the joke in that?

"You don't like the Engineer much?" Vitya asked, hanging his travelling suit in the ancient wardrobe.

"We quarrelled."

"What about?"

"Children."

"Children?"

"Little girls. Prostitutes. He spends Alexandra's money on them. Or he did."

"You stopped him?"

"He told me to mind my own business, but he stopped anyway."

Vitya began to arrange his books on the desk. She watched him, puzzled. "How are you sorting them? By author? By subject? I can't see your system."

"By colour," he replied.

Sonya smiled.

"That wasn't even a joke," Vitya said and burst into cheerful laughter.

She liked him. Perhaps now she could get rid of Yurkovsky and pass the job to this new man, Pelin, the Coalminer. First, of course, she'd have to find out if he could be trusted. They'd met twice in Petersburg. She'd told him about the job, and he'd understood it immediately – better in fact than she'd understood it herself. He'd only made one condition: his final exams were in the summer, so he'd take his books with him. After his exams, he was planning a model project, a mine on his own land run as a commune. But he'd dig their tunnel for them – he could see how important it was. And there was a cousin, her name had come up at their second meeting: Evgenya. He'd asked if she could come with him to Kherson. In time he'd learn not to ask questions like that. If Kherson was impossible, he'd said, the girl wanted to leave home. Could the Movement find her a place somewhere? Sonya had promised to talk to her, but there hadn't been time – with news of the tunnel collapsing and the workers walking off the job, Sonya had left Petersburg in a hurry. She'd given the Coalminer a week to arrange his affairs and follow her. Now she'd stay in Kherson till things were running smoothly – a week maybe, if the new man was as good as he looked.

## III

Sonya waited till Vitya had finished unpacking and then showed him round the house and the untended garden. The house was a good thirty years old. It had been built by a brewer on a plot between his brewery and the Old Believers' cemetery. Originally there had been a view from the south veranda across the distant estuary of the Dnieper, but now the new State Treasury blocked off the river completely. Then the brewery had lost its roof in a Black Sea storm, and the brewer had moved to Odessa. He'd tried to sell the house, but, cut off from the sea by the State Treasury and sandwiched between the roofless brewery and the graveyard, it was sometimes impossible to find even a tenant.

The house was run-down but spacious and comfortable. The garden, on the other hand, was reverting to nature. A tussocky field that had once been a lawn sloped down to a fence, entangled now with briars and wild clematis. Scrawny trees screened the redbrick, windowless walls of the Treasury. They found a mossy path in the shrubbery and pushed their way through laurel bushes and myrtle, already green with the hint of new buds. Somewhere underneath their feet the tunnel would soon be running. They searched for an opening onto the track that ran behind the house, but there was no way through. Though it was early February, the day was warm. St Petersburg was still crusted with ice and choked with fog. The Black Sea was another world.

"So what do you really think?" Sonya asked him, as they went back to the house. There were wooden steps up to the veranda and she sat on the highest. He sat beside her. The sun warmed and soothed them. It would be easy to talk.

"About the tunnel?" he asked. "It's an engineering problem, quite a simple one as it happens. The real problem is the people."

"Come round the other side," she said. "I'm deaf in that ear." Whenever she was forced to confess her deafness, her voice took on an edge of bitterness that she couldn't disguise. She hadn't been born deaf – the diphtheria which had attacked her voice had left her hearing intact. The deafness had struck when she was thirteen. Her governess had thought she'd caught little Sonya 'touching her private parts' in the bath. The woman had dragged the child off to her mother, as governesses are paid to do. Her father in the next room had overheard everything. In a rage, he'd shouted at all three of them, then he'd hit Sonya – hard enough to rupture her eardrum. After that, to make sure she didn't miss the point, Sonya had been taken to the women's jail to see the lunatics. The sickening display of fiendish women, caged with their fellow-prisoners and putting them through the torments of hell had been intended to teach Sonya what happens to young girls who pollute their bodies. For Sonya, her deafness, the pain when her father burst her eardrum and the spectacle of the insane tormenting the insane had become agonisingly fused.

Vitya moved to sit on her other side. "I'm sorry," he said, "I didn't know."

Sonya struggled to clear her mind of the devils that pursued her. "I can get you workers," she said shakily, her hands clenched hard together. "A couple of men. But they won't be miners. It's easier to get women. Like Rakhel."

"What's wrong with Rakhel? I couldn't get a word out of her."

"I told you she was a prostitute. In Kiev. Jewish. Her father was killed in a fire when she was eleven. Pogrom, as always. Her mother disappeared not long after. A woman got hold of Rakhel and sold her virginity, like they do, to fifty foul-minded bastards. A kid of eleven. Then... not hard to guess. Drink. Men. She was mostly in a house, not on the streets. She still has her looks."

"Why did she come to us?"

Sonya heard hesitation in the *us*. It pleased her. Most newcomers saw themselves as a mixture of John the Baptist and Stenka Razin. "The Engineer recruited her," she said.

"So she has a pure revolutionary heart?" Vitya quipped.

"No," Sonya replied soberly. "She's a prostitute."

"Once a whore, always a whore? No way out?"

"Coalminer, do you have any idea of the lives those women lead?"

"Some," he shrugged.

"Then use your imagination."

"So why accept her?"

"She's useful. She found out where they keep the money in the Treasury. *Exactly* where. Wheedled her way in with the sergeant of the guard."

"And why was she so quiet with me?"

"You?" Sonya smiled. "She thinks you'll despise her when you know who she is."

"Why should I? I mean, if anyone was ever... a victim..."

"That comes from the heart," Sonya observed sharply. "You have your own victims?"

He looked at her narrowly, surprised at her shrewdness. "Yes," he replied. "One anyway."

"One of your own people? Your own *souls* as they used to say?"

"How did you know?"

"I didn't. I just know in a fucked-up society like ours, it happens all the time. But at least you learned a lesson. Most men carry on regardless. Like our friend the Engineer."

"Can you see through me so easily?" Vitya asked, uncertain.

She didn't smile. Why should she? Such a transparent young man, but his heart was in the right place. "In any case," she said, "there's... Evgenya? That's her name, isn't it?"

"Yes," he said evasively, "but shouldn't we be measuring the coach-shed?"

"Coalminer," she said, hardening her tone. "In the Movement we have a tradition. Some of us anyway. We try to be direct and open with each other. I'd like to give you this job. Get rid of the Engineer. So I have to talk to you. Properly."

"You need to know about Evgenya?"

"Yes," she said. "I don't ask from curiosity."

"She's my cousin. I live with her family. For years I've half-planned to marry her."

"Do you love her?" Sonya's tone implied exactly what she thought of the love that entices men to commit themselves to overgrown children.

"Love?"

"Can you walk away from her? She wants to join the Movement. That will separate you. The Movement has no place for lovers."

"I need to know more, Sonya. And so does she. I don't think I'm part of the Movement yet. Am I? I'm building you a tunnel. But..."

"You have a plan for your own mine. And this Evgenya is part of it." She said the girl's name without sarcasm, but already Sonya had taken a dislike to her.

"Plans? Dreams really. I'd have to raise a lot of money."

"And the Movement? What do you need to know?"

"What does it want?" He hesitated. "I've read the pamphlets. I know what it *says* it wants. But you're the first person I've met who's actually part of it."

"You've met Countess Anna?"

"She's not like you. Not at all. But she impressed me. I've never seen a woman with so much authority."

"A *mere* woman, you mean."

"That's not what I said." Sonya heard disappointment in his voice, as though he'd expected better of her. He stood up and went down the steps, away from her. He stopped, his back to her, his hands in his pockets.

"Viktor Pavlovich," she said. "I'm sorry. It was a stupid thing to say. Tell me about Anna Petrovna."

He turned to face her again but did not sit down. "I don't know," he replied slowly. "Perhaps she doesn't have your convictions."

"What do you know about my convictions?"

"Your face is outside every police station in Russia. And every time I post a letter I see 'Sofya Luovna Perovskaya, known as Sonya, wanted for...' You know as well as I do."

"That's my history, not my convictions. But I agree there's a price on my head." She touched the wooden step beside her, hoping he'd sit down again. He was sensitive as a girl, she thought. And his shaved face made him look curiously different from other men. Girl-like? Perhaps. But none the worse for that. If men and women were ever to be equal, it wouldn't mean women acting like their brothers. Quite the opposite – men would learn how to behave from their sisters. That would be the way of it.

"A price on your head," he repeated. "Somehow, talking to you, I can see why." He sat down again but on a lower step.

"So what are *your* convictions?" she asked, flattered but not smiling. "Say it all in three sentences, so think carefully."

"Three sentences?"

She nodded and watched him struggle to find the words.

"First, I think our society is fucked-up, like you said, and I think people like us have a duty to straighten it out." He was digging with his fingernails into the soft, rotted wood of the veranda steps.

She nodded.

"Then I think the worst thing in our society is the way women are treated. I've thought about it a lot, Sofya Luovna. It pains me, I don't know why, that I had tutors and my cousin had nothing, but…"

"Three sentences," she interrupted him.

"Then, third… I think…" he fell silent, pulling out a splinter from under one of his nails. "I think small steps are better than none at all, but if I thought a single giant step could change everything at one blow, I think I'd… I'd do what I could. Though it might not be much."

Six years before when she and her generation had 'gone to the people', most of them would have echoed Vitya's words. Her own answer at that time would have been much the same. Going to the people. The great fiasco. They'd gone to the villages full of hope, eager to teach and longing to help. The police had picked them up by the hundred. The landlords had denounced them, and the peasants had refused them shelter. Prison, death – they'd been ready for the worst, but that didn't make their failure more bearable. The worst was the cynicism that tainted so much of their thinking afterward. Nothing had been achieved – nothing would ever be achieved. Only a handful had kept faith. And where were they now? In Petersburg, the 'new women' and the 'new men' talked economics and social science. They used Hegel's logic to prove that society must eventually achieve perfection, with or without their efforts. History was not a matter of individual effort but of unstoppable forces. It was a long time since anything had warmed her as much as Vitya's stumbling words.

"Thank you for telling me," she said. Impulsively she stood up. She hurried down the steps and sat next to him, hugging him to her. She wanted him. She wanted him for the Movement.

They sat now as comrades, arm in arm. "I know I sound shallow," he said. "I'm sorry."

She laughed. "You take me back ten years," she said. "That's how we all used to talk."

"Still," he replied, "talk doesn't make a programme. I've no idea what I really want. Just change. An end to the way things are now."

"Coalminer, let me tell you something. There *is* no programme. In fact there's not really a Movement – just a lot of people, like you and me. No structure, no control, and no discipline."

"But the Committee?"

She shook her head. "Nobody knows who's on it and who isn't. Just a group of us who stick together. Most of the time."

"But you're on it?" he insisted.

"It doesn't exist, Vitya. Not in the way people imagine."

"Pure anarchism then," he said.

"Pure nothing. But every '-ism' you ever heard of, all bundled together. If we want to get anywhere, we'll have to change. And soon."

"But no nihilism?" Vitya argued. "You all… I mean, we all believe in something. Don't we?"

"Not even that," Sonya replied. "We have our nihilists. Bent on destruction and nothing else." Her weak voice had dropped to a spiritless whisper. "And a lot of them are women," she added, "young women especially. Sometimes I think I've lost touch."

"How old are you?" he asked.

"Twenty-six," she replied. "And Evgenya? How old is she?"

"Eighteen."

"And could you – this is important and you didn't answer before – could you walk away from her?"

"Let me finish this job first."

"That's not the answer I want, Coalminer."

"You want the truth, and I don't know what it is."

She nodded. It was a fair answer. "Tell me about your mine," she said.

"Antimony. My grandfather had a silver mine. There was a lode, but it ran out. They dug tunnels to find more silver, but all they found was antimony. At the time no one knew what to do with it."

"And now?"

"They use it to make alloys, dozens of them."

"And you'd run the mine?"

"As a co-operative. A phalanstery." The strange word did not trip off his tongue. She guessed that he'd never said it aloud before.

"Your own revolution." Her words sounded condescending, but his idea was admirable enough. How many people had their own revolution, big or small? "With Evgenya as your wife?" she asked, knowing her question was disingenuous but asking it all the same.

"No. She doesn't want to get married, and I think she's right."

"She's read *What is to be Done?*"

"Like everyone else. But in the story Vera *does* marry. Twice. If marriage is such a bad thing…"

"I'll talk to your cousin, Coalminer."

"I wish you would."

"She's eighteen. A rebel by the sound of her. But rebellion isn't revolution – she'll learn that one way or the other."

"What's the difference?"

"Discipline, Coalminer. Discipline is the difference. Now let's measure the coach-house."

# IV

Sonya had said there was no Movement. She'd watched and planned, but nothing had crystallised out of the splinter-groups and affiliations scattered across the Empire. Even so, some things were in place. For instance, the Guardian had created a more or less unbreakable code system. When a prearranged message was sent by telegraph, one apparently harmless word, 'harvest' for example, could carry a lethal meaning. To send longer messages, the Guardian's code was based on a published book. Currently the book was *Anna Karenina*. The key was the start-word, at that time 'Dolly'. The first letter of the first occurrence of the start-word counted as 1. If Tolstoy's sentence ran *'Dolly, whom he had always thought of as busy, bustling and rather foolish, now sat motionless, looking at him with an expression of horror, despair and anger'* and if the coded message ran 1, 11, 21, 23, 62, 66, 67, 69, 99, 80, 100, 118, 114, 5, then the decoded message was *'Detonator ready'*. As long as the book and the start-word remained secret, the code was unbreakable. Because nearly all letters were opened and read by the Third Section, long strings of numbers were disguised as household accounts or as arithmetic exercises for schoolchildren. Using the code, Sonya put together in five days promises from Odessa, Sebastopol and Kharkov that Vitya would get the workers he needed. The Engineer was tactfully persuaded that if a factory girl from Sebastopol could do his work there was little point in his staying in Kherson. To Sonya's surprise, the cook, Yevdokia, did not go with him, even though her kitchen budget was halved on the day he left.

The timber for the new outbuildings arrived. Sonya and Rakhel took turns working with Vitya, sawing the timbers into props for the tunnel and into planking for the roof. As they worked, Sonya saw how gingerly Vitya treated Rakhel. Subtly he steered the conversation away from anything that might bear, even indirectly, on Rakhel's life as a prostitute. He spoke of history, geography, mining – anything that could cause her no pain. Rakhel became curious about some of the things he told her. She began to ask questions. Sonya saw a timid affection for him take shape in Rakhel's corrupt and shattered mind. Once after dinner, when Vitya was in his room studying his textbooks, Rakhel had confided in her: "Surely there's no one like him in the whole of Russia," she'd said.

"Well, compared with the men you've mixed with…" Sonya had replied brusquely.

After that, of course, there were no more confidences, but Sonya was not displeased. In the end every man took a woman, and if Vitya picked Rakhel… he could do worse – as long as he knew how to stay healthy. Maybe she'd have a word with him. For sure, a woman would stop him pining for this cousin of his – Evgenya. No good would come of his hankering after an eighteen-year-old ninny.

On the day that the first of the new workers arrived, Sonya left for Petersburg certain that the project in Kherson was in good hands. She was mulling over new plans. A tunnel, a long tunnel, could be dug under a railway or under a road. If the end were stuffed with dynamite, many otherwise inaccessible targets might become vulnerable. A train carrying the Tsar, for example, or the imperial carriage as it drove through St Petersburg. With a miner like Vitya working for her, many things became possible.

# V

"Sofya Luovna Perovskaya, known as Sonya," was born, according to the police posters, in 1853. The correct date was, in fact, a year later. She was the daughter of General Perovsky, who had been governor of Petersburg for almost a decade during the 1860's. General Perovsky's brutal mismanagement had become a legend that reached the ends of the Empire. Even Vitya, buried in rural Chernigov, remembered his mother threatening him with punishment at the hands of General Perovsky. Sonya was a rebellious child, a tomboy who preferred climbing trees to practicing the piano and who refused to keep herself pretty, tidy, or sometimes even clean. She had a series of governesses who beat her with a rope or whipped her with a cane, depending on whether they were Russian or English. According to the law, a noblewoman could not be subject to corporal punishment, but a governess had little choice when her employer told her to thrash some manners into her little charge. From the beginning, Sonya rejected the nursery and the drawing room. She enjoyed the processes of the great house: the jam-making, the soap-boiling, the feeding of the horses, the washing down of the carriages, the polishing of the silver and the cultivation of the kitchen garden. She was often rebuked for her low tastes, but she wouldn't give them up. So, when Sonya was just eleven, the General went into action. Sonya was led by her governess to the stables. There a housemaid was tied over a cart, her back exposed for flogging: the day before the girl had shown Sonya how chickens were plucked for roasting. It took fifteen minutes for the coachman to beat the maid senseless. When she revived, she was given her quarter's wages and dismissed, her back so pulped that it was agony for her to put on a blouse, let alone walk through the streets. Sonya wept at the unfairness of it, she wept at her own powerlessness, and she wept because she knew as she watched the flogging that she hated her father with a vicious and undying hatred.

Not long after this, Dmitri Karakozov, a student living in Petersburg, made the first of many attempts to assassinate Tsar Alexander II. The repercussions on the Perovsky household were severe: the General lost his governorship and quickly descended into debt, selling estate after estate to keep up with his expenses. He'd always been a domestic tyrant – now he was a tyrant with time on his hands. After her deafening when she was thirteen, Sonya separated herself from everyone in the world but her mother. Shame, frustration and anger – with these emotions Sonya had to content herself for a year or two more. In 1869, with her mother's help, she joined an informal school where women of all ages prepared themselves to study at a university, though at that time no academic courses were open to them. At fifteen, she was the youngest of the group. She read revolutionary tracts, brought home friends who drove her father into apoplectic outbursts, and refused to improve her manners. Finally her father pitched her out of the house. At this point, Sonya fell in with a circle of puritanical young women centred round

Alexandra Kornilova. The circle enrolled her in the school of midwifery. It was Kornilova's friends and a group of equally puritanical young men who, in 1873, led the movement of young idealists 'to the people'. Most of them were not yet twenty, but they were ready for sacrifice. They wanted one thing only – the chance to break down barriers, to teach reading, writing or whatever the villagers needed, to bring hope to the wilderness of despair that was the Russian countryside. Sonya inoculated villagers against smallpox. Although she'd never delivered a baby on her own before, she worked as a midwife in country towns where no doctor would attend a woman in labour without payment, and the wise women, as they were called, had no way to stop a haemorrhage, no idea what caused puerperal fever, and no way to treat a new-born baby but to swaddle it in cripplingly tight bands. To her despair, the brutality and violence of the people she was helping appalled her. In the countryside she was friendless, poverty-stricken and threatened day and night by drunken bullies and vicious women. For Sonya, the collapse of the Movement to the People was a personal and bitter failure. When the round-up of political suspects began in 1873, Sonya was arrested. She was sent to her mother's estate in the Crimea to wait for her trial, and she stayed there four years. Then in October 1877 the great trial began. 193 men and women were charged with spreading revolutionary propaganda and similar crimes. But Sonya, like most of the others, was found not guilty and released. The verdict of not guilty did not prevent the police from trying to re-arrest and deport her to Siberia. But she escaped, and that was the start of her life underground.

# VI

Sonya had a price on her head, but even so she travelled by train, walked city streets at all hours of the day and night, and took only simple steps to disguise her appearance. Her best defence was a set of false papers made out in the name of a young girl who had died in Novgorod some ten years earlier. The name was real. The papers, supplied by the Guardian, were good enough to buy a railway ticket, register at a hotel, or pass through a police barrier. Even so, Sonya was always cautious when meeting someone new, even someone as insignificant as Evgenya.

She knew that Anna Petrovna had visited the Grishin family, and she asked Anna to send Evgenya a note: 'Please meet me at the Nevsky Slide. Two o'clock on Tuesday. Anna.' Anna would keep the appointment and walk with Evgenya in the direction of the Winter Palace. Sonya would join them unless she thought Anna was being followed.

The Nevsky Prospekt at lunchtime was crowded with shoppers and diners from the ministries. Every January, as soon as the deep frost descended, the city council built an enormous ice slide outside Sazikov's, the most famous silversmith in the Empire. The slide itself scarcely obstructed the traffic, but the crowd around it — children, onlookers, daredevils with their sleds — blocked one side of the Prospekt completely.

Sonya waited at the foot of the slide, where the sleds flew from the ramp and down the street on polished ice. There was always a policeman at the door of Sazikov's about ten steps from where she stood, but she was sure he wouldn't recognise her. For one thing her photograph on the wanted-posters was unrecognisably flattering. For another, her shawl was clenched tightly round her face. At two minutes to two by the big clock in the window of Fabergé, she saw Anna approach the slide, dressed in fashionable black. Anna was wearing a hat that would have fed a small village for a month if she'd spent her money on potatoes instead of millinery. The hat annoyed Sonya, but then something about Anna always annoyed her — it was a sensation she'd learned to expect. And where was Evgenya? The girl was becoming a nuisance. Sonya had received a letter from Kherson — Vitya's work was going exactly to plan. But the coded part of the letter had six unwelcome letters in it: HVUCNE. 'Have you seen E?' There was no rose without a thorn, Sonya reflected. Though this thorn might, with a little ingenuity, be broken off.

Anna turned her head – a girl was approaching her. Evgenya perhaps. Or possibly one of Anna's friends – Anna knew dozens of women who might be shopping in the Prospekt in the early afternoon. Sonya saw Anna and the girl shake hands and then, on second thoughts, kiss each other three times like intimate friends. The girl was not badly dressed – a fur collar, an almost matching fur hat. A pretty girl. Strong and lean. Anna offered the girl her arm, and they walked off together in the direction of the Winter Palace. It was Evgenya then.

Sonya watched as the two women sauntered down the crowded, well-swept sidewalk. No one seemed to be following them. Sonya hastened after them as they wove their way across the Morskaya, zig-zagging through the almost stationary chaos of sledges, sleighs and drays.

"I love that slide," Anna was saying, her voice raised above the din of the traffic. "Years ago, two of us dressed up like boys and went down it."

"Girls go down it too," Sonya cut in coldly from behind without saying hello. "Always did."

"That wasn't the point," Anna replied smoothly, ignoring the strangeness of the interruption.

"You can leave her to me, Snowman," Sonya told her. "Thanks for your help."

"You're welcome," Anna said cheerfully, turning on her heel and making her way back to Sazikov's.

"You're Evgenya," Sonya said to the girl who was standing bewildered amid a line of sledges that had just begun to move. "I'm a friend of Viktor Pavlovich. Come with me."

They reached the sidewalk again. Sonya led the way in silence through an arcade of expensive shops and a tangle of streets. They reached a *salon de thé* just opening for the first afternoon shoppers. Sonya knew the place. There were tables on the ground floor and upstairs. It would be an hour before the place filled up.

They sat at an upstairs table overlooking the street. Sonya let her shawl fall back from her face. "Let me look at you," she said to Evgenya. "Take off your hat."

She saw the flash of rebellion in Evgenya's lively brown eyes. "Take it off," Sonya repeated.

Fumbling a little, Evgenya took off her gloves then pulled out the two long hatpins that kept the hat in place. She took off her hat and put it on the table with the pins. Her hands went to her hair, tidying, smoothing, coquetting even with Sonya.

"Viktor Pavlovich asked me to talk to you," Sonya explained. "So tell me who you are."

"Who am I? You know who I am."

"You're Evgenya."

"Yes."

"That all?"

"Evgenya Antonovna Grishina."

"That's your name. It's not who you are."

The girl looked bewildered. Her mouth opened to say something, but she closed it again. Sonya saw that she had strong, even teeth. Altogether she was a charming girl, though apparently not intelligent. Or maybe she was just another example of the unmitigated ignorance in which Mother Russia drowned her womenfolk.

"Viktor Pavlovich is working for me now," Sonya said. "He asked me to find you something."

"Find me something?"

"Something to do. For us."

Another blank look.

"For the Committee."

She saw the sudden light of comprehension. And more. With the word *Committee*, Evgenya had recognised her face from the police posters. "Don't say anything," Sonya warned her urgently. "The waiter's coming up the stairs." It had been a mistake. She should have taken the girl to a safe house. There was no guessing how she'd react now, sitting in a tearoom with the most wanted woman in the Empire.

But an ambiguous "Oh" was all Evgenya said. She turned to the waiter who was wheezing up the stairs and gave him a brilliant smile. "You were quick," she said, "and such steep stairs." Sonya watched the waiter's sour face melt into the imbecile grin that afflicts men when a girl is pleasant with them. And the grin, Sonya saw, included her too. She shook her head in acid amusement and ordered black tea with lemon.

"Viktor Pavlovich has told me about you," Sonya began again as soon as the waiter was out of earshot.

"There's not much to tell," Evgenya replied easily.

"He says you don't want to get married. Is that true?"

"You're not married?" Evgenya retorted. "Are you?" Then more softly, "I'm sorry. It's none of my business."

"But I think you're fond of him." The conversation was moving quickly, but that was what Sonya liked – no one knew what to expect.

"Fond of him?"

"Love. You love him."

"Did he tell you that?" Evgenya asked.

Sonya smiled ruefully – a little girl guarding her precious secrets. "No," she said. "But it's obvious. Isn't it?"

"I suppose it must be," Evgenya replied, out of her depth and struggling.

"You think that's appropriate? In this modern age? For a woman to love a man?"

"Or a man to love a woman?" Evgenya questioned.

"Men can't help it. They have no control over their feelings." She watched Evgenya struggle with this new view of things.

"You think it's wrong?" Evgenya asked.

"I didn't say right or wrong. I said appropriate. Or inappropriate." Sonya sighed. The girl wanted things spelled out. "Imagine a situation like this. The Committee has an important job for you, but the man you think you love is injured and needs your help."

Evgenya nodded.

"Would you do the job? Or nurse your boyfriend?"

Evgenya understood now, but she didn't reply at once. Then, slowly: "Vitya didn't tell me about the work he's doing. Nothing. Not even where he is."

It was an indirect answer but useful. Sonya nodded. "Has he written?"

"No. He said it was forbidden."

"Yes it is. So he puts the work before you. Rightly so. And you'd do the same?"

Again Evgenya hesitated, seeing the trap, but there was no escape. "I suppose so," she said.

"Yes or no?" Sonya pressed home her advantage.

Evgenya picked up one of the hatpins and began to twist it in her fingers. She tested the sharpness of the point against the ball of her thumb. Sonya saw the flesh dent inward. Then a sudden ooze of blood as the pin broke through the skin. Evgenya put the pin back on the table beside the other. Sonya saw that the pins didn't quite match. Evgenya looked at her opaquely and then folded her arms. "You decide," she said.

"How can I decide a thing like that?" Sonya exclaimed, startled and suddenly at a loss. What did the girl mean: *you decide*?

The tea arrived. Evgenya was all smiles again for the waiter. With the tea he'd brought a plate of little meringues that neither of them had ordered. They were 'on the house'.

Sonya sensed an obstinacy in Evgenya that she found attractive. She was tougher than most girls of eighteen, and a lot wilder. And that *you decide* had the mix of submission and rebellion the Movement needed. As the older woman, she poured the tea, saying nothing more until the waiter was downstairs again. Then: "I have work for you in Odessa. There's a press. You'd learn typography. Print pamphlets. That sort of thing."

"I don't have the train fare," Evgenya replied. "I've only got ten roubles in the world."

"So you accept?"

Evgenya shrugged. She'd put her fate in Sonya's hands – of course she accepted.

"I can give you a ticket and money for the journey. When can you go?"

Evgenya shrugged again by way of reply.

"I ought to tell you, so you understand me properly," Sonya explained. "Viktor Pavlovich is not in Odessa."

Evgenya picked up one of the meringues. It had a coating of rice paper underneath. A red stain quickly suffused the paper from the blood on her thumb. She looked at the stain for a moment but ate the meringue anyway.

Sonya's calculation was this: Viktor Pavlovich, if things went on as they'd started, was the best man the Committee had recruited for many months. Unfortunately he'd fallen for an extremely pretty, wilful and possibly wanton young girl. If the Coalminer was to work successfully, Evgenya would have to be 'neutralised' as the chemists called it. Sending her to Odessa would create an obstacle – 1500 versts of imperial territory. But there was more. Mischa Trigony, who ran the operation in Odessa, was a ladies' man. His codename was *Milord* because of his princely dress and his easy way of spending money. The group he'd established was half men and half women – young women, slack in their ideology and loose in their behaviour. A certain way of life had developed in Group South, and Sonya found it distasteful. She'd planned work for herself in the south in the spring. Odessa would be her base, but she wasn't looking forward to it. And Evgenya? It seemed she had a way with men. Compared with most women in the Movement, she was pretty. Vigorous, strong, attractive. Obstinate and submissive. Sonya wondered if the girl was still a virgin – probably she was. In Trigony's group, Evgenya would be besieged. It would help. Viktor Pavlovich would certainly lose interest in her if she began to play the whore. And if she didn't… if she didn't, the Movement would find a place for her – either way it wasn't a problem.

Sonya wrote to Trigony in Odessa, but his reply was slow in coming. Meanwhile Evgenya stayed at home squabbling with her despairing mother and her fatuous father. To ease things, Sonya asked Anna Petrovna to invite the girl to stay with her – the invitation gave Evgenya a reason to pack her bag and leave home without scandal. As soon as word arrived from Odessa, Evgenya would be on her way.

# Extract 3

Political assassination has been with us as long as politics itself. Judith and Holofernes, Brutus and Julius Caesar, Charlotte Corday and Marat: there is no need to multiply examples. Until the death of Alexander II, the most celebrated assassin in the history of our Movement was undoubtedly Vera Zasulich. Armed with a miniature pistol, she approached General Trepov ostensibly to make a petition; he was Governor of St Petersburg at the time. At close range, she shot him in the chest. The pistol was too small, the wound was trivial, and a few weeks later Trepov was riding round Petersburg in his carriage as though nothing had happened. The extraordinary thing about Zasulich's case was, of course, what happened next: she was arrested, tried, and acquitted in the face of plain evidence. A jury of twelve middle-class citizens found her not guilty. Perhaps they were all would-be assassins. Whatever the reason, when the police tried to re-arrest Zasulich outside the courtroom, the crowd rescued her and she escaped to Switzerland. That was in early 1878.

From then on things began to change. In 1879, Prince Mirsky made an attempt on the life of General Drenteln, head of the Third Section. Despite police precautions, Mirsky was able to gallop up to the General's carriage, fire a shot through the open window, and gallop off again without pursuit. In fact, the Prince was a poor shot: he fired twice and missed his target by yards.

As it developed, Mirsky's case did not follow the same lines as Vera's. Unlike her, he did not escape for long. He'd been recognised, and the Third Section began what the newspapers called a 'man-hunt'. If the reader is familiar with *Les Misérables*, he will recall that Inspector Jouvert took an entire lifetime to track down Jean Valjean in a country as small as France. The Third Section, with the aid of the telegraph, picked up Mirsky in Taganrog exactly four months after his attempt on Drenteln. Taganrog is 900 miles from St Petersburg. Mirsky was arrested, tried and sentenced to life imprisonment.

Mirsky's arrest should have alerted us to the potential reach of the police, but it did not. If we had improved our planning and tightened our security in 1879, we might have created an organisation strong enough to conduct a revolution. As it was, we remained amateurs while the Third Section, with Drenteln at its head, became the most effective nemesis of revolution since Caligula's praetorian guard. (*Memoir of the People's Will*, Chapter 3.)

# Chapter 4

## I

Anna told the sleigh-driver to stop opposite the Austrian embassy. The runner ground against the kerbstone and the sleigh stopped. She paid the driver, glancing back down the street to see if other sleighs had stopped. She saw nothing suspicious, but in the chaos of evening traffic, she couldn't be sure. She was poorly dressed – a dark cloak over a black, shopgirl's dress and a brown shawl over her head.

Anna owned an apartment block on the Obuchovsky Prospekt just near the Haymarket. It was a gloomy building with cavernous, unfashionable shops at street level. One of these shops sold pianos, though the stock never changed and the owner existed entirely on a subsidy paid to him by his landlady. Through the shop and then through an obscure inner doorway, Anna could slip in and out as she pleased. In one of her flats she kept the old clothes she wore when she wanted to disguise herself. She had make-up there too, grey hair powder, bags, umbrellas – everything she might need but nothing that could incriminate her.

It had snowed all afternoon and the street was bright with reflections from the shop windows. A few innocent flakes of snow were still falling – somehow they made the yellow gaslight seem less sinister.

Two streets away, as they'd agreed, Evgenya would be waiting in a second-hand clothes market. Evgenya was a puzzle, Anna reflected as she waited for her sleigh to disappear into the traffic. As soon as the sleigh was gone, she turned into a side-street, avoiding the brooms and shovels of the shopkeepers busy now heaving snow into the roadway. She'd invited the girl to stay with her – it had been Sonya's idea, but it was no great imposition. Anna's townhouse was a handsome building, not quite a palace, on the embankment of the Catherine Canal. Twenty rooms, fifteen servants, and stabling for four horses. It was completely safe – the police could search it as often and as thoroughly as they liked – there was nothing for them to find. Illegals like Sofya Perovskaya avoided the place completely. Anna had told her servants that Evgenya was to be governess to a distant niece and that she'd stay with them till spring.

Leaving the Austrian embassy behind her, Anna walked slowly, keeping close to the shop-fronts. Abruptly she turned into a dark entranceway. An ill-lit passage led from the street into an inner courtyard. Halfway down the passage, she stopped by the yardkeeper's door and pretended to rummage in her shoulder-bag. No one followed her into the entrance. She waited a moment longer, shivering in the evening air, and then set off again. The raw passageway and the courtyard beyond smelt of sewage, the eternal smell of Petersburg, worse in the winter when the drains froze. The filthy courtyard ended in a snicket between towering walls. There was another courtyard beyond, then a street with the clothes market at the corner. Without difficulty she spotted Evgenya – the girl was poorly dressed, trying on hats in a foxed mirror by the light of a paraffin lamp.

Anna approached her quietly from behind and stopped at arm's length, waiting for her to turn. The wait wasn't long. The two women nodded a greeting, behaving with the churlish restraint of the poor – even a handshake would have betrayed them immediately.

"How did you know I was behind you?" Anna asked.

"I just knew," Evgenya replied, taking off a battered hareskin helmet and putting it back on the trestle table.

"Fifty kopeks?" the stallkeeper offered.

"It's a nice hat, but not today," Evgenya replied, pulling her shawl over her head.

They set off together. It was a long walk. First they had to cross the river, heading north. The Alexander Bridge had been dismantled for the winter and the roadway led across the icy river. The ice-way pinged alarmingly under the iron hooves of horses. New snow covered the treacherous, slippery ice. For a while they raised their skirts an inch or two to keep them clean, but they soon gave up – walking without falling over was hard enough. Every few yards they passed a fishing-hole bored through the ice, sometimes lit by a lantern on a tripod.

"What's the lantern for?" Evgenya asked.

"To attract the fish I think," Anna said, "though how anybody could eat what comes out of the Neva I've no idea." As she spoke, she slipped, falling to her knees. Evgenya helped her up.

"Some of those fish-holes are big," Evgenya said. "Be careful." And they trudged on.

"So you delivered your package this afternoon without breaking your neck," Anna said.

"I'm more used to the ice than you," Evgenya replied indirectly.

It was the first job they'd given Evgenya – to collect an envelope from an anonymous courier who'd be standing in the Carriage Museum. Then she'd hide the envelope in a collapsed wall of wattle and daub on the Vassilyevsky Island. That was what the Guardian wanted: documents to be moved secretly, anonymously and with the couriers ignorant of what they were carrying.

"It's already spring in Odessa," Anna told her. "It'll be a shock when you get there."

"If ever I go," Evgenya said. "Have you heard anything?"

"In a way, yes."

"What? Tell me!"

"This evening – where we are going – it's all connected."

"So where *are* we going?"

"It's near the embankment. Opposite Kammeny Island. I've only been there once."

"And what's going to happen?"

"I asked Sonya if I should tell you. She said probably not. But she didn't forbid it."

"You do what Sonya tells you, don't you."

"Everyone does."

"But you're rich. You can do what you like. Your servants are petrified of you."

"There's only one Movement," Anna replied, "and I'm part of it." It was a shallow answer, she realised, not enough to satisfy even Evgenya.

"Why? What sort of part?"

Anna always felt uncomfortable when her motives were questioned. Only one person, a Scottish engineer who worked for her in Rostov, had any idea what she was planning. "Maybe I have the same reasons you do," she replied evasively.

"I don't know any reasons. Not proper ones anyway."

"Goose," Anna said laughing. "But at least you're honest about it."

"Am I going to be part of it?" Evgenya asked. "Is tonight...? What do they call it?"

"... an initiation?"

"Is it?"

"In a way, yes."

"What does that mean, initiation?"

"It means you'll know things, you'll have done things, that make you... that make you like the rest of us."

"How like the rest of you?"

"Apart from society. Outside the law." She hesitated. Evgenya had to understand, with no chance of ambiguity or misunderstanding. "Criminal," she said finally.

"Criminal?"

"Of course. What you did today was criminal, though you didn't know what was in the package. If you're caught, they'll be lenient – hard labour for a few years and Siberia for the rest of your life. What your cousin, Vitya, is doing is criminal. If they catch him, they'll hang him."

"I know that," Evgenya objected flatly. "We talked about it. Me and Vitya."

"Doesn't it worry you? What happens to you?"

"Yes, of course." She shrugged and added: "It does, and it doesn't. I don't know really."

Anna said nothing. How could a girl of eighteen be so casual about prison, about hanging, about hard labour? Perhaps she felt invulnerable. Or perhaps she simply lacked imagination. Maybe she lived only for the moment. She remembered Evgenya's words to the stallkeeper: *it's a nice hat.* It was a horrible hat. Why say something like that? Just to keep the moment sweet. A craving for admiration. *What a sweet girl!* As long as the stallkeeper felt she was a sweetheart, Evgenya didn't care what lies she told him. A girl without principles. A nihilist in fact. A nihilist by nature. Though, of course, such people had their uses. Maybe Sonya had understood the girl already. Attractive, obedient, and reckless – if that was what Sonya wanted…

"But what I don't understand," Evgenya was saying, "is why? Why make me a criminal?"

"A criminal can be threatened," Anna told her. "If you get out of line, you can be denounced to the Third Section. It's a way of enforcing discipline."

"Out of line? Sofya Luovna's line?"

"Usually. We tend to do what she tells us – as you've already seen."

"And me? Tonight?"

"You'll see. It may be rather horrible. Try not to throw up."


## II


Anna led the way down icy streets, each more squalid than the last. They passed a barracks and the guard at the gate greeted them with cheerful obscenity. Evgenya opened her mouth to return his gibe, but Anna stopped her: "If you say anything, he'll remember you," she warned. "We must be as anonymous as the rats in the sewers."

They trudged on. Anna's steps grew less certain, and finally she stopped. "I think we're lost," she said. The nearest streetlight was a hundred yards away, dim and yellow. "I hope that light's on the embankment," she said, "or God knows where we are."

They reached the light and an iron railing that ran along the frozen river. A row of gaslights disappeared in both directions into the murk of snowflakes and night.

The street they were looking for had a tavern on the corner. They found the tavern a hundred yards down the embankment. It was in darkness and surrounded by leafless trees. Sleighs with drivers waited in the snow. From inside came the sound of an accordion playing a waltz.

"One more check in case we've got a tail." Anna rested her back against one of the chestnut trees and held out her arms to Evgenya. The girl hesitated for a second, then put her arms round Anna's ice-covered coat and shawl. Anna felt the supple young body adjust to hers, seeking warmth and perhaps protection. It was bitter cold, but at least there was no wind. They watched in silence. Along the embankment, nothing moved.

They waited, each thinking her own thoughts. This meeting tonight – it was an unpleasant business, Anna reflected. A tangled history lay behind it, though the facts were clear enough. The old Section South had run a printing press in Odessa. Mischa Trigony – Milord – had taken it over when he'd formed his new group. Somehow the Third Section had found out about it and raided the place. Six girls had been arrested: three of them were already dead – two had hanged themselves, or so the authorities said, and the other had died of prison fever. The press and the type had been lost as well as a great deal of paper. The Committee had found out who'd squealed and picked him up: Reinstein, a Jew. He'd been uncovered in Moscow early in January, but there had been a knife fight and he'd escaped. Then he'd shown up again, this time in Petersburg. This time he hadn't got away. Tonight he'd be tried, found guilty and executed. A plain act of murder – why call it anything else? When the Committee ordered an execution, Mikhail Popov, the *Hangman* as they called him, did the dirty work. Anna had met Popov only once – she shuddered at the memory. His broken, blue, nerveless hands and his cropped head with its inhuman bull-neck – better not think about him at all.

"Time to go," Anna whispered. On a sudden impulse, she kissed Evgenya's ice-cold cheek. The girl was in for an ugly evening. Now they'd found the side-street, Anna began looking for an *isba* with two candles burning in the window. If it was safe, one candle would be above the other.

They found the candles. The *isba* was separated from the street by a fence. There was a gate standing wide open on broken hinges. Even in the dim light of the candles, Anna could see the prints of many footsteps on the snowy pathway. "Better clean the path afterward," she whispered to Evgenya. "Too many footprints."

Anna rapped with her knuckles on the door. The rhythm was the first phrase of 'An der schönen blauen Donau'. Five-two-two. The door opened. "In," Anna said.

There was no light in the entranceway. Anna felt wooden steps and a wooden floor beneath her feet. She smelt the peaty, rotten smell that wooden houses never lose in the swamps of St Petersburg. Someone was standing by the door. She sensed it was a woman, but she could see nothing. Then a woman's voice: "You brought our little *Mimi* with you. Good."

It was a cold, small voice, incisive and compelling – Sonya. And evidently Evgenya had been given a code-name: Mimi. It was always Sonya who decided these things. But it was an odd choice, to name her after the slut in Henri Murger's mean little story.

"Don't take your coats off, the place is freezing," the voice continued. Anna felt her arm gripped and Sonya propelling her toward the sound of restrained voices in an inner room. A curtain parted. The light of a single oil-lamp was blinding after the darkness outside. Half a dozen people were in the room, two sitting on simple chairs and the others sitting on the floor, their backs to the bare wall. Three of them were women. There was a samovar on a table, but it was unlit and there were no glasses for tea.

Anna felt the eyes of the group on her.

"Snowman!" A thin man stood up and shook Anna's hand, as one man might greet another. The women nodded to her without warmth. The two remaining men sat immobile, backs to the wall. They were Georgians, dark-eyed and black-haired – one of them was Popov.

"Did you tell Mimi why we're here?" Sonya asked.

"Yes," Anna replied. It was a stupid name for the girl, they'd have to change it.

"We're waiting for the Guardian," Sonya explained. "When he's here we'll start."

"We weren't late?"

"No," Sonya replied vaguely. She was scrutinising Evgenya's face critically and without ceremony. "You did your job this afternoon," she said. "I already heard. Sit down now, over there by the wall. There aren't enough chairs. And keep quiet. Later on you'll be asked to say one word: *yes* or *no*. Otherwise, keep your mouth shut."

Evgenya sat down as Sonya told her. She left her shawl round her head, waiting perhaps for Sonya's order to remove it. Why was Sonya so harsh? Anna wondered – Evgenya opened up so easily to a word of praise. But Sonya had her ways, and disconcertingly often she was right.

The thin man who'd greeted Anna now offered her his chair, a kitchen chair made of bentwood. A similar chair stood in the middle of the room with short lengths of cord hanging over its back. Anna accepted, despite Sonya's ironic scowl. As Anna sat down, Sonya went and stood behind her. She felt Sonya's hands pull back her shawl from her head. She sensed Sonya's face, inches from her head and heard a tiny indrawing of breath. No, her hair wasn't scented, whatever Sonya had expected.

Sonya began to ask casual questions and to listen carefully to the answers. Had Anna heard the talk about giving the police guns? And what about the new idea of putting photographs in passports? A batch of prisoners had left Petersburg for Siberia the week before, but passers-by had given them no alms for the journey – what did Anna think about it? Questions. What was the point? A glance at Evgenya made it clear – the girl was gazing at them intently, maybe trying to fathom their relationship. And Sonya wanted it to seem friendly, intimate even.

"Don't call her Mimi," Anna said quietly. "That's not who she is."

"Not yet," Sonya shrugged. "Give her a name yourself if you want."

"She reminds me of a gypsy sometimes," Anna suggested. "All that black hair and her white skin. Wild. Canny."

"Call her that then: *Gypsy*. I'll tell the Guardian."

They fell silent. The other women in the group exchanged occasional whispers. The two Georgians said nothing. No one spoke to Evgenya.

Finally Sonya broke the silence. "I don't think the Guardian is coming," she said. "We have to start." She nodded to the Georgians. "Popov," she ordered. "Bring him in." The two men stood up and tramped out of the room.

"Olga," Sonya said at length, "check the two candles. The Guardian might come late." The woman called Olga opened the thick, dusty curtain in front of the window.

"The candles are good for another half hour," she said.

The Georgians burst back into the room, half carrying, half dragging a thin, dirty man with a rag tied round his mouth. He was barefoot and thinly dressed, shivering with cold and fear.

"Walk, you bastard," grunted Popov, jerking the arm of the prisoner.

Everyone stood up.

"Take that thing out of his mouth," Sonya ordered. The Hangman untied the rag. With his free hand, the prisoner pulled a pad of wet cotton out of his mouth and spat on the floor.

"Reinstein," Sonya said.

The man looked at her.

"Sit on the chair," Sonya ordered him. The Hangman pushed the chair into place behind the prisoner.

Reinstein glanced at the doorway, perhaps hoping for rescue, perhaps calculating his chance of making a dash for it.

"Sit down when you're fucking told," the Hangman said, his blunt hand clenching into a fist. Reinstein sat down.

"You know why you're here?" Sonya asked. Her breath came so weakly from her lungs that her voice was hardly a whisper.

"No," Reinstein said.

"You certainly know why you're here. You know what you did. You remember Akim Nikonov – so you know how we deal with traitors."

"I know what you think I did," Reinstein said.

"And you deny it?"

"It's ridiculous," Reinstein retorted.

"Reinstein," said Sonya, "on 13th September last year, you reported to Colonel Shuvolsky of the Third Section in Odessa the existence of a printing press. Do you deny it?"

Reinstein looked at her, the shadow of defiance in his face draining away. "I deny it," he said flatly.

"Don't waste time," Sonya warned him. "Why deny what we both know?"

"I deny it," Reinstein repeated weakly.

The Hangman moved behind the chair. He took a piece of cord, knelt on the floor, and lashed Reinstein's wrists together behind his back. Then he stood up and put his hands on Reinstein's shoulders. Sonya nodded. With his thumbs firm behind Reinstein's neck, the Georgian felt with his fingers for Reinstein's collarbones. At another nod from Sonya, the Hangman pressed the bones hard into Reinstein's body. Reinstein began to squeal and then to scream. Sonya made a slight gesture with her head and the pressure stopped immediately. Sonya waited till Reinstein was quiet again.

"Have you changed your mind?" Sonya pursued in a voice that hardly disturbed the ugly, silent air in the room.

"What difference does it make if I deny it or not?" Reinstein panted.

"If you mean, will you go free, the answer is no," Sonya replied. "It makes no difference."

"So?"

Sonya nodded again at Popov. "Put the gag back," she said. "He makes too much noise."

At first the prisoner clenched his mouth against the filthy, wet gag, but then the Hangman squeezed the muscles of Reinstein's jaw. The gag went in and the Hangman tied it tight with the rag. Reinstein was trying to say something, perhaps the admission that Sonya was demanding, but she signalled the Hangman to continue. The Hangman took his place again behind Reinstein's back and the terrible pressure began once more on the thin collarbones. Reinstein was screaming still, but all Anna could hear was a frantic ripping of the soft flesh in his throat and an inhuman squealing trapped somehow inside his head.

Olga, the woman who'd checked the candles, vomited suddenly across the floor and sank against the wall, trembling. "I'm sorry. I'm sorry," she whimpered, wiping her mouth angrily with the back of her hand.

The torment continued till something cracked in one of Reinstein's shoulders. It was a faint sound, muffled and sinister, but Anna heard it as loud as an axe splitting a log. She glanced at Evgenya; the girl's dark eyes were blazing with astonishment and fascination. The Hangman relaxed his grip. The other

Georgian removed the gag, stained now with fresh blood, and untied Reinstein's hands.

"You're a Jew," said Sonya. "You should be preparing to meet your maker, not making us wait for the truth like this."

"Bitch," Reinstein said. The Hangman must have tightened his grip because Reinstein squirmed again and started to shriek.

Sonya shook her head. "Snowman," she said, "see what you can do."

Anna had left her chair and was standing now by the table with one hand on the cold samovar. She crossed the room, motioning the Hangman away from the chair. He looked at Sonya for confirmation. She nodded.

As Anna approached him, she saw something strange flicker in Reinstein's tortured, defiant eyes. She went behind his chair, where the Hangman had stood. Reinstein tried to turn his head to see her, but a stab of pain in his shoulder stopped him. He cried out and tried to take the weight of his head in his hands.

"Reinstein," Anna said. "How many times can a person die?"

He made no answer.

"Once," Anna said. "And you gave six of us away. Six that we know of. Your miserable death pays us back for one of them." Her voice throbbed. "The Hangman hurt you." She glanced across the room at Olga, who sat trembling like a child lost in a dark and sinister place, still wiping at her mouth with the back of her hand. "And as you see we find it hard to cope with your pain, some of us. The Hangman won't touch you again, not till we're finished with you. Then he'll kill you – if we tell him. But he won't hurt you again."

"Stand where I can see you," whispered Reinstein, his voice distorted by pain.

Anna moved a few paces and stood in front of Reinstein. She hated him: his rat's face, his treacherous, bloodshot eyes. "You've got a chance," she said. "Before you die, you can show which side you're on. Ours or theirs."

"Jews don't have a side," Reinstein replied in his crippled voice.

"So why betray us?"

"Is it important?" Reinstein said. "I did what I did. Somehow you found out. We find out all sorts of things in our trade, don't we? I made a mistake."

"What mistake?"

Reinstein said nothing, staring up at her face, strangely without fear.

"What mistake?" Anna persisted.

"Or you set your torturer on me? Is that it?"

Anna straightened her back angrily. "No," she said. "I told you he won't hurt you again."

"And him?" With wild eyes he gestured at the other Georgian. "And her?" This time it was Evgenya. The girl had moved forward on her knees – she was glaring at Reinstein like a hungry cat.

"No one will hurt you."

"And you?"

"Me?"

"Yes Countess Shestakova, Snowman, I know you."

"You know nothing." Anna's voice faltered, suddenly less certain.

"Of course I know you. I know a fucking bitch when I see one. I know you. I know you. I know you…"

Anna swung her right hand across her body and struck backhanded against Reinstein's face. She felt his jaw wrench to the side and saw his body crash to the floor, driven by the force of her blow. He lay where he fell, blood running from his mouth. He was trying to talk, spitting blood and a clot of flesh that looked like the end of his tongue. The confused sounds bubbling from his mouth were like names. And something that sounded like *baby*. He'd fallen close to Anna's feet. Blood splashed the wet hem of her dress.

Then, with deliberate fury, she drew back her foot and kicked him full in the mouth. "I forbid you," she said viciously. "I forbid you."

Reinstein curled up his body, trying to protect his head. "That's enough," said Sonya sharply. She crossed the room and took Anna roughly by the arm. "Calm down," she said quietly. "He confessed."

Reinstein was still trying to force words out through his broken mouth. Then he lay sobbing and hopeless on the floor.

"Pick him up," Sonya said to the Georgians. The Hangman grabbed Reinstein by his shirt collar and sat him back on the chair. The blood made Reinstein's face unrecognisable.

"We have to agree," Sonya said decisively. "We all heard what he said: 'I did what I did. Somehow you found out.' We agree he said that?" She looked round the group. Most of them nodded.

"Is that a confession? Do we agree it's a confession?" Now Sonya wanted a response from each of them in turn. She asked Anna first.

"Yes," Anna said. Her voice was congealed with fury – she could scarcely pronounce the simple word.

"Hangman?"

"Yes."

"Ilarion?"

"Yes," said the thin man weakly. "I think so."

"Is that yes or no? If you're not sure, say no."

"Yes then," came the uncertain reply.

"Evgenya?"

"Yes," the girl said without hesitation.

The round continued. Olga was the last. She was still trembling. "He betrayed us," Olga said. "It sickens me, and I want him to suffer. But…"

"That's enough," Sonya said. "Does anyone else have anything to say?"

No one spoke.

"The Guardian isn't here," Sonya continued, "so I'm the only member of the Committee present. The Committee gave an order: if Reinstein confesses and if we agree he's guilty, he'll be executed. We agree he confessed. Do we agree he's guilty?"

Again no one spoke.

The Georgians lifted Reinstein to his feet. Anna looked at his hanging jaw and his blood-spattered face. She shivered. The smell of Olga's acrid vomit became suddenly intolerable. A spasm of fear shook her whole body. She went to the wall and hid her face from the others.

"Reinstein," Sonya pursued. "Are there Jewish prayers you want to say before you're executed?"

Reinstein must have signalled yes, but Anna could hear nothing for the ringing in her ears – the names, the threats.

"Ten minutes then," Sonya told them. "You can all go. Unless you want to help the Hangman with the execution."

Anna forced herself to turn and face the room again. Reinstein was kneeling and whimpering some words in a language she didn't understand. Ilarion left quickly with most of the others. Olga, who lived in the *isba*, was discussing with Sonya how best to clean the bloodstains off the floorboards. Evgenya, she saw, was talking to Mikhail Popov – he was explaining something to her and she was nodding to show she understood. The other Georgian stood beside them, looking with blatant admiration at Evgenya's pretty face.

"The inside pump isn't frozen. I'll get some water," she heard Olga say. When Olga had gone, Sonya glanced across the room in Anna's direction, concerned and uncertain. It wasn't a suspicious look – not suspicious at all. Anna tried to smile.

Sonya crossed the room, her arms outstretched in comfort. Anna let herself be embraced and listened closely to the words Sonya whispered to her. "Of course it's upsetting. Such a revolting little shit. But, as soon as he's finished his prayers…"

Reinstein's prayers came to an abrupt end. With a groan of agony, he collapsed in a dead faint.

"Evgenya," Anna said. The girl was still talking with Popov, chatting it almost seemed. "We must go."

"I'm going with Mikhail," she said. "I'll find my own way home."

Anna shrugged. Mikhail? When had the girl found that out? "Take a sleigh from the tavern," she said coldly. "You've got money?"

"Yes," the girl replied. "Enough for a sleigh."

The Georgians and Sonya took Reinstein to a fishing-hole in the river ice to drown him. Evgenya went with them. When everyone had left, Anna cleaned up the floor with Olga and helped her sweep the front path. Occasional flakes of snow were still falling.

"Strange, that new girl," Olga remarked, grateful for the help. "Going off like that with the Hangman. He gives me the creeps."

"Not so strange really," Anna replied. "She's a normal, healthy young woman – she likes violent men. Killers, I should think, she finds irresistible."

"What's normal and healthy about that?"

"Well, of course, Popov isn't in uniform like most of our killers. For some strange reason, Olga, most of the girls I know marry *officers*. And no one thinks it the least unhealthy. Maybe it's because soldiers only kill factory workers and foreigners." She remembered Popov's broken knuckles gripping Reinstein's shoulders, caving in the collarbones till one of them fractured. And the gaudy troops of hussars and cossacks that clattered down the streets of Petersburg at all hours of the day and night – what were they? Popovs in pretty clothes. No better and no worse than the Hangman when you thought about it. Still, it *was* unexpected, Evgenya going off like that.

"I suppose you're right," said Olga. "Depends how you look at it."

They finished the path. One of the candles in the window had guttered out. The other still burnt, feeble and meaningless.

# III

Anna was back in her flat on the Obuchovsky Prospekt, transforming herself into the Countess Shestakova. She realised that Evgenya might well be home before her. The girl had gone off with the Hangman. But Sonya was with them too – Sonya would see no harm came to her. No harm? Nothing but harm ever came to Mimi and her kind. They went with men by the dozen, got sick, and that was it. The Haymarket was full of them. Mimi – that had been Sonya's name for her. Anna brushed the thought aside. She was beginning to like Evgenya, her hard-bodied, dark-eyed Gypsy. Maybe the girl *should* marry her cousin and go mining with him in the Ukraine. Though Evgenya didn't want to marry. Or so she said. Fashionable claptrap probably. The girl had no convictions, just second-hand theories she only half understood. But she had a sweetness – a wild, reckless sweetness. She remembered the girl's body hugged against her in the snow under the chestnut tree… she brushed that thought aside too. She had other worries, especially now, after Reinstein's confession. *I know a fucking bitch when I see one. I know you. I know you. I know you…* And he did. She knew what he'd been trying to say as her boot smashed his face: *Babe*. But no one had understood. Thank God, no one had understood.

Dressed now in her simple, expensive clothes, Anna slipped into the street through the piano-shop and found a sleigh at the corner of the Haymarket. In a few minutes she was in front of her town-house, with two servants in livery opening the wings of the front door and a third handing her from the sleigh to the house.

"Is Evgenya Antonovna back yet?" she asked.

"Yes Ma'am. Ten minutes ago. She went straight to her room."

Anna allowed the maid on duty to help her off with her coat. She unpinned her hat herself and handed it to the girl. "Have them bring some chocolate," she said, "to Evgenya Antonovna's room."

She'd given Evgenya a pretty room. It had been her own till her father had died and she'd moved into his pompous bedroom. She knocked.

"Come in." Evgenya's voice. Anna caught her breath, realising with surprise how much she wanted to see the girl. Someone she liked, someone who liked her, someone she could talk to.

Evgenya was already in her nightgown. The cheapest cotton, Anna saw. She was hanging up her day dress on the front of the wardrobe so the hem could dry. Anna had offered her a maid, but Evgenya said she didn't want one – the maid would know more about everything than she did.

"You! Anna Petrovna!" the girl exclaimed with obvious pleasure. She dropped the dress on the floor and stepped nimbly across the room, holding out her arms to Anna. Then she stopped and folded her arms self-consciously across her breast. The nightgown was thin and she was evidently unsure about her figure.

"Did you try the wrap?" Anna asked. She'd left an embroidered silk dressing gown hanging in the wardrobe for her young guest.

"Not yet." Evgenya fled back to the wardrobe and slipped her arms quickly into the dressing gown. "It's beautiful," she said, catching sight of herself in a long mirror.

"On you it is," Anna laughed.

Evgenya gave her a quick, childish grin. "You alright now?" she asked.

"Almost," Anna replied. "You don't mind if I come in? They're bringing up some chocolate."

"How could I mind?" Evgenya exclaimed. "It's your house."

There were two comfortable chairs on each side of the blazing fire. Anna sat down in one of them. "Hang up your dress," she said. "Or shall I do it for you? You've had a long day."

"I'll do it," Evgenya said, shocked, as she was meant to be, at Anna's condescension.

"That was horrible tonight," Anna said. "I don't think you should have been there."

"They drowned him," Evgenya said, suddenly sober. "In a fishing-hole. But I think he'd passed out by then. They didn't hurt him anymore."

"You saw it to the end?" Anna asked.

"Yes."

The next question was one that Anna dared not ask: *did he say any more about Babe?* Cautiously she changed the subject from victim to executioner. "You were talking to Popov, I saw," she said.

"Yes."

"Do you like him?"

"Like him!" Evgenya flashed indignantly. "He frightened the life out of me."

"I thought you liked it, talking to him."

"Why?"

"You were smiling. Chatting, I thought. You knew his name was Mikhail."

"He told me. I didn't ask him. I saw you go to the wall and hide your face. I thought you wanted to be left alone. He talked to me. What could I do?"

"Yes, I hid my face," Anna agreed. "I was angry. I needed time to control myself."

"You didn't look angry," Evgenya contradicted her. "You looked frightened."

"What makes you think that?" Anna retorted, quick to defend herself.

"You were. I could see."

"Come here, Evgenya." It was a plea, not an order. Evgenya came immediately to the fireplace and knelt beside Anna's chair. "You're right, I was frightened. But did anybody else see?"

"That you were frightened? I don't know. I think they were sorry for you, being called those filthy names. That's how it seemed to me."

"And you were sorry for me too?"

"No. I was afraid for you."

"I kicked him. In the mouth. A man with a broken collarbone. There was blood on my boot."

"Yes," Evgenya agreed. "That's why I thought you were afraid."

"Do you read palms, my little Gypsy?" Anna said, holding out her hand for Evgenya to examine.

"Why call me that?" Evgenya asked, puzzled.

"It's your new code-name. Sonya decided."

"Gypsy. That's what Valentina called me because of my black hair. She's a friend of mine. She's got five brothers."

"And they all want to marry you."

"Not exactly *marry*," Evgenya laughed.

"Oh…" Anna said. "Well, I hope you refused."

"So far," Evgenya said, with a sudden peal of merriment.

"It still amuses you, does it? Accepting? Refusing? Wondering if?" Gently Anna took Evgenya's hands and held them in her own. "Sit by me," she said. Evgenya turned, lithe and slender, and sat at Anna's feet, facing the fire. Anna felt the pressure of the young body tentatively against her skirt. She moved to make the girl more comfortable.

A maid brought in a silver tray with chocolate and milk warming over a flame. Anna told her to leave the tray on the bedside table and to turn out the lamp. Alone again, in the firelight, the two women sat in silence, watching the birch logs flame.

"And Sonya?" Anna asked at length. "Did she see I was… afraid?"

"I don't think so. But even if she did… why is it so important what she thinks?" Evgenya paused, but Anna didn't reply. "Of course I like her," Evgenya continued, "I admire her a lot. But she's not…"

"She's not what?"

"She's not like you." Anna heard diffidence and affection in the simple words. How strange, this moment of comfort between them after the awfulness of the day. Who was she, this Gypsy who could watch the murder of a helpless man and laugh an hour later about her boyfriends?

The girl's thick, black hair glowed in the firelight. "Do you brush it every night?" Anna asked, stroking the crown of Evgenya's head with her fingertips.

"Not really," the girl replied. "That's another reason Valentina calls me Gypsy, because I'm a mess half the time."

"Get the brush, I'll do it for you."

"No," Evgenya objected. "Let's stay like this. Such a beautiful fire."

"You don't have a fire at home?"

"Hot water pipes. It's horrible where we live. You've seen it: the railway, the gas-works."

"You have another place? In Yaroslavl?"

"It's mine. But not for much longer. I told my father to sell it. Or mortgage it."

"Why?"

"They need money," Evgenya shrugged. "The house is all that's left. And what good is a house to me?"

The girl had burned her boats, Anna thought. Walking out on her family, but leaving them enough to live on – for a year or two. Through her skirt, Anna felt the girl's arms clasping her, hugging her legs. It had been so long… She remembered sitting at the piano in Rostov and her father standing behind her, stroking her hair as she played. And she remembered him sitting in the same chair she was sitting in now in front of the bedroom fire, gossiping about the guests they'd entertained that evening. Her dear, dead father.

"So," Evgenya broke into her thoughts. "Why were you afraid? That's what you want to talk about, isn't it?"

"Take my shoes off for me," Anna said. "It's warm here."

Evgenya knelt to unlace Anna's elegant little boots. Her fingers were clumsy, her hands undeft – not at all like a maid's. "You know, Anna Petrovna, when Valentina and I have secrets to tell, we lie on the bed and whisper them. Somehow it's easier."

"That's you and Valentina," Anna objected. Half struggling, half submitting, Anna let herself be pulled to the bed. The old-fashioned bed-curtains were open. Then, for a second, she froze with doubt. What was Evgenya up to? Was the girl corrupt? In that way? No, she realised. It was impossible. For Evgenya, bed was simply a place where you could exchange secrets. At least that bed. At that moment.

"What are you waiting for?" Evgenya laughed, and pushed her companion with innocent freedom onto the silk counterpane. Anna felt Evgenya's body crash beside her, and then she heard: "Move over. I want some space too."

Anna lay on her side, her back turned to her mad gypsy-girl. She felt Evgenya curl behind her and then the girl's arm across her body, feeling for her hand. Their fingers locked. "Tell me now," Evgenya whispered. "But only if you want."

Anna did want. The girlish fight had, for a moment, shattered the seclusion in which she lived. No one wrestled with her, no one was boisterous with her or even playful. And no one had been since she was twelve. She wanted to tell, but how? "Six years ago I got back from Zürich…" Anna said slowly. "Tell you like that?"

"Yes," Evgenya said. "However you like."

"I was older than you are now, quite a lot. I got sent to Section South. They weren't political – just boys who liked blowing things up. Not terror like it is now; they used to call it 'propaganda by action'. It was more or less mindless violence. So, three boys and me. They told us to blow up a factory near Kherson."

"What sort of factory?"

"Soap."

"Soap?" Evgenya repeated. "Why blow up a soap factory?"

"I don't know. Those were the orders."

"Soap," Evgenya said thoughtfully.

"The soap isn't important," Anna said. "Shall I go on?"

"Yes."

"So the four of us rented an *isba*. I was in charge because I was older and I'd met Bakunin in Switzerland."

"Who?"

"Bakunin. He's a famous writer."

"I think I've read about him," Evgenya agreed doubtfully.

"The boys knew gunpowder, and I was supposed to know everything else. They were so young – younger than you, but they didn't like taking orders from a woman, even if I had flirted with Bakunin in the Lindenhof. It takes a while to get enough gunpowder together – so we were there for three months. Gunpowder's not like dynamite. You need much more of it." She stopped, unsure if Evgenya understood. "Am I explaining too much?" she asked.

"We've got all night," Evgenya replied, squeezing her hand.

"It was something new then – a woman telling men what to do – and we argued about it endlessly. We got drunk most nights and they started joking with me about what everyone nowadays calls 'free love'. In those days, that was completely new – at least in Russia. "If love is free, why aren't you free with us?" We went through it all, like you will in Odessa. Your right to your body; modesty is a kind of lying; your body's no different from any other woman's, so why hide it; all that eighteenth-century stuff about appetites – eat when you're hungry, drink when you're thirsty, and… Maybe Valentina's brothers talk that way – you hear it everywhere."

"Sometimes," Evgenya agreed.

"It's all rubbish if you think it through. And they had trouble with the democracy of it: did free love mean I had to choose one of them? Or could they choose who was going to have me?

"Anyway, we were due to blow the factory on July 14th – Bastille Day."

"Bastille?"

"It's a prison in Paris. They stormed it during the revolution."

"Oh," said Evgenya uncertainly.

"Everything was ready at the factory. And then I ruined it, Evgenya. I lost my head. It started with a stupid dare about taking off my blouse. I was drunk, and I did it. I don't give a damn about things like that. Sometimes it's even fun. Well, it didn't stop there, it never does, and I ended up in bed with one of them. It wasn't my first time. Not at all. In Zürich... It doesn't matter about Zürich. That kind of thing, well it goes to my head. I can't... I can't control myself. I couldn't think about anything else, and neither could he. This boy – just a boy."

She felt Evgenya's body grow tense and heard her breathing quicken – the story had begun to interest her. She tightened her grip on Evgenya's fingers.

"That's why I didn't make a proper plan to get away. There was a train at six in the morning. We blew up the factory just after midnight – long after the workers were in their barracks. Then, after the explosion – so stupid – we went back to the *isba*. Can you imagine? Escape is the first rule, unless you want to get hanged. We finished a bottle of vodka to celebrate. And Babe... We called him Babe because he was the youngest. Sixteen... I don't have to tell you, do I? The group was falling apart by then. They were Georgians – they understood rape and they understood marriage, but a Russian woman who couldn't stop..."

"I can imagine," Evgenya said. "I think so anyway."

"Well, in the end they crossed themselves before they spoke to me."

"Crossed themselves? Really?"

"No, not really. What I mean is – somehow they thought I'd come from hell."

"Oh..."

Anna paused – it was hard to guess what Evgenya was making of the story. "So," Anna began again when Evgenya asked no more questions. "The other two were waiting to leave. I was... I was with Babe. You understand?"

"With him?"

"In bed."

"Oh…"

"Then the soldiers came. Not the police. Just soldiers, checking addresses after the explosion. They saw the packed bags and decided to search the place. I'd sent my trunk ahead that afternoon, thank God. Babe was pulling on his clothes when they started on the bedroom. 'Who's the girl?' they asked. 'Just a whore. Leave her out of it,' Babe told them. So I played the whore. It wasn't difficult under the circumstances. I put on a dialect. Asked who was going to pay me if they took the men away. I stood up and told them to pass me my drawers – anything so they wouldn't ask for my papers."

"With your real name in?" Evgenya asked.

"Yes, we couldn't fake passports in those days. The boys knew me as Anna, but that was all. They had no idea who I really was."

"So what happened?"

"They took Babe away. And the others. I got away. That was it. The end. All three of them disappeared. Completely. It was my fault, Evgenya. Thinking with the wrong part of my anatomy. I killed them – the most stupid thing I did in my life."

"But why were you afraid tonight? I still don't understand." Evgenya's simple whisper was tempting. Evgenya had been in the *isba* – she'd seen everything, perhaps more clearly than Anna had seen it herself. And Evgenya had gone to the fishing-hole. She'd heard exactly what Sonya had heard. And she'd seen how Sonya had reacted. Did Sonya suspect? Anna had to know, and she had to know now. Nothing could be more dangerous than staying within Sonya's murderous reach if Reinstein had made her suspicious.

"Yes, I was afraid," Anna conceded. "Very. But you're not shocked? About what I just told you?"

"Not really. It's so easy to imagine. And it makes me feel… You with him. And in Tsurik before. It makes me feel I know nothing. I'm a stupid nobody."

"No," Anna contradicted. "One day you're going to surprise everybody. I know you are."

"I don't think so," Evgenya contradicted her modestly. "Not me. You're the one with the plans, not me."

"What do you know about my plans?" What did the girl mean? What could she have found out?

"Nothing. Only that you have them." Evgenya said nothing more, waiting like a child to hear the end of the story.

It was a moment or two before Anna could interpret the silence correctly. Then, driven by her fear of Sonya, she explained what had happened after she'd parted from Babe. "Afterwards…" she whispered. "Afterwards I thought no one knew, so I made up a totally different story to tell Sonya and the others. I told them I wasn't at the *isba* when the soldiers came. I was walking already, heading for the next station up the line."

"So you wouldn't look like an idiot," Evgenya surmised.

"Not really. So Sonya wouldn't think I'd given the boys away to save my own neck."

"Yes," Evgenya's voice was startled. "That's exactly what it might look like. To someone like Sonya."

"As long as no one knew I was there, in the *isba*, it made no difference what story I told. It wasn't true, but it didn't hurt anyone."

"But did someone know?" Evgenya asked, suddenly understanding. "That you were there?"

"I think Reinstein knew. I think that's what he was trying to say. He was working in Odessa then, with the Third Section. He must have been there when they questioned Babe and the others. They died in prison, all of them. So-called suicides. All they knew was my name, Anna. And what I looked like. They didn't even know I'd been in Zürich, so they couldn't have told much. But I'm sure Reinstein put two and two together later."

"He joined the Movement? Reinstein?"

"About a year later. None of us dreamed he was working for the Third Section. He was a Jew – no one even asked where he came from." She paused. "I'd never met him face-to-face, but when he saw me tonight and heard the word *Snowman*, then he knew for sure who I was. 'Yes Snowman, I know you.' He said it, didn't he?"

"Yes, he did."

"And he was going to tell Sonya."

"Tell her you'd betrayed the others?"

"I think so. I didn't betray them, but in the end it comes to the same. He'd have taken me with him – wherever he's gone."

"But it was gibberish what he said," Evgenya objected. "No one understood a word."

"You heard. *Babe*, he kept saying. *Babe*."

"Yes," Evgenya agreed, remembering. "He did say *Babe* – or something like it."

"And later at the fishing-hole? Did he say anything then? Tell me, Evgenya."

"No, nothing. Not a word."

"Thank God. If…"

"… if Sonya thought you'd been lying, there'd be two bodies under the ice. That's why you're so scared."

"Exactly." Anna let go of Evgenya's hand and turned over on the bed to face her. In the distorting red glow of the fire, Anna was startled at how young the girl looked – her smooth skin, her gleaming eyes.

"But you definitely heard it? That word?" Anna asked, hoping even now that Evgenya would deny it.

"Yes. He said *Babe*. Definitely."

"And Sonya didn't hear it?"

"I don't think so. But I'm scared stiff for you. My God!"

"Yes," Anna agreed, realising suddenly how far she'd gone. This chit of a girl knew enough to get her killed. The warm room, the affectionate arm clasped round her legs by the fire, the playfulness on the bed. It had been sweet. And there'd been no one, absolutely no one, for so long. Isolation – that's what she'd wanted. And for good reasons. But now to throw it all away, to put herself in the hands of an ignorant, unknown girl – it was beyond anything stupid.

"But, I still don't really understand. I mean, you came back from Tsurik. You were rich. Why do something like that? Blow up a soap factory? Or any factory at all?"

Anna said nothing.

"Tell me," Evgenya said, kissing her cheek, coaxing. A kiss? How much distance was there between Evgenya and Judas Iscariot? A million versts surely. Surely?

"Well," She took Evgenya's hand, held it to her lips and kissed her fingers, not once, but several times. "When I got back to Russia, my father was dead. The lawyers told me I'd inherited everything, but they couldn't promise me that the court – the court of probate it's called – would approve. It's unheard of for a daughter to inherit so much."

"Was that the lawsuit Mama told me about?"

"Probably. My uncles…"

"Yes, that's what Mama said."

"It took nearly two years. I had an allowance – not a big one. I could live in any of the houses but mostly I lived here, in this room. But everyone told me I'd lose. And if I lost, I wouldn't get a penny." She felt a throb of remembered pain – those days had been very bitter.

"So?"

"I'd made friends in Zürich. In the Movement. And I was sick of the endless, endless talk about money. Someone told me about a case like mine that had dragged on for twenty years."

"And then you won!"

"It was sudden. No one expected it."

"But you didn't give up – the Movement? I mean, most people would have."

"No they wouldn't. The Movement had me. I was a criminal. A blower-up of soap factories. And some other things. You can't walk away. You can never walk away."

"They wanted money?"

"Sometimes."

"How mean."

"Maybe. But you know, in most ways I wanted to be with them."

"Why?"

"Because, they're right for one thing. One day, somehow or other, they're going to win. So little by little, I got more involved. I paid for things, I helped with the planning. It can be very exciting. I mean, for you, even tonight…"

"Yes," Evgenya admitted. "Nothing in my whole life…"

"But you see what happens," Anna broke in. "Once you know *too* much, they can't turn you in to the police anymore. So either you do what they say, or it's Popov and a hole in the ice."

"Oh." In that *oh*, Anna heard a dream fall apart. The enviable, sophisticated, independent Anna who'd lived till that moment in Evgenya's imagination was gone.

"That business with your cousin Vitya – at the Drentelns – they *mobilised* me. That's what they called it: mobilisation. They tell me what to do, and I do it whether I like it or not."

"That's what I didn't understand," Evgenya said. "What made you do that, with Vitya. And tonight. I think… I think you're very brave."

Evgenya's voice was eager and filled with awe. *Brave.* Was that how she'd behaved in the *isba*? The old dream was gone, but a new one had swept into its place. Anna relaxed. For a while at least she could trust Evgenya's loyalty – affection even. "May I?" she asked softly.

"May you what?"

"Stay here tonight? With you?" She kissed Evgenya's hand again. Then the pang of guilt: maybe Evgenya would misunderstand – would think something was expected of her. Demanded of her even.

"Don't be silly," Evgenya laughed, a naughty child enjoying a new game. "Of course you can stay. The bed's big enough for a whole family."

# IV

Anna's maids came next morning at eight o'clock with hot water as usual. They found the mistress and her governess friend curled up on the bed together, fast asleep. The bed-curtains hadn't been closed. The mistress wasn't properly unlaced, and the governess was wearing a pretty embroidered kimono. The maids gave each other a knowing look. They crept out of the room and left the hot water outside the door.

"No wonder she ain't married," one of them giggled.

"Sh-sh," said the other. "Long as she pays our wages, what do we care?"

"And don't pester us with it."

"She never has, has she?"

"Not so far, no."

"Would you do it? If you had to? With her?"

"Course I would. So would you, if you got any sense."

"Better than factory work anyhow."

"You really think she's that way?"

"Never. We'd of known before. And anyhow, she didn't even unlace herself. What could she do in a dress like that?"

"Tight as a drum, she likes it. Hurts your hands, stringing her up like that."

"Well, the other one's young enough."

"Nice girl. Always gives you the time of day."

"Something odd about her though. Wild look in the eyes. Know what I mean? Don't think she'll make much of a governess. They like 'em prim and proper."

"Another few years and they'll all get their throats cut anyway. Or so Gerasim says."

"It's alright for him. Throat-cutting here, hole in the ice there. Who's going to pay our wages when they're all dead? Don't think about that, do they?"

"I asked him that, and he says, come the revolution, they'll take women in the army. We can sign up for the infantry."

"The army! They ought to lock him up. Fucking revolution. What's it for? Eh? What's the point of it?"

# Extract 4

I would like to write a few words about terror. The world has often seen terror exercised for political ends: Caius Julius Caesar Germanicus, known to the world as Caligula or 'Little Boots', was one exponent. Robespierre was another. Their terror was what we now call 'state terror' or terrorism from above. What our Movement invented was something new: terrorism from below. If a small group of people, acting secretly and with seeming invulnerability, can perpetrate acts of murder and destruction on such a scale that society goes into a state of shock and ceases to function, then that is terrorism from below. In itself terrorism achieves nothing. Rather it creates a climate in which change, perhaps massive and irreversible, can occur. The terrorists themselves, though they dream otherwise, can never steer this change. Their logic is the logic of despair: nothing can be worse than society as it is now, and therefore any change must be for the better. The practitioners of terror are inspired by dreams of utopian societies without hunger, without disease, without ignorance, without conflict and sometimes even without work. None of these conditions has ever existed in any society. Terror has not promoted and will never promote such conditions. Quite the contrary.

How was it that a group of idealistic youngsters invented this devastating social phenomenon? To instil terror in the minds of so many people that widespread and catastrophic panic ensues, terrorists must organise quickly and distribute orders in a flash. Writing a letter and sending it by a dispatch-rider is enough for a *plot*, but it cannot put enough resources in place quickly enough for *terror*. And the terrorist must be able to move fast, in and out: attack and escape. Finally, the attack must be devastating. Killing a provincial governor, burning down a country house, kidnapping the wife of a minister: these acts are trivial and can be achieved by the simplest peasant. The terrorist must blow up the Winter Palace, blast the imperial train off its tracks, kill the best guarded and perhaps, at least among the peasantry, the best loved man in the Empire. That is terror: to achieve the unthinkable, to shatter the bourgeois world. "Why would anyone do a thing like that? It's so pointless, so unthinkably horrible!" That is the reaction the terrorist hopes for. The telegraph and the railways gave us, of course, instant communication and high-speed travel. When in 1866 Alfred Nobel patented dynamite, he supplied the missing piece of the terrorist puzzle. A stick of dynamite is worth ten barrels of gunpowder. It wasn't long before the People's Will learned to put the new technologies together. Around the world since our time, our techniques have been copied and perhaps improved. Terror has taken root: it is an idea that will perhaps haunt mankind until those utopian dreams are finally realised. (*Memoir of the People's Will*, Chapter 20.)

# Chapter 5

## I

Evgenya's birthday fell on 26<sup>th</sup> March. By coincidence, it was Mischa Trigony's birthday too. Evgenya had been only a few days in Odessa, but, with Sonya's help and her own easy manners, she'd quickly found her feet in Trigony's new Section South. She'd worked at the press during the daytime, learning to set type. Each evening she'd gone back to the villa where Section South was living.

Mischa Trigony was not called Milord for nothing. His family was rich. The wealthiest of them was an uncle, his mother's brother, who'd emigrated to Canada leaving Milord in charge of his Ukrainian property, including the villa now in the hands of Section South. The villa was on low cliffs to the south of the city, with a view of the Black Sea through a spinney of pine trees. Milord himself lived in his old family home in the best part of town. On the least occasion he liked to throw a party in one of the city's pleasure gardens or, during winter, in a fashionable restaurant.

With the coincidence of his birthday with Evgenya's, Milord was in his element. The long table, with silver and cut glass, seated twenty guests. Milord presided from the middle of the table, with Evgenya on one side and Sonya on the other. Sonya sat with a frown of disapproval: the risk was abominable, the expense inexcusable, and the food too rich for her abstemious northern digestion. She drank no wine and made no attempt at small-talk. Yet she was not ignored. She was a legend – a disgruntled legend perhaps, but heroines are forgiven their idiosyncrasies. Luckily her bad temper had no effect on the others, the party was a celebration of Milord's birthday and the birthday of the pretty girl sitting next to him. The company rose to the occasion.

Evgenya took little part in the conversation – in fact she didn't understand much of it. Even so, her wry smile and her readiness to laugh when the others laughed, was a lively begetter of conversation in others. Taking her cue from Sonya, she drank little, mostly the cheerful Crimean champagne. She drank her wine from a cut-glass *coupe* which Milord told her had been modelled on the breasts of Marie Antoinette. The story was immediately disputed. The same story, someone shouted, was told of Diane de Poitiers, 200 years earlier.

"No!" argued another voice, strong and aristocratic. "Champagne wasn't invented till the seventeenth century, and anyway we have *coupes* in our family made in Venice when Marie Antoinette was still a flat-chested little girl."

"Well," insisted Milord. "This I know for sure – the girls at the *Folies Bergères* have to fit their…" He hesitated, "… their charms into a champagne *coupe,* or they don't get a job."

"You see how travel broadens the mind," the owner of the Venetian glasses hit back. His name was Oleg. He'd returned from a trip to Sebastopol that afternoon. He raised his *coupe* and drank a toast to his excellent friend, Mischa Trigony, the unsung lord of the *Folies Bergères*.

"I don't understand." Evgenya raised her *coupe* and studied it with a coy disbelief. She looked from her *coupe* to her breast and back again. "But the champagne would spill out," she said.

Milord laughed as though she'd said something worthy of Marie Antoinette herself. Evgenya drank her glass empty and put it down with a comic little shrug. She turned her head to catch Sonya's eye. Sonya wasn't laughing. She mouthed the word *Gypsy* and stood up.

"Evgenya and I are going back to the villa," she said. "We'll find a cab. You enjoy yourselves."

Evgenya stood up immediately with no hint of reluctance. The success of her little joke pleased her. Of course she knew exactly what Milord was talking about, she'd even read about the *Folies Bergères* in an article denouncing such things in one of Valentina's magazines. Women dancing naked on a stage. She'd sometimes wondered what it would be like. To watch. Or to be one of the dancers. She'd never been to a theatre, but the idea interested her – it gave shape to one of her fantasies.

Milord made no protest when Sonya stood up to leave. He was in awe of Sonya, just as they all were. That was something Evgenya had learned on the long journey south – there was no point in opposing Sonya. None at all. Milord escorted them to the door, helped them on with their coats, and waited while the doorman whistled for a cab.

As soon as the cab had turned the first corner, Sonya told the driver to stop. "We can walk," she said to Evgenya. "It's cheaper, and the exercise will do us good. They eat too much down here. All of them."

## II

Evgenya still couldn't quite believe that she'd travelled half-way across the Empire with the notorious Sofya Perovskaya, or that in Odessa they shared a bedroom, ate together, washed their clothes together, and walked arm in arm through the streets. Her abrupt passage from family domesticity through ease and luxury to conspiracy and adventure had left her bewildered but passionately aroused. There was danger now at every turn. Police, soldiers, agents of the Third Section – they'd passed hundreds of them on their way south. That evening, a room full of strangers had been aware that the terrorist *known as Sonya* was among them; betrayal was in the air they breathed. Yet Sonya was not at all the romantic heroine Evgenya, and thousands of girls like her, imagined. She was ugly and terse, more like a cattle-drover than a Russian Jeanne d'Arc.

"You didn't mind leaving the party early?" Sonya asked. Like many of Sonya's questions, it was closer to an order.

"Not at all."

"They won't be back till three or four," Sonya said. "Shall I put on a samovar?" They were in the kitchen where the big stove was still warm. The long night walk had left them shivering.

"You didn't drink any champagne," Evgenya said.

"Mischa drank enough for all three of us."

"He's funny. The things he comes out with."

"Do you like him?"

Evgenya hesitated. The question was leading to something. "Of course," she replied evasively. "Everyone likes him."

"That's not what I meant."

At the kitchen pump Evgenya filled one of the small samovars with water. She dropped half a dozen scraps of charcoal down the samovar's narrow chimney. Then she took the fire-tongs and held another piece of charcoal in the stove till it glowed red.

"I didn't want to stay too late," Sonya told her. "I'm leaving early tomorrow. I'll be back in a day or two."

"Where are you going?" Evgenya took the hot coal now and dropped it onto the others.

"Kherson."

"Is there a train?" Evgenya asked, carefully fitting the long chimney.

"Yes. It takes four hours. Change in Nikolayev."

"Kherson? Is that where Viktor Pavlovich is working?"

"What makes you think that?"

"You asked if I liked Mischa. Mischa? Vitya? I thought there might be a connection."

"You have a devious mind," Sonya remarked, "and such an innocent face." Then, "Why don't you blow on the coals? They catch quicker."

"You mean he *is* there, in Kherson. Four hours away."

"As it happens, yes."

"Why didn't you tell me?

"Why do you need to know?"

"Does he know I'm here?"

"No."

"Will you tell him?"

"What good would it do?"

"He might want to send me a birthday card." Obediently Evgenya knelt by the table and began to blow on the coals.

"Mischa gave you a present, didn't he?"

"Earrings. Opal."

"Why aren't you wearing them?"

"Opals are unlucky."

"So they say."

"And I *am* wearing them anyway." She pulled back her loose, black hair to show Sonya one of the earrings. "Why shouldn't Vitya know where I am?"

"The job he's doing is dangerous. If he's caught..."

"... he'd give us away. You think so?"

"You think he's too strong for them?" Sonya probed.

"No," said Evgenya. "I saw what you did to Reinstein. No one's strong enough..."

"Exactly," Sonya nodded. "If they catch you, they ask you what you know. When you say the word 'nothing', it's important they believe you, so it helps if you're telling the truth."

"Poor Vitya," Evgenya said quietly, a little sob choking her voice.

"The fewer people who know where he is, the safer he'll be." Sonya crossed the kitchen to where the girl was still kneeling. She put her hand on Evgenya's shoulder. "Pull yourself together," she said. "And don't drink so much. It makes you sentimental."

"Get off! Let me be," Evgenya snapped, shaking her shoulder free of Sonya's hand. It was detestable, the idea of Vitya in the hands of men... of men like Mikhail Popov.

"That's better," said Sonya quietly.

In her imagination, Evgenya began a passionate assault on Sonya and her cold-hearted bitchery. The samovar began to seethe.

"Shall I put some tea in the pot?" Sonya asked.

Evgenya eyed her spitefully and didn't answer. Yet, even in her anger, she saw that Sonya was right. Why get sentimental about the inevitable future? Sooner or later everything would end in unendurable pain, broken bones, and a hole in the ice. Reinstein's miserable end, or something like it, awaited them all. Even Vitya.

"Sonya," she said. "If I wrote a letter to him. Just personal things. Would you take it?" She stood up and found the tea caddy on the dresser. She put five spoons of tea into the little teapot.

Sonya said nothing, watching her measure tea into the pot. "No," she replied at last. "Let him work in peace."

# III

Evgenya worked each day at the press. The machine and the type were well concealed in the cellar of a cottage on a low chine about a mile from the villa. Two lobstermen lived in the house. Their simple boat was moored just off the beach and their lobsterpots were piled in front of the cottage. Behind the cottage was an overgrown garden with a fence and a gate into a narrow lane. It was easy enough for the women alone or together to slip in and out of the gate. The cellar was dark and smelt nauseatingly of printer's ink and paraffin. The work was tedious. The simple pamphlets and flyers went quickly enough, a single page printed on one side. What took time were the booklets they were printing on a dozen subjects: history, economics, the woman question. Sixteen pages of text simple enough for a factory worker or a study group to struggle through. Four pages were printed with engravings. In some groups, especially in the fish canneries, hardly a soul could read – the pictures helped them puzzle through the argument.

Writing these booklets was the work of two men and a girl of sixteen. The illustrators, an artist and an engraver, were both men. They all stayed in the villa, ostensibly preparing for John Murray of London, an illustrated guide to *Crimea and the Black Sea*. In case the Third Section visited the house and asked awkward questions, Milord himself had drafted a contract for the book in English, a fake – but a good one.

Another aspect of the work was holding meetings and making speeches among the factory workers of Odessa and the smaller cities nearby. None of the speech-makers lived at the villa, but they often stopped there for a night or two, picking up material and suggesting new ideas for booklets. Some nights there was quite a crowd.

The press work went smoothly. Evgenya saw that Sonya had no reproaches for Section South beyond a regular carping about their extravagance and a periodic denunciation of their depravity. Since their arrival in Odessa, Sonya had shielded her from much of what was happening. They shared a room at the top of the house. Each evening Sonya took her off early to bed, much as they'd left the party before the end. Evgenya hadn't complained. The close work in bad light and bad air gave her a headache. It was a relief to go to the cold, airy room and lie on the bed, talking to Sonya. They chatted about the booklets Evgenya was typesetting but couldn't always understand. Often Evgenya saw Sonya repress a flash of sarcasm. A repeated question, a word wrongly used, a missing fact of history – anything could trigger it. But there were no rebukes and no reproaches. With the others Sonya was different; she had a biting tongue and used it freely.

"Does your mother know where you are?" Sonya asked her quietly one evening.

"I sent her a letter," Evgenya told her, "when I was staying with Anna. I said I was going south – but I didn't say where of course."

"She'll want to know you've arrived safely, won't she?"

It was a question for a ten-year-old and Evgenya bridled:

"Do *you* write to *your* mother?" she asked.

"Yes," Sonya said simply. "Every month. To tell her I'm alright."

"But…"

"When I was arrested," Sonya said quietly, "I had to wait years for my trial. They let me stay with my mother in the Crimea. We got very close. I can't write her proper letters of course – the Third Section opens everything. So I write her notes with my left hand. From a servant."

"What's her name? The servant?"

"Kolya. He's a footman."

*We got very close.* Evgenya couldn't say that of her own mother. But all the same, Sonya was right, she should write home. "So how do you post them?" she asked. "The letters?"

"Always from Moscow. If I'm not there, someone who's going to Moscow posts them for me."

"Then perhaps…"

The morning after the party Sonya went through her morning exercises an hour earlier than usual. She was washed and dressed in her travelling clothes long before dawn. Half asleep, Evgenya got out of bed to hug her goodbye.

"Evgenya," Sonya said factually. "The cab's waiting. I heard it arrive. But… I want to say… just a few days we've been together. And I've come to… well, to like you. You may be ignorant, but you're not stupid. You'll be someone in the Movement, I'm sure of it. Now go back to bed. Do your exercises later. No one will stir till lunchtime."

In fact no work at all was done that day. They drifted together for lunch and sat round the big table all afternoon. As the wine went to their heads, one of the men, Timofey, produced a champagne *coupe* and suggested they hold an audition for the *Folies Bergères*. The idea was unanimously rejected, though on the grounds that it was too early for such frolics. Too early? Evgenya wondered.

"Well then," Timofey pursued, "who's most likely to get the job?"

"Certainly not me," said Larissa who ran the press. Her breasts were heavy and shapeless under her blouse. "They like skinny things."

"Don't look at me either," said the young writer, Darya, who was sixteen. Not at all pretty, Evgenya thought, and perfectly flat-chested. Of the three writers, Darya was the most convincing, or so Sonya said. Darya touched her breasts playfully and pursed her lips: "All I've got is nipples." Darya enjoyed the *frisson* of saying aloud things that many girls would hesitate even to think. It was expected of her, and she lived up to her reputation.

Evgenya sat with folded arms, hoping no one would drag her into the discussion. Though she'd wondered several times what her breasts would look like moulded in a champagne glass, she wasn't ready to try the experiment, at least not in public. As it happened no one so much as gave her a meaningful look, and she was grateful. Another girl, Elif – Azeri and Moslem – they let her alone too. Elif worked for Larissa at the press, saying little, though her translations of Caucasian curses made everyone laugh. Her Russian spelling was accomplished too, good enough to check the proofs. Evgenya envied her – how could an Azeri spell better in Russian than she did?

Then the subject changed – why not publish a booklet on contraception? With illustrations. As the merriment grew, Evgenya went to sit beside Elif. "I've got a bit of a headache," Evgenya whispered. "Do you know the way to the beach?"

Elif nodded.

"Could you show me?"

"Of course."

The two girls made their excuses and wandered through the spinney down to the beach. They talked about Petersburg and Azerbaijan, interested in each other's lives, but lacking the words to explain what was important or to pose the questions that would bridge the gap. The wind blustered from the east, and the huge rolling waves that presage a Black Sea storm crashed onto the sand. A stone jetty ran out into the sea. The waves surged against it, a wall of black water and white spray, tremendous and frightening. Dark clouds hid the setting sun, but the two women wandered on, almost as far as the cottage where the press was hidden. When they returned to the villa, the kitchen-maids were clearing the lunch table. In the drawing room, the owner of the Venetian glasses, Oleg, was playing Chopin on a handsome Bösendorfer. Nothing in all her years of hammering at her miserable piano had prepared Evgenya for that moment; the power of the huge instrument, the purity and intensity of the sound, overwhelmed her like one of the waves crashing on the sea-wall. The E-major *étude*. She heard the melody and the accompaniment together in the right hand, the melody strong, *legato,* and played with two fingers. She understood at last what Chopin wanted. How many wasted hours had she spent on that *étude*? She sat down entranced, lost to Elif, lost to everything else in the world.

Near the end of the piece Oleg caught her eye. "Do you play?" he asked across the room.

"No," she said, "I never learned, but I like to listen." She stood up again, smiled at Elif now, and took her by the hand. They went to the piano.

"Maybe you sing," Oleg said pleasantly, bringing the *étude* to its harrowing end.

"No," Evgenya confessed. "I have no accomplishments." She said the word sarcastically, as though accomplishments were somehow unrevolutionary.

"Nor me," said Elif.

Oleg turned over his hands, studying the soft, white palms. "In a few years," he said, "hands like these will be a disgrace to a man. Or a woman. Chopin will be altogether forgotten. And this magnificent beast…" He played an awesome sequence of chords on the Bösendorfer. "… will be firewood."

"What's that?" Evgenya asked in amazement. "That music?"

"Mussorgsky. *The Great Gate at Kiev*," Oleg told her, still playing. The chords softened and then returned, nobler, overwhelming.

"Too much fucking noise. I can't hear myself think." It was Darya's voice coming from the depths of an armchair.

"Sorry," Oleg said. He stopped playing and shrugged his shoulders. "Only two music lovers here," he sighed. "You and me, Evgenya Antonovna."

She nodded. "And Elif?" she asked.

The Azeri girl shook her head. "It's just noise to me," she said.

"Mmm," Oleg began. "Evgenya. While you were out, they thought up a plan. It involves you. Don't…"

"Don't what?" Evgenya asked, suddenly unnerved. A plan? Against her?

"Don't do anything you don't want to. That's all." He paused again. "They won't take it very far. Unless you go along with it. Which, of course, you might. But just as long as you know. And choose for yourself."

"Maybe I should go to my room."

"No. Please stay."

"I don't know."

"If I play Chopin, will you stay?"

At the strange question, tears came to Evgenya's eyes. She felt alone, helpless and surrounded by barbarians. People who called music 'fucking noise'. She stood, weeping, making no attempt at concealment.

Oleg grinned at her. "Cheer up," he said and began the tenderest of Chopin's nocturnes, the late E-minor.

Evgenya took the handkerchief Elif offered her, and they sat down together to listen. The swelling sadness of the music stirred in Evgenya a longing for a life she'd never known, and which had no positive shape in her mind. Now, as Oleg played, the desolation and the tragic sense of loss in the music expressed this unattainable life in a way that deeply disturbed her. She burst into uncontrollable tears again and fled upstairs to her room. The music faded behind her. It vanished altogether as she closed her door. Alone in the cold room, the sense of tragedy induced by the music degenerated into bitterness. She was on her own. No one cared what happened to her. Sonya had gone. She'd refused to take even a message to Vitya. And him? Even if he knew she was in Odessa, would he come to her? Just a few hours by train? No. He'd carry on with his precious work. Not stupid work like hers that a child of ten could do. But real work. Dangerous. Work he shared with Sonya. She opened the window and let the storm outside batter the curtains and rip at her hair.

When Elif knocked on her door about an hour later, she'd closed the window and was sulking in an armchair by the bed.

"Yes?" she said as the dark, Azeri face peeped into the room.

"Darya sent me to say she's sorry. She didn't mean it about the music. She didn't know you were enjoying it."

"But you? You said it was just noise too." She had to reproach someone, and Elif was an easy target.

"Not the last piece he played. It was so sad. Anyway, he won't play any more unless you come down."

"Hmmm," Evgenya replied.

"Oleg's a wonderful writer, you know. Like Darya. They're friends."

"They sleep together you mean?" Evgenya said, rebuking Elif again, this time for her lack of candour.

"Sometimes perhaps. I don't really know. I find it all... It's against my religion..."

"It's against everyone's religion, but I suppose you take yours more seriously." Evgenya stood up. "I'll come," she said. "I don't want them to think I'm stuck-up or anything."

The drawing-room was full now. The lamps were lit and the stove was roaring hot. There was a smell of wine and olives. As Evgenya entered, Darya immediately jumped to her feet. "I'm sorry," she pleaded. "Truly."

Darya wasn't pretty with her mousy hair and freckled face,

but she was animated and quick-witted. "It's nothing," Evgenya replied. "We'd been out in the storm. Maybe it upset me."

Darya took her hand and led her back to the sofa where she'd been sitting. "We were just discussing a new booklet," she explained, beckoning Elif to join them.

"About…"

"No," Darya laughed, "not the one about contraception. A special one for women. On health and exercise – that kind of thing."

"If the booklets are for working women…" Evgenya said, trying to sound interested. "I mean, they get enough exercise, don't they? A bit too much sometimes."

"Right," said Oleg. "But there might be other audiences. You, for instance. Would you read a booklet on exercise? Or your friends? And would you like a glass of wine? It's Crimean, but drinkable."

"Yes, I would… read it," Evgenya said. "Definitely. And yes to the wine too."

Exercise? She'd wrestled with Anna on the night they'd murdered Reinstein, and she'd been amazed at Anna's unexpected strength. She'd seen Anna knock Reinstein off his chair with a terrible backhander. She'd asked Sonya why – why Anna was so strong. 'She exercises. Every day. We all do,' Sonya had said. Then, on their first morning in Odessa, Sonya had dragged Evgenya out of bed before it was light. She'd lit the lamp and taken off her shift. She'd told Evgenya to strip off too, and then they'd exercised hard for an hour. 'You're tough,' Sonya had told her. 'Not at all the young lady – pigeon-breasted, knock-kneed, short-winded bunch that they are.' Evgenya had explained her childhood in the country, then her rowing on the lake with Valentina, running, sledding, walking in the forest, even the arm-wrestling she'd learned from Valentina's brothers. 'You don't know how lucky you are,' Sonya had said. 'They forgot to educate you.' Evgenya had thought over the strange compliment as she'd washed and dressed. Tough? Her whole body was aching from so many unfamiliar movements. But yes, she was tough, though not half as tough as she could be.

"So who's going to write it, this booklet?" Evgenya asked.

"I know some of the routines," Larissa said. "I learned them off a woman called Anna. Five years ago maybe. She went to Zürich – one of that lot – to be a doctor. I can't remember her other name."

Evgenya said nothing.

"I can show Darya the routines," Larissa concluded. "She can do the writing."

"There will be pictures. Many pictures. *Strichzeichnungen*. To show movements." Albrecht, the illustrator, was German. He spoke with a German accent and often used German words to eke out his sentences. Milord had met him on a trip to Berlin. Albrecht had been in trouble with the Prussian police for publishing seditious cartoons, and Milord had invited him to Odessa. Though Albrecht's Russian was primitive, his drawings were clever, easy to engrave and simple enough to reproduce on their equipment.

"Oh no," said Darya. "I can hear it coming."

"Darya is good model. *Keine Frage*." Albrecht said dogmatically. He turned to Larissa. "You show Darya the position. Then she model for me."

"Alright," Darya agreed. "But I'm not taking my clothes off."

"What she say?" asked Albrecht, pretending not to understand.

"*Sie will sich nicht frei machen,*" Oleg explained.

"*Quatsch!*" Albrecht exclaimed. "I get my things. *Moment*."

"Fucking artists!" Darya exclaimed in her turn.

"I get my things," Albrecht repeated, striding out of the room. "You talk with Lavritsky. He explain you."

Josef Lavritsky was nineteen. For a while he'd been apprenticed to an engraver. Then after one semester at the Academy of Fine Arts in Petersburg, he'd been expelled because his roommate had been caught with a package of Land and Freedom leaflets. The leaflets weren't illegal, but they aroused suspicion. Josef also had a gift for improvisation. "It's not a pleasure," he began now in the style of a fairground huckster. "It's not a duty. No! It's a privilege to pose for a great artist. For a female to bare her all in the holy cause of aart! I ask you, ladies and gentlemen, what could be more rewarding? More fulfilling? More exciting? And it ain't just trulls and trollops as do it. No! Aristocratic ladies, ladies from families – no less! – claw each others' eyes out for the privilege of dedicating their aristocratic boosoms to the great cause. Not to mention their even more aristocratic parts lower down."

"Josef," Darya said laughing. "Shut up, will you."

Albrecht returned busily with his sketchpad and half a dozen pencils. "The problem!" he announced. "Is how to show movement? Drawing is position. *Turnen ist Bewegung.*"

"Gymnastics is movement," Oleg explained.

"Larissa!" the German instructed. "One movement. Now. Show please."

Larissa got to her feet. She stood with her elbows raised and her hands under her chin. Then she threw her arms wide, pressing back her shoulder blades.

"You see, Darya?" the artist queried.

"I'm not blind," Darya replied. She stood, as Larissa had done, and opened her arms.

"That is *Scheisse!*" Albrecht objected. "You look same like Larissa. *Dick und schlabberig.*"

They all looked at Oleg. "Not quite the perfect gymnast," Oleg translated.

"You are *straff.* You have beautiful *Körper.* Show me."

Darya made the movement again, neat and precise.

"Exact so," said Albrecht. "Now *nackt bitte.*"

"I fucking hate you," said Darya. She kicked off her shoes. She unbuttoned her blouse and took it off. Underneath was a simple chemise. She pulled it free of the waistband of her skirt. She smiled at Evgenya: "Be a sweetheart," she said, holding up her arms.

Evgenya hesitated – but how could she refuse without

looking ridiculous? In any case, if Darya wanted to go naked in front of everyone, that was her affair. And obviously it wasn't the first time. Evgenya stood up and helped the girl pull the chemise over her head. Without hesitation, Darya unbelted her skirt. Underneath was a red petticoat. It dropped to the floor with the skirt. Darya stepped out of her clothes, naked apart from long socks that came up to her knees.

Evgenya caught her breath. It was so easy. Nothing depended on it. Just that in this overheated drawing-room, a girl was naked, perfectly immodest, not making the least attempt to hide herself. And nobody seemed to find it out of the ordinary. Albrecht had asked her, she'd done it, and the roof hadn't fallen in. The rule book had been rewritten.

"*Socken*," said Albrecht.

"Bastard," Darya replied.

With a sudden movement, Evgenya knelt at the feet of the naked girl. "I'll do it for you," she offered. She was one of them now – the outsider had vanished.

"Thank you," Darya said. She raised her right foot for Evgenya to pull off her sock, and then her left.

Evgenya looked up at the girl's body. Her skin glowed white. Her breasts were small, almost flat. Albrecht was right – her body was beautiful. Exposed, at ease, beautiful. She was sixteen, and already she slept with men – that's what Elif said. And part of her beauty was her shamelessness.

"Stop," Albrecht cried. "No move. *Ich muss es zeichnen! Mit so ein Bild wird man berühmt.*"

"He wants you to stay where you are, both of you," Oleg translated. "He wants to draw you. But Evgenya…"

She looked at him.

"… you don't have to if you don't want to."

Was this the plan? It didn't seem so dangerous. "I don't mind," she said. "Honestly."

"*Perfekt*," Albrecht exclaimed. "*Absolut perfekt.*"

As Albrecht wanted, Evgenya stayed on her knees, her face level with the girl's belly. But where should she look? Her eyes flickered up and down. She looked at Albrecht and then at Oleg. Finally she allowed her eyes to rest on what interested her most – Darya. She'd never looked at a girl properly, except for herself in the dim mirror in her bedroom. And now she was kneeling, in a roomful of people, confronting what was always hidden, always private. Her mind swirled with images, nothing added up, but somehow she sensed a victory.

"*Perfekt,* Evgenya," Albrecht muttered, drawing masterfully. "Don't move."

"I don't want to be doing this," Darya moaned playfully. "And which booklet is it for anyway?"

"This go to Paris," Albrecht said. "*In the Studio of the Albrecht Kelterbach.* I see it now."

In twenty minutes the drawing was finished.

"Show me," Darya said. Evgenya stood up stiffly, her knees aching from the hard floor, and the two girls examined the sketch together. It showed a vain, rather silly model flaunting her nakedness at a girl on her knees. The naked girl was frontal, the kneeling girl in half profile from behind. Yet the focus of the sketch was the elation, the astonished awe in the pose of the kneeling girl. Evgenya was startled – Albrecht had understood the moment exactly.

"You see!" Darya complained with mock-outrage. "She kept her clothes on and you've made her much prettier than me. And look at me. I look like a trollop. Thanks very much. If you need a model next time, you know who to ask."

"I can ask. But she will say no. I am certain." The artist looked pathetically at Evgenya.

"Not like Darya. Definitely not," Evgenya said quietly. "But…" The word was so soft it was hardly spoken.

Albrecht nodded.

"Don't send the picture to Paris. I mean, could I have it?" Evgenya asked, still in a voice no one but Albrecht could hear.

He caught her eye. It was enough – he'd give it to her. But he made no move to tear out the page. The first time she modelled for him, he'd give it to her – she understood perfectly. It was a fair bargain. The idea excited her – excited her greatly. But she wasn't committed to anything. She'd ask Sonya when she got back. Sonya would tell her what to do.

The drawing session moved to Albrecht's atelier, but Evgenya stayed in the drawing room – so much had changed and she needed time to take stock. Oleg caught her eye and patted the seat beside him on a big, comfortable sofa. She liked Oleg. Oleg Kryukov. He wasn't like Sonya, he didn't protect her – just explained things and then let her decide for herself.

"It all seemed strange to me when I first arrived," he said easily. "Is that how it seems to you?"

"I had some friends in Petersburg," she said. "We used to talk, but…"

He nodded, "Talk is one thing."

"It doesn't upset me," she said. "Not at all. I'm nothing like…"

"… like Sonya?"

She glanced at him. Was he teasing her? No. He was interested – he wanted to know what she thought.

"No one's like Sonya," she said safely.

"She's taken you under her wing. That can't always be comfortable – for you I mean."

"She's very patient," Evgenya laughed. "She needs to be with someone as ignorant as me."

"Don't misunderstand me," Oleg said, "without Sonya this Movement wouldn't exist. But she's a bit of a slave driver."

"And I'm a bit of a slave?"

"I think you could be submissive," he replied seriously, "to someone with a strong will. But only till you chose to rebel."

"I'm not a rebel," she objected. "More of a gypsy. That's what they call me."

"Well, whatever they call you, you're the prettiest girl I've seen since I left Petersburg."

"Only since then?" Evgenya replied with mock-disappointment, wondering where the conversation was going. Oleg was surely too intelligent to be flirting with her like one of Valentina's brothers. Or maybe intelligent men were the same as the others. She didn't know.

"Can I ask you something?" she said.

He held his hands open in invitation.

"You're a friend of Mischa's?"

"Yes."

"We all live here in luxury – at least it feels like luxury compared with…"

"… Home?"

"Yes."

"Why? Is that what you want to know? Why someone like Mischa play-acts revolution?"

"Is it play-acting?"

"In a way. He's a bit like you really – he hasn't found himself. You haven't given up teasing every man who likes the look of you, and he hasn't given up a taste for luxury."

"But would he give it up? If he had to choose?"

"Would you? Give up teasing?"

"Of course I would. Obviously."

"People join the Movement for all sorts of reasons. What was yours?"

"Tell me first, what was Mischa's?"

"Power." Evgenya watched him hesitate and reflect – maybe the answer was too glib. "Yes, power," he repeated. "I think so."

"Power?"

"Evgenya, the Movement is going to win. If we didn't think that, we wouldn't be here. And when it does, a handful of people will have power – real power."

"But if you wanted power… I mean, the government…"

"You could join the bureaucracy – work your way up? Is that what you mean?"

She nodded.

"Yes, you might get power that way."

"You're nearly as patient as Sonya," she said shyly.

"Is your father in the service?" Oleg asked.

"No, he's nothing. I don't think he did a day's work in his life."

"But it isn't easy, in a hierarchy. You have power over everyone lower down. But they can get you into trouble whenever they like, make you look stupid. And everyone above you – you're their slave. It doesn't feel like power."

"Did you do something like that? Yourself?"

"My father was a deputy minister. A horrible life actually."

"So Mischa hopes…"

"Mischa has fun. He keeps us all in luxury. But one day…"

"But it's so risky. I mean – he risks his life the same as the rest of us."

"Men join the army. Isn't that risky?"

"My brother's in the army."

"So tell me – why are you here?"

"I'm not very good at explaining things," Evgenya said evasively.

"Try."

"I've thought about it," she said. "A lot. And – I know, I just know – that something's not right. In the way we live. I never went to school. Millions of girls never go to school. They just have babies, and half of the babies die. How can that be?"

"You want a new way of life?"

"Yes. I think so."

"And the fact that the Third Section could bang on the door one minute from now and we'd all finish up in Siberia?" Oleg prompted.

"If it doesn't worry Mischa and it doesn't worry you, why should it worry me?"

"But it does worry me. Greatly."

"But you stay. Why shouldn't I stay for the same reason?"

"So your reason for being here is that I have a reason for being here? Me, Sonya, the rest of us?"

"Doesn't that make sense?"

"Perfect sense – in a way."

"Can you play for me now?" she asked. "The noisiest piece of headache music you know."

"How about some Liszt? Some fake gypsy music?"

"For a fake gypsy?"

"You're not any kind of gypsy. Actually, you're an angel."

## IV

Evgenya was pleased when Sonya returned from her three days in Kherson, though the others were not. Milord had met her train at the station in Odessa and brought her to the villa in time for the evening meal.

There had been talk of rules to be published by the Committee – precise regulations on how men and women in the Movement should behave to each other. Freedom was doubtless a principle of revolution, but in practice there was something unrevolutionary about the unrestricted exercise of personal liberty. In Sonya's absence, Josef had been parodying the new rules. He'd worked up a little show of Sonya dictating them to her scribe: "No punishment shall be imposed for performance of any sexual act whatsoever…" He shook his head, imitating Sonya's trick of raising her eyebrows when she was dissatisfied. "Change that: for any *normal* sexual act whatsoever. No… for any act other than an *abnormal* act… including but not limited to… No, a list might give people ideas." He folded his arms across his chest exactly as Sonya folded hers. "No punishment for *heterosexual* acts performed between the hours of 8 and 10 p.m. Make that 8 and 8:30." It was funny but pointless – what Sonya decided to forbid would be forbidden.

"Did you tell Vitya? That I was here?" Evgenya asked as she helped Sonya upstairs with her travelling trunk.

"I said I wouldn't."

"But did you?"

"No," Sonya grunted, heaving at the trunk.

Evgenya was crestfallen. "Did you talk about me at all?"

"Several times."

Evgenya brightened. "What did he say? About me?"

"He sees the problem," Sonya replied cautiously, implying there was more and that she was reluctant to tell it.

"I didn't know I was a problem," Evgenya retorted. "Is that how he thinks of me?"

"Don't be childish," Sonya reproached her. "There's a problem. You know it as well as we do."

"We?" Evgenya exclaimed. "You and Vitya?"

They were turning an awkward corner in the stairs. Sonya seemed more concerned with the trunk than with Vitya's feelings. "Lower your end," she said sharply.

In the bedroom Evgenya sat on her bed watching Sonya unpack her cheap, shapeless clothes and hang them on a row of nails hammered into the wall. Near the top of the trunk was a package wrapped in red tissue paper.

"Something for you," Sonya said. She held out the package to Evgenya.

"For me?" Evgenya weighed it in her hand. A book, she guessed. She opened the package. The book was called *Exercises for Women*, and it was illustrated with stiff little sketches of overdressed women in unlikely poses. She looked at Sonya uncertainly. "Thank you," she said. She looked inside the cover, not expecting to find a dedication, but there was one:

*Tighten the knot of my shawl when we say farewell.*
*Like its two ends, during these days we have been drawn together.*

*The Gypsy Song*

"The message... it isn't from Vitya?" Evgenya asked, puzzled at the handwriting.

"No. He didn't send any message. It's from me."

"Who wrote the poem?"

"Polonsky. There's more." She began in her weak, unvibrant voice to recite another verse of *The Gypsy Song*:

*"Will someone tell my fate? Tomorrow, my falcon,*
*Will someone else undo the knot you tied in my heart?"*

"Does he?…" Evgenya began. "Does Vitya?…"

"Is there any way…" Sonya asked gently. "Is there any way you can forget him?"

"Has he forgotten me then? Already?"

"He's working. The tunnel will be finished in a few more weeks. Then he has his examinations."

"I know," Evgenya said. "I know more about his examinations than you do."

"I'm sure you do. But you'll be here. And he'll be in Petersburg. Evgenya…"

"For the work you want him?" Evgenya asked doubtfully. "Nothing else?"

"It's for the work, that's why I want you both."

"And him? What does he want?"

"He doesn't want me, if that's what you mean. Nobody does. Nobody ever has. And nobody ever will."

"If only I could talk to him."

"Evgenya. I like you. I like you very much. I don't think… I don't think talking to him would help. You'd be better off…"

"… To forget him."

"Yes."

"Is that what he told you?"

"Not in those words exactly." She paused as though sparing Evgenya the ugly truth. "But yes. Yes… forget him."

"Then…" Evgenya flung herself on her bed and burst into sobs. Sonya finished her unpacking, left the room and closed the door behind her.

Mischa Trigony stayed for dinner. He sent his driver back to town for some good wine and for some of the sweet Turkish *lokum* that was just coming into fashion. In the meantime he was sitting four-handed with Oleg at the Bösendorfer playing sentimental waltzes. Oleg, had studied at the Conservatoire in Petersburg under Anton Rubinstein; Milord had been taught

131

by his mother. But they were enjoying themselves, and their good humour was infectious.

Evgenya heard the piano and it tempted her downstairs. She stood outside the half-open door of the drawing room listening. As one of the waltzes rolled to its predictable end, she heard Trigony ask: "Where's Evgenya?"

"Upstairs," Sonya told him. "She may not be down."

"The work gives her headaches," Larissa added.

"Does she complain?" Trigony asked. He didn't like complainers.

"Never," Larissa replied. "She suffers in silence. But you can tell."

Evgenya decided it was time to show her face. She'd brushed her hair in her room and put on a clean blouse, prettier than the one she wore for work. Anna had given it to her, and Anna's maid had taken it in – taken it in considerably. "Sorry to be late," she apologised opening the door wide.

"When you so illuminate the room with your beauty," Trigony said, "we'd wait for you all night."

There was a chorus of booing and whistling.

"I'll fight any man who denies it," Trigony declaimed from the keyboard, rising heroically to his feet. "Or woman!" Oleg hammered out the trumpet call from *Lohengrin* that summons Elsa's champion.

Evgenya stood behind the sofa where Sonya was sitting. She wanted to say something funny, to show Sonya she wasn't going to pine, not outwardly anyway. "Keep it for the girls in the *Folies Bergères*, Mischa," she said. There was a laugh. She caught Oleg's eye. She saw his amusement turn to concern – he'd guessed something was wrong.

"Well that's gratitude for you," Trigony exclaimed ruefully and started to play a gloomy Cossack lament.

Evgenya saw Sonya turn and felt Sonya's hand give her own hand a little squeeze of solidarity. It reassured her. Her life was approaching a crisis. More than anything she wanted someone to tell her what to do, and Sonya's approving touch came very close.

Dinner was announced by a maid dressed in the neat French style. As revolutionaries, Group South had debated the issue of maids and cooks extensively, reaching the comfortable conclusion that, if the police were to visit the place, a house with servants would appear less suspicious than a house without. At first the meal was as lively as the waltzes that had gone before it.

"Sonya!" It was Josef Lavritsky across the table. "While you were away we had a discussion, and we'd like to hear your opinion." There was a sudden silence. Sonya was going to be baited – it didn't often happen.

"By all means," Sonya agreed, ready for confrontation.

"The girls pose for us, for Dürer and sometimes for me."

"I know," Sonya replied. "I've seen them. Is that a problem?"

"Not for me."

"For the women?"

"Not for them either."

"Then what do you want my opinion about?"

For a second Josef hesitated. He'd lost the first round miserably. "We know," he tried again, "that the Petersburg Section has different views from Section South on such matters."

"Possibly."

"Our practice here is somewhat freer. You've commented on it several times."

"Your practice is freer," Sonya replied. "Is that a problem for anyone? Larissa?"

"Not for me," Larissa replied.

"Darya?"

"Not at all."

Evgenya remembered the last time Sonya had gone around, counting votes – an hour later Reinstein had vanished under the ice.

"Zhenia?"

"No."

"Elif?"

"Such things are against my religion. For Christians…" She shrugged her shoulders.

"Evgenya?"

"No," Evgenya said uncertainly, and then more definitely: "No."

"No point asking the men," Sonya said, looking round the table. Half a dozen propagandists were visiting that night and the table was crowded.

"And what's your opinion?" Josef pressed, not liking to lose the game so obviously.

"If no one has a problem, then my opinion is of no importance. In any case, you already know what it is."

Everyone waited in case Sonya had more to say, but she'd finished, and a babble of conversation erupted again.

"You think it's wrong?" Evgenya asked quietly. Sonya was sitting next to her – there was no need to raise her voice. "Modelling? The other things?"

"Did they say anything to you? While I was gone?"

"Not directly. A few hints."

"Did he ask you to model? Albrecht?"

"Not really. He did a drawing of me."

"One of Albrecht's interminable drawings. Will you take your clothes off? If he asks you?"

"I don't know. Tell me what to do, Sonya."

Evgenya watched Sonya's expression turn serious and then, for a second, sour. She was wrestling with something tougher than posing for a picture. It made Evgenya uneasy.

"If they ask you," Sonya said at length, "I don't see why not."

"Take everything off?"

"Yes. If you want."

"I'm not sure."

"You're strong. You're good-looking. You don't have to be shy."

Evgenya was startled – she'd expected a lecture not a compliment. Perhaps it was a good moment to ask the question she'd wrestled with since Sonya's fateful *'Yes, forget him.'* Forget him! No, she couldn't forget him, but at least she could get her own back – the faithless bastard.

Sonya waited, saying nothing.

"And …" Evgenya hesitated. "And what if they ask me to?…"

"To open your legs?"

Evgenya nodded. *Open her legs* – Sonya's ugly phrase. But ugly or not, it would show she'd forgotten him, wouldn't it? Vitya! To send her a message like that. Poor Sonya hardly had the nerve to pass it on.

"It's up to you," Sonya said. "But… objectively…" Sonya hesitated, thinking through a decision. "It's probably time you found out what it's like – I know you spend half your life thinking about it."

"No I don't," Evgenya protested.

Sonya looked at her ironically.

"Not half anyway," Evgenya smiled, relieved that the decision was taken. Yes, it was time she found out about this thing. Larissa, Zhenia – they had no qualms about it. Hardly a night went by… It was exciting giving yourself to someone – or so they told her as they set type and printed flyers together. And yet… Vitya. She'd never promised to wait for him. But in her imagination it had always been him. Always. If Sonya had told her to wait, she'd have waited. But Sonya had told her to go ahead – *open her legs*. It sounded so cheap – a midwife's view of a bodily function. But maybe that's all it was. She didn't have to, of course. She could do what she liked. Or not do it. But if Sonya thought it was right… that made it all much easier.

And Sonya would stand by her. If any of them got pregnant, Sonya helped them out – the women had told her that too. *It's time you found out…* It was strange advice, coming from Sonya – strange but not shocking. In any case, Evgenya's interest had been piqued beyond bearing. Darya was two years younger, and she hopped in and out of bed all the time. No one thought any the less of her. No one. It was nicer than frigging Darya said. Some men weren't so good at it, of course, so afterwards you still had to… The others agreed. The whole thing was more than flesh and blood could bear.

# V

Evgenya made no definite plans after her conversation with Sonya, but for a girl of eighteen living away from home, opportunity seldom lags far behind inclination.

The next day, Sonya received an urgent message: for some time a group of officers in Sebastopol had been edging toward conspiracy. Now they wanted Sonya to visit them, to set up, they hoped, a link between the conspirators and the Committee. Everyone knew that without an army, no revolution had a chance. Through propaganda and terror the Committee might create a revolutionary moment, an opportunity, but only well trained and well armed men could exploit it. From the Committee's point of view, the officers in Sebastopol were ideally situated – they were a long way from headquarters in Petersburg, and they were sitting on a mountain of arms.

Sebastopol was a three-day journey from Odessa with changes in Nikolayev and Kherson. Sonya would be away ten days – maybe more. As Evgenya helped her find the train connections in the huge imperial timetable, she asked her timidly: "Sonya? If you're in Kherson, will you see Vitya again?"

"No reason to. His job's going perfectly."

*Always the work*, Evgenya thought. But so what anyway? So what if Sonya spent the next six months in Kherson? If Vitya had forgotten everything they'd dreamed of, if the work had taken over, if Sonya had taken over, then to hell with him.

Sonya left by the first train next day. All morning Evgenya worked at her task in the stinking press-shop. Not long after lunch, Larissa sent her back to the villa with a bundle of leaflets to be collected that afternoon and taken to Kiev.

Back at the villa, Evgenya dawdled a little, gossiping with the writers. Oleg had offered to give her piano lessons but she'd refused, unwilling to admit that she'd lied to him about her 'accomplishments.' They chatted about some music Oleg had played the night before. *The Seasons* – Tchaikovsky. Silly stuff he thought. He didn't say any more about her looking pretty or being an angel, so she stopped teasing him. Maybe it was better that way.

After Oleg, she drifted up to Albrecht's *atelier*, a big room under the roof with light from the north. Josef was there too. He was standing naked in the middle of the room, leaning on a beggar's staff with a heavy pack on one shoulder.

"Oh," Evgenya exclaimed, backing out of the doorway. "Excuse me."

"*Kein Problem*," roared Albrecht. "Come in. You see now. Why a model is always *nackt*. Tell her Lavritsky."

Without moving and with no sign of embarrassment, Josef began to explain how the weight of the bag drew down one of his shoulders, how the support of the staff raised the other, and how all the bones and muscles in his body followed that line. If he wore clothes, even a simple shirt, most of the distortion would be invisible, and the figure would never come to life.

"Sit down," Albrecht invited Evgenya expansively.

"I can't stay," Evgenya replied, "I'm expected back at the press."

And then: "*Ach* Josef! *Benehm dich!* You think bad thoughts. What will Fräulein Sophia say when she return?"

Evgenya looked puzzled.

"He is useless now. You take him," said the artist, throwing down his black crayon in disgust.

Evgenya glanced from one to the other and back again, finally catching sight of the problem that had upset Albrecht.

"Oh!" she said.

"You don't have to do anything you don't want," said Josef, dropping his bag and letting his staff clatter to the floor. "But – if you want – we can go…"

"No," said Evgenya. "Absolutely not." She left the *atelier* quickly, but not so quickly that Josef couldn't follow close on her heels.

"If I don't get back, they'll think I've been murdered in the lane. I just need to change my boots – these are pinching my toes."

"Evgenya."

"No – absolutely not."

Amid these and similar prevarications, Evgenya gave up what she no longer valued in exchange for something no money can buy – a gentle and affectionate introduction to the mysteries of lovemaking. It wasn't quite what she'd expected, but there was some pleasure in it, enough at least to convince her that she still had a lot to learn. As for Vitya, he could go to hell. Really.

The women at the press expressed no surprise when she returned hours late. Sonya had had her way.

# VI

Evgenya had soon learned to set type quickly and accurately. In the evenings, though, her eyes were tired after a day at the press, too tired to tackle the dense books Sonya wanted her to read. So she drifted downstairs and joined the others in the drawing room. Usually Oleg played the piano for a while and the others danced. Most of the time they sat around, drinking brandy and joking.

The evening after her encounter with Josef, Evgenya was sitting on a deep sofa, subdued, drinking brandy and mulling over what had happened. Suddenly she heard her name. It was Albrecht.

"You must model now," he said, "perfect, exactly as you are, lost in thought."

She shrugged her shoulders and agreed, trying to be as casual as Darya but without the back-chat. She stood up, still in a half-dream, took off her clothes and kicked them into a heap. Quietly Elif left the room with tears in her eyes. Evgenya watched her, tempted for a second to put her clothes back on and go down to the beach with her little friend. But instead she shook her head and stood for a moment by the sofa, her awareness sharpening. Everyone was looking at her. She caught Oleg's eye. He was sitting at the piano, watching and waiting. Better not seem too shy. Better not flaunt herself either. Be like she was with Sonya when they started their exercises. It wasn't easy in a room full of alerted eyes and subtle glances. But it was possible. She knew what she was doing – she was in control. She turned a little as she stood, waiting for Albrecht to pose her. There was tension; it thrilled through her body and crackled around her. If she could calm her movements and feign tranquility, she'd be free. If there is such a thing a perfect liberty – it touched her at that moment.

Albrecht was delighted. He told her to sit down, to let her mind drift away, to lose herslf in thought. He made half a dozen sketches, all of them subtle and inoffensive. Evgenya was pleased. Could he continue the next evening? Albrecht wanted to know. Naturally she refused – not in earnest but to tease him. To tease all of them. In fact, the next evening turned into a game – thinking up new poses for Evgenya. She played along but she made a bargain: she'd pose any way they liked, but if she didn't like a drawing, she could burn it in the stove. Wilfully she burned them all. Albrecht complained bitterly as his work went up in flames, but the others took a legalistic view – a contract is a contract.

Darya lived for popularity, and the new arrangement wasn't much to her liking. She put up with two evenings of Evgenya stealing the limelight and then suggested that they pose together. From Albrecht's point of view, this was not a success. Spurred on by the brandy, the comments of the onlookers, and their own tight nerves, the two girls found it impossible to keep still. They began to jostle, pulling each other's hair, pretending to wrestle. Then to kiss, though the experience was unfamiliar to both of them. With half a dozen excited young men in the room, the two girls fighting and then seeking reconciliation had an inevitable sequel, and Albrecht gave up the evening as lost. Evgenya, high-strung, bewildered and generous, gave herself freely just as they asked. "It's probably time you found out what it's like," Sonya had said. What Sonya had meant by *it* had not been clarified. But Sonya wasn't there and Evgenya could do as she pleased. Anyone who didn't like it could do the other thing.

In the warm days of early spring, Evgenya let a tide of physical excitement sweep her away. At the same time she drew closer to Oleg. In quiet moments they talked and he played the piano for her, trying different interpretations and asking her preference. He'd studied to be a professional pianist, he told her – in another life. They talked about her childhood in Petersburg, about her posing, about sexual feedom. He took a view she found hard to understand at first. It came to a head one night when one of Milord's vistors, a propagandist called Fomin, called her a 'slut' – it was playfully meant perhaps, but Oleg broke out in fury: "You don't understand! None of you understands. Take it back – such a filthy word."

Fomin apologised, blamed his slip on the brandy, and went to bed.

After he'd gone, Evgenya led Oleg into the kitchen where they could be quiet together. "I'm not sure I understand either," she said. "I mean, it *is* sluttish, isn't it? What I... I mean standing here with nothing on in the kitchen. Only a slut..."

"No," he insisted, "you're breaking everything down. You're trampling on history, on everything society thinks about women. I've never seen anything so blatant in my whole life. Or anything half as revolutionary."

"Oh," she said, surprised. "And the others? Darya?"

"Darya wants everyone to like her. Larissa is simply addicted. But you..."

"I like it," Evgenya said quietly. "Spending and all that. I told you that already. Honestly there's nothing revolutionary..."

"Wrong!" Oleg exclaimed. "That's the beauty of it! You like it. You do what you like, and the whole world can go to hell. I told you already – you're an angel."

Next evening as Evgenya and the other women left the printshop and started the long walk home, Evgenya heard footsteps behind them. It was Oleg. He could think more clearly if he took a walk in the spring air, he told them, and by some chance he'd gone in the direction of the printing press.

Larissa laughed. "I don't believe a word of it," she said. "Evgenya, be careful. He wants you all to himself."

Evgenya made no objection. The women laughed.

"Oleg wanted to show me something on the beach," Evgenya told them. "We'll see you back home."

When they were alone, Oleg made no move to take her hand or put his arm round her. They went down to the water's edge, took off their shoes and walked along the fringe of firm sand. They talked about music. Evgenya went back to *The Seasons* – the Tchaikovsky piece Oleg had been playing. She wanted to know why he didn't like it.

"It misses the point," Oleg told her. "It's not the seasons themselves that are interesting but the transition, how one moves into the next. Winter into spring. Spring into summer."

"Maybe you should compose something yourself?" Evgenya suggested.

"If I did, would you dance it for me?"

"You're as bad as Albrecht," she chided, "and anyway, I can't dance."

"You can. It's what you do. Posing is frozen dancing."

"Dance?" she said. "Me?"

"Can we try?"

That evening Evgenya ruled him some music paper. On the first page he wrote the words *Winter Turns to Spring: For Evgenya. By Oleg Kryukov*. Fragments of music quickly took shape, and as April smothered the Black Sea coast with flowers, it seemed to Evgenya that her life was taking an entirely new direction.

Sonya did not arrive back from her trip to Sebastopol until 30th April. The train was many hours late. She took a *droshky* from the station and when she arrived at the villa no one was expecting her. She went straight to the drawing room where there was still music, though it was nearly midnight.

Oleg stopped playing as the door opened. Evgenya saw Sonya at once, standing travel-weary and enquiring in the doorway, and stopped dancing. She ran lightly across the parquet floor, put her arms round Sonya and kissed her. "Come in," she said. "Let me take your coat. We'll take your luggage upstairs in a minute."

Sonya let herself be fussed, let herself be led to a comfortable chair. Darya brought her some tea from the samovar.

"Oleg's been writing music. I've been dancing," Evgenya said to her.

"So that's why you're stark naked is it? Is that how girls dance these days?"

"Don't be so grumpy," Evgenya chided her. "Watch. See what you think."

Sonya sat stiffly in her chair and began to sip her tea.

The dance lasted five minutes. Albrecht had worked it out – the white cloak of winter cast aside for the blinding nakedness of spring. After the last crashing chords had finally put paid to winter, Evgenya went again to Sonya's chair. She knelt at Sonya's feet and bowed her head.

Everyone in the room looked at Sonya. There had been rumours that she wanted to break up Section South altogether. Maybe this was the opportunity she'd been looking for. Sonya passed her empty teacup to Darya, then leant forward, resting her hands and then her lips on the crown of Evgenya's head. "You are beautiful," she said. "Absolutely beautiful."

There was more to come. Nobody moved.

"But… if you will listen to a word spoken in love by someone who is not beautiful and who has no right to direct you, none whatsoever – enough is enough."

Next evening, this little scene had its consequences.

Mischa Trigony had not been there when Sonya had returned the night before, but he knew about Oleg's piece and Evgenya's dancing. He'd planned a party for 1$^{st}$ May with *Winter Turns to Spring* as the centrepiece. But it was not to be. The party had been in full swing for about an hour when Mischa called for silence. Everyone knew what was coming. Immediately, however, Evgenya interrupted: there would be no dance – she'd decided against it. At first Mischa thought it was a joke, but Evgenya stayed firm. He reproached her – she had no business changing things when it was all decided. Oleg stepped in: Evgenya should do exactly what she wanted – she could dance or not dance as she saw fit. The two men began to argue. Mischa called Oleg a "brainless fucking aristocrat."

"In that case," Oleg replied, "I'll take my brainlessness elsewhere," and he left the room.

The next morning he'd left the house. Evgenya followed not long after.

# Extract 5

It is curious how often a trivial detail decides the outcome of a great project, and even more curious how often this detail derives not from chance but from character. In the winter of 1878-1879, the Movement rented a house in Kherson, on the estuary of the Dnieper. The house backed onto the State Treasury where the pay for the Imperial Army South was secured. The Committee planned by means of a tunnel from a rented house to the cellars of the Treasury to perform the greatest burglary of the nineteenth century: ten million paper roubles according to one version. The tunnel was dug by a young mining engineer whose name I have forgotten, even though he was engaged in all the Movement's later tunnelling projects. Sofya Perovskaya ran the project: he dug the tunnel.

Imagine that all the notes in the Treasury were three-rouble notes. That is three million pieces of paper, each about half the size of a book page. 3000 fat books. Once the cellar wall had been breached, it was no mean task to convey all that paper along a tunnel just over three feet high and two feet wide. It was done with ropes and sleds. When time ran short, half the money was left behind. In the villa the equivalent of over a 1000 books had to be loaded into trunks and suitcases ready for carting to the station. This was done, but nobody could lift the cases. The idea of carrying them unobtrusively on to the train was abandoned. The cases were lightened and again huge sums of money were left behind. This was where a single detail destroyed the plan completely and with it months of work. Sofya Perovskaya, for all her cunning, hated waste in all its forms, or maybe this hatred is central to cunning such as hers. The mining engineer wanted a dray and a drayhorse to move the load, but she insisted that a haycart would be enough. A dray would have cost ten roubles, a peasant cart only three. And, as always, Sonya prevailed. The hired cart was loaded with the bags and cases on the morning of 3rd June, 1879, though later than planned. The plotters now made their way individually to the station. The cart was to arrive an hour before the train pulled out, leaving each of the group time to pick up two cases. But the cart never got there. The driver took a corner too fast, the flimsy cart overturned, and the horse was injured. By the time the cart was upright again and a new horse had been found to pull it, only fifteen minutes remained. Finally, in the square in front of the station, one of the cartwheels fell to pieces, and that was the end of the adventure. Luckily one of the women had taken 10,000 roubles in her handbag, thinking it a shame to leave so much money behind. Otherwise the venture was an abject failure. In a way it symbolises all our efforts. It is no simple task to construct a tunnel through sand and to pierce the wall of a huge brick building. We achieved it. The money was there, the cases were there, the transport was there, but to save seven roubles, and, if I remember her clearly, to allow Sofya Perovskaya to win an argument, the whole venture dissolved in failure.

What came out of this failure was a passion for tunnels, as the later events in this account will show. (*Memoir of the People's Will*, Chapter 4.)

# Chapter 6

## I

Evgenya climbed the stairs to the apartment, sniffing the air. Something was different. There was a strange box in the hall and a man's voice in the living room. Rakhel stood at the kitchen door, looking flustered. Her cheeks were more hectic, her eyes brighter than usual.

"Who is it?" Evgenya asked quietly.

"The Coalminer," Rakhel whispered. "You remember. He was in Kherson."

"Viktor Pavlovich?"

"Yes," Rakhel replied. "You know him?"

"I used to. I haven't seen him for ages. Not since he went to Kherson."

"He's so nice," Rakhel said. "So different from the others."

"What's he doing in Moscow?"

"Brought some letters and a box for Anna... for Viktorya, sorry."

The Guardian had established a rule that the head of a safe-house must always be officially registered but under false papers. The papers he'd sent Anna were an undetectable forgery. The seals and signatures were genuine. They'd been supplied by a connection the Guardian had formed inside the Third Section. The name was genuine too: Viktorya Nikolayevna Rakovskaya. Viktorya had died the previous summer in Novgorod: twenty-eight years old, fair hair, blue eyes and a member of the nobility. There was no central registry of deaths, so illegals living on forged papers became the resurrected children of typhoid, dysentery and suicide. Things would get more difficult if the new German idea spread to Russia – passport photographs embossed with a seal. But photography was getting easier, and the Guardian was planning a darkroom – if they could make dynamite, they could fake pictures.

"Is Viktor Pavlovich staying?" Evgenya asked. "Here? With us?"

Rakhel shook her head in disappointment: "Anna didn't say to make up a bed or anything."

"Listen," Evgenya said faintly. "I forgot some of the shopping. I won't be long." She gave her loaded basket to Rakhel and fled back down the stairs.

Moscow. October. The cold street. She walked aimlessly toward the Pokrovka. Vitya! There in the house. It was ten months since he'd left for Kherson. In the summer he'd passed his examination – Sonya had sent her a newspaper clipping with the result. But that was all she knew – except for what everyone knew about the disaster in Kherson. And how much did he know about her? About how she'd spent the summer? Leaving the house in Odessa. The months in Kiev with Mikhail Popov, the Hangman. Her baby… aborted. The safe-house she was setting up with Anna. He knew nothing – how could he? Who would have told him? Certainly not Sonya.

When she reached the Pokrovka, she turned fitfully back toward the house. She went into a baker's shop and waited for bread. When she reached the head of the line, the baker asked her what she wanted. "Nothing!" she replied, as though the question made no sense and went back to the street again. She walked in a tangled circle through backyards, streets and snickets, ending again in their own yard. It was evening – the lamplighters had passed down the street an hour before. She slipped into the stairwell and then stopped, staring upward at the flight of steps. Perhaps he'd gone. He wouldn't wait for her. Probably he wanted to see her as little as she wanted to see him. Except she *did* want to see him. Vitya!

She ran up the stairs, her latchkey ready in her hand. She opened the heavy front door. His voice. He was saying goodbye to Anna. Shaking hands. He turned and saw her.

"Evgenya," he said diffidently. "Viktorya Nikolayevna thought you might be back earlier."

"I had to get some extra shopping." She was empty-handed. Her words were senseless. "They didn't have any... what I wanted. They'd sold out."

Rakhel was standing beside Anna. The three of them had been gossiping together, and now they were silent.

"If you want to talk to Evgenya, you can stay," Anna prompted. "As long as you like."

Evgenya saw him glance at her.

She shrugged to show it didn't matter to her either way. Though it did.

"I'll be going then," Vitya said.

Rakhel pushed past Anna and found Vitya's fashionable ulster on the coat-stand. She helped him on with it. "Wonderful to see you settled like this," he said to Rakhel. "I thought after Kherson I'd never see you again."

"I thought so too," Rakhel replied. "Maybe the 10,000 had something to do with it." The legendary 10,000 roubles that she'd salvaged from Kherson had bought her a grudging recognition, even from Sonya. "Will you stop by again?"

"I don't think so. It's only by chance I'm here today." He hugged Rakhel and shook hands with Anna as old friends take leave of each other.

"Goodbye, Evgenya Antonovna," he said, extending his hand to her, his face suddenly expressionless.

"I'll walk with you a little way," she said, not taking his hand. "There's another shop I ought to try."

"But you don't know which way I'm going," he objected.

"To the station," Anna broke in. "Evgenya's shop is on the way."

Vitya shrugged much as Evgenya had done earlier. The two of them left the apartment and walked in silence down the stairs.

"I wanted to congratulate you on your exam," Evgenya broke out, desperate for something to say.

"I passed. Not very well. I didn't have enough time."

"No," she agreed. "It must have been hard."

"And now?" he asked. "With all the new organisation. You're here? In Moscow?"

"With Anna, I mean Viktorya, and Rakhel. Yes. The safe-house."

They walked the length of the next street in silence. "Where's your shop?" he asked at last.

"There is no shop."

"Where are you going then?"

"I wanted to ask you something."

He said nothing and she balked at his silence. What was the point?

"Well?" he asked finally.

"Why didn't you write to me?" She tried to sound casual, but her voice choked.

"Is that what you wanted to ask?"

"One of the things."

"You know why."

"I mean, *really* why?"

He thought for a second: "Why didn't *you* write to *me*?"

A cheap answer – it surprised her. "I didn't have an address," she replied curtly.

He said nothing.

"And anyway," Evgenya continued, "when Sonya said you were in Kherson, I wanted to send a note, only she wouldn't take it."

"*Sonya wouldn't take it*," he jibed. "That's not true."

"Vitya!" The word was a cry of pain. "She wouldn't take it. I asked her. She said no."

"That's not what she told me."

"What did she tell you then?"

"She said you were…"

"What?"

"She said you were… enjoying yourself. In Odessa. She said she'd offered to take a note. And you'd said no."

"Enjoying myself? Is that what she said?"

"No. She said 'fucking around'."

"Did she now?"

They'd reached the courtyard in front of the new Kursky Station. "I have to get my train," Vitya said. They stopped, looking gravely at each other. Evgenya could hardly breathe – something had gone agonisingly wrong.

"And I know it's true," he said. "You *were* fucking around. I heard… Forget it Evgenya, it doesn't matter anymore."

"But Vitya, that was after."

"After what?"

"After she told me you weren't… interested in me anymore."

He pondered over the words. "Possibly," he said at last.

"Is that all you can say? Possibly?"

"I have a train to catch, Evgenya."

"Do you believe me? Or do you believe her? Vitya. Tell me."

"What difference does it make?"

"What do you mean, what difference?"

"You were three months with Mikhail Popov. In Kiev. Did you fuck around with him too?"

"Yes," she admitted freely. "But who told you? Was it her again?"

"Does it matter?"

"It matters to me."

"Yes. It was Sonya."

"So she did what she could to split us up, and now she's made sure we can't even talk to each other properly."

"Our lives have gone down different roads, Evgenya."

"Don't talk shit to me, Vitya. *Our lives have gone down different roads.*" She mimicked his dead, emotionless voice. "Why can't you talk to me? Because Mikhail Popov fucked me? A lot of people fucked me. I'll give you a list if I can remember all the names, and Sonya can sign off on it. But that doesn't mean…"

"What doesn't it mean?"

"Anna's not exactly a virgin. But you talk to her. And Rakhel. I mean, Rakhel of all people. *I thought after Kherson I'd never see you again.*" Maliciously she mimicked his almost brotherly concern.

"But I never…"

"Exactly. You never spoke to Rakhel like you spoke to me. You never looked at her like you looked at me. Vitya, for heaven's sake."

He glanced up at the big clock outside the station. "The train's gone anyway," he said.

"Do you want to go to a café?" she asked. "It's cold out here."

"No," he replied. He held out his hand to her, though not to say goodbye. She didn't take it, and he let it fall to his side again. "I think Sonya was wrong – what it seems she did," he began. "I haven't taken it in properly yet. It hurt me, what you told her. I couldn't believe it. Really."

"What did I tell Sonya?"

"That I'd better forget you."

"That's exactly what she told me *you'd* said!" Evgenya was aghast at Sonya's absolute treachery.

They stood for a long time saying nothing, sharing their misery.

"But you can see it another way too," Vitya said at last.

"What way?"

"Two people, like we were. In love…"

Evgenya looked at him viciously. In her long summer with Mikhail Popov, she'd learned a great deal about pain – how to bear it and to some extent how to inflict it. She knew that her face, when she scowled, hinted evil things, and she was scowling now.

Vitya fell silent, frozen by her intensity.

"Don't say it," Evgenya threatened. "'The Movement has no place for lovers.' That's shit, Vitya. I don't want to hear Sonya's drivel second-hand from you."

"You want to break my arm by the look of you," he said, unnerved.

"Why should I?" she retorted. "You're not worth the effort. I wanted to talk. We were close. We could be close again, I thought. But I don't think so any more." She turned on her heel and walked away from him, hoping that nothing in her walk would betray the tears that were streaming down her face.

## II

Anna sat at the big table in the drawing room decoding the messages Vitya had delivered. They were from the Committee of the People's Will. It was slow, tedious work, and her mind wandered. The Committee. The new leader was a man with ideas, Andrey Zhelyabov – a rough diamond everyone called him. He came from a family of house serfs, though he'd studied for a while in Odessa. Two years before he'd been tried along with Sofya Perovskaya and the others who'd 'gone to the people.' Like Sonya, he'd been acquitted. Then, after the fiasco in Kherson, he'd called a meeting – almost everyone in the Movement had been there. Anna had gone, though with no great expectations. But what she'd heard had excited her. At the meeting Zhelyabov – Andrey – had fought for a new organisation and for terror with unflinching terrorists behind it. The fence-sitters and drawing-room communists rejected the whole idea at once and vanished. Those who stayed were revolutionaries, fired by Zhelyabov's rhetoric and by his demands for action and self-sacrifice. His new organisation was called the People's Will, the *Narodnaya Volya*.

Andrey was a peasant, physically strong, alien and attractive. Anna liked him. In August Andrey's new followers had met again in the Lesna Forest. He'd laid out his programme. One goal was enough: the assassination of the Tsar. A Committee would produce the plans, and the rest would carry them out. Alexander Mikhailov, the Guardian, would enforce discipline and establish procedures which would be followed – on pain of punishment. Though the conspirators took no oath, after the meeting in Lesna they understood the price of disloyalty to the People's Will – a bullet in the neck or a hole in the ice.

Anna had been close to the Movement for many years. Zhelyabov wanted her on the Committee. Her money would help of course, but he seemed to have taken a liking to her in his blunt way. Sonya, however, took a different view: Anna didn't belong on the Committee – she'd be better running a safe-house in Moscow. The Committee would lose all credibility if it leaked out that 'Countess Agriculture' was a member. It wasn't much of a reason. Most of the group sided with Andrey: Olga, Mischa Trigony, Vera Figner and her sister. Sonya, however, refused to give in, and Anna conceded defeat, making a virtue of it. As compensation Andrey gave her a role that fitted her own plans perfectly – liaison with the army conspirators in Sebastopol. That would allow her…

The street bell rang and then the key turned in the doorlatch. Evgenya was back, her dark eyes red with crying. She pulled off her coat, tearing at the buttons.

Anna was sorry. "Can you help me with the code?" she asked. "You count the letters quicker than me." She stood up, abandoning the work to Evgenya.

"And you never land on a wrong letter," Rakhel added ruefully. The code was more or less beyond her.

Evgenya sat down without a word. Anna went to the piano and began looking through the music that nobody played. Perhaps the tedious task and the quiet, familiar room would calm Evgenya's nerves. It wasn't such a bad room, Anna reflected: Moscow-Parisian, *bourgeois,* but they felt comfortable there. She'd rented the place from a knife-maker who'd gone to live in Solingen, but she'd replaced nothing, not even the frightful chromo-prints. If the police ever searched the place, nothing should hint at elegance – or even at good taste.

Evgenya settled quickly to her work. Anna retreated to the sofa to gossip with Rakhel, who was flicking through the latest edition of *La Mode Illustrée*. Anna and Rakhel shared a love of finery and had strangely similar tastes – tastes which Rakhel now had the money to indulge for the first time in her life. Though Anna was mistress and Rakhel was maid, when they walked out arm in arm, the distinction was far from obvious. The swish of Rakhel's skirts was as *épatant* as the swish of Anna's, and her figure, Anna accepted grudgingly, was a shade more fashionable: narrower at the hips and fuller in the bust. Though not for much longer. Rakhel's days were numbered; her body was rotten with the diseases that went with prostitution. If she looked after herself, she'd have a year of normal life. Maybe two. If she let herself go...

Anna's willingness to translate French fashion news for Rakhel was quickly exhausted. She went back to Evgenya's table. "Vitya catch his train?" she asked easily. "He cut it a bit fine."

"He can throw himself under it for all I care," Evgenya muttered. Then: "There's a miscount here. That has to be an *m* not a *d*."

"Let me see," Anna said, though Evgenya was always right.

"Viktor Pavlovich?" Rakhel queried coming to the table too, *La Mode Illustrée* still in her hand. "Anna just told me he's your cousin."

"No one's responsible for their relations," Evgenya jibed back. "Specially not when they're total shits."

"Viktor Pavlovich?" Rakhel exclaimed in disbelief.

"Oh for Christ's sake!" Evgenya stood up and flung out of the room in the direction of the kitchen.

"There isn't any," Anna called after her. "You drank the last yesterday."

Evgenya came back into the room. "I'm sorry, Anna," she said. "It's not your fault." She glanced at Rakhel: "Nor yours. I'm going out for ten minutes. Is there anything you need?"

"If you just want to forget him," Anna told her wryly. "Opium's quicker."

"Keep your stupid advice to yourself!" Evgenya cried in sudden rage. Then, on the opposite impulse, she threw her arms round Anna and kissed her cheek. "I love you," she whispered.

"Go on with you," Anna replied.

"I mean it," Evgenya objected, "and I'll prove it one of these days."

"Well, you can't marry me," Anna said with pretended relief. "At least I'm spared that." She held the trembling girl until she was calm again. Rakhel went back to the sofa looking puzzled – most things seemed to puzzle her softening mind.

"Let me get on with the message," Evgenya said at last. She sat down resolutely at the table, picked up her pencil and began counting letters.

Anna went to the kitchen to set up a samovar. She glanced back at Evgenya, and the two women exchanged an enquiring frown.

Evgenya had been pregnant when she'd arrived at the safe-house half way through September. Occasionally, when the mood took her, she drank brandy till she passed out, and her time in Odessa had radically changed her attitude to men. Kiev had been entirely different. The frightful Popov had abused her, made her suffer, demanded instant obedience to his unpredictable orders. Yet strangely, her submission had been free and whole-hearted. It had brought her something Anna couldn't quite understand. Evgenya had tested herself to find her limit, but a lot of girls did that – especially the ones who joined the Movement. But there was more. Evgenya recounted the facts, but she had no explanation for them. It was puzzling.

Anna had dealt with Evgenya's pregnancy swiftly and without compunction. The girl had accepted the simple procedure with little comment and almost no reaction – or so it seemed. Her drinking had been easily curtailed – Evgenya wasn't addicted. Perhaps she wasn't the type. And men? Secluded in a household of three women, Evgenya sometimes spoke nostalgically of their household in Odessa, but she accepted the absence of Oleg and the others, just as she accepted the fact that there was no brandy in the house when she wanted a drink. And what about the men? There'd been quite a few apparently. It was a time-honoured revenge to pay back a faithless lover with a little infidelity of one's own, though it seemed Evgenya had made a science of it. On the other hand this Oleg – more perhaps than any of the others – had brought her something important. He'd written a piece of music for her – that was how Evgenya put it.

Anna listened readily to Evgenya's tales. Not much was left of the girl who'd gone to Odessa six months before. The Movement was moulding Evgenya, toughening her, sharpening her for its own purposes. Now that the Movement had become the People's Will, Evgenya, who'd not been at the meeting in Lesna and who'd never met Andrey Zhelyabov, belonged to it heart and soul. Anna saw it in the way she exercised. For an hour each morning and an hour each night, Evgenya worked fiercely with dumb-bells and a chest-expander of caoutchouc that Anna could hardly stretch. That all came from Popov. Evgenya had told him she wanted to be strong, so he'd taken her to a gym in Kiev where he sometimes picked up a few roubles sparring with a sporting gentleman or an occasional prize-fighter. The trainer, a Chechen called Yakub, had shown Evgenya some of the heavy routines. He'd been surprised how quickly she'd picked them up. Even Popov had been impressed.

At Yakub's gym, Evgenya had discovered something else, something that Anna found alien and strangely exciting. As Popov's girl, Evgenya had fallen in with a handful of women fighters who worked for Yakub. At serious fight meetings, the practice had sprung up of using women boxers as a *divertissement* between bouts The women didn't fight for long – five or ten minutes. Some of it was playacting, but not all – the boxing crowd knew a pulled punch from a real one, and they preferred punches that hurt. The women boxed in flimsy skirts and not much else. They boxed with bare knuckles or with gloves, with rules or without. Sometimes there was a prize fight – one of Yakub's women against a woman from another gym. That was rougher: no gloves, no clothes and no time limit. Evgenya had watched the women train and watched them fight. It had interested her. She'd asked Yakub if she could join in. He'd talked to Popov. The men had agreed it was up to her, if she wanted to get herself killed…

At first the women had been too tough for Evgenya, but to please Yakub they'd shown her the basic moves, let her spar with them, and enjoyed giving her ugly bruises. Popov had nicknamed her his Spitfire and looked on while she took her beatings. In a month or so Evgenya had been able to take care of herself. She was young, quick and her brain was still undamaged. And she was a good-looker. Yakub had begun to wonder if he might give her a fight one day. Popov had said she wasn't ready. But given time…

Anna was engrossed. Like every woman in the Movement, she knew the value of being tough. Prison, exile, hard labour – that's what threatened them all at any hour of the day or night. If you weren't tough, you'd never survive. Worst of all were the transports where politicals were herded with criminals, men and women together, night after night on the long march to Siberia. Terrible stories were told and retold. The women talked, obsessively sometimes, about making themselves strong, about discipline and exercise. About hunger, cold, pain.

Years before, in the winter, Anna had climbed with two friends into an attic. They'd taken off everything but their shifts and shivered in the icy cold till they could endure no more. They'd done it day after day, trying to go longer as their bodies hardened. After that, the idea took hold: they'd starved themselves, they'd walked their rooms all night to deprive themselves of sleep and then driven themselves to exhaustion next day – walking, swimming, riding. In a barn where horses were trained, they'd run round and round in the filthy sand till they'd collapsed and could only crawl a few more rounds on their hands and knees.

Anna and her Gypsy explained these things to each other as they exercised. Anna ordered boxing gloves and a punchbag from a shop in the Kitay Gorod. They hung the punchbag in the empty bedroom where they exercised. Evgenya nicknamed it Romanov and beat it to death twice a day. But they didn't fight. Evgenya couldn't bring herself to hit Anna, not even a friendly tap on the shoulder. On the other hand she teased Anna often with a "Come on, hit me." But swing and lunge as she might, Anna never landed a punch – Evgenya was quick as a weasel.

In Petersburg the winter before, Anna had found Evgenya shrewd but ignorant – an attractive child but not much more. Even so – often as she'd regretted it since – she'd confessed to the Gypsy her entanglement with Babe. Now in Moscow she formed an intimacy with Evgenya that went much further. She felt driven to explain herself – justify, define, condemn. She'd wanted passionately to become a doctor, she told Evgenya. She *was* a doctor in all but name. She'd planned to work in neurology and begun a thesis with a professor in Zürich who'd specialised in the nervous diseases of women. He'd been happy to absorb a rich, well-connected Russian into his little group of researchers. After a while, he'd become her first lover. Anna still wasn't sure if a professor of female neurology had been a good choice. Evgenya smugly suggested that an artist might be more imaginative. When Evgenya finally realised what female neurology was, she was shocked.

"Is that what you... studied? In Tsurik? Spending? Frigging?"

"Partly."

"Like Vitya studied mining?" Evgenya began to laugh.

"Very similar I expect."

"But he had to do experiments, in a lab, with coke and coal."

Anna began to laugh too. "We did experiments too. In a way."

"How? You didn't...?"

"Not ourselves, no. The professor hired women. Whores, models – I don't know."

"And that's what happens at university?" For a second, Evgenya was helpless as a child with laughter.

"Not in Russia. Stop being so silly."

Evgenya clung now to Anna, merrily recovering her breath. "So that might be something for me?" she teased.

"Study?"

"No. What the whores did. Unless they have a course on dynamite."

# III

Anna read again the message that Evgenya had decoded. At 13:15 next day, Stepan Shiraev would arrive at the Kursky Station. He'd have with him two suitcases of dynamite. He'd walk from the station to the safe-house carrying the cases. Anna was to store the dynamite at the safe-house till she received further instructions. All 'Alert One' procedures for safe-houses were to be followed.

Anna took the Guardian's handbook from its hiding place and studied the procedures with Evgenya and Rakhel. Alert One meant a risky operation of the highest importance. If a visitor arrived at a safe-house, he might perhaps be followed. The safe-house had to ensure that the visitor wasn't being followed – in other words, watch him and warn him if he had a 'tail.' The warning was simple: a woman known to the visitor would approach him at least two streets away from the safe-house wearing a bright red shawl over her head. Given this danger signal, the visitor would avoid the house at all costs. Who wore the scarf if the visitor knew none of the local women or what happened if he failed to see the signal – these details the handbook did not discuss.

Anna decided that they should go to the Kursky Station and check out the streets that evening, though Shiraev wasn't due till the next day. It was already eight o'clock – they shouldn't leave it much longer. The three women dressed for the street and strolled together toward Kazenny Lane.

"Suitcases of dynamite?" Evgenya asked as they entered the quiet lane. "What for?"

"I don't know," Anna replied. "Viktor Pavlovich is working on a tunnel. So he told me."

"More than he told me," Evgenya retorted. "Where is it? His tunnel?"

"Near Moscow somewhere?"

"Is it under the railway? Like you said before?"

"That was Zhelyabov's plan in the summer: three mines on Romanov's way back from the Crimea. Two in the south and one here."

"So we blow up his train three times."

"If one fails, the next one gets him."

"Do you think so? You think blowing up his train will kill him?" Evgenya was evidently in a mood to contradict everything and everybody.

"Zhelyabov thinks so. And so does Kibalchich."

"And you? What do you think?"

"I have my doubts. But I don't know much about dynamite."

"Lots of trains come off the tracks, but hardly anyone is killed. And maybe the Tsar's train is different. Maybe it's strengthened. Underneath. With iron."

"How do you know about such things?" Anna asked, surprised.

"Popov. He taught me more than how to take a licking."

"I'm glad to hear it," Anna said with a shrug. Though Evgenya's experiences as a fighter interested her, Mikhail Popov was not her favourite subject.

From the timetable on the station wall, they saw that the 13:15 train arrived at the south end of the long, main platform. It was coming from Nizhny Novgorod. That made sense – the Committee, Anna knew, had set up a workshop in Nizhny to make dynamite. They began to plan. Shiraev knew Rakhel from the meeting in Lesna, and she knew him, so Rakhel could wear the red scarf. Anna would meet the train and follow Shiraev closely, looking for a tail. Rakhel would be standing at the corner of Pokrovsky Square with a red shawl in her basket. She'd see Anna and Shiraev approaching. If Anna had taken off her hat and was walking bareheaded then Rakhel was to put on the red shawl immediately and walk straight at Shiraev. Not speak to him though. Nothing was more dangerous than talk – the tail would certainly see what was happening, and Rakhel would be picked up. Evgenya would watch from a distance in case Shiraev took a different route. In that case, if there was danger, Evgenya would run ahead and meet him outside the safe-house, wearing a red shawl of her own. He wouldn't recognise her, but there must be no talk. The signal was the red shawl – that had to be enough.

"You tell me what to do, and I'll do it," Evgenya agreed. "That's how I worked with Popov."

"Well I'm not Popov," Anna objected. "I don't want you hurt."

"No, you're definitely not Popov," Evgenya laughed. "Afterwards he always…"

"Enough!" Anna admonished her. "Only pure thoughts, Evgenya. Otherwise I'll put you in a cold bath. All night."

In the station yard they bought scarves and shawls of various colours from a street peddler, two of them bright red.

There was a famous restaurant in the Sadovaya, not far from the station. It was sufficiently elegant for ladies to dine there without male company. The three women went there once or twice a week. The head waiter knew them and welcomed them with an air of discreet irony. Though a whore's fine clothes might deceive the rest of the world, a head waiter can tell her at a glance. He admired Rakhel of course. Of the three he gave her his deepest bow and poured her wine with the most eloquent flourish. But he sometimes glanced curiously at the three of them, wondering, Anna guessed, what brought together a whore, a hard-muscled gypsy, and a dressed-down aristocrat.

"So tell me," Anna began when the head waiter had poured the first glass of wine, "something I never asked you about Popov. Why did you go to Kiev? Did Sonya send you?"

"Milord told her to get rid of me," Evgenya replied bluntly. After her quarrel with Vitya, even the sound of Sonya's name was an irritation.

"Milord didn't like you? I thought everyone liked you."

"Some liked me more often than others," Evgenya said sourly. She explained the quarrel between Trigony and Oleg.

"So he kicked you out. But why go to Popov of all people?"

"Sonya – it was her idea."

"So what was Popov supposed to teach you? How to hang people?"

"I never hung anyone."

"Then…"

"In Kiev a lot of Group South are in jail and a lot end up killing themselves. Suicide, that's what the prison calls it. You know how it is. We had a list. Some of the guards were… very rough. Specially with the women."

"A list of guards," Anna nodded. "And now the list is shorter?"

"The list doesn't exist anymore," Evgenya agreed.

"And did things get better in the jails?"

"So they say."

"We don't have a proper word in Russian for 'hangwoman'," Anna said, raising her glass and staring into the dark red wine.

"We don't need one. I only kept watch," Evgenya replied. "But I learned a lot."

"Will you work for me one day? If I need you?" Anna asked.

"Work? Yes." Evgenya raised her glass to Rakhel, and the three women drank a toast. "Work."

The head waiter raised an eyebrow, wondering perhaps what sort of work these curious women performed together.

As they exercised together before going to bed, Evgenya finally told Anna what she'd learned from Vitya that afternoon

– Sonya had lied to them both. Obviously she wanted to keep them apart. And she'd succeeded.

"So you can't forgive her?" Anna asked, breathlessly trying to keep up with Evgenya's rhythm.

"Not as long as I live."

"Which won't be long if you pick a quarrel with Sonya," Anna observed, putting down her dumb-bells on the wooden floor.

"I think it was vile of her," Evgenya continued. "And she said she liked me!"

"Probably she does. But she doesn't want you getting in the way of her blue-eyed Coalminer."

"How would I get in his way?"

Anna laughed and flexed her aching shoulders. "Think, Gypsy. You're a very demanding young lady. It sounds as though Popov had you beaten up twice a week to take the ginger out of you. Poor Vitya – you'd have worn him thin as a candle."

"Even if I would," Evgenya admitted. "What business is it of hers?"

"She doesn't like that kind of thing to get in the way of the work. And in principle she's right."

"You think so?"

"I know so. From what happened to me."

"But she could've been open with me, couldn't she?"

Anna picked up her dumb-bells again and swung back into Evgenya's rhythm. "Answer that yourself," she said. "Could she have been open? Or put it another way – decide if you'd rather be what you are now, or what you would have been if you'd stayed in Petersburg with Mama and Papa."

"And what *am* I now?"

"Now? This minute? A very sweaty, very pretty, bad-tempered gypsy."

Evgenya laughed. "If ever I hit you," she said. "I'll kill you."

# IV

Evgenya watched next day as disaster struck. A porter at the station told her where the luggage van would stop and she waited beside a bench on the other side of the platform. Shiraev's train was more than an hour late. A moment after it pulled in, a crush of passengers formed, as always, beside the luggage van, shouting, demanding, pointing. Evgenya had no idea what Shiraev looked like, but she saw Anna on the fringe of the crowd, her eyes fixed on a man in a dark blue chesterfield. Then something unexpected – the man in the chesterfield, turned, saw Anna and, without thinking, held out his hand to greet her. Anna turned away in horror, and Shiraev pulled back his hand with a show of mistaking her for someone else. Shiraev dawdled now at the luggage van, waiting patiently, too patiently Evgenya thought.

Finally he identified his suitcases and walked off with them down the almost empty platform, shaking off porters and cab-drivers. Anna followed him. She was not alone. Two men, one a railwayman and one an anonymous clerk in a dirty trench-coat, were tracking him. When Shiraev stopped in the station yard to ease the muscles in his hands, the two men stopped. When he moved again, they followed. Anna took off her hat and hurried away down Kazenny Lane to the meeting place with Rakhel. Evgenya knew her job – watch to see if Rakhel's warning was successful. If it was, she could go back to the safe-house immediately. If it failed, she was to warn Shiraev with her own red scarf. She scurried after Anna. But then she saw something they'd never thought about – Anna now had a tail too. Two men, one on either side of the street, dogging her footsteps. Bareheaded, Anna reached the corner where Rakhel was waiting. Rakhel saw her, pulled on the red shawl and then scanned the lane for Shiraev. Casually Rakhel moved across Shiraev's path, avoiding a collision with him only at the last second. Shiraev understood the warning – at the corner he turned away from the safe-house.

Anna stopped by a shop window, using the reflection to put her hat on again and to scan the street behind her. Evgenya's first impulse was to rush to Anna and stay with her whatever happened. The orders, however, were different – send a telegram to Petersburg if anything goes wrong.

From the other side of the Pokrovka, Evgenya watched. She saw Rakhel fifty yards down the street watching too. Suddenly Anna seemed to take a decision. To shake off a tail in the street, the first step is to get into a cab. There were cabs back at the station and a cab rank on the Pokrovka, a hundred yards away. Anna moved, quick and resolute, heading for the rank. Instantly the men tailing her were in pursuit as though they'd guessed her intention. One of them was running – he'd be at the cab rank before Anna. She was trapped. She reached the first of the *droshkies* and spoke to the driver. She had her foot on the step when the two men closed in on her from either side. They said something. Evgenya hurried nearer. If she could hear what the men were saying...

Anna took her papers from her handbag. "Viktorya Nikolayevna Rakovskaya," she said.

"What were you doing at the station by the luggage van?" The two men were dressed alike in worn-out office suits, though one clearly outranked the other.

"A friend of mine was due to arrive. I thought she might be looking for her case."

"Was that the man who recognised you?"

"No one recognised me. My friend is a woman and she wasn't on the train."

"That's not what I saw," said the superior.

"Nor me," added the other.

"Perhaps you'd be so good as to come to the Central Office with us, Ma'am? So we can get everything down in writing. Start a file. It won't take long."

A sudden wave of shouting and screaming echoed down the Pokrovka. People were running toward them – screeching, panicking women, men punching and fighting to gain a pace or two. "Dynamite!" A moment later the street was all but empty, though every thirty yards a poorly dressed man was standing, stripped suddenly of his cover and trying to look inconspicuous.

"Dropped his cases and ran," said one of Anna's captors.

"They'll get him," said the other. "Half the department out today." They bundled Anna into the cab and told the driver to go to the Central Office. Anna made no resistance. As the cab creaked away, Evgenya felt her arm gripped as the men had gripped Anna. She pulled away, ready to run, but it was Rakhel.

## V

Evgenya composed her telegram from the list of standard expressions in the Guardian's handbook. She'd read them through with Anna the night before. A safe-house was a 'cowshed', the head of the house was the 'farmer'. An arrest was 'catching cold', disappearance 'catching the pox', and death 'catching TB'. Evgenya's telegram read: 'Farmer caught cold. Farmhouse still habitable. Latest consignment of fodder is lost. Please instruct. G.'

"But they won't understand that, about the fodder," Rakhel objected.

"Of course they will. They're not stupid."

For more than three hours Evgenya and Rakhel waited in the telegraph office for a reply. The benches were crowded – some people had been waiting all day. As always, the answer, when it came, was cryptic: 'If farmhouse roof is safe, go there. Help follows. Polonsky.'

"Who's Polonsky?" Rakhel asked.

"A poet. He wrote a gypsy poem. It's from Sonya."

She remembered the poem: '… *during these days we have been drawn together*'. Why had Sonya written like that if all the time she was planning such treachery? '… *a word spoken in love, enough is enough.*' It was unforgivable. All of it. However the immediate problem was not Sonya's dirty tricks – but Anna. She was gone. They'd lost her without a fight – Evgenya trembled with frustration. Why all the toughness? Why all the training? If only she'd had a gun! But Evgenya knew nothing about guns, and the street had been full of Third Section men.

Evgenya said little to Rakhel on the way back to the safe-house. In five minutes they reached their building and turned under the arch into the yard. The yardkeeper was standing, arms folded, gossiping with the housekeeper from the top-floor apartment. He greeted them cheerily: "Did you hear, Evgenya Antonovna? Dynamite. In the Pokrovka. Two cases of it. What's the world coming to?"

"Everyone's talking about it," Evgenya agreed. "Did they catch him yet? Did you hear?"

"They'll catch him. Then he'll catch it," the yardkeeper quipped.

"Viktorya Nikolayevna..." Evgenya began.

The yardkeeper sighed, preferring chat to business. "What about her?"

"She's gone for a few days. To see her parents in Novgorod, I think. I'm not sure though." She paused casually. '*Help follows*' the telegram said. "And we're expecting a visitor, tonight or tomorrow. Might stay a while." The yardkeeper had to report anything suspicious to the police. It was best to keep him informed, though vaguely and without fuss.

The top-floor housekeeper studied the middle distance carefully, as people do when they're interested in a conversation that doesn't concern them – there were plenty of strange stories about the first-floor tenants.

To Evgenya's surprise, their visitor was a man – Viktor Pavlovich. Sonya had sent him. He was to shut down the safe-house, remove the codebooks and destroy any incriminating trace of the inhabitants. For the time being, Vitya was to take Evgenya and Rakhel back to the house where he was working on his new tunnel. It was ten miles south of Moscow.

"No," Evgenya refused. "We don't give up on Anna so easily."

"Those are your instructions from the Committee," Vitya said.

Evgenya bit her lip. Disobedience was disloyalty.

"Sonya says Anna will talk when they find out who she really is," Vitya explained. "We must cut off any trails she opens up for them."

"She'll talk, will she? You're talking rubbish again, Vitya. It's a lousy habit."

Vitya turned to Rakhel, obviously expecting her to side with him.

"Viktor Pavlovich," Rakhel countered, not looking at him directly. "If you think we're giving up on Anna, that's..."

"That's what?"

"We won't. We agreed. Me and Evgenya. We'll get her out."

"Get her out of jail! You're mad. There's a manhunt out there. Everyone in a blue chesterfield between here and Yalta is being picked up. Anyone even half-way suspicious is in jail. It's never been so tight."

"So," Rakhel retorted. "You ever been in jail?"

"No," he replied.

"Well I have, lots of times."

"We have a plan," Evgenya broke in. "Or the start of one anyway. We'll tell you what it is. You can be part of it. Or not. If you won't help us, there's other men who will."

"Who? Popov?" he jeered.

"One day Popov will cut off your nose and stuff it up your arse, you cockroach," Evgenya said.

"Evgenya," Rakhel pleaded. "Calm down, sweetheart."

With an effort Evgenya bit back her temper. For a while no one spoke. Then: "Viktor Pavlovich," she began. "Vitya..."

He looked at her, expressionless.

"Can I get you a glass of cognac?" she asked politely. "We have some. From France."

"No thank you," he said dryly.

"I think you should," Rakhel broke in. "While we tell you the plan. Please Viktor Pavlovich."

"Just a small one then," Vitya compromised. "Tell."

"First," Rakhel began, "one of us has to talk to Anna and agree what story she's to tell. All the details. They think they've arrested someone called Viktorya. Who was this Viktorya? What was she doing here? When they know she was registered here, they'll come to check. Bound to. If we all tell the same story, they'll probably believe she's Viktorya and let her go in the end."

Evgenya brought back three kitchen glasses and an untouched bottle of cognac. She uncorked the bottle and poured the glasses half full.

Vitya's face took on a superior, sarcastic look. "That's a wonderful plan, Rakhel. But there's a fatal flaw."

"Tell us," said Evgenya, flushing for a new confrontation.

"No one," Vitya said dogmatically, "No one can talk to Anna or agree a story with her."

Evgenya scowled, half ready to carry out in person the threat she'd just delivered on behalf of Popov.

"Shut up, Evgenya," Rakhel said. "Let me handle it."

Evgenya shrugged and took a gulp of the cognac. She had to calm down. Unless they could win Vitya over, Sonya would take against them and everything would be lost.

"If I knew a way of talking to her," Rakhel said. "Would you go along with the plan?"

"I suppose so," Vitya conceded.

"Good." Rakhel took a sip of her cognac. "Because that's actually the easy part."

"Vitya," Evgenya began in a nervous, conciliatory voice. "We're going to need help. If it came from you, I think Rakhel… and me, we'd both like that. Very much." Surely he could hear in her voice how bitter it was for her to quarrel with him.

He looked at her doubtfully, and then at Rakhel. He cleared his throat as though to announce his refusal with authority and finality.

"Viktor Pavlovich," Rakhel interrupted before he could begin. "In Kherson the tunnel collapsed on you, and I got you out. Remember?"

He nodded.

"Then in return at least you can listen."

Evgenya stood up quickly and went behind Rakhel's chair. She put her hands on Rakhel's shoulders, so that they faced Vitya together. Rakhel was doing well.

"If you put it like that..." Vitya conceded. "So tell me, how will you talk to her?"

# VI

Evgenya was cold. When they came to a tavern she suggested to Rakhel that they wait in the warm. Arm in arm, they swung into the bar. It was a quiet place – two students in one corner, a well-dressed man sobering up with a mug of raw eggs, and a bored girl sitting at the bar staring at an empty glass. They found a corner table and sat down. Everyone glanced at them but then looked away again – there were so many streetwalkers in the district and they were no different from a hundred others.

"So how does it feel?" Rakhel asked. "You look as though you've done it all your life."

"It feels a bit different," Evgenya replied, "with nothing on underneath. And all this make-up. I'm going to look at myself. In that mirror over there." She stood up and went to the bar. She looked at herself in the big mirror behind the glasses and bottles. With a shock she saw what a short step it was to the gutter. And she was cold. Despite the chilly autumn night, Rakhel had said no coats and no shawls, the better to flaunt their figures. "Two brandies," Evgenya said to the girl at the bar, roughening her voice.

"Money?" the girl asked.

Evgenya took a three-rouble note from her bag and waved it at the girl, who shrugged and went to get the drinks.

"What time shall we make a move?" Evgenya asked as she got back to their table.

"It's busier out there than I thought," Rakhel replied. "Give it an hour."

The girl brought the drinks and Evgenya paid for them.

"You needn't have come, you know," Rakhel said. "I'd be alright on my own."

"It's interesting somehow," Evgenya replied, "and anyway…" She squeezed Rakhel's hand in a friendly way. They were not friends and never would be, but if they worked together it might help Anna. There was no other way. "You've got the note?" she asked.

"You know I have."

"The note's not really important. Just to encourage her. Only take it if you're sure they won't search you."

"They never search whores. Feel you all over for 'concealed weapons' or so they call it. But they never search you for bits of paper."

"If you can only talk to her…"

"If she's there, I can. It's not a problem. They pull in whores all night. You make trouble – inside you go. And they always keep the women separate from the men. In a big cell usually. Benches to sit and nowhere to lie down. Bucket or two in the corner. I told you already."

"And we come by in the morning to get you out."

"Ten roubles, like I said. Might be less. They don't know me in Moscow. And tell His Honour not to look so respectable. He's supposed to be my pimp, and yours. He's too shaved and polished like he is."

"Same clothes for me as now? And make-up?"

"Yes. Just like you are. But remember, he owns you. You're just a piece of dog-shit under his shoe. Flinch every time he turns in your direction, like he hits you all the time."

"How did you stand it?" Evgenya asked. "All those years?"

"I was in a house mostly, not on the streets." Rakhel sighed. "It's not so bad."

Evgenya shook her head.

"And now," Rakhel said, "with you and Anna. It's all so different. I've never been so happy – not in my whole life. Not even in Kherson – when Viktor Pavlovich came. He's so different from the rest."

"You always say that."

"Well he is. Doesn't talk about the one endless subject all the time."

"Would you?" Evgenya asked mischievously. "If he wanted? With him?"

"I'm not his type," Rakhel replied, avoiding the question. "He prefers young ones. Specially when they look like gypsies."

"Never. He hates me."

"Well, after the way you talk to him! But if you played your cards right..."

"Rakhel! I don't have any cards and I don't want him."

Rakhel nodded – she knew better. Then she said: "Rather be a whore, right?"

"I can't imagine it. Not really. No proper clothes and freezing cold – at least I've got that bit clear."

"It's not that cold tonight," Rakhel said. "Wait for a hard frost and try it then. But listen, you want to try it? Just unbutton your blouse a bit more and go over to that old drunk. Sit down, pull your blouse open so he can see down it and say: 'You can fuck me for fifty kopeks. I'm clean. No syphilis. No nothing.' He'll tell you to piss off. Then tell him everything you'll do for him. In detail. And drop the price to twenty-five. Go on, what you waiting for?"

"What's the point?" Evgenya objected. "We'll get thrown out."

"Course you get thrown out. So what? Try your luck again next door."

"Twenty-five kopeks?"

"I thought you liked it so much you did it for nothing."

"Not with old men though."

"He's not so bad actually. Maybe I'll try him myself."

"Rakhel. Don't. That's not what we came for."

"Course it is. How else do I get pulled in? Be a pest, talk dirty and make sure the law is round the corner."

As Evgenya looked at Rakhel, she was suddenly unsure. In her garish makeup and skimpy clothing, she was unmistakably a prostitute. Her movements were different, her tone of voice was wheedling and repellent. Her eyes had an unaccountable glitter. Why did they trust her? With her feeble brain and rotting body?

# VII

Evgenya arrived at the Central Police Office with Vitya at ten o'clock the next morning to pay Rakhel's fine and take her home. Vitya hadn't shaved and was trying to look raffish without much success. The building was in uproar: anxious fathers demanded the release of sons and daughters picked up, so they insisted, because of idiotic police blunders – blunders that would be reported to the highest authorities. There were threats and high words. Lawyers backed up their wealthy clients with paragraph numbers and the Latin names of obscure writs. No one was let out, except an occasional prostitute whose pimp had managed to struggle to the front desk and pay her fine.

When she was finally free, Rakhel's news was interesting. She'd spent most of the night agreeing details of their story with Anna. Then, early that morning, the politicals had learned that they'd be shifted to an overflow prison as soon as transport could be organised. The location of the new prison was whispered among the prisoners – some of them had been there before. It was a warehouse by the Moskva River, east of the city, near the marshes. That was where Anna would be before nightfall.

# Extract 6

The single purpose of the People's Will after the meeting in Lesna was to assassinate the Tsar as a deliberate act of terror. Andrey Zhelyabov addressed the work with apostolic zeal. During the late summer of 1879, the *Court Gazette* announced that the Tsar would travel to St Petersburg by ship and by train, crossing the Black Sea to Odessa and journeying on by rail. The Tsar's route was the backbone of Andrey's plan. He left little to chance. The railway track was to be mined in three places between the Black Sea and St Petersburg: Odessa, Alexandrovsk in the Ukraine and Moscow. The Tsar normally travelled in three trains, one for baggage, one for officials, and one for himself and his immediate circle. The key was to know in which coach of which train the Tsar was travelling. Andrey's plan was to station our people at crucial points along the line, watching the three trains for the necessary signs. We had a system of telegram codes so that word could be passed ahead.

The Moscow attack was the third and last, but it is the only one that survives in popular memory. Sofya Perovskaya found an old house near the railway on the southern edge of Moscow. It is often called the Hartmann House because Lev Hartmann, who was still a legal, signed the lease. It was in a desolate quarter taken over by Old Believers. My non-Russian readers may not have heard of the Old Believers. They are a sect, persecuted by the Orthodox for hundreds of years. Apparently the worst crime reported of them is their refusal to accept Patriarch Nikon's reformed way of making the cross with three fingers rather than two. I have no idea where the sin might lie, but then I have never understood religion. In any case, they were schismatics and, in the manner of schismatics, they were serious-minded, fanatical in their support of each other and suspicious of outsiders. Within this dour and scattered community, the Hartmann House stood isolated and close to the railway embankment. Around it were rubbish tips and abandoned ponds. The location was perfect. (*Memoir of the People's Will*, Chapter 8.)

# Chapter 7

## I

Evgenya sat huddled with Vitya and Mikhail Popov in the fo'c'sle of an all-but derelict steam barge, the hull rusty and the boiler dismantled. The barge had been guarded by a Kazakh watchman. Vitya had given him fifty roubles to disappear from Moscow. The barge was moored for the winter just upstream of the old customs warehouse where Anna was imprisoned.

The warehouse rose straight out of the river, five stories of yellow brick and windows with square iron grilles. The wooden jetty that had once run between the building and the river had been ripped out during the conversion of the warehouse into a jail. A catwalk had replaced it, a flimsy walkway of new yellow pine perched over the water on struts. Day and night a sentry patrolled the catwalk from end to end, 150 yards.

At first Sonya had flatly refused to send Popov, even though the plan of attack depended on the warehouse guards being silenced, and no one but the Hangman could do that. Vitya had done his best to change her mind but she'd been obstinate – Anna Petrovna, she'd insisted, was not one of the Committee's priorities. Then, unaccountably, she'd changed her mind; a risky jail-break might be just the thing to put some fight into the *Narodnaya Volya*, and it would divert police manpower away from protecting the railway and the Tsar's train – even if the breakout failed, it would still be a diversion. That wasn't how Sonya's mind usually worked – perhaps she'd asked Andrey Zhelyabov for his opinion. Whatever the reason, Popov had arrived earlier that afternoon.

There was a small porthole in each side of the fo'c'sle, close enough to the blunt curve of the bows to give a view of the warehouse. The barge was empty and sat high out of the water. Further upstream, empty lighters were moored two or three abreast, little more than hulks. The Hangman had been studying the warehouse all afternoon, asking questions, contriving, planning. "You're sure about her window? There's about sixty of them in all."

"Second level up, fourth across from our end," Evgenya said.

"With the smashed glass?"

"She smashed it to show us where she is."

"How'd you know it was her?"

"A white rag. It's gone now."

"Who saw it?"

"We had people watching from the other side of the river."

"Good," the Hangman said, confirming each detail with a nod. "This Anna? She set up that rag idea with the Jew-girl?"

"Yes," Vitya told him. "With Rakhel."

"Clever. And does Anna know we're coming?"

"Not exactly, but she agreed with Rakhel that she'd sleep in her clothes. She'll be ready."

"I liked that Rakhel. We met her, didn't we? In Kiev? She came through with a bag of money."

"You met her," Evgenya agreed. "I didn't."

"You were in bed with a black eye, I remember now."

"Black eye!" Evgenya exclaimed. "I had so many bruises I could hardly breathe."

"You should see her fight, Coalminer. Regular little spitfire. Took a lot of beatings though, till she learned to keep her right in front of her chin."

"She told me," Vitya said flatly.

"At first she ducked too low. Walked into uppercuts and knee-jerks. Mistake a lot of people make."

As he talked Popov stared out of the porthole, studying the bleak shape of the warehouse. His growling voice reverberated round the cabin. He pulled a small telescope from the pocket of his pea-coat, opened it and focused the eyepiece. "You can see them behind the glass," he said. "Poor bastards."

"And you think it's possible?" Vitya asked. "The basic idea makes sense to you?"

"Don't see why not," the Hangman replied, snapping his telescope closed and turning toward them. "Who thought it up?"

"Vitya," Evgenya answered quickly. "He's an engineer."

The Hangman nodded. "The river's slow. But you can feel it pulling at us all the time. We'll drift down alright."

"Till we're opposite the warehouse? I still don't understand that properly," Evgenya asked.

"Let's go over it again," the Hangman said. He took pieces of kindling from a box beside the pipe-stove. He arranged four pieces of wood in a square. "That's the warehouse. Wall on three sides. Fourth side's the river with a catwalk right along the river side. Guarded."

"Yes," said Vitya. "Guarded."

"This is the barge." The Hangman picked up a chunk of bark. "Upstream of the warehouse and pointing upstream. Right?"

"Yes," Evgenya said.

"We're tied up with two longish cables, one front, one back. The cable at the front is on a capstan. So what happens when we release the capstan?"

"The cable unwinds and we drift down with the current," Evgenya said. That was something she liked about Popov – he explained things so she could understand them.

"We drift down till we're opposite the warehouse. I jump up onto the catwalk and fix the guard."

"And the barge?"

"Coalminer jams the capstan and the barge stops… here." He put the chunk of bark next to the square of the warehouse. "Then Spitfire here shins up the window bars with her ropes. Up to the *third* level."

"That'll be easy, won't it?" Evgenya asked. "With those criss-cross bars?"

"Might be if you was wearing a skirt, like a proper lady," Popov replied. "But…"

"Two ropes," Evgenya interrupted. "One I shackle to the bars on the third level above where Anna's is, and the other goes on the bars of Anna's window."

"You know how a shackle works?" Popov asked. "A spring shackle?"

"She's been practicing," Vitya said.

"And don't muddle up the ropes. One will have a red rag tied to the shackle. That one…"

"… goes on Anna's window."

"Right. And that rope goes back to the winch where the Coalminer's ready to haul in."

"So after the shackles are on, I…"

"You shin down and get back to the barge. Double quick," Popov said and fell ominously silent.

"What?" Vitya said.

"And you, Coalminer, you wait," he said grittily. "Till she's on the barge. Safe – understand? You don't start to winch till she's back."

"Of course not," Vitya shrugged.

"Don't shrug your shoulders at me," Popov growled. "If that cable snaps, you could kill her. Easy. And if you did, Coalminer, you'd have the Hangman to answer to. Understand?"

"I know what happens when a cable snaps. Don't worry," Vitya reassured him.

"You know why I'm here?" Popov growled on. "Because of her. That Sonya asked me: 'You want to do it Hangman?' I said: 'Spitfire be there?' She said yes, so I came."

"I understand," Vitya said.

"You better."

Vitya nodded. "As soon as I see Evgenya on the barge, I winch in. The window bars spring, Anna climbs out of the window, down the other rope and onto the barge."

"Good," said Popov. "Then there's this skiff." He took a scrap of wood and placed it behind the barge. "We all get in and row away. What could be simpler?"

"Can either of you row?" Evgenya asked.

"Nothing to it," Popov grunted, "but there *is* one other thing."

"Yes," Vitya agreed. "When you said 'We all row away', I thought of it. How many of us will there be?"

"Exactly," said the Hangman. "Must be dozens in there."

"That's good," Evgenya said. "If a lot get away, it's less obvious we're after Anna."

"Too many for our little boat," the Hangman replied. "We'll all finish up in the river."

"Then we have to be quick," Vitya agreed.

"Another idea," the Hangman suggested. "At the end of the catwalk, there's some new railings. Thin stuff. If we roped them to the barge and then set the barge adrift, they'd pull out. Probably. So everyone could get away easy. Spitfire?"

"I could do that," Evgenya agreed. "If the rope was ready. With a shackle on the end."

"Who is this Anna that you want her so bad?" Popov asked.

"You know her," Evgenya said. "She was there the night we did Reinstein. She was the one who broke his jaw."

"Her," Popov grunted in approval. "A real lady. Not like you, Spitfire. Knows how to keep her knees together, I'll be bound." For a moment the three of them sat in silence, listening to the sounds of the empty iron hull shrinking in the afternoon cold.

As night fell, lamps started to burn here and there among the jetties and warehouses, but the riverside was largely deserted. In the last daylight they explored the boat together, examining the winches, the mooring ropes and the big capstan. In the chain locker they found good rope and heavy shackles to spring the window bars – everything was ready with nothing to buy at the last minute.

Vitya went back to the fo'c'sle – he was hungry, he said,

and there were leftovers from lunch, unless the rats had eaten them already. Left alone, Evgenya and Popov fell silent – the link to their life in Kiev was broken.

"Come on," Popov said at last and led her back to the capstan. She followed without question.

"Take off your pea-coat," Popov told her.

"I shall freeze," she said, removing it. The air struck cold, cold enough for snow.

"Shirt sleeves are too long," he told her. "Thought they might be." He took one of the shirt-cuffs in his scarred, broken fingers and ripped it back to the elbow. Then he tore the bottom of the sleeve away altogether. "Get in the way of your hands," he said, starting on the other sleeve, "and tuck your trousers in your boots if you're going to climb those window-irons."

Evgenya did as he told her.

"Take your cap off."

She took it off. Her black hair was short now, not even shoulder length.

"You're keeping it short? Not still fighting are you?" Popov asked.

"Rakhel did it for me."

"Stay still." On one finger he collected black grease from the big gear-wheel of the capstan and drew stripes across her face. Then he smeared the grease more evenly into her skin. "You'll be a target up there if they start shooting. Anything white they aim for. Give me the backs of your hands."

She held up her hands for him, palm down, and he smeared them with grease.

"Thank you," she said. "Can I put my cap back on?"

"Course," he agreed. "So what happens to you next? After this?"

"I don't know. Sonya hasn't told me."

"Come and work with me again, if you like…"

"You? And Yakub?" she asked, pushing her hair under her cap until none of it showed.

"Yakub? Only if you wanted to. Anyway that was your idea. With those harridans."

"You agreed."

Popov nodded. "So how about it? You could ask Sonya anyway."

"Mischa," she said, "I don't think she'd agree. She wants me here."

"You don't want to come, you mean," Popov grunted. Then: "So he's your lover-boy, is he?"

"Who? Vitya?"

"Who else?"

"What gives you that idea?"

"Way he looks at you. Like a hungry dog. Same way I look at you probably."

"No, he doesn't," she retorted with a nervous laugh. Rakhel had said the same thing in the tavern.

With harsh fingers Popov unbuttoned her shirt, exposing her breast.

She didn't stop him. This was how she'd been in Kiev. Letting him have his way with her – whatever he wanted. It would be the last time. She steeled herself against the icy cold. That was what he'd taught her – resistance.

He took black grease again on his finger and wrote on her white skin P P V leaving her breasts to fill in the O's.

She spelled out letters, saying nothing.

He stroked her breast with the back of his knuckles.

"No," she said, pulling her shirt together.

"What do you mean, no?"

"You're breaking your own rules. You always said: 'Save it for afterwards'."

She began to button her shirt. Kiev again? It wasn't what she wanted.

"You've changed," Popov said, with a hint of resignation.

"Maybe," she agreed.

He sniffed. "Smells like snow," he said. "Too early though."

As if to contradict him, a few white flakes of snow drifted

down, grey against the distant lights. Evgenya put on her coat, and they went back to the fo'c'sle. The attack was planned for 2.30. It was a long wait, and they had nothing to do but prepare the ropes.

## II

Evgenya went to the cabin door every half hour or so to report on the snow. At first it didn't settle, but around midnight it began to build up. They decided to go in early.

A dirty light filtered from the warehouse windows, enough to work by – but also enough to be seen by if they were careless. The first task was to swing the skiff out on its davits and lower it into the river. Vitya had greased the blocks – nothing squealed. As the skiff settled in the water, the current tugged at it, banging it against the iron side of the barge. They unfurled a ladder of rope and slats. The lowest slat easily reached the skiff – the escape route was open.

Popov crept to the stern. His walk was furtive and silent, and his rubber-soled boots made no sound on the iron deck. Hidden by the bulwark, he waited until the sentry was at the far end of the catwalk and then unhitched the mooring rope. It was slack and dropped with a hiss into the river.

Vitya waited with Evgenya by the capstan. They heard Popov's rope hit the water and saw the sentry turn, now at the far end of the catwalk, trudging back toward the barge, his position marked by his lantern. Although the building protected the man from the wind, he'd pulled his cap down over his eyes and turned up the collar of his greatcoat for warmth. With his monotonous, weary tramp, he neared the barge, some thirty yards from where they were crouching. They heard his muttered curse as he turned like a patient farm-animal, changed his old-fashioned smoothbore wearily from shoulder to shoulder, and set off back down the catwalk.

Vitya had worked with capstans in a mine he'd visited one summer – he understood the pawls and the big ratchet wheel, and he'd explained them to Evgenya. They watched the sentry's lantern move away. Vitya took the crowbar from its rack. The capstan, when it unwound, would be noisy. He let the sentry take a few more paces, then wrenched up the pawl with the crowbar. With a jolt and a growl of worn bearings, the capstan began to unwind. Close-to, the noise was enough to wake half of Moscow, but the sentry kept up his slow, even shuffle, still moving away from them.

The barge was drifting downstream, nudging its way along the wharf. Somewhere ahead of them, the Hangman was waiting to jump onto the catwalk.

"Can you see him?" Vitya asked. "Are we opposite the catwalk yet?"

"Yes," she said urgently "we're opposite but I can't see Mischa." In a few seconds she'd be on the catwalk herself – her body was tense and ready.

Vitya jammed the pawl closed. It caught the slow-turning capstan with a jerk that echoed like a hammer blow through the empty barge.

No sign of the Hangman. Where was he? Then they saw the lantern on the catwalk jerk violently. The Hangman was there, one dreadful hand at the sentry's throat, the other working a knife somewhere below his heart. In shadow play, Evgenya saw the sentry collapse against the flimsy wooden railing and fall at the Hangman's feet. The Hangman braced himself against the wall. With one foot he pushed the body off the catwalk and into the river. He kicked the lantern after it.

Again Vitya released the capstan. "Go," he said urgently. The barge picked up speed, drifting under the windows of the warehouse a few feet below the catwalk.

Evgenya knew exactly where her ropes lay. Popov had given her a belt with two rings. She snapped the shackles to the rings – she'd never make the climb unless both hands were free. She waited breathless. She heard the capstan *clack* to a stop again.

Seconds later she was on the catwalk, clinging to the first barred window. She counted again – fourth across – and started to climb.

"Alright?" Popov's voice was just below her. "Rope not too heavy?"

"Not so far," she said, already near the second grid.

Popov disappeared. They'd put together three extra ropes. Popov would tie two of them to window bars on the first floor and the third to the railing laced with American barbed wire that protected the warehouse upstream. When the barge was set adrift, it should drag the window bars and the railing with it.

The ropes were heavier than she'd thought. Dangerous seconds lay between releasing the shackle from her belt and clamping it to the bars – if she dropped the rope, she'd have to go down again and find it in the dark. She paused, gathering her strength. Don't hurry, Popov had said – slow but sure.

A sudden sound distracted her. Anna's voice at the broken window pane. "Who is it?"

"Me. Evgenya." She heard her own voice shrill and excited. "The bars are coming out. There's a rope for you to climb down. Just wait."

Evgenya's hands were powerful and quick from years of piano playing and months of exercise. The shackle was clamped in seconds. She was climbing again, making for the third level. It was easier now with only one rope at her waist. The second shackle snapped shut. She shinned a few feet down the rope. "Anna!" she shouted through the broken pane.

"Yes?"

"The glass comes out with the bars. If it doesn't, smash it." She dropped nimbly, hand over hand to the catwalk.

Popov was waiting for her. "Perfect," he said. "No shooting yet. Get back to the barge. Now. I'll check the skiff."

"Why not stay here? Help Anna?"

*185*

"No. When that iron pulls out, it's like a bomb going off."

Vitya had moved. He was crouched now beside a heavy winch. The window-rope was already tight on the roller. Evgenya clambered over the bulwark and landed beside him. The instant he saw her, Vitya swung the crank-handle with one hand, taking up the slack. The rope tautened.

"Where's the Hangman?" he asked.

"Back on board I think," Evgenya replied. "Getting the skiff ready."

Vitya put both hands to the crank now and began to turn. The winch hardened. The rope stretched. The ratchet clacked into position notch by notch. Then the winch seized. It was rigid. Immovable. Vitya strained at the crank, fighting to turn it further. The barge seemed to keel upward, lifting out of the water.

"Help me," he gasped.

Evgenya put her hands next to his, struggling to move the ancient handle. The ratchet clacked again. And again.

"The whole thing'll give," Vitya warned her, "any second now. When it does dive behind the bulwark," Vitya said. "It's a killer."

A sharp flurry of wind caught the barge, rocking it in the water. As the barge eased, the iron grille came away with the smack of a giant cross-bow. Evgenya felt Vitya grab her and force her down against the iron bulwark as the grille smashed into the winch with the force of a cannonball.

The appalling noise of the flying iron was pierced by a ghoulish sound that started as a scream but broke off suddenly with the finality of death. As the scream exhausted itself, the warehouse erupted into a bedlam of shrieks and shouts. Glass and fragments of window frame smashed and clattered onto the catwalk.

Evgenya leaped to her feet. High above her a black-clad figure was climbing out of the unbarred window, grabbing at the rope that trailed across it. A woman, but surely not Anna. She watched as the figure struggled free of the window, gripping the rope with both hands. She saw the woman's feet grapple wildly for the rope without finding it. Hand over hand the woman lowered herself. Evgenya sprang onto the catwalk. She grabbed the loose end of the rope, steadying it. "Hurry," she screamed. For a second the woman dangled motionless. Then, with a shriek, she let herself down, the rope playing through her hands. Evgenya grabbed her as she landed on the catwalk.

It was Anna.

She pulled Anna off the catwalk and onto the barge. She heard a shout and a gunshot from the roof. Anna stood, trembling, unable to move. Evgenya tugged her by the arm and ran with her to the ladder where the skiff was tied up. No sign of Popov. "Go down," she shouted. Anna struggled onto the ladder, groaning aloud at every movement, pathetic, agonised. She let herself fall the last few steps into the skiff. Evgenya scurried down the ladder after her. She heard running footsteps. Vitya. He'd released the capstan for the last time – the barge would drift free. His voice, urgent: "Anna with you?"

"Yes!"

He was down the ladder in a second. "Where's the Hangman?" he demanded.

"No sign," Evgenya said.

"What's happened to Anna?" Anna was lying huddled on the bottom boards, writhing in silent agony.

Together the barge and the skiff yawed into the stream, slow at first but ever faster. Then, with a wrench and a scream of tortured metal, the iron fence on the jetty was ripped from its footing. Seconds later window grilles tore free, one after the other. The flying metal smacked into the barge above them, mangling, destroying, ripping into the bulwarks and the wheelhouse. In the confusion of screams and gunshots from the shore, Vitya untied the painter and let the skiff drift away from the barge.

"What about Mischa?" Evgenya cried.

"He's dead. That was the scream. I'm sure." As Vitya said the words, Evgenya knew they were true. Mischa was nothing now but a streak of human pulp in the chaos behind them. She shuddered.

The skiff, picked up by the current, drifted away on the black surface of the river. Wet snow fell, a grey, lifeless curtain between them and the warehouses, slowly obliterating the city. Sounds faded. Distantly Evgenya heard a long volley of gunfire and then no more.

Anna began to moan again, still curled as she'd fallen in the bottom of the skiff. Vitya pulled off his pea-coat and gave it to Evgenya. "Keep her warm," he said. "I'll row."

He found the thole pins, banged them in with the heel of his hand and then slipped the oars between them, ready to row. "We'll make Danilov if we're quick," he said. "The Monastery."

Evgenya laid Vitya's coat over Anna's shoulders. She took off her own coat and wrapped it round Anna's legs. "What's the matter?" she asked. "Where have you hurt yourself?" Anna made no reply beyond a gasping little moan that hinted some devastating pain.

"Say something," Evgenya begged, shaking Anna's shoulder through the thick coat.

"My hands. My hands," Anna moaned. It was the rope. She'd lost control. The rope had cut her into her palms agonisingly deep.

There was nothing they could do. In the freezing darkness Evgenya could scarcely see where the boat ended and the river began – how could she look at Anna's hands?

"We've missed Danilov," Vitya grunted, heaving at the oars. "I don't know what comes after. Just marshes I think."

The skiff and the oars were heavy. Clumsily Vitya urged the boat toward the dark bank. The snow stopped. Distantly on the far bank they glimpsed lights. Then blackness. There was nothing to guide them in.

"Keep a look out," Vitya whispered. They heard the hiss of wind through dead reeds and the rustle of dry bulrushes. With a scrape, the skiff went aground. The riverbank was shallow and sandy. Vitya took one of the oars to the stern. The bow lifted. With the oar, he levered the skiff hard onto the shore.

"Don't get your feet wet," he said, "or Anna's. You'll get frostbite."

Evgenya tried to rouse Anna but the injured woman could only moan in reply, close to her last strength. Vitya carried her off the boat. Evgenya brought the pea-coats and the bundle Anna had been carrying, the bundle that had cost her her grip on the rope. It was a shawl, one of those they'd bought at the station. The wind that had brought the snow was freshening and the sky was clearing. Already there was enough light to tell the white of the snow-sprinkled shore from the black of the river.

The skiff behind them rolled on a slow wave and an oar settled against the bottom boards. Pushing fiercely with his foot against the bow, Vitya heaved the skiff out again onto the river. It drifted away and disappeared into the night.

They stood in the darkness, safe from pursuit for a few hours, but lost and with Anna injured, badly it seemed. They listened into the darkness for a dog barking or a cow in a barn. Nothing. Then a rhythmic thudding, starting suddenly, cutting off again, and the nicker of a horse that smells humans.

"If there's a horse, there's shelter," Vitya said. "Straw too. We can start a fire."

They stumbled up the low bank, dragging Anna with them. The wind was tearing ragged holes in the clouds, letting the starlight shadow their way. The ground was soft under their feet, patchy with wet snow and hard-grazed grass. They heard the thudding of feet again and turned to face the sound. For a second Evgenya glimpsed the outline of skimpy trees and a low byre against the sky.

"There's a hut over there," she said.

By the light of a straw fire, Evgenya unfolded Anna's fingers and looked at her hands. One palm was slashed to the bone, a deep, mutilating burn. Blood began to spurt as the wound unclenched. Evgenya closed the useless fingers. Anna's left hand was burnt too, but not so deep – her fingers opened and clawed together again as Evgenya touched them.

"Oh God," Anna groaned. "It's finished."

The straw fire was almost out. Vitya sprinkled more of the filthy litter over the flames. He had a flat flask of brandy in his shirt pocket. He uncorked it and pressed it to Anna's lips. She sipped the brandy and groaned again.

"Tell me what to do," Evgenya said as calmly as she could.

Anna told her in a dead, grieving voice: clean round the wounds with brandy and bandage her crippled hands so the wounds wouldn't open. And get Vera. Vera knew about injuries. Vera would help.

When the wounds were clean and bandaged with strips of shirt-cloth, Evgenya buttoned her own jacket round Anna and then secured her hands across her breast with the shawl.

A track led away from the byre. They followed it. A low moon dodging among the clouds lit their way. They found a cart-track, then the straggling houses of a settlement. There were no lamps anywhere – just the shape of each isolated *isba* and the leafless fruit trees round it.

Then distant music – a clarinet and an accordion. As they got nearer, the buildings rose higher and drew closer together. They heard the stamp of feet and noisy dancing. A brothel. The house was shuttered, but outside the lights of closed coaches burnt dimly. There was a *droshky*, but only one, the driver and the horse fast asleep. Vitya bargained quickly – the driver was waiting for another fare, he said.

"Take us and come back," Vitya argued. "Five roubles."

"Ten. And what's wrong with the girl?"

Vitya pointed to the shuttered house and shrugged. The driver shrugged in reply and set off for the Pokrovka.

## III

Evgenya had taken money to the Figners twice. The family

house was twenty minutes away through the empty streets. Vera Figner had studied medicine in Zürich but she was not a doctor; her passport, like Anna's and like Alexandra's, had been cancelled two months before her final examination. What interested Vera now were industrial injuries. She ran a project for women who'd lost fingers or even hands working in Guchkov's mills. That was the money Evgenya had delivered – for 'Vera's women'.

In Anna's ornate, tasteless bedroom, Vera took charge. She gave Anna morphine and started to work on her hands. She'd seen enough injuries at the mill to know that Anna's right hand was permanently crippled – the immediate problem, though, was to save both hands from gangrene. She took an enamel basin from her medical bag, poured in a good measure of carbolic acid and topped up the basin with water. She let her instruments sterilise in the basin while she scrubbed her hands and dosed Anna's hands with carbolic. Then with a magnifying glass and tweezers she removed hundreds of splinters of hemp embedded in Anna's torn palms. With a scalpel and scissors she trimmed back flaps of ripped skin that were certain to die anyway. While she worked, she told Anna her conclusions in plain language and without much sympathy. Evgenya was shocked, but Anna was not – she'd seen the severed tendons and scorched bones for herself, and she nodded pathetically as Vera worked on. Her drugged brain grasped the message – her left hand might recover, but her right was finished.

Vera dressed the wounds, explaining each step to Evgenya. First a layer of silk soaked in oil of eucalyptus. Then thick gauze soaked in carbolic and squeezed nearly dry. On top of that, layer after layer of clean, white gauze. Finally she wrapped each hand in a thin film of caoutchouc, impermeable to dirt or water.

Vera took the revolutionary view of injuries: dirt caused putrefaction and only clean wounds healed properly. She told Evgenya to change the dressings in three days' time and left her everything she needed. In a week, Evgenya would have to debride the wounds again – cut away the dead flesh. Anna knew how to do that and by then she'd be strong enough to explain it herself. Vera explained what food to cook and offered to find a nurse – Anna would need tending. Vitya protested immediately – they'd look after Anna themselves. When they asked Anna what she thought, she simply fell back on her pillow in tears of hopelessness.

"I'm sure the Coalminer is needed elsewhere," Vera said stiffly. "You'd better talk to Sonya. This is a safe-house, not a sanatorium." She looked down again at Anna. "Discipline, Anna Petrovna," she said. "That's what we worked for, wasn't it? Self-control when things got tough. Well, they're tough now. And they'll get worse. The police will be here soon. Decide now what you're going to tell them." Vera's voice was merciless. "And not too much morphine. Remember in Switzerland – you couldn't get off it." She turned to Evgenya: "Twenty milligrams every four hours. Five drops from this dropper. Not a milligram more."

"I remember," Anna replied weakly. She closed her eyes and let the morphine take over. They watched her exhausted body collapse into sleep.

"You think the police will be here?" Evgenya asked. "When?"

"Soon," Vera replied. "Tomorrow maybe. They know Viktorya escaped from jail. They know she lived here. They'll want to see her things. Where's the Jew?"

"Rakhel? She's out getting newspapers, seeing what she can find out," Vitya replied.

"You trust her?"

"With my life," Vitya said. He told Vera how Rakhel had got herself arrested, and how she'd saved 10,000 roubles from the robbery in Kherson.

"Oh her…" Vera almost smiled. "The famous 10,000."

"And Anna?" Vitya queried. "Should she be here when the police come?"

"Who rents the place officially?"

"Anna rents it," Evgenya told her. "She didn't have her papers as Viktorya when we first arrived."

"Then she can be here as Anna – Anna, Countess Shestakova: drunk and deviant. Laid up by an overdose. What else do you expect of the idle rich?" Vera paused. "And another thing. The yardkeeper? Where's he tonight?"

"In a coma," Vitya said. "I gave him fifty roubles."

"A hundred bottles," Vera added. "You've probably killed him."

"Vera," Vitya hazarded, unsure of his ground. "What did you mean, calling Anna an addict? I thought that was years ago. In Switzerland."

"Switzerland then. Russia now," Vera shrugged.

"She's not addicted now," Evgenya said. "Not to anything."

"You live with her. You should know."

"Would it help if we know what happened?" Evgenya asked, intimidated. "In Switzerland."

"It might," Vera replied. "How much do you know about her?"

"Not much," Evgenya replied.

"You know about her father?"

"The Count. I know he was rich."

"He brought her up. She had no brothers or sisters and her mother died when she was born. The old man let her run the household when she was far too young. It amused him, Anna at fifteen ordering the servants around, playing hostess to princes."

"I thought she had schemes – schools, things like that," Evgenya argued.

"Yes," Vera sighed. "Schools. A pump instead of a pond. A midwife instead of a wise woman. That's how she still is. Look at my poor women, how she helps them. Anna's a good woman. When I look at her hands, I just want to weep."

Anna stirred – a plaintive cry that sounded like 'Gypsy'.

"So what else do you want to know?" Vera pulled herself

together. *Self-control when things get tough.*

"Zürich? Getting addicted?"Vitya reminded her.

"Yes that.Well, she had a fearful row with her father. I think he'd found a husband for her – something of the sort. Her idea was to go to Zürich and study medicine. So she stormed out of the house and went to Switzerland. That's where I met her."

"And her father?"

"He died a year later. Left her everything. Absolutely everything."

"But she stayed on in Zürich?"

"Yes. She'd got in with a professor. She wasn't exactly his guinea pig, but they both had an experimental side to their nature – let's put it that way. She acquired… appetites."

"Addictions?" Evgenya asked.

"Yes. Morphine. Other, more physical, things.You can get addicted to that too – if you're the type." She glanced a question at Evgenya.

Evgenya shook her head. "Not with me," she said. "Nothing like that."

Vera nodded. "Discipline," she said. "The morphine will weaken her. If you love her, don't get too close to her."

"No, of course not."

"Please,"Vera said. "Please. It's important."

"You're talking about me as though I'm not here," Anna muttered, rousing for a second. "It makes me feel dead already."

"Well you will be," Vera replied, "if those hands go to gangrene. A crippled Anna for a healthy Popov. What a lousy bargain."

Evgenya flinched at the rough words. Anna, though, seemed to draw comfort from them, as perhaps Vera had foreseen – they were old friends.

"So Vera, will any of us come out of this half-way intact, or is it completely hopeless?"Vitya asked her.

"'The revolution eats its children,' Viktor Pavlovich – that's what Lamartine said. Saturn devouring his offspring, the sun swallowing the stars, time swallowing the hours – in any case, the right of the great to devour the small. Does mythology interest you?"

"No," Vitya said. "Not in the least."

"Your bedside manner is shit," Anna moaned. "All of you. Now let me sleep."

# IV

Evgenya sat in a comfortable wing chair beside Anna's bed waiting for Rakhel to return with the afternoon papers. Vera was gone, Anna was asleep, and the house was quiet except for the sounds of Vitya cooking *solyanka* in the kitchen. Silence, warmth, exhaustion. Evgenya awoke only when Rakhel threw a heap of newspapers onto her lap with the first accounts of the breakout. The stories varied. One paper said twenty, another said 2000 prisoners were on the run. The details were sketchy and exaggerated. Rather than two men and a girl, the Minister of the Interior was hinting that a fleet of insurgent ships had magically appeared on the Moskva River leaving the loyal garrison outnumbered and outgunned. Stampede the public into panic and then take reprisals – that was the tactic they always used.

Rakhel had been to the warehouse. Sightseers had gathered on the wharf, kept at a distance by a cordon of soldiers. Even from the wharf the damage was clear – much of the catwalk torn away; three windows ripped out; the railings and part of the wall smashed. Rakhel gave them her news at the kitchen table, weary after her tramp round town. Vitya's thick soup bubbled on the gas stove. It would be ready in half an hour.

"Rakhel," Vitya explained, "we have to plan for tomorrow. It's Saturday, but the police will be here, checking on Viktorya. Probably."

"Yes," Rakhel agreed.

"So it's better if you're not here. Evgenya can say you've run away."

"Why?"

"It seems odd, you and Anna setting up house together."

"You mean my yellow papers?"

"Exactly."

Rakhel nodded agreement. "When did I run?" she asked.

"Last Sunday, and on Monday they picked you up, soliciting."

"But the next day I came back here. With you. The yardkeeper must have seen me."

"He hasn't seen anyone. He's been blind drunk for days."

"And Evgenya?"

"Evgenya's leaving in a day or two. With Anna."

"Where will she go?"

"She'll hide Anna for a while."

"Where?"

"You needn't know. It's not important."

There was a long silence. Finally Rakhel said: "And where do I go? Or isn't that important either?"

"You're coming with me," Vitya told her. "To Sonya."

"So you won't be here tomorrow either?"

"Exactly," Vitya said. "Just Evgenya and Anna."

The police made their first visit the next morning as Evgenya was clearing the breakfast table. Two men, both in uniform, one near retirement and the other early thirties with a pale face and narrow shoulders. A routine inquiry, they told her politely. A woman, Viktorya Nikolayevna Rakovskaya, had given this apartment as her address in Moscow. Was that possible?

Evgenya saw how little they were telling her. She'd have to be equally cagey. "Yes," she agreed. "She was staying here, Viktorya."

"When did you last see her?"

"On Sunday."

"That was the day before the dynamite was found in the Pokrovka."

"Yes," Evgenya agreed.

"She didn't come home?"

"No. She went out about twelve and didn't come home."

"Did you try find out what happened to her?"

"Yes. I telegraphed her family," Evgenya replied.

"When would that be?"

"On Tuesday I think."

"Any answer?"

"No, the form came back in the mail – yesterday – marked 'undeliverable'. The address was wrong. Do you want to see the telegram?"

"Yes, ma'am," said the older man. "Please."

Evgenya found the returned form in the big desk. It had been Vitya's idea. He'd sent it to an imaginary address in Novgorod four days before.

"And that's all you can tell us?"

"I hardly know the woman at all. She's a friend of Anna Petrovna."

"A friend?"

"Not really a friend. Someone she knows."

"And this is the Anna Petrovna who rented this apartment." He checked the name elaborately in his notebook. "Anna Petrovna Shestakova?"

"Yes," Evgenya said.

The younger man was studying the room negligently, saying nothing and taking no notes – even so, he was the senior, Evgenya saw.

"Member of the nobility," the older man said. "Estates in Rostov and elsewhere."

"Yes," Evgenya said, catching the point. The widow's apartment was hardly shabby, but it wasn't up to Shestakov standards.

"Can we speak to her?" the older man pursued.

"You can try," Evgenya said. "She's in her room."

"Would you ask her to come in here?"

"I can ask." Evgenya left the room. She tapped on the door of the big bedroom. "Anna Petrovna," she called. "Can you come? The police. They want to talk about Viktorya." She waited and banged again, louder. "Anna," she shouted. She returned to the two men. "She's asleep. She's hard to wake sometimes – you know what I mean."

"Drink? Morphine?"

"Unfortunately," Evgenya said. "Sometimes both." Anna's character would have to suffer – that was the hint Vera had given her. Something had to explain her renting a tasteless apartment in a middle-class backstreet.

"Maybe I should try," the older officer said. "A strange voice might have more effect." The two officers looked at each other with professional disbelief.

"Of course," Evgenya said. She showed the older man the bedroom door.

The officer raised a gloved fist and tapped on the centre panel. "Excuse me, ma'am. Could I have a word with you? I'm a police officer." He listened at the panel.

"You're sure she's in there?" he asked dubiously.

"Try the door," Evgenya suggested. "She sometimes locks it, but…"

The officer turned the china doorknob and the door cracked open. The officer looked at Evgenya questioningly. She shrugged. The officer pushed the door half open and peered into the room. He pulled back his head quickly. "She's there," he said.

"She often sleeps till midday," Evgenya told him.

"Just confirm it's her, will you ma'am?"

Evgenya put her own head round the door. Anna was deep asleep – or so it seemed. She was naked to the waist, her hands hidden below the sheet. A bottle of Madeira they'd spilled onto the carpet filled the room with its warm aroma.

"That's her," Evgenya said. "Why don't you come back this afternoon? You can talk to her then." She went back to the drawing room with the officer and they both sat down.

"We talked to the yardkeeper," the older man said.

"Yes."

"Is he always so drunk?"

"Yes."

"He gave us the impression a woman was living here with yellow papers. Would that be you, ma'am?"

"Certainly not!" Evgenya exclaimed. "I am Evgenya Antonovna Grishina."

"Exactly, ma'am. I was certain it wouldn't be you. If we might just see your papers."

Evgenya, as planned, had left her papers in a drawer of the *secrétaire* and was several minutes finding them. She passed them to the younger man, who studied them carefully and returned them to her without taking notes.

"You live here?"

"I'm staying here."

"And the prostitute?"

Evgenya looked embarrassed. "Rakhel?" Evgenya said. Then after a long silence she added: "She was recommended to Anna Petrovna as a housekeeper."

"Housekeeper? Where is she now?"

"Her mother's dying. She asked if she could go and spend some time with her. Anna Petrovna said yes."

They didn't believe her. The older man sat forward on his seat, suddenly alert. "When did she leave?"

Evgenya felt the game slipping away from her. What did they know about Rakhel? All she could do was disown her. "Last week. Saturday or Sunday. I'm not exactly sure."

The two officers exchanged a knowing look.

"Can I be frank with you?" Evgenya asked with deepening embarrassment.

"Please," said the older man. "It makes things so much easier."

"She wasn't a housekeeper. She did simple things – went shopping, things like that. Anna Petrovna doesn't have proper servants – not here. Elsewhere, but not here. Anna Petrovna was trying to help the girl – give her a new start. It was a stupid idea. She started sneaking out at night. Last Sunday she went out in the evening and never came back."

"Is Anna Petrovna in the habit of befriending prostitutes?" The old man eyed her shrewdly as though to add: *And juveniles?*

Evgenya hesitated – alcohol, morphine and a taste for girls. If that was how Anna spent her time it was no wonder she hid herself in a street off the Pokrovka. But it might be a mistake to blacken Anna's character too far. "She helps people," Evgenya said ambiguously. "All sorts of people. And she… We…"

"Do you know where she went? The prostitute?"

"No idea. It was a mistake," Evgenya said. "People like that… you can't help them. They don't understand."

"Are you missing anything? Money? Silver? Do you want to lodge a complaint?"

"I don't think so."

"And if she shows up anywhere, do you want us to tell you?"

"You should ask Anna Petrovna, not me."

The older man made a conclusive note on his pad and snapped it shut. "We did pick her up in fact, ma'am. On Monday last. Jew, wasn't she?"

"I think so," Evgenya replied. "Not a Christian anyway."

"One last thing, ma'am. This friend of Anna Petrovna's, Viktorya Rakovskaya, did she leave any luggage behind? Personal effects? Anything like that?"

"There's a suitcase," Evgenya replied. "We packed her things so she could collect them. It's a bit heavy – books and papers. Do you want to see it?"

"If you don't mind. Or perhaps we could take it with us. Take it off your hands."

"No. I don't think so," Evgenya said. "She left the things here. I think she should collect them herself. Or her family."

"If there's papers, ma'am, I think we'd better take care of them."

Evgenya conceded the point. They'd stuffed the suitcase full of old clothes and papers: feminist tracts in English and German, two of Anna's psychology textbooks, and a thumbed copy of *What is to be Done?* They'd left a strip torn from a recent flyer of the People's Will as a bookmark in Professor Stricker's *Studies in Consciousness* – it was enough to incriminate Viktorya. Evgenya showed them the suitcase standing by the coat-rack. "Do you want to see her room?" she asked. "There's nothing there – as far as I know. But you can check if you like."

"Yes, we'll do that," said the older man, standing up. "You packed the suitcase yourself, I think you said."

"Yes."

"And you didn't throw anything of hers away? Anything that might have got her into trouble?"

"If I'd found anything – I have to say in all honesty – I'd have thrown it out."

"But you didn't?"

"No."

The younger man sat hunched in his chair, listening with professional cynicism. Abruptly both men stood up. "We'll check the room," said the older man, "and be back at about five. If you can arrange for Anna Petrovna to be presentable by then?"

When the officers returned at five, Anna was taking a bath. Evgenya told them to come back at six. At six, Anna was sitting in a big armchair in her bedroom, draped in shawls. The gaslight was turned low and the fumes of English gin mingled with the rich smell of Madeira. Fighting every other smell was half a bottle of cheap perfume. Evgenya had sprinkled it onto a Tartar rug to cover the lingering traces of zinc ointment and carbolic in the air.

The officers wanted to talk to Anna in the drawing room but she refused: she'd vomit if she stood up, she said. Evgenya fetched two kitchen chairs for the men to sit on. She herself stood by the door, watching Anna struggle to perform her role.

The older man looked at Anna for a long time without saying anything. Evgenya tried to see her through his eyes. She was seriously ill, that was obvious; her skin was grey and sweaty and a nerve in her neck shuddered uncontrollably.

"Viktorya Nikolayevna Rakovskaya was a friend of yours?" the officer asked at last.

"No," Anna said weakly. "I met her in Petersburg in September – a few weeks ago."

"In what connection?"

"In a bookshop. We got talking."

"And you invited her to stay with you here?"

"No. She was coming to Moscow. I gave her this address in case she needed help."

"Help?"

"She was pregnant. She came to Moscow for an abortion."

Evgenya was shocked, as they'd planned. "You didn't tell me that!" she exclaimed. They all looked at her.

"There was no need," Anna replied. "It had nothing to do with you."

Evgenya glared at her. "We can talk about it later," she said sullenly.

The two men returned to Anna. "She could go to jail for something like that," said the older man gravely.

"I know," Anna said. "I told her not to do it."

"But you offered to help her?"

"Not with the abortion, but she might have been bleeding. She might have been dying. How much do you know about abortions, officer?"

"Not a lot," he admitted.

"Well, I worked in a hospital in Switzerland. Cleaning up the mess women get into through men." Anna's tone was sharpening – her arms were beginning to work against the carefully arranged shawls.

"I understand," the officer said, calming her. "And she came here?"

"Yes."

"Was that before or after the... operation?"

"After. She had very little money. I let her stay here."

"When exactly did she come here?"

"I don't know the date. It think it was a Friday."

"The fifth?" the officer queried, making a note.

"Yes, it was the fifth," Evgenya confirmed.

"One other question you might help us with perhaps," the older man turned to Anna again. "It turns out that Viktorya Nikolayevna and the prostitute Rakhel were in the women's cells at police headquarters at the same time on Tuesday night. That seems a strange coincidence."

"Yes," Anna agreed.

"For which you have no explanation?"

"Do I need one?"

"We thought you might be able to give us a hint. For example, perhaps you could tell us if the two women knew each other before they met here."

Anna shook her head: "Not as far as I know. Where could they have met? Though anything is possible."

"They hadn't formed any sort of liaison?"

"What do you mean?"

"Some prostitutes specialise in... sapphic relationships."

"I know nothing about that. Nothing at all."

"No, of course not, Your Honour," the older man said slyly.

After the men had gone, Evgenya helped Anna back into bed and settled her for the night. She cleaned the room, carrying away the rug still damp with perfume and leaving it on the kitchen balcony. She opened Anna's window to clear the smell. In the courtyard, the early snow lay one finger deep, still unswept.

"Evgenya!" Anna's voice behind her was stronger than she'd heard it for days.

"Anna?" she replied, turning toward her at the open window.

"You're risking a lot to help me," Anna said.

"So did the others," Evgenya replied. "Popov's dead. Somehow I still can't believe it."

"Grieve for him," Anna said. "I can't, but you can."

"I do," Evgenya said flatly. "He wanted me to work with him. I can't bear to think about... how he died. That awful cry."

"'A crippled Anna for a healthy Popov,' that's what Vera said. And she's right. I'm nothing now. Nobody at all." Anna's voice was weak again and full of pain.

"We'll get away," Evgenya told her. "Get you strong as quick as we can."

"Away? Where away?"

"Yaroslavl. It was Vitya's idea. My house is there – you know, the one that was going to be my... dowry." At the word, a sense of catastrophe overwhelmed her. She knelt beside Anna's bed, sobbing. Popov was dead. And Vitya... nothing, almost nothing that she remembered about him was touched with pleasure. Once, only once, they'd dressed up and gone out together – one Sunday afternoon to a concert. A year ago. How beautiful she'd tried to look for him that day. Her hair shining and perfect. That day no one could have called her Gypsy. And now! In her grief she half rose to her feet – she'd cut off the rest of her hair, down to the scalp. With scissors. Like a mad woman. Then she sank back to her knees. No. Anna needed her. Anna with her poor, mutilated hands. What good would she be to Anna, looking like a scarecrow? They'd go to Yaroslavl as soon as Anna could travel. And in Yaroslavl, they'd disappear. Maybe forever.

# Extract 7

The Third Section did everything it could to insinuate its agents into the People's Will. Its only success, as far as I can remember, was Nikolai Reinstein, whose execution I mentioned earlier. I also mentioned how we came to suspect and finally unmask Reinstein. As the reader may recall, it was the work of our agent in the Third Section, Nikolai Vassilyevich Kletochnikov. I would like to say a little more about him at this stage. For the convenience of my European readers who have trouble with our exotic Russian names, I will use his codename: because of his underground work, we called him the *Ferret*. The Ferret was recruited by Alexander Mikhailov, the Guardian, in the days of Death or Freedom. He was a student from Perm who was too sickly to finish his examinations. Mikhailov told him to apply for a job in the Third Section: the St Petersburg office needed a clerk and the Ferret was given the job. His handwriting was excellent and after a while he was promoted. In his new job he had access to personal files. This gave us a priceless opportunity to inspect the files the Third Section was collecting on us; the Ferret alerted us whenever the Section started a file on a 'legal'. We tried to keep fake passports ready for exactly such emergencies. He warned us of impending raids in St Petersburg. He also saw many of the documents requested by the Ministry in St Petersburg from regional headquarters. This was especially useful to us in the aftermath of the Moscow mine explosion. He even stole Third Section stamps to help the printers forge passports…

Mikhailov set up a special safe-house where he could meet the Ferret and pick up his latest discoveries. The house was run by Maria Olovennikova, and it had no other function than to accommodate these meetings. I've been told that Maria complained bitterly about the triviality of her assignment. She was wrong. Nothing was more vital to the survival of the People's Will than the safety of the Ferret. (*Memoir of the People's Will*, Chapter 9.)

# Chapter 8

## I

Sonya went every day to the food market and the *poste restante*. One rainy afternoon she returned to the tumble-down villa soaking wet despite her waterproof. She found Vitya standing at the kitchen door, looking out at the rain. He hadn't heard her come in. Sonya eyed the dejected curve of his back and his filthy, wet clothing. The work was going badly. The autumn snow had melted days before, purged away by incessant rain. The ground was saturated. Water trickled through flaws in the earth – good, firm earth for the most part but now it was waterlogged and unstable. Even with full boarding and props every two feet, the tunnel was a death trap.

"We must be nearly there, Coalminer," she said. Her small voice was hoarse – every kind of sickness plagued them in the dank, mildewed house. It was impossible to stay warm and dry. Everything was soaked after a few minutes in the tunnel. Wet clothes and boots, hanging round the stove to dry, filled the house with their foul smell.

"Look out there," he muttered, not turning round. Standing beside him, she looked at the desolate waste of mud and weeds between the house and the railway embankment. "I've absolutely no idea where the end of the tunnel might be."

"You say that every day," she reminded him. "Ten times."

"There's a faint chance," he pursued, "that we're under the railway and out the other side." He glanced round at her. She smiled – it was a poor joke, but she couldn't let him lose heart.

How often had he explained to her the problem of direction? From the cellar to the embankment he kept the tunnel horizontal within a few inches by following the level of the water that slopped between the props and planks. For direction he had the hand compass he'd used in Kherson – but something was wrong. He'd paced the distance above ground and measured it below many times – they should be under the railway embankment by now, but they weren't. There was no gravel and no foundation. The compass, he knew, was erratic underground; there was too much iron in the reddish soil. But how else could he keep direction?

"And that business I told you about. With the aquifers," he said. "The pump can't keep a head of water, and all that bailing is killing us. If we hit an aquifer out there…" Even in a well managed coal-mine, miners drowned when water broke through into a gallery; in their muddy little confine, nobody would stand a chance. She knew and shared his horror of being trapped down there, underground, drowning in the dark.

"There was a note at the *poste restante*," Sonya said, breaking his train of thought. "About the dynamite. '*The dentist will see you on Monday*'." She rested her hand on his shoulder, a quiet companion. He smiled at her wearily. In Kherson they'd learned to trust each other. Then there'd been that clumsy business with Evgenya – they'd never spoken about it but he seemed to have forgiven her. And now during the last, crushing weeks in Moscow, their trust was turning into grim reliance.

Of late an intimacy of touching and holding had grown up between them. As they talked, her hand might rest comfortably on his forearm. Sometimes he gave her a quick hug as though he were a fond brother. The others were surprised and teased Vitya about it. But nobody teased Sonya.

Over the rest of the house, Sonya exercised absolute authority. She made no demands and gave no orders – she simply left no room for disagreement. She *was* the People's Will. But she understood weakness too. Not everyone in the group was strong. Grigory Goldenberg had joined them; ten months before he'd become a hero when he'd assassinated Prince Kropotkin. Around the house, however, Goldenberg was painfully unheroic, querulous, and given to self-glorification. Sonya let him make beds and wash dishes when his asthma or a fit of lassitude made him too weak to work.

"A pity we lost so much with Shiraev," Vitya said. "Two suitcases. Thirty kilos."

"Shiraev!" she replied. "On the Committee and making a mistake like that." Sonya's voice was small and childlike. She knew that Vitya found it disconcerting. 'You talk about terror like a nine-year-old discussing her dolly's headache.' Something like that he'd said to her once.

"He cost us Anna too," Vitya added, "and Popov."

"Popov was a strange man, but…" Sonya shrugged, "… a serious loss."

"You mean Anna isn't? A serious loss?"

"Loss or not, she's gone. And taken the Gypsy with her. As if she couldn't pay a nursemaid." Sonya was testing the ice – Evgenya's name was hardly mentioned in the Hartmann House.

Vitya fell silent immediately, withdrawing into himself. Then at last he said: "Can I ask you a question?" he said. "About Evgenya?"

"More than one if you like." She leant against him now, letting him take part of her weight, unsure what might follow.

"You like her," he said.

"Yes."

"And you like me?"

"Why ask?"

"But you tried to break us up…"

"Yes," Sonya admitted. "Yes, I did."

"Why?"

"Several reasons."

"Well?"

"You were dangling after her. She was… is… extremely attractive. I wanted you to dig tunnels, not chase skirts."

209

"You lied to us. Both of us."

"Yes," Sonya admitted. "I lied to both of you." She took her hand from his shoulder, wishing she'd let sleeping dogs lie.

Vitya said nothing, gloomily watching the rain. "And the other reasons?" he asked finally.

She thought for a second — perhaps it was time for bluntness. "Innocent Evgenya is less use to the Committee than Evgenya…" She went to the rack of clothes that stood round the stove, feeling for a dry skirt.

"Corrupt?" he prompted. "Sexually corrupt?"

"That's your word, Coalminer, not mine. Unlike you, she's lost most of her bourgeois prejudice." How much did he know? What had he heard?

"So you sent her to Popov — to iron out any last hint of her upbringing?"

"She could have been very useful… in Popov's line. If you'd hung on to her, she'd be a breed-sow in Chernigov by now." She found a dry skirt and shook out the creases.

"So you depraved her in Odessa and let Popov finish her off in Kiev."

"Certainly not."

"What then?"

"No one forced her into anything. Ever." She went to him with the dry skirt over her arm. It was going to be hard, making him understand. He seemed to know the details, and he'd been letting them fester in his mind for months now.

"And then with that other girl? Darya? That was her name, wasn't it?"

"They were posing, Vitya — posing for an artist they have down there. Sometimes it got out of hand. But even if they weren't? What sort of prejudice says women can't love each other?"

"We're not talking about my prejudices," he said, "but about what you did to her."

"Somebody told you," she asked. "Who?"

"She told me herself, and I met someone who'd been down there. In Odessa. Nilo. He didn't know she was my cousin."

"Probably he didn't," she agreed.

"But you! You hate that kind of thing. You could have stopped her."

"Vitya." Her voice was choking. "I could have. Yes I could." She remembered *Winter Turns to Spring*. "And in the end I did. But really, you know, she's…"

Vitya waited, not prompting her, his breath tight in his chest.

"… different from anyone else I ever met. In a strange way, perfectly beautiful," Sonya said quietly.

"She was whoring around. What's so beautiful about that?"

Sonya shrugged.

"'For women, it's part of the revolution.' Don't say it Sonya. I've heard it all before."

"Then for once stop hearing! Listen!"

How could she explain to him? He wasn't a hopeless case. In many ways he was the pick of the crop. And if *he* couldn't understand… "When it comes to sex," she began, "men have more freedom than we do. Agreed?"

He nodded.

"So why shouldn't women have exactly the same freedom?"

"You do, Sonya. You're free. You can't deny it. But it doesn't mean you act like a whore."

"Free? Me? I say what I like, but when it comes to living… Yes, I got over my fear of nakedness – in a second I'm going to take this wet skirt off and put on a dry one. You can look at me or not as you choose. But that's as far as it goes. I'm as stuck in convention as I was when I was twelve, and suddenly your cousin smashes down every convention there's ever been. Not that she went to extremes. She wasn't showing off. She wasn't trying to prove anything. She just did whatever she liked just because she felt like it! With Darya – with anyone. To be honest, I was…"

"What?" Vitya asked hoarsely. "What were you?"

Sonya weighed her next word nervously before she could say it. "In a way I was jealous," she whispered.

"You were *jealous*?"

Sonya had made her confession, and he'd echoed it like a village yokel.

"Look at me," she demanded. "It may surprise you, but I'm not actually a virgin. A few years back I opened my legs to prove... I don't know what anymore. That I was a woman, probably. Polemical fucking. Utterly despicable. And then Evgenya – shameless and beautiful. It *is* a kind of revolution, Vitya."

"Is the Committee making it compulsory? Will she be giving lessons?"

"Don't talk rubbish. I've explained it as well as I can. Try to understand." She moved away from him, unbuckled her belt and wriggled her wet skirt to the floor.

"And Popov?" he pursued. "Are you jealous of that too?"

"I only know what she told me." She took the belt out of the wet skirt and threaded it through the loops of the crumpled skirt she was wearing.

"Which was?"

"I'll quote her exact words if you like: 'In his own way he was kind to me, but when he wanted to put me through it...'"

"What then?"

"'... he half killed me.' That's exactly what she said." She arranged her wet skirt on the rack round the stove. It began to steam.

Vitya visibly winced at her words. "Why? It makes no sense."

She went to him and stood behind him at the window, looking out at desolation. "I suppose she wanted to be obliterated. Annihilated."

"And why?" he pursued.

"Maybe it's something women have to cope with."

"Annihilation?"

"Vitya, from the moment I was born they made it clear to me – a daughter's nothing. You know how my father treated me, with my ear, and taking me to the madhouse to see the lunatics. He'd never have done that to a boy. A girl... she's a nuisance and you pay another man to take her off your hands. Maybe Evgenya followed the trail to the end. She let Popov reduce her to nothing, *nihil*. Knowing she'd have the guts to come back." She paused. "Or maybe not knowing. That would be worse."

"That's all very tidy. Is that how *she* explained it? Or you?"

"She doesn't explain. She does things. Just does them."

"So Popov finally found his victim."

"No. There you're totally wrong. Popov had no problem finding girls. He fed them and clothed them, and, till he kicked them out, they only had one master. Some girls have unspeakable lives, Vitya. Letting Popov rough you up now and again would be paradise in comparison."

"Oh God," he said. "I know, I know. But Evgenya? Why her? She is... she was..."

Sonya watched him struggle, trying to make sense of ideas that lacerated his feelings. If only more men were like him, she thought, there'd be no need for revolution. And she wouldn't be half-deaf, trapped in a stinking, mildewed wilderness plotting murder.

"Anyway," she struck out in a less threatening direction, "for the time being our favourite Countess has turned Evgenya into a nursemaid."

"That was my idea. And you approved it," Vitya muttered.

Yes, Sonya thought, she'd approved it. It seemed so long ago – Anna rescued, Popov dead. Between that life and this stretched three weeks of incessant rain, of bailing out the cellar with buckets, of sawing wood for props and planks, of ceaselessly pumping air to the end of the tunnel so the miners wouldn't suffocate, and of endless, endless quarrels. It had been the hardest time of her life.

"Yes, I approved," Sonya agreed. "I wanted Evgenya out of harm's way for a while."

"And Anna?" It wasn't a real question. His mind was elsewhere.

"I'm sorry about her hands, but I don't like her."

"Why not?"

"I have my reasons."

"They can't be very serious," Vitya objected, a little less distant, "or she wouldn't be in Yaroslavl. She'd be feeding the fish in the Neva."

Sonya ignored the distaste in Vitya's voice. "It's not what we know about Anna," she said. "It's what we don't know. There are rumours. And she disappears for weeks on end, no one knows where."

"Maybe you could ask her."

"Maybe *you* could ask her, Coalminer. She trusts you."

"No," Vitya said coming suddenly to life. "I'll build you tunnels, but I won't spy for you." Whipped by a sudden squall, the rain lashed into the landscape of puddles and garbage. The chimney sighed and breathed black smoke into the kitchen. Vitya folded his arms.

Tentatively, Sonya reached out to lay her hand on his shoulder, but he shrugged her off. How stupid she'd been, bringing up Evgenya like that – arguing, quarrelling.

"You'd better change," she said. "Stay here in the warm. I'll get your dry things."

Sonya fetched dry clothes from upstairs, while Vitya stripped off in the kitchen. When she returned, his mood had subtly changed.

"You're not planning to 'do anything' about Anna, are you?" he asked. "In Popov's line?" He wasn't looking at her, pulling on his clothes.

"I know you like her," Sonya replied indirectly. "Most men do."

"And most women," he retorted. "Vera even. And you didn't answer my question."

"We haven't had many traitors," she said, "but we know how to deal with them. And we'd deal with Anna if we had to."

"Or me?"

"Or you, Viktor Pavlovich."

Vitya finished dressing. "You know what I was thinking when you came back from the shop?" he asked. "We need two things, you and I – a miner's compass and a marine bilge pump. And both of them cost a fortune. Get them for me, or this tunnel won't be ready on time."

Before Sonya could answer, they heard a woman's footsteps running up the cellar stairs. "Coalminer, come quickly." It was Rakhel, soaked and shivering. At the end of the tunnel they'd hit something – wood it seemed. The three of them hurried down to the cellar. Vitya grabbed an already lit lantern from the rack, crawling into the black hole and the drenching mud. Sonya waited with Rakhel and the others in the cellar, listening at the mouth of the tunnel. Goldenberg worked the sobbing air pump, each *clunk* of the handle a breath or two of air for the miners. Lev Hartmann was still at the workface – Rakhel had been helping him. Far away, distorted, Sonya heard excited words, but she couldn't make them out. Then Vitya's shout, ringing toward her: "It's a telegraph pole. I know where we are."

Sonya waited as the two men splashed back to the cellar. Hartmann was first. "Coalminer's hooking up the air hose," he said. "It's come off its bracket."

"Brilliant," Vitya exclaimed, emerging from the mouth of the tunnel. "Now we can angle up. Up and dry. We'll hit the packed stuff tomorrow."

The questions began, jubilant, intoxicated with relief.

"Celebration," Sonya said. "Tidy up and get dry. No work tonight."

## II

Sonya was sitting at the kitchen table mending a torn shirt, wrangling with Lev Hartmann and the others about what the army would do when the Tsar was gone. It was late evening, 9th

November. The rain had stopped and the tunnel was finished. Already they had half the dynamite they needed and more was on the way. The kitchen was warm. Ten more days.

Sonya's idea was that the soldiers would mutiny and turn their guns on their officers. Lev disagreed: the troops would follow orders – the penalties for mutiny were savage. If the government told its soldiers to massacre civilians, they'd do it. And perhaps massacres were necessary – anger would force more workers to rise. Maybe even the peasants.

Vitya sighed. "My family owns a village," he said. "Pelinskoye. Our people might murder an overseer or burn down a barn. But revolution?" He shook his head. "You know how they think: 'If there's revolution, Your Honour, who'll get the harvest in?' And perhaps they're right. You're not country people. You don't know what it's like when a family loses its breadwinner. Young men without a family of their own – you might fire *them* up. But the rest of them live in families because that's the only way they can survive. And the elders decide what's what. I don't know in the towns, but…"

The knocker on the outside door rattled abruptly. Weak-strong-four times weak: the rhythm of *Narodnaya Volya*, the People's Will. Sonya put down her work and left the room quickly. As the woman of the house, she always answered the door. It was Rakhel, soaked with rain and soiled with mud. That afternoon she'd taken the train to Moscow to meet Nikolai Kibalchich, 'Kib' as they called him. Coming back from the station through the dark wilderness of the ponds, she'd been attacked. Her coat was gone and so were her shawl and her bag with money. Her dress was soaked, and the hem dripped red mud. Sonya brought her to the stove. Lev set a chair for her and poured her a glass of the *weinbrand* they were drinking.

"I couldn't run," Rakhel stammered, shaking with fear and cold. "Three of them followed me from the station. I wanted to run, but… I've got the stuff on me." With muddy hands she pulled up the hem of her underskirt and nervously drew something from a hidden pocket – a bottle of transparent liquid, enough to fill a small beer mug. "Take it," she said. "For God's sake." It was nitroglycerine.

"You got it!" Sonya said excited.

"Kib says if you shake it, it explodes. So what could I do? They took my coat and my shawl. I just gave them everything."

Sonya took the bottle. "Is it enough?" she asked doubtfully, standing it on the table.

"Kib says if you fire into it with a revolver, it'll bring down a cathedral," Rakhel told her. She gulped down the *weinbrand* and Lev refilled her glass.

"Perfect," said Sonya.

A train rumbled distantly toward them. In a moment it would clatter along the embankment, shaking the house. The embankment was in bad condition. The track was worn and uneven, slowing the trains to a walking pace. The bottle of nitroglycerine stood on the table, an inch or two from the edge. Lev picked it up cautiously and positioned it again in the middle of the table. Around it he arranged a circle of knives and spoons. The oily liquid in the bottle trembled and glinted as the train went by.

"Nothing else goes in the circle," Lev said.

It was Sonya who'd asked Kib for the bottle and the others had agreed. The Tsar's journey would bring him to Moscow in just over a week, and the police were stepping up patrols along the line. In the *Moskovskie Vedomosti* they'd read that the army was searching random houses along the Tsar's route. If their house was picked, Sonya would blow it up – and all of them with it. A revolver shot would be enough. Or she could smash the bottle on the stone floor.

Sonya saw the doubtful look on Vitya's face. She put her arm round his waist. "Better blown apart than in the hands of the Third Section," she said.

"We took a vote," he agreed. "That's what we all said."

"And what all of us said, some of us meant," Sonya replied. "Either way, it's better than dying of old age in your bed."

"I didn't know you'd given us the choice," Vitya said wryly.

# III

Sonya crouched in the cellar, waiting. Vitya knelt beside her. In each hand she held a wire, heavily insulated but with the last three inches stripped. When the wires touched, the revolution would begin. They waited, silent, the world shrunk to Sonya's bony hands and the gleaming inches of naked copper wire.

They heard Lev's warning shout from his lookout in the kitchen: "Train!" For a second Sonya felt her hands tremble – a weakness she corrected with a curse.

She heard Vitya counting quietly as they'd practiced with a dozen trains since the warning telegram arrived. When he reached sixty, Lev would shout again, and she'd detonate the mine. Fifty-eight, fifty-nine, sixty. But still no shout from Lev. Long, empty seconds. What was happening? Then the word: "Now!"

Sonya drove her hands together. Vitya had warned her about the back-blast down the tunnel, but its force stunned her. She felt herself lifted helpless and slammed against the wall of the cellar. The light flashed out. Bricks, planks and mud pounded against her. As the shock died away, she heard Lev shouting, "We did it! We did it!" She couldn't move – the cellar stairs had blown apart and she was caught in the rubble. She began crying out their names: "Vitya! Lev!" Her voice rose to a strangled scream. She struggled against splintered woodwork. Her arms were pinned, but her legs were free. Then she felt strong arms grab her knees, trying to pull her free.

"Lev! Bring a light!" Vitya was shouting. "She's trapped."

Sonya wriggled against the heavy planking, helping Vitya to pull her out. She felt a sharp, stabbing pain beneath her ribs – the splintered wood had pierced her. "Stop!" she screamed. A few seconds later Vitya and Lev had pulled away the rubble, and she was free. She clung to them for a moment, shaking with uncontrollable emotion. "He's dead," she kept saying. "He's dead."

"We got the train. He might be dead," Lev said soberly. "Or he might not."

"I'm going to see," Sonya exclaimed, still trembling. She put her hand to her breast. Blood was seeping through her shirt.

"From the kitchen window," Lev urged her. "No further. We get away now. That was the plan."

"I'm going to see," Sonya repeated with sudden viciousness. "Maybe he's just injured. If we get close enough, we can finish him." She began the difficult climb to the kitchen over the rubble of the stairway.

"That's not what we agreed," Lev objected.

"Go if you want," Sonya retorted. "I'll find my own way." She stopped climbing and turned to Vitya: "And you?" she asked, still angry.

"I'll come," Vitya said.

"Good."

"I'll wait for you by the crucifix," Lev said, "the one on the main road."

In the kitchen the samovar was hissing. A lamp glowed in front of a cheap, printed icon of Saint Olga, 'The Butcher of Kiev' as Sonya called her. The bottle of nitroglycerine had disappeared from the table – at the last minute Vitya had added it to the dynamite in the mine.

Sonya flung open the kitchen door and then stopped, gazing at the wreck of the train. Vitya stood beside her. The night was clear, stars shone through the faint haze. The train stood in profile against the starry sky. Two coaches – the third and the fifth – hung down the embankment. The fourth coach, where the Tsar slept, had blasted clear; a wreck, twisted and smashed in the blackness and the mud. Lanterns were everywhere – shouts and shrill orders.

Sonya put her arms round him and hugged him. "We did it," she said. "Bring the light."

Lanterns glittered across the landscape – already some of the Old Believers, awoken by the noise, were nearing the crippled train. "Slowly," Vitya said, holding her back.

"You've got a gun?" she asked.

"Yes."

"I've got my knife."

They were half way to the wreck already, but something was wrong. The fourth coach was lying on its side in the mud, but that was not where the guards were gathered – instead their lanterns glittered on the skyline in the gap where the fourth coach had been.

As they neared the wreckage, a sickly sweet smell overpowered them. Strawberries and sugar. "Vitya!" The pain in Sonya's voice made him shiver. "It's the wrong train," she said. "It's the baggage." Her breath grated in her throat. She crouched suddenly in the mud, struggling for air and beating her fists against her chest. "He's still alive." It was a wail of grief.

"Get up," Vitya said. "There are people. Control yourself." He held the lantern away from her, his shadow making a place for her to hide. She stood up, still gasping for breath. A bitter fury consumed her.

Under the cover of the crowd, they climbed the embankment. They listened painfully to the excited questions and the answers of the soldiers. Fragment by fragment they put the story together. The baggage train – too long, too slow. The Tsar? Gone ahead hours before. Embankment must've collapsed. Rain undermined it. Smell of gunpowder? Better not be. Accident – problem with the track. Thank God the Tsar was in the first train – another delay and they'd flog half the regiment. Poor bastard in C-Company got it yesterday, a hundred. Really laid 'em on. He was dead by sixty, but they gave him the last forty anyway. And he won't be the last now the baggage is late. Jam. Strawberry fucking jam.

Sonya clambered down the bank. Vitya followed with the lantern. "Come with me," she said curtly. Her voice scratched like a branch on a window. She was breathing in erratic little gasps.

"You alright?" Vitya asked.

Without answering she crashed to her knees in the mud again and beat the earth with her fists.

"Sonya," Vitya said quietly. "Stand up. Stop behaving like a half-wit."

Her body froze. She stood up without looking at him. "We failed." She spat the words out like venom. Grimly she walked back to the house. At the kitchen door she stopped, pressing her forehead against the wood.

"We should go," Vitya urged her. "Now."

"No," she insisted. "Come with me. There's something I have to do." They went into the kitchen and she closed the door behind them. The house was warm and smelled of dynamite. She extinguished the lamp on the table. "Put out your light too," she said. He turned down the wick. Only Saint Olga's icon lamp flickered wickedly in the corner. Sonya took off her shawl and dropped it to the floor.

"What are you doing?" Vitya asked. "We've got to move."

"Everyone thinks it was an accident," she said, her voice ominously level. "There's plenty of time. Wait." She crouched stiffly on the stone floor and pulled her knife from a sheath strapped to her boot. It was a sharp forester's knife with a bone handle – a present from Vera Figner. She put the knife on the table and crossed to the kitchen shelves. She took down a block of cooking salt wrapped in blue paper and put it beside the knife.

Vitya was watching her intently. "Come," she said, moving to the window. "Print it in your mind." He stood beside her, looking out. "We failed," she said. "This is terror? Three attempts Andrey wanted. Two failed completely. And ours... You, Vitya! And me. Working together, and this is all we could do! Jam! Like he said out there: *strawberry fucking jam*."

"No, it's worse," he said. "Look at the fourth coach." Slowly she saw his point: the explosion had rolled the coach clear of the track, but that was all – to kill the occupants they should have blown it to matchwood.

"Just like before," Sonya said. "When Zasulich failed with Trepov."

"Trepov? He was just a governor – this was supposed to be…"

"He wasn't just a governor," Sonya repeated sourly. "He was governor of Petersburg. Like my father." So often the three men blurred together in her mind – her father, Trepov, Alexander Romanov.

"And now?" he asked, staring into the night, his eyes reflecting the glitter of lanterns from the embankment.

"Now," she repeated in a voice so tense, he turned to look at her. "We trust each other. Don't we?"

"What do you want?" he asked.

"Vitya," she said. "Something feels wrong. In my head. There's something I have to do. If I do it on my own – I don't know how it'll end. Stay here. Be with me. Please. I feel so weak, it frightens me."

"You're the strong one," Vitya said. "You're the one who keeps us going."

"I think I'm bleeding," she said. She unbuttoned her shirt. "Wait," she said. "Please." She wriggled her shoulders free and slipped her arms out of her shirt-sleeves. She looked down at her shallow breasts, gleaming amber in the icon light. The wound under her ribs had stopped bleeding but it was painful.

"My scar," she said. "You saw it before." She touched an ugly cross, badly healed on her left breast.

"Yes," he said.

"It was a punishment. I did it myself when Zasulich failed. It was a crisis. For a lot of us. And now we've failed again. Miserable, ludicrous failure."

She took his hand. She wanted him to feel the rage of impotence and humiliation that overwhelmed her. She lifted his hand so his fingers could trace the scar on her breast, deep and roughly healed.

"You understand?" she said.

He shook his head. "Not really."

"Take the knife," she demanded.

"No," he shook his head, suddenly guessing her intention.

"Then hand it to me. Be with me that much." He looked intently at her face. She knew how ugly she must look, ugly as a succubus, her mind bent on self-mutilation. "Please, Vitya," she begged. "There must be blood. If it can't be his…"

He touched the cross on her breast again. She grasped his fingers and pressed them hard into her flesh. He went to the table. She stood with her back to the icon light and held out her hand for the knife. He picked up the knife by the blade and handed it to her, handle first. She took it. Then she took her right, unmarked breast in one hand and pressed the tip of the knife into the white skin. A bead of blood swelled in the tiny cut. "Do it for me," she said.

He shook his head. "I'll be your witness," he said quietly. "But…"

She cut quickly but not deep, three inches across her breast, and a hand's breadth below her collar-bone. Blood welled slowly in the clean white line. They both watched it, Vitya struggling to understand, Sonya with a grimace of self-contempt.

She handed him the knife. "Finish it," she said. "Cut me."

He took the knife. She saw his eye ran along the sharp edge and his grip tighten. It was an awkward knife, though it was surgically sharp.

Sonya gasped – a hungry, passionate indrawing of breath. "Do it," she whispered. "Make me strong."

He cut her, a long vertical slash ending just above her nipple. His cut was deeper than hers and the blood flowed instantly, flooding across her white skin. She watched the blood trickle from the wound and run across her stomach. "Blood," she said. Her breathing slowed, her body softened. She closed her eyes.

When she opened her eyes again, they wouldn't focus. "You think I'm insane," she said, trying to see him clearly.

"No," he replied. "We failed. Pain drives out pain."

"If I'd been on my own I'd probably have killed myself," she said quietly. "Break off some salt. It stops the bleeding."

He unfolded the block of salt from its blue waterproof wrapping. With the knife he cut a wedge from the corner of the block.

"Break it up," she whispered. He crunched the salt with the handle of the knife, gathered the crumbs together and put them in her outstretched hand. She tensed herself and pressed the salt into the fresh cuts. She waited for the pain. When it came, it calmed her. Vitya's face lost its blur. She could see again.

Vitya turned away. "Get dressed now," he said with his back to her. "We have to go."

She pulled on her shirt, not stopping to clean off the blood or the saturated, red salt. The pain was hard to endure, and she was grateful for it. She buttoned the shirt quickly, found her thick coat and her simple bag with papers and money. She pulled an old shawl round her shoulders. With Vitya she hurried out of the house and through the settlement toward the crucifix where Lev was waiting.

The three of them stood together, crushed and baffled. The pain in Sonya's breast and under her ribs sharpened – she trembled, trying to control it.

"You'll go to Petersburg?" Vitya asked.

"It's a four-hour walk into town. Then we'll get the morning train," Lev replied. "What will you do?"

"Go to Chernigov maybe."

"Your estate's there."

"Yes."

"Go to Evgenya. Go to Yaroslavl," Sonya broke in. "Stay there till…"

"Till?…"

"God knows," she replied. "Maybe we're finished. Maybe. I don't know."

"I'll walk with you. Into town."

"No," Sonya said. "You go ahead, Coalminer. We'll be slower."

"Are you sure?"

"Lev will look after me." She fell back with a groan against the crucifix, clutching the wound below her ribs. "I think a piece broke off inside me," she said. "But go. You go. Don't hang around here."

# Extract 8

The story of the Moscow mine has been told many times, but it is still rich in revolutionary lessons. In 1879 the November storms in the Black Sea were the worst for years. Alexander Romanov decided to travel overland rather than go by yacht to Odessa. Our preparations for a mine in Odessa stopped immediately. That left two mines: Alexandrovsk under Andrey Zhelyabov and Moscow under Sofya Perovskaya. She saw that the now-useless supply of dynamite in Odessa would double hers if she could only get hold of it. On 9th November she sent Grigory Goldenberg to Odessa to collect as much dynamite as he could pack into a small trunk. On 13th November on the way back to Moscow, Goldenberg changed trains in Elizavetgrad. His luggage was suspicious: far too heavy for its size. The railway police arrested Goldenberg. I think the mistake was Sonya's. When the police are alert, they are all-powerful. The revolutionary's main weapon is surprise. We should exploit weaknesses, not pit our strength against theirs. We were a handful; they were Legion. The reaction of the Third Section to Goldenberg's arrest was also predictable: they tightened security along the Tsar's whole route.

Goldenberg was tortured, but he followed Guardian's rule: hold out, if you can, until your information is useless. Goldenberg held out. It was a heroic effort.

Some days later *[17th November. Trans.]* the Tsar began his journey north. His three trains were due to pass through Alexandrovsk during the night of 18th November. North of the city, the track was mined with two giant cylinders packed with dynamite: Zhelyabov's work. When the Tsar's coach was over the mine, Andrey fired the detonator, but nothing happened; the train rattled on through the night unharmed. The cylinders were abandoned. That was Andrey's mistake. Revolutionary procedure dictates that all traces of failed activities must be obliterated. After the failure of the two southern plans, nothing was left but Moscow.

On 17th November, a telegram was delivered to the Hartmann House: *Price of flour two roubles. Our price four*, an exceedingly unlikely message, but it was delivered. It meant: second train, fourth coach. The house was cleared: three of our people stayed behind to handle the mine. On 19th November there was no traffic on the line for many hours. Then, in the late afternoon, the first of the three trains steamed through, decorated with flags and painted a brilliant red. Night fell, but even in the dark Alexander's trains were easy to identify by the extra headlight they carried. It was almost midnight when the second train approached the embankment. The fourth coach was blown off the track, but, as is well known, it contained not the Tsar but strawberry jam. At this point the Committee failed absolutely to understand what it had achieved. The fiasco of the jam was in almost all respects a brilliant success. The engineering was sophisticated and carried out under appalling conditions; an imperial train had been blown apart, and none of the conspirators brought to justice by the investigation. An immediate propaganda effort should have capitalised on this success, but we were too downcast by our sense of failure. It is a mistake for the same people to run operations and propaganda. They are completely separate activities. (*Memoir of the People's Will*, Chapter 8.)

# Chapter 9

## I

Evgenya's dowry, the Grishin estate, had stretched at one time from the Volga to the outskirts of Tunoshna, ten miles to the south. It had included three villages and a manor house in the Palladian style. The house was surrounded by what Evgenya's grandfather had planned as an English park, but the project had never been completed – the clumps of beeches and the belt of oaks had done badly and were chopped down for firewood. By 1879, all that remained of the layout was a silted-up lake crossed by a stone bridge and an immense structure designed to look like the ruins of a Roman aqueduct. On the plans, the aqueduct was labelled in English 'Grishin's Folly'. The Folly stood half a mile from the manor house. It marked the furthest extent of Evgenya's property.

Though it was neglected and shabby, Evgenya had happy memories of the place. Until the family finally ran out of money when she was fourteen, she'd spent long summers there, swimming in the lake, climbing trees and joining the rough games of the children who lived on the estate. Barked shins, splinters in her bare feet or a bloody nose from a fight – her mother had tutted and threatened but Evgenya had run with the pack. She was tough and daring. She'd enjoyed roughhousing and sometimes got into real fights, mostly with girls but sometimes with boys too. The fights had taught her the truth of an old proverb – boys fight to win, girls fight to kill. Boys had a ritual of victory and defeat: a concession, a few insults and the whole thing was forgotten. Girls gave in far later and then stayed enemies for months. On the whole, she found fist-fights with boys more to her liking. They left no scratches and bites which were hard to explain – just bruises, and she had plenty of those anyway. Despite anything her mother could say, Evgenya always played, ran or fought in a cotton smock like the other girls. Naturally her mother told her to wear 'something underneath' and Evgenya agreed – but only as far as the stable. The worst that could happen if her mother found out was a good slapping. That was simply part of being a child – but not the mockery of the other girls. Imagine if she was fighting or climbing a tree and they saw she was wearing drawers like a lady. With no governess and a mother who counted for nothing, Evgenya, for better or worse, ran wild.

When Evgenya arrived with Anna at the station in Yaroslavl, no one was there to meet them; Evgenya had decided against sending a message. In the station yard, she rented a *troika* and a driver for two days. Anna gave her money to fill the sleigh with everything they might need, and they drove out to the estate.

No one but an elderly housekeeper and her two sons lived in the sprawling house. Though the sons were only in their thirties, they were already habitual drunkards. Grudgingly the old woman admitted Evgenya into the house, lamenting that the place wasn't fit for the family, let alone guests. How could she keep it properly on the pittance Their Honours sent? Even so, bedrooms were opened up, chimneys unblocked and fires laid. That afternoon Evgenya drove round the old family villages in the *troika*, seeking out families who'd worked at the big house in her childhood, paying them three months wages in advance and stirring the place back to life. She drove into Yaroslavl, extended the hire of the *troika* for two months, and found a cook who understood plain cooking. Her most important find was in Tunoshna: Dunyasha, a calm, sweet-faced woman of fifty who had once been her mother's maid and for that reason had never married.

Dunyasha lived on a tiny pension paid erratically by Evgenya's father. Anna told the old woman that she'd taken a fall from her horse during a wolf-hunt and that her hands had been badly cut. The story was never accepted by the household. The most popular theory was that 'Her Honour's guest' had been injured running away from a cruel husband. Some said she'd murdered her husband and was on the run from the police, others that she'd broken out of jail after she'd murdered him, or her baby, or, in some versions, both. Evgenya picked up the tattle from childhood companions who came to the house partly out of curiosity and partly to see what they could steal. Dunyasha never questioned what she was told and tended Anna without fuss, calling her 'ma'am' in the modern style rather than 'Your Honour'. Anna patiently accepted her care and they quickly settled down together.

Evgenya was kept busy attending to the house and running Anna's errands. Three times a week she drove back and forth to Yaroslavl, finding books and newspapers for Anna, sending mysterious telegrams to Anna's steward in Rostov, collecting the money he wired to Yaroslavl and buying whatever Anna's fancy demanded, or, more frequently, the best substitute the little town had to offer.

On 20th November they read about Sonya's mine in the *Moskovskie Vedomosti*. As report followed report, the government's thunder was increasingly laced with frustration and impotence. Even so, it was two agonising weeks before the *Narodnaya Volya* threw off the lethargy of defeat and claimed the mine as a victory. Terror now had a name: the People's Will. The telegraph broadcast it across the Empire and round the world.

The Tsar had escaped and the revolution was delayed, but apparently none of that grieved Anna. In fact, as Evgenya saw, the postponement was somehow a source of strength to her. She certainly needed strength from somewhere – her mangled hands tortured her. On some days she fought to master the pain without morphine, but she never got through till evening.

It is not easy for a girl of eighteen to establish control of a household. Evgenya quickly saw that her estate had been stripped of anything the local traders would buy for cash – the housekeeper's sons had seen to that. Over the years they'd also drunk Evgenya's cellar dry – not a single bottle remained in the carefully labelled system of wine-racks. Anna told her to buy claret in Yaroslavl. The racks were set up by dozens, and Evgenya filled two of them with the wine she bought. On the first evening that Anna came downstairs to dinner, Evgenya went to fetch one of her bottles. Inexplicably her stock was not twenty-four but twenty-three. There were only two keys to the cellar, her own and the housekeeper's. Furious, she went straight to the coachman's room above the stables where the housekeeper's sons had been living for years. She stamped up the stairs and flung open the door. Tyomka and his brother were playing cards by the light of a candle.

"Which of you took my wine?" she demanded.

The two men looked at her in disbelief and denied everything. "What wine?" Tyomka protested. "First I heard of any wine."

The candle that lit the room was rammed into the neck of a wine-bottle – a claret bottle. Her wine.

"Stand the fuck up when you talk to me," Evgenya stormed.

Tyomka slid off the bed, eyeing her now in real astonishment.

"Your candle is in my bottle," she said viciously.

"What do I know about the bottle?" Tyomka pursued. "Lopka? You know anything about Her Honour's bottle?"

Evgenya's next move took Tyomka completely by surprise. She lunged forward onto her right foot, smashing into his face with her left fist and battering his mouth with her right as he staggered backward. His nose spurted blood. His weak, unhealthy gums split as his teeth drove inward.

"Stay out of my sight in future," she spat at him. "Both of you." She flung away, turning her back on the routed enemy, and hurried to the cellar – it was nearly time for dinner.

Anna had scarcely left her room for three weeks. She came down for dinner now, dressed in a warm wrap that Evgenya had bought for her in Yaroslavl. At least Evgenya's bout with the brothers was something fresh to talk about.

"So your lessons with the Amazons of Kiev weren't completely wasted," Anna observed.

"I did what Popov said," Evgenya replied modestly. "Surprise them when they're off balance."

"Do you still exercise? Twice a day, like you did?"

"I've set up a room just for that."

"Maybe..." Anna began. "Maybe I could come and be with you?"

"Of course you can. I didn't suggest it because..."

"... because I'm a cripple and it would hurt my feelings."

"No, not at all."

"Well, I am a cripple. Most things people do for themselves, I can't do anymore." Dunyasha was sitting next to Anna, feeding her and trying to be invisible. "And maybe I never will."

"Please come," Evgenya said simply.

"But..."

"What?"

"It might be better if..."

"If what?"

"Listen... is there anywhere in Yaroslavl they sell... outfits?"

"To wear you mean?"

"Yes. It's none of..."

"I understand," Evgenya said. "One by one, you want to cure me of all my bad habits."

"Being naked isn't a bad habit. It's healthy – helps you sweat. It's just that..."

"I understand," Evgenya repeated. But she didn't. Anna's feelings were a mystery.

The episode with Tyomka did Evgenya no harm among the servants. Next day, when her temper had cooled, she allowed Tyomka to apologise, looking with some satisfaction at his battered face. Tyomka's mother apologised too, fearing for her place. Evgenya was politic. Like a good mistress, she forgave mother and son, but like a prudent bailiff, she planned to kick them out as soon as she had the house under control.

## II

Evgenya and her guest began to lose track of time. The silent, snowy days and interminable evenings blurred in to each other, like the facades of buildings in a Petersburg fog. Two days before Christmas, however, an unexpected visitor broke the tedium – Vitya.

He told them little about where he'd been beyond the fact that he'd stayed in Moscow with Rakhel, lying up quietly in the apartment off the Pokrovka. He had no special reason for visiting them and no plans. He'd sent to Sonya for instructions, and she'd simply repeated what she'd said on the last night at the Hartmann House: '*Go to Yaroslavl'*.

"And what about Pelinskoye? Your mine?" Anna asked him, as they sat drinking tea on the first evening of his visit. "Why don't you go there in the spring?"

"I talked to the banks in Moscow," he explained, "every one of them, I think. I can't borrow the money. And do you know why? They say with all the terrorism, they're not lending so much, especially for vulnerable projects."

Anna began to laugh, her sweet, clear aristocratic laugh. Vitya laughed with her. Evgenya watched them – nothing struck her as funny, but then she'd been nervous and humourless as a cat ever since Vitya had shown up at her front door.

"But you, Anna Petrovna!" Vitya exclaimed. "You seem amazingly recovered. Drinking tea even."

"Yes," Anna replied, more soberly, "I can lift a cup with my left hand."

"We've written to a doctor in Germany," Evgenya explained, "in Wiesbaden. Tell him, Anna."

"No, you tell him. You wrote the letter."

"*Professor Arnson's Institut für Orthopädie, Heilgymnastik und Massage. Taunus Strasse, Wiesbaden.*" She screwed up her face. "Say it for me in proper German, Anna."

"Vitya doesn't care about your accent, sweetheart."

"What sort of doctor is he?" Vitya asked, avoiding Evgenya's eye as she was avoiding his.

"After the war... ten years ago?..." She looked at Anna for confirmation. Anna nodded. "... the Germans started using electricity on wounds. On patients everyone thought were maimed for ever. From the war, you know?"

Vitya nodded.

"We told him in the letter what had happened to Anna. The rope burns. Anna told me what to write. He said something might be done with her left hand."

"But at best my right hand would be a claw – a working thumb and four stiff fingers."

"I'd give you one of my own hands," Evgenya broke out. "Willingly. If only I knew how." She saw Vitya turn to her with a puzzled expression, but a deep light of approbation in his eyes.

"My darling," Anna said to her mournfully. "Nothing..." Her voice choked with tears, and she couldn't finish her sentence.

From the first hour that Vitya was in the house, Anna had watched him closely. Evgenya knew the question that preyed on Anna's mind, and in her own way, she answered it.

"Anna?" she asked as she started her morning exercises on Christmas Eve. "I'm having nightmares again. Can I sleep in your room tonight?"

"Did you ever hear of Tristan and Isolde?" Anna gave a little frown as she said the words – Evgenya never had nightmares.

"The opera?"

"There is an opera, by that awful Wagner man. But, I meant the story."

Evgenya shook her head.

"Well, Tristan has to sleep with Isolde in the forest, and to be sure that they stay chaste, he puts his sword between them."

"I don't have a sword," Evgenya said, half understanding her point, "but I can probably imagine one."

"Then you're welcome."

Early that afternoon, the mid-winter sun and the hard frost turned the park into a marvel of iridescent diamond light. Evgenya wanted to walk to the Folly and she asked Vitya to go with her.

As often happened, the Folly was covered in magnificent icicles. Evgenya broke one from the shattered architrave, as long as a rapier. She turned and pointed it at Vitya's heart. He broke off another. For a moment they fenced with the icicles, laughing, smashing them blow by blow into stumps. Their gloved hands touched and the laughter froze.

"Such a pity you're selling," Vitya said, avoiding a hundred more urgent subjects that hung in the cold air between them. "It's beautiful here."

"What will happen now?" she asked, brushing aside the insoluble problem of the estate. "Is it finished? The People's Will? The Committee? All of that."

The snow was clean and powdery. The wind had blown one side of the Folly clear. Huge blocks of red sandstone lay in artistically contrived chaos. Evgenya knew every stone from countless games of hostage and bandits; she remembered the bonds chafing her ankles when she was hostage, and the joy of storming the Folly when she was captain of hussars. The upward path climbed half a dozen icy steps cut in the rock. Evgenya stopped and Vitya offered her his hand. She pulled away, startled – what sort of hussar needed help?

"Sorry," he said, "I'm not used to girls who beat up their servants."

"I let him have it," Evgenya retorted. "So what?" Then provokingly she added: "But I suppose… living with someone as docile as Rakhel…"

"I wasn't what you'd call 'living' with her,"Vitya objected, "for one thing, she's ill, you know. Seriously."

"Anna said she's consumptive."

"Syphilis as well. The consumption got much worse working in that filthy tunnel. She's a wreck."

Evgenya smiled and held out a ladylike hand, letting him help her up the steps. She was sorry for Rakhel, but there was no hint of brotherly concern in Vitya's voice and she was pleased.

They climbed as high as the hollowed-out cornice that channelled the water. In the summer, artfully placed cracks created a waterfall. On hot summer days, children fought and splashed in the cold, exhilarating water. Now it was a wall of glittering, transparent stalactites. With her gloved fist, Evgenya smashed a row of icicles from their anchorage. They tinkled together and clattered down the rocks.

"Why did you come here?" she asked. "Tell me the truth."

"I came because I wanted to tell you…"

He had something to tell her, a conclusion he'd come to perhaps. She wanted no conclusions. She'd say nothing to help him.

"At first, when I heard about…"

She listened in obstinate silence.

"… Odessa…"They stopped clambering over the stones. He could say no more.

"You came all this way… to say that?"

"More or less," he replied.

*Odessa.* The word stood for a whole indictment. But she wouldn't defend herself. Why should she? Even so, after a brooding silence she said: "Did Sonya explain to you? About Odessa?"

"Yes," he said flatly. Was he accusing her? Perhaps not.

"She explained it to me too," Evgenya lightened her tone. "She made it sound quite heroic. And I thought I was just…" she shrugged, "finishing my education."

He smiled. "She told me she was jealous."

"Of me? Yes, she told me that too. God knows what she meant."

"Do you remember…" he began, his voice tightening.

"In Petersburg?" she offered.

"Yes. In the old apartment."

"I remember all sorts of things. But mostly…"

"Yes?" She heard a sudden anxiety in his voice.

"We could have…" She rejected all the unseemly possibilities of language. "… become lovers." Her breath froze in her body. "I certainly wanted to."

"Yes," he whispered.

"Well…" she blurted out. "It would have been a mistake." A mistake? The word was said, but her doubt remained. Vitya, love, and an inescapable marriage? Or Sonya, Popov, Anna… a life of feverish activity, painful, brutal? Her choice was long made – made in Odessa. In Kiev. And yet…

"So…" His breath released itself in a white mist of relief. "A mistake. And you don't hate me. For being such a…"

"… Limp dick?" she suggested. She saw him wince. "Sorry – an expression of Popov's." She thought it over. "But you were."

They began to clamber down the frozen avalanche of sandstone. Caves, cells, tunnels suggested themselves. One place she knew well, a tiny cave with a slit for a mouth. Half a dozen boys had taken her there. They'd imprisoned her, forcing her to take back some hasty words: '*This is my waterfall. These are my rocks. It all belongs to me.*' She'd held out for a long afternoon, refusing to go back on a single word. Then the boys outside the cave had gone frighteningly quiet. She'd called out to them, fearing their silence more than their demands. But they'd gone. The next day she'd agreed they were right – the waterfall, the Folly, the whole world for all she knew, belonged to everyone.

She stood, looking at the narrow mouth of the cave, remembering. Vitya went ahead. As she caught him up, he turned to her almost fiercely.

"What's to stop us?" he asked. "Being comrades?" He held out his hand to her again. His woollen gloves were crusty with flakes of broken ice. "Start again," he said. "Forget everything." His face was bright in the low afternoon sunshine.

"Not forget," she offered, "just think of it in a new way."

He shrugged his shoulders, laughter welling up suddenly inside him. "Call it what you like," he said. Crystals of ice flashed in his hair, then his laughter broke out suddenly, ringing uncontrollably across the icy fields.

She took his arm, exactly as she had when they'd roamed the streets of Petersburg a year before. "Let's walk round the lake," she said. "It's where I learned to swim. It isn't ours any more, but there's no fence."

The snow made walking difficult – they sank deep at every step. Evgenya hiked up her skirts to her knees. Laughing they struggled on, their hot breath steaming the air around them. Finally Vitya fell against her, unable to drag his feet any further. She let go of her skirts and held him. She felt his panting breath swell and relax against her breast. She kissed his forehead and then his lips. He was nervous, as though they'd never kissed before.

"We have to turn back," he said. "I can't go any further."

"Yes," she said, turning away and walking back ahead of him the way they'd come. Like a child, he eased his way by planting his feet in her deep footsteps. When they were back at the Folly, she took his arm. "Vitya," she said, "there are lots of guns here. Will you teach me to shoot?"

# III

Anna was presiding at the afternoon samovar. "So," she said, "You two have signed a peace treaty."

"No," Evgenya said. "We've started again." Anna saw how the warmth of the fire flushed the girl's cheeks. The lamplight made everything in the room sparkle.

"Started *what* again?" Anna asked.

"Started…" Evgenya shrugged. "You know what I mean."

Anna glanced narrowly at Vitya. "Does Vitya know what you mean? Perhaps that's more important."

"I know what *I* mean," Vitya said. "Tomorrow Evgenya starts shooting. There are guns in the gun-room, chained up, but we found the key. There's even a Mauser. I'd never seen one before. We can do some proper shooting."

"Mauser. 1871," Anna said. "Prussian army. I saw it. Amazing that Tyomka couldn't find a buyer."

"I didn't know you were interested in guns?" Vitya said.

"Oh yes," Anna replied. "I know nearly as much about guns as I know about the nervous disorders of women."

# IV

Evgenya had made sure long before Christmas that all the proper decorations would be hung up and the necessary ceremonies performed. She'd bought simple presents for the servants, even Tyomka. The ritual feast with twelve foods, one for each apostle, was prepared in traditional Volga style. Christmas Day, Dunyasha warned them, wasn't a good day to go shooting, so Evgenya's lessons had to be postponed till the day after.

Evgenya was feverishly excited by the guns, by the noise, by the pain in her shoulder and by the feeling of power it gave her to destroy something twenty yards, or fifty yards, away. There was gunfire, but there were no more kisses. She could see that Vitya was waiting for a sign from her, but she refused to give it. Vitya wanted her, he loved her. What held her back? She had no clear idea. Perhaps it was the same dark conflict that had made her say: 'It would have been a mistake.'

Vitya was a good shot and Evgenya an eager pupil. Within a few days, after the pain of countless recoils had eased, she could hit a bucket at fifty yards. Then, well away from the barn, Vitya rigged up a machine that tossed china plates high into the air.

With the barn door wide open, they knelt together all afternoon on the dry floor and annihilated crockery. She couldn't hit all the plates, but her score was 'respectable', Vitya assured her.

Respectable! She picked up the word in mockery, and for a while, everything was 'respectable'.

On the third afternoon of shooting, after she'd missed three plates in a row, Evgenya stood up quickly. "Let's go back," she said. "Anna will worry." Her voice was shaking with the excitement the guns aroused in her. "I think your machine is so clever, Vitya. But we'll have to buy more plates in Yaroslavl tomorrow, and more ammunition."

Vitya stood up too. "Evgenya," he said.

Something in his tone alerted her – he didn't want to talk about cleaning guns or picking up empty cartridges. "No," she said. "No."

"Evgenya," he repeated.

"Vitya, I know what you want to talk about."

"Then…"

"Try to understand," she reproached him. "What was important in Petersburg… it doesn't matter anymore. I wanted you then. Just you." She watched him closely, reading his reaction on his face.

"And Valentina's brothers?" he teased.

"That was nothing," she laughed, "just a way to get out of the house."

"No," he contradicted. "You played hell with Aunt Betty's nerves when you got home. You couldn't sit still for five seconds."

"Maybe," she conceded, "though you never seemed to notice… things like that."

"And now?" he pressed.

"Now? Nothing's the same anymore."

"Does that make you happy? Or sad?"

This was the argument, this was the fight that had lowered between them for days. "Why ask when you know the answer?" she said dismissively. "So tomorrow, how many plates shall we buy?"

"I don't want to talk about plates."

"You want to talk about fucking, I suppose. We're back to that."

He said nothing.

"Ask then. What do you want to know?"

"Why. I want to know why."

"Why what?" she replied harshly. "Why I went overboard in Odessa? Why I put up with Popov?"

He said nothing, but the intensity of his silence was unnerving.

"You want me to tell you? Or not?" She saw him wince. Then perhaps she should really spell it out, provoke him till he called her a whore and have done with it.

"That's not what I meant," he whispered.

"Yes it is, Vitya."

"Nilo told me. He was down there."

"Danilo? Yes, he was one of them. So what does that make me? In your opinion?" She was shouting in his face, clamouring for him to insult her.

He turned away. "It doesn't make you anything," he said mildly. "If that's what you wanted... why not? And anyway — you left Odessa a long while ago." He turned toward her, took her hand and kissed it.

"That's not what you really think," she said, disbelieving.

He dropped her hand, with a shrug. "How do you know what I think?" he said.

She shook her head in confusion. "Time to pick up the cartridges," she said. "We'd better get back."

"Yes," he said, kneeling in the dirt where they'd just practiced. "Get the box. It's by the water-butt."

She fetched the box and knelt too, picking up their spent ammunition. "You know," she began, "I hope you meant what you just said. It helps a lot. But there's something else. I've been thinking about it." She threw a handful of cartridges into the box. "When Anna talks to you, you listen even when she talks nonsense. Maybe you think you'll learn something — I don't know. But when I talk, it's just the prattling of a child. And you can't change that. I'll never be a woman for you. A schoolgirl too stupid to learn French – that's how you make me feel. You know, in Odessa…"

"I don't want to talk about that."

"No. Something else. In Odessa there was someone – a pianist. Very good. He was a writer as well. He used to ask me what I thought, and he listened when I told him."

"Where is he now?"

"I don't know."

They were on their hands and knees just a few feet apart, looking at each other like bewildered animals. Then, slowly, she reached for her gun. She raised it until the muzzle caught him under the chin and forced back his head. "Vitya," she said. "Is there any reason I shouldn't blow your head off?"

"There's one," he said calmly. "Your gun isn't loaded."

"Yes it is," she said. "That's what Popov told me. Always keep one in reserve." She stood up, took aim and fired the gun at Grishin's Folly, though it was well out of range. The rooks which had settled back into their elm tree took flight again, cawing bitterly at the new disturbance.

"Every time we get nearer," he said quietly, "we end up further apart. I don't understand why."

They picked up the guns and walked side by side across the icy meadow that had once been a lawn. Halfway to the house, Vitya stopped. "Listen Evgenya," he said. "I have to know something. Just answer yes or no."

"What?"

"Would you marry me?"

"Would I?"

"If I asked you."

"You know what Mama used to say? I ought to try harder with you. You're my only chance, now we're so poor. You or some spiteful old man."

He shook his head. "Say yes or no."

"What do you think my answer would be? Yes or no?"

"I honestly don't know," he said ruefully.

The wind was cold. As they spoke, their breath iced their scarves and the upturned lapels of their jackets. "I'm going to ask you anyway," he pressed.

She looked at him and shook her head. "Don't," she warned.

"Shall we get married?"

"No," she said. "Absolutely not. Not now. Not ever. Nothing." She pulled away from him in tears. "After all we've said… how could you?"

At dinner Evgenya took her place opposite Vitya. She was wearing a handsome silk dress she'd not worn before during his visit. It was red, almost orange. She'd had it made in Yaroslavl. It was not particularly fashionable, but it was low-cut and showed off her slight breasts. She wanted the dress to shriek at him the words she'd said on the icy lawn – I am not yours. Not now. Not ever.

She leant forward, coquetting almost with Anna. "Do you think it's too low?" she asked, running her fingers along the lace trimming. "I wish I had your figure, Anna."

Anna eyed her clinically and glanced at Vitya. "Your cousin is in need of a compliment," she said to him. "Why don't you pay her one?"

"No need to state the obvious," he replied, his voice dry with emotion. The two women looked at him with different expressions of enquiry in their eyes.

"You know why I put this dress on, Vitya?" Evgenya asked bluntly.

"I think so."

"Good." She stood up and looked at Anna. "I'm tired," she said, "I think I'll go to bed."

# V

Anna was sorry to see how little success Vitya's visit had brought him. "You've had words," she said when Evgenya was gone.

"How observant," he replied.

"Why do you think she wore the dress?"

"Because it cost an engineer's salary for six months," he said sourly.

"Vitya, you're impossible. You attach yourself to a girl who's as vulnerable as a new-born lamb, and you blame her when you drive her to despair. What did you do, for heaven's sake? Ask her to marry you?"

The question startled him. "Yes I did. How did you know?"

"That's why you came here, wasn't it? Honestly, you don't have much idea about women, do you?"

"What should I have done then? Bedded her like those animals in Odessa?"

"That's not the kind of man you are, Vitya. Don't be ridiculous."

"Ridiculous or not, it's over."

"Is that what she says?"

Vitya nodded. "It's over, Anna. Finally, terminally, irremediably over."

"I'm sorry," Anna said. There was a catch in her voice – suddenly she was crying. "For both of you."

"It was a dream from another time."

"She's an extraordinary girl. You're so alike, the two of you. So obstinate and so sensitive. I wish I knew how to make you happy."

Next morning, Vitya announced that he was leaving. If the *troika* could be harnessed to take him to Yaroslavl, he'd make his way back to Moscow and perhaps on to Chernigov. Anna told him to wait a day longer. After that she'd go with him, and so would Evgenya, at least as far as Pereslavl. She had something to show them.

Anna owned many estates, but, as the newspapers correctly reported, only one was run as a model farm – a huge tract of fertile land near Rostov where her father had once tried out the latest machines from England and America. A few of the imports worked well in Russia, but mostly they'd been too delicate or too complicated. Old Shestakov had employed a Scottish engineer and equipped a workshop to keep the machines running or to strengthen them for Russian handling. After she'd inherited the estate, Anna had kept up the experiments with machines, in the same way that she'd rebuilt the hospital and extended the school, though her heart wasn't in such things any more.

Anna explained it all to them in the *troika* they hired from the station-master at Pereslavl. She told them about a conversation one afternoon in the repairshop with David Campbell, her father's engineer and now hers. He'd been working on the sight of a rifle, and she'd asked him what the word *rifle* meant. He'd told her about hunting rifles, and then about the repeating rifles the Russian army so desperately lacked in 1877 when the Turks beat them back from Plevna. Not a single Russian regiment had such rifles. Winchesters – Campbell had one himself. He'd shown it to her. A battalion with guns like that would be worth half the Russian army, he'd told her. Add a couple of machine guns – Gatlings… It had started her thinking.

The *troika* was a good one with strong horses. They were making for one of Anna's small estates deep in the forest. It had been a hunting lodge once, but now it was shut up and empty, without even a housekeeper.

The thudding of the hooves, the creaking of the harness and the swishing of the runners: the magical sounds of a *troika*. For a mile or so nobody spoke. Then, as the birches changed to oaks, Anna dropped her voice so the driver could hear nothing and told them the real reason she bought so much farm equipment. With the help of David Campbell, she was buying American rifles, Winchesters, and smuggling them into Russia together with her farm machines. With shining eyes, she poured out her dream. Only she and Campbell knew where the guns were hidden – nobody on the Committee even knew the guns existed, not even Vera Figner. When the revolution started, she'd arm a thousand fighters: an elite, soldiers who'd desert from the Tsar's armies. Nobody knew who they'd be or who'd lead them, but they'd come. She'd find a commander for them – maybe a strong man who'd emerge from the Committee, or maybe someone else altogether. In the chaos of revolution, her battalion with its overwhelming weaponry would seize power. Real power.

"There's a last consignment," she whispered, "coming through Helsinki. Not rifles this time. Machine guns."

They swung off the main road. The track through the oak woods was drifted deep in soft snow. The horses began to flounder. "Slow down," Anna told the driver. "We still have ten versts to go."

"Why?" Vitya asked. "Why keep it to yourself like that? It's so unbelievably… disloyal."

Anna sniffed. "You know how the Committee is. Even the People's Will. It's better now than before, but… Andrey, Sonya – all of them. Maybe they can start a revolution, but they'll never control it. When the Tsar is killed, there's going to be chaos. Sonya will burn alive in her own inferno. She knows it – they all know it. There's nothing in them but terror and assassination. None of them can keep a secret, and none of them thinks a single day beyond the revolution." She looked at Vitya wryly. "I'm right, aren't I?"

"You really have enough guns for a regiment?" he asked.

"Yes. You'll see when we get to the house."

"Is that where you're taking us? Now?"

By way of answer, Anna took her bandaged hands out of the fur muff where she'd hidden them for most of the journey and held them up. "I was strong enough before. Now I'm not," she said simply. "I can't force you to keep it a secret. If you tell Sonya and the others, I'm dead – we all know that. But… I thought you'd see the sense of it."

The horses were strong and well fed, but they made slow headway through the big drifts. Twice they stuck. The driver wanted to turn back. Anna settled the argument by doubling the fare to fifty roubles. Then she sat back and wormed her hands into her muff, sensing Evgenya's shock and Vitya's scrutiny. Finally Vitya said: "This power you're talking about. It's enough, maybe, to change everything. To change history. But if you choose the wrong man... if you choose a Bonaparte, what happens then? Do you really want power like that?"

"I already have it," Anna replied. "The question is whether either of you wants to share it."

A sudden turn through the trees, an open patch of ground swept clear by the wind, and the old lodge, shuttered and deserted, was in front of them. The *troika* swept up to the front door and stopped, the horses sensing shelter and rest.

"I'll show you where we hide the keys," Anna said. She shrugged off the sheepskin rug and slipped down from the *troika* without waiting for the driver to help her.

After they'd found the keys, Anna led the driver to the stables and told him to stay there. There was hay for the horses in the loft and a stable pump that hardly ever froze. In an hour they'd go back to Pereslavl – well before dusk.

As they entered the house, Anna was strangely anxious, as though she were late for a tryst with an impatient lover. "Open the shutter," she said as soon as they were inside, "the first one by the door." Vitya opened the window and the shutter outside it. The hinges were greased and swung easily. The thin winter light showed the house stripped of furniture.

"There's nothing here," Anna said, pulling her bandaged hands free of her muff and dropping it on the floor. "Nothing to tempt a thief. The steps go down by the kitchen." She led the way.

At the bottom of the cellar stairs were three locked doors just visible in the light from above. "That one," Anna said waving a bandaged fist at the middle door, "the brass key with the mitre on the end." Evgenya opened the door. It was a wine cellar with dusty racks to the ceiling – all empty.

"Leave the door open," Anna said. "There's enough light to see if you wait a minute."

They waited.

"David made it," Anna explained. "It's not really a rack. Pull the top level down. To the right." Evgenya fumbled for a second, then discovered how part of the rack hinged down.

"Further," Anna said. As the lever reached its extremity, the whole rack swung away from the wall. "There's a hole. Down there." Anna pointed to the base of the wall. "Crawl through. There's a lamp on the floor inside and matches. You have to feel around for it. Be careful with the match." Evgenya crawled through the hole. Anna breathed gratefully the smell of oil, beeswax and explosives. Light glowed from low down as Evgenya lit the lamp. Anna crawled in after her, using her elbows instead of her hands to pull herself through. Vitya waited till Anna was clear, then slipped through himself.

"The air circulates from outside," Anna told them. "David thought it out."

"Good God," Vitya exclaimed, staring at the heaped-up gun boxes.

"The cellar used to be huge. We split it. What do you think?"

"It's well hidden," he said.

Rifle boxes were piled to the ceiling, each painted with a large white number. The highest number was 210. In each box were five rifles. Ammunition boxes were piled high against both side walls. "A thousand Winchesters," Anna said. "The Gatlings will be the last."

The lamp on the floor lit their faces weirdly from below. They stood in silence. Anna suddenly understood how much the sight of the guns had changed everything for Vitya and for Evgenya – their future with the Movement, their feelings for each other, and their understanding of what might, and what might not, be possible. The three of them retreated into defensive silence, and Anna resigned herself to the exhaustion that follows a supreme effort.

Back in Pereslavl, the two women said goodbye to Vitya on the platform. He was heading south to Moscow. They would take a later train back to Yaroslavl. After he'd gone, the women waited on the platform, shunning the crowded waiting room and the overheated restaurant.

"You're very quiet," Anna said wearily when they were finally alone.

"I'm overwhelmed," Evgenya replied. "I had no idea."

"But you knew I had plans." It was an effort to talk, but she needed to reach some kind of understanding, at least with Evgenya.

"Not plans to start a private army," Evgenya said. "I thought you were part of the Movement. I thought…"

"The Movement will die at the moment of its triumph," Anna said. "They'll kill the Tsar. I believe that. But they'll never rule Russia."

"And you will?"

"No, not me. Certainly not now. Perhaps I had dreams once…"

"You, Anna…"

"I don't know what will happen or who will take over. But the man I choose…"

For a moment their talk collapsed in a tangle of half sentences and lost ideas.

"Is that why you wanted to talk to this group in Sebastopol?" Evgenya asked at last. "The army officers?"

"Exactly." Anna felt suddenly faint. Evgenya helped her to an empty bench and they sat down. "You think I'm wrong?" Anna asked hesitantly.

"Do you care what I think?"

"Please, sweetheart," Anna said gently. "I'm not Vitya. You don't have to talk to me like that. I care what you think. If you haven't understood that much…"

A distant train-whistle from the south alerted them. They went to the far end of the platform where the first-class carriages would stop, as far as possible from the smoke and soot of the engine. It was eighty miles to Yaroslavl – over three hours.

"I want to ask you something," Anna said when they were sitting comfortably in their compartment. "It's important to me."

Evgenya smiled. "Ask," she said.

Despite the clear invitation, Anna hesitated. It was a delicate subject. "Vitya asked you to marry him," she began, "didn't he?"

"Yes."

"You refused?"

"Of course. I don't want to marry him. I don't want to marry anyone." She grinned suddenly: "Except maybe you."

"Be sensible," Anna warned her.

Evgenya shrugged. "It's been a serious day," she said.

"Is Vitya important to you?" Anna pursued. "Do you love him?"

"I don't know what you want to know," Evgenya said quietly. "Or why you want to know it?"

"I have some important family business," Anna said. "My uncle is trying to take away what my father left me. I may need…"

"… a husband?" Now that Anna had given her the scent, she pursued it without hestitation.

"And a son," Anna said. "An heir."

"Take him," Evgenya said without hesitation. "You won't find a better man. Anywhere."

"It wouldn't hurt you. I couldn't do anything that would hurt you. I'd rather marry Tyomka."

"It wouldn't hurt me. Not at all," Evgenya said bravely. "In fact I've half predicted it, ever since that night you came to our apartment."

"And really," Anna argued, "it's no different from *What is to be Done?* Vera Rozalskaya and Lopukhov."

"He married her to save her life," Evgenya said. "But he never… It was never a proper marriage."

"No," Anna agreed. "That wasn't a proper marriage. Vera Rozalskaya didn't need an heir."

"And you do," Evgenya shrugged.

"Would it hurt you? If I asked him and he agreed?"

"No. As long as I can be bridesmaid," Evgenya said flippantly.

"Bridesmaids have to be virgins," Anna replied, trying to rise to Evgenya's tone. "Or they bring bad luck."

"I know I'm not much of a virgin," Evgenya said, "but I'm good with my fists. If you need anyone beaten up…"


# VI


Sonya was the next unexpected visitor to the Grishin estate. She announced her visit with a telegram: *Arriving Yaroslavl Wednesday 11:30 Polonsky*.

Sonya's problem was this. Just before the Moscow mine fiasco, Grigory Goldenberg had been picked up on a railway station near Odessa with a trunk full of dynamite. He'd stayed heroically silent for six days, but then he'd begun to talk. But what had he said? The key to affairs like this was the Ferret, Kletochnikov. In the aftermath of the Moscow mine, hundreds of files from around the Empire had been requested by St Petersburg. In a list of Third Section informers, the Ferret had seen the name *Elif Akbarova*. She'd started to work for the Third Section fifteen days after Goldenberg's arrest. The Ferret had traced the link through Goldenberg's own file: in his deposition Goldenberg stated that he'd collected the dynamite in Odessa from an Azeri girl — Elif was her name, and that he knew no more about her. The Third Section had quickly identified her and started a file on her: Elif Akbarova, registered as living in a villa belonging to a certain Vassily Vashetko, now living in Canada. With their usual subtlety, the Third Section traced Elif's family in Azerbaijan before they picked her up. She had a brother in Moscow who might find his studies abruptly terminated — that was their hold over her. The Ferret had passed on the information about Elif to the Guardian, and the

Guardian had alerted Sonya. Sonya worked quickly – Section South had sent Elif on a meaningless mission to Yalta to get her out of the way. The press had been moved and the villa purged of any trace of revolutionary activity.

And now Elif had to be eliminated – that was obvious. But how? It wasn't so easy with Popov gone. Sonya's immediate thought had been Evgenya, but the girl had never worked on her own and Sonya wasn't sure that she was ready for such a job. First it wasn't easy to approach someone as alert and sensitive as a police spy and execute her. Then strength – the Hangman preferred to work alone, but he was strong as a drayhorse. Evgenya was tough for a girl, but real strength, like Popov's... In any case Evgenya might well refuse to execute someone who'd been, in a way, her friend. She might refuse to do anything in Popov's line at all. The more Sonya thought about it, the higher this final hurdle rose. She'd have to talk things through with Evgenya herself, even though it meant a trip to Yaroslavl. If Evgenya wasn't ready or wasn't sure she could do it, they'd have to find another way.

On the morning Sonya arrived, Evgenya had dismissed her housekeeper and kicked the woman's two sons out of the house. She was still in a vile temper when she met Sonya at the station in Yaroslavl. She cursed the *troika* driver all the way back to the estate for driving so slowly, and screamed at the cook when they arrived because the samovar was cold. Anna kept to her room. Worse, Sonya realised, there'd been some kind a quarrel *with* Vitya or *about* Vitya – it was all very confused.

At lunch they talked about the railway connection from Moscow, the mildness of the weather, the unusual stucco in the decaying rooms. At last the rustic footman put a bowl of pine nuts on the table to end the meal and the servants gratefully withdrew.

"What's it all about, Gypsy?" Sonya asked as the door closed.

"None of your business," Evgenya replied.

Sonya stood up immediately, went round the table to where Evgenya was sitting and slapped her face. "No one talks to me like that," she said.

If there was a clash of wills, it was brief. "I'm sorry," Evgenya said gritting her teeth. "Really. Maybe if we went for a walk. The cold air…"

Sonya turned away on her heel. "As long as you keep a civil tongue in your head," she agreed.

The two women walked toward Grishin's Folly, still decorated with icicles but looking like a gloomy and abandoned prison under the threatening sky. Sonya explained the few facts she knew about Elif. Evgenya was immediately interested. "Did they put pressure on her?" she asked.

"Through her brother. He's a student in Moscow. It was in the file."

"Did she give away anything important?"

"We don't know. Probably not yet. Informers usually tell lies at first."

"Did she tell you the Third Section had picked her up?"

"No, unfortunately not. We had to find out for ourselves."

"And you're certain? They really did recruit her?"

"Yes."

"Then…" Evgenya hesitated to put the next step into words.

"Yes," Sonya agreed.

Evgenya stopped, kicking at a chunk of ice with the tip of her boot. "Who will do it?" she asked.

"There is someone. He used to help Popov."

"Stepka? You can't use him. He's half blind and totally stupid. He'd get lost on the train between here and Odessa, and you'd never find him again."

"Was that what Popov thought of him?"

"Yes."

They walked on again in silence, making for the Folly. "So she's a traitor," Evgenya said at last. "There's no doubt? None at all?"

"None."

"When Reinstein… I think it was right what we did to him."

"Yes. We all agreed," Sonya reassured her. "And it wouldn't matter to you that Elif was, in a way, your friend?"

"Not if she's like Reinstein. I utterly hate such people, Sonya. I've been thinking a lot about it recently – disloyalty, divided loyalty."

"Why?" Sonya asked shrewdly. "Have you seen any signs of it? In Vitya perhaps?" She laughed. "No, impossible to imagine. What about in Anna?…"

The hint was too obvious. Sonya saw Evgenya move instantly to cover her tracks.

"Anna? Good heavens no," Evgenya exclaimed. "Just that housekeeper, the one I threw out. In some ways she was loyal, but she robbed me – day in and day out."

"If we kicked out every thieving servant, we'd soon be blacking our own boots," Sonya agreed. "And you haven't quarrelled with Anna? She's a hard taskmaster. You must have a lot to put up with."

"Not at all," Evgenya replied. "She's teaching me so many things. Filling in the gaps in my education."

It was another way of saying 'none of your business' but harder to cope with. For the moment, Sonya gave up the attack. "Whatever is that building?" she asked brightly, eyeing the aqueduct ahead of them.

"Grishin's Folly."

"What's it for?"

"It takes water from a stream in that hill over there."

"Yes?"

"And brings it here."

"Why?"

"I don't know," Evgenya said. "It was my grandfather's idea. But listen…"

As so often, Sonya was a jump ahead of her: "If you're going to volunteer to remove Elif," she said, "the answer is no. You're far too young, much too weak and hopelessly inexperienced."

Faced with such a challenge, Evgenya argued and pleaded for the job until Sonya finally gave in with well-feigned reluctance. "No one can say I forced you to do it," Sonya concluded. They strolled back to the house, discussing exactly how the execution might best be managed.

Anna came down for dinner. "You've worked a miracle on the Gypsy," she remarked to Sonya, "she's halfway human again."

Sonya's visit was a short one. The day after she arrived, the women left the old manor house together, and two of them never saw it again.

# Extract 9

In October 1879, one of our people, a carpenter called Stepan Khalturin who worked on the imperial yacht, was transferred to the maintenance staff at the Winter Palace. One of the corporals of the palace guard was impressed with Stepan. The corporal had a daughter and, the story has it, Stepan and the daughter came close to getting married. I mention this because Stepan was the type we almost completely lacked in the Movement: working men, normal people who marry, drink vodka in the evening with their friends, set up home and have children. Stepan lived with the maintenance crew in a cellar of the Winter Palace. Above his cellar was the guard room and above that the Tsar's dining room. Stepan's intimacy with the corporal meant that smuggling dynamite into the Winter Palace, little by little, was no problem. Stepan planned to increase his store of explosive until it was large enough to destroy the imperial dining room when Alexander Romanov was at dinner. An enormous quantity was needed, but Stepan was prepared to wait, for years if necessary. A little detail Sofya Perovskaya once told me: as a Christmas bonus in 1879, Stepan was given a hundred roubles by the palace management. A hundred roubles: he must have been a wonderful craftsman.

In February 1880, on orders from Andrey Zhelyabov, Stepan exploded his mine. In Stepan's opinion it was too early: far more dynamite was needed. Even so, he destroyed the guard room and wrecked the dining room of the palace, such is the power of even a small quantity of dynamite in a constricted space. Unfortunately the Emperor was late for dinner that day. Of course there was consternation in the government: terror had penetrated the Winter Palace itself. Security was tightened another notch. This failure, though once again the propaganda value was incalculable, led to a blazing quarrel between Andrey and Stepan. Stepan turned his back on the People's Will and never spoke to any of us again as far as I know. Looking back I think Stepan was right, but in 1880 when my wisdom might have had some effect, I agreed with Andrey. We wanted quick results: time was the enemy. After twenty years in the Schlusselburg, time and I have become old friends. (*Memoir of the People's Will*, Chapter 9.)

# Chapter 10

## I

Evgenya decided to say *no*, and she said it in such a way that everyone believed her. They were disappointed, of course, especially Albrecht, who'd apparently been ecstatic with anticipation ever since they'd received Sonya's telegram: *Gypsy dancer will be appearing in Odessa February 3. Reserve a seat.* Now at last he could perfect the drawings he'd made of her, exactly right, he was sure, for *La Vie Parisienne* – not too brazen, not too coy, erotic with a hint of violence, and ingenuous with a hint of brimstone.

No, she told him, she wasn't going to pose for his drawings, and he needn't try to wheedle her because she wasn't going to change her mind. And it was the same with Lavritsky and the others – whatever they wanted, the answer was *no*.

Sonya had planned things carefully. Trigony was to recall Elif so that she'd arrive the day after Evgenya. Apart from Trigony, nobody in Odessa knew why the house had been purged or that Elif was an informer – it was possible that Group South had been infiltrated by other police spies. And Evgenya was to present herself as a completely reformed character – that way she might get close to Elif again.

During Elif's first evening back at the villa, things went well. "They pester me all the time," Evgenya complained to her, "but I suppose I deserve it really."

"In a way you do," Elif agreed, "but it's good that you've… changed."

"I spoke to our family priest," Evgenya told her. "He helped me a lot."

"I'm sure he did," Elif replied. "You have to do what your religion says. I think that's true even though you're a Christian and I'm a Moslem."

"I wish I'd understood that better when I was here before," Evgenya agreed, "but there's always hope. I mean, one of Jesus' best friends was a prostitute."

"Who?"

"Mary – Mary of Magdala. She's a saint."

"I don't think we have any saints like that," Elif said, only half believing the story.

"We certainly do. I pray to her for strength. Quite often."

Evgenya wasn't in the habit of lying, and she was amazed how readily Elif accepted the most blatant nonsense. She waited until the following evening to take her next step. Almost a year before they'd walked on the stormy seashore. Despite the drenching wind, they walked there again now, exchanging commonplaces, touching sometimes on religious differences and trying to bridge the gaps. She was winning Elif's trust again – of that Evgenya was certain. That was a vital first step – Sonya wanted Elif removed, but in such a way that the police could never establish for sure that their carefully recruited agent had been uncovered and eliminated.

The next step, as Evgenya planned it, was to get the girl up onto the breakwater at a time when the sea ran strongly but the spray wasn't enough to drown them on the spot.

The daytime hours were tedious – the press wasn't running and revolutionary writing was stalled in fear of a police raid. There was little to do beyond eat, sleep and exercise. The afternoon after her first walk with Elif, the sea was oily calm. Evgenya stayed in her room finishing a book she'd found at the station bookstore in Moscow – *The Possessed*. Evgenya found the story confusing and Dostoevsky's language difficult, but the obsessed, suicidal characters fascinated her. One of them, according to the introduction, was based on Sergey

Nechaev. Anna had told her about Nechaev, Bakunin and the other anarchists – she'd known them all in her Zürich days. *The Possessed* wasn't a book like *What is to be Done?* full of useful sentiments and fine conversations. It was frighteningly close to Evgenya's daily world, where she was stalking an Azeri girl with the vile intention of drowning her in the hungry black sea. Elif was a sweet girl really, with shy brown – almost black – eyes, trusting and fundamentally without guile. Evgenya didn't particularly like her – she preferred tough little cats like Darya – but even so…

The next afternoon the wind was up again and the sky was dark with storm-clouds. Evgenya was walking and gossiping with her victim, bent into the blustering headwind. They'd been out a long while and were nearly back at the villa. "Let's go out along the breakwater," Evgenya shouted, her voice flurried by the wind.

"I'm worn out," Elif objected, "and we'll get wet through."

"Who cares?" Evgenya replied. "We'll have to change when we get back anyway." She took the lead, climbing easily on to the breakwater. She turned back to give Elif a hand – the girl was exhausted. "I'll help you!" Evgenya shouted.

The top of the breakwater was drenched with spray, but it wasn't slippery. The waves spilled over it only at the deep-water end, 200 yards away. Even so, the sea on the windward side was malignant, alive with overfalls, swelling and groaning like a monster jealous of the air they breathed. The fierce wind whipped the tops off the waves, charging the air with spume.

"I'm not sure," Elif cringed.

"Don't be silly. Come on, at least as far as that… whatever it is." Half way down the breakwater, two iron bollards offered moorings, though no boats were tied to them now.

Whipped and exhilarated by the sea and the wind, they reached the bollards. "Elif," Evgenya said, her voice suddenly hard with authority. "Sit down. On that iron thing."

"Why don't we go back," Elif objected, glancing at Evgenya uneasily. "I think we'd better."

"I said sit down," Evgenya told her. "So sit." She put her hand on Elif's shoulder, feeling the thin bones through the girl's coat.

Elif sat down, frightened now. It seemed she'd guessed what was coming and her body quivered, urgent for escape.

"Sonya wanted me to ask you some questions," Evgenya said, pitching her voice above the roar of the sea.

"What about?" Elif's face contorted with fear. She tried to stand up.

"Sit down," Evgenya said, forcing her back on to the bollard. "You know what about."

"What are you going to do to me?"

"Questions first," Evgenya said.

A shower of sea water drenched them as an angry wave lashed into the breakwater.

"First – what did you tell them?"

"I can't hear you."

Evgenya waited for a lull in the waves and shouted her question again.

"Nothing."

"Names? Did you tell them names?"

"Only nicknames."

"And that we had a press?"

"They knew already."

"So you confirmed it?"

Elif hesitated as though the idea was new to her. "I suppose so," she whimpered. Evgenya understood the reply without hearing it.

"Did you say where the press was?"

"I said I didn't know. I told them it was in the middle of town somewhere."

"Why didn't you say anything? To Mischa? To any of us?"

Elif was speechless, shaking with fear.

Evgenya tightened her pressure on the girl's collar-bone. Popov had shown her how. "Why didn't you?"

"How could I? My brother…"

"At the university?"

"Yes."

"Him or us? And you chose him? Is that it?"

"No. I never told them anything. Never, never, never." Elif's voice degenerated into a howl whipped away by the wind.

Another wave, higher this time. It surged across the breakwater, pulling at the hems of their dresses, washing into their shoes. With a vicious *hiss,* the hard-driven water crashed into the seething, restless sea beyond the wall.

"Stand up," Evgenya said.

Elif stood up. "Evgenya, please…" There was resignation in her words – she knew it was over.

"Go and stand on the edge. Over there. Facing the wind. I don't want to see your face."

Elif didn't move. Evgenya grabbed her wrist, turned her, and twisted her skinny arm up behind her back.

"Stop it!" Elif screamed in panic.

Evgenya pushed the girl forward, tightening the pressure on her arm. The girl's feet reached the edge of the breakwater. For a long moment Evgenya stood behind her prey, unsure. What Sonya called the logic of events was driving her forward; it was impossible now for Elif to return alive to the villa. But the awful sea – to hurl the girl into the devouring, spiteful waves, to let her body be battered against the wall till she was dead…

Then, rolling toward them, Evgenya saw a huge wave, high as an *isba.* Ahead of it, a chasm was forming as the mountainous wave sucked up everything in its path. When the wave hit the wall, it would sweep them away. There was no escape. She must decide – let the wave kill Elif or do the job herself. Instantly she understood – it had to be her. Her wet skirt dragged heavy at her leg as she raised her knee and thrust hard at Elif's back. With a scream Elif toppled forward into the appalling, all-devouring chasm. Evgenya flung herself flat on the stones, grasping her arms round the bollard where Elif had sat. A tumult of water broke over her, crushing the breath out of her body. She held on, her lungs bursting out of her body, the furious water tearing at her limbs. Then air, sounds, breath returning. She clung to the bollard for a long while, half-drowned and shivering. There was no sign of Elif.

Evgenya hurried back to the villa and went straight to her room. No one saw her, and she had nothing to say to any of them. She changed into dry clothes and packed her suitcase. She had a warm shawl but no dry coat – she'd buy an old one at the station. She had money, not much, but enough for a coat and a train ticket. She slipped out of the house, still unobserved. Where to? Where could she disappear? Disappear – there was more to it than disappearance. Evgenya Antonovna Grishina had existed till that afternoon – but now her existence was cancelled. Sucked up by a giant wave. Annihilated.

Kiev. She'd go back to Kiev. Sink there into the underworld. She'd talk to Yakub. At the boxing gym. Popov's old friend. She'd work for him. Fight for him. He wanted young fighters. Hurt and get hurt. Take her punishment. While men looked on and gloated. Anything was possible. But not... but not...

## II

Anna's father had been told by his doctor that he had a weak heart and could drop dead without warning. Anna had been sixteen at the time, and her father had decided to bequeath to her the entire Shestakov fortune. The family lawyers, Kreuzotter and Beil, had drafted the will for him. They'd assured him that such a will, despite some provisions that had never been tested in front of a judge, was in accordance with the new Civil Code. The law itself wasn't the problem – the difficulty lay in a long-established family tradition: the income from certain estates had always been set aside for the support of younger brothers, and certain houses were reserved for their accommodation. There would be trouble with Anna's uncle if the will changed that. But the old man insisted. He'd quarrelled with his brother, broken with him for ever. If the will could throw his errant brother out of his comfortable home and send him to rot in the street – then let it happen.

The quarrel was an old one. At the time of the emancipation of the serfs, Anna had been twelve. Twenty years later, she still remembered her father and his younger brother shouting, swearing, insulting each other – emancipation with land or without land? The Count had refused to give up a single *arshin* of Shestakov land to any damned peasant. His brother had taken the opposite, liberal view. At the height of the quarrel, the Count had tried to cancel the lease under which his brother held his estate. Kreuzotter had drafted the lease himself – it was inviolable until the Count's death. When that happened, the lease would automatically fall in. After she'd inherited her fortune, Kreuzotter suggested that Anna present a petition to the high court seeking to evict her uncle from his estate since he now had no lease – none at all. But Anna had refused. Lease or no lease, her uncle could keep his house. The best Kreuzotter could do was to divert the tiny income from the estate into Anna's coffers.

Her uncle was not grateful. For years now, he'd attacked her on two fronts, the sentimental and the judicial. On the sentimental side, he'd entreated her to make over to him some part of her absurdly large income – he had children to be brought up and provided for. Surely an ancient quarrel with her father about serfdom was no grounds to impoverish her own nieces and nephews. The judicial attack was more deadly. Anna, her uncle believed, was mentally unstable. If he could take it one stage further and prove she was insane, the estate would be taken from her. With Anna still unmarried and childless, her uncle was first in line to inherit.

The easiest defence on both fronts, as Kreuzotter had impressed on Anna ever since she'd come of age, was marriage. As a married woman she could make no disposition of her property without her husband's consent.

A severe husband would block the sentimental attack, and an heir, even a girl, would block the judicial. For years Anna had resisted these arguments, but with the injuries to her hands, she felt vulnerable and helpless. Seeing no way out, she decided to marry, and of twenty possible candidates, she'd chosen Vitya. He was poor but presentable. He was idealistic enough to marry her without love, and decent enough not to exploit her afterward. And she liked him. She liked his humour, his dedication, his simplicity. If she was to have a son, it wouldn't be a bad thing if he were another Vitya. The only snail in the salad might be Evgenya – but as it turned out Evgenya, though not exactly blessing the marriage, had quietly stepped aside. Kreuzotter approved Anna's choice – provided the penniless heir of the Pelins signed a marriage settlement that threatened no inroads into the Shestakov fortune. Vitya would receive a fortune-hunter's dowry each month, 10,000 roubles, but no more. If he ran up gambling debts, the estate would not pay them. Kreuzotter approached Vitya, and Vitya, sure now that Evgenya would never marry him, agreed to go through the legal formalities of marriage with Anna. She would keep her name so that her heir, if she had one, would be a Shestakov. The settlement was drafted and signed.

On Anna's estate near Rostov there was a lake with an island. On the island was a small wooden church dating back to the time of Ivan the Terrible. It was dedicated to Saint Olga of Kiev. There, in the presence of Kreuzotter and David Campbell, the happy couple were married on 26th February, 1880, Vitya's name-day.

Oddly perhaps, they *were* a happy couple. As a wedding present, Anna gave her husband three wishes. His first wish was that Anna would buy the Grishin estate and give it to Evgenya with enough income to keep it in shape. The second was that she'd set up with him the Pelinskoye Antimony Mining Trust. His third wish was that Anna should travel to Wiesbaden to see what could be done about her hands.

The purpose of the marriage, however quiet the celebration, was to inform the world in general, and Anna's uncle in particular, that Anna was now under the management of a husband and might well produce an heir. To that end, Kreuzotter busily drafted newspaper announcements and congratulatory advertisements wishing the couple all the good things that God heaps upon the deserving, in particular the blessing of a son.

During the second week of March, Vitya took his new wife as far as Minsk on her journey to Germany. While she went on to Wiesbaden, he was to go to Helsinki with David Campbell to see Anna's Gatlings through the customs, along with a gigantic American reaper. After that, Anna wanted him to join her in Wiesbaden, but he refused. He wouldn't put their marriage above the Movement – that was something she had no right to ask. Anna agreed in principle, though her smile was wistful as she said the ill-starred words, "Yes, you're right."

Marriages of convenience as Chernyshevsky depicts them in *What is to be Done?* inevitably pose problems of consummation, and Anna was far from certain how this aspect of her marriage would work out. In fact, with prompting from his new wife, Vitya turned what might have been sober duty into a promiscuous and repeated pleasure for them both. Anna would be unlucky if she was going to Germany without what Kreuzotter called 'an heir to her body'.

Apart from Stepan Khalturin's mine in the Winter Palace, the spring of 1880 was a dead time for the Movement. The government, on the other hand, was uncommonly active. The old Third Section was abolished, taken over by the Ministry of the Interior, the MVD, with more money, more men in the streets, and the cleverest heads in the civil service on secondment. For most Russians, however, the spring of that year was simply a time of anxiety. In the Ukraine, the autumn rain in 1879 persisted till Christmas. Without its protective covering of early snow, the spring wheat was devastated by frost. The germinated seed was frozen in the earth and destroyed. Across the Empire, summer would bring famine.

# III

Evgenya was allowed an hour for lunch. Her first fight was coming up in three weeks, and Yakub wanted her fit. As always, a blood-red beefsteak and a pint of black beer were brought in from a nearby tavern. As she ate, she scanned Yakub's newspaper. The name *Shestakov* caught her eye – one of Kreuzotter's advertisements. When she climbed back into the ring and threw off her robe, she was ready for naked murder. Her sparring partner, a stocky peasant girl with no physical talents beyond stoic endurance, was quickly felled with a broken rib. Yakub was annoyed. It was hard enough to recruit girls for the ring – impossible if bad-tempered bitches half-murdered those he did find. For the next three weeks, she'd have to fight with men. But he was pleased with her too – she had no qualms about taking punches, she was extraordinarily pretty for a fighting girl, and she was still unmarked.

Evgenya's first public appearance was a bout halfway through a long evening of heavily backed prize-fights. She won a purse of twenty gold roubles after half an hour of unbroken ferocity with no bell, no rounds, no compulsory count, no gloves and no rules as to where kicks and punches could be landed. The referee stood outside the ring, waiting till one of the fighters submitted. The roars of the cheering men overwhelmed her. The battering she took clouded her brain and bruised her half-trained body. For three days afterward Yakub kept her in a haze of morphine. When she came round, she remembered that she'd won and offered to pay him back the money he'd lent her – sixteen paper roubles. But he refused. He'd bet on her halfway through the fight when she was on the floor and taking a hammering. Her opponent, a broken-nosed, tatooed Arab, had got to her feet and walked away, thinking the job was done. But she'd been wrong. Evgenya had staggered to her feet, lurched forward and rammed her head into the small of the woman's back. The fight ended not long after, and Yakub had cleared 200 roubles. A few days later Evgenya was training again, slow and stiff and keeping her elbows much tighter across her chest. She was learning. Yakub had already booked her next fight for double the prize-money.


# IV


Sonya was not expecting visitors. The jangling of the doorbell from downstairs startled her. She glanced at the window – even though it was daylight, two candles were burning, one above the other.

St Petersburg was at that unpleasant time of year when the ice on the Neva was too dangerous to cross, but the summer bridges to the islands were not yet built. The streets were clogged with heaps of left-over snow, rotting ice and mountains of cinders. The packed ice over the cobbles was not thick enough for sleighs, but the surface was too potholed for anything more delicate than rustic cartwheels. Enshrouding everything, the resinous smoke of log fires mingled with the spring fog of the Gulf.

Sonya hurried to the apartment door and slid open the peephole. Footsteps approached slowly up the stairs. Two people – a man and a woman. The footsteps stopped and the woman began to cough, a long, tortured, ugly cough. Steps again – leather boots on the oak stairs.

Vitya? It was Vitya. With Rakhel. In Petersburg? Why? She opened the door before Vitya could knock. She beckoned them in and quickly closed the door behind them.

"You weren't followed?" she asked. She eyed Rakhel closely. A sick whore – Rakhel had degenerated rapidly and irreversibly. Her skin was unwholesome, her eyes bloodshot. Suppurations disfigured her neck, though they were mostly hidden by a scarf. Syphilis.

"No," Vitya assured her. "We double-checked everything."

"So what do you want?" Sonya didn't invite them further into the apartment or suggest that they take off their coats. For her the news of Vitya's marriage to his Countess had been as bad as the news of Khalturin's failure at the Winter Palace.

"It's not so simple," Vitya told her, accepting her hostility. "Can we come in? It might take a while."

"If you insist," Sonya agreed. "Take off your coats. Hang them there." She indicated a loaded coat rack.

They followed her into the living room. It was cheaply furnished and untidy. "Sit down," she said. "Well?"

They sat down uncomfortably. "Sonya," Vitya began, "you know I married Anna."

"You didn't exactly keep it secret," Sonya retorted. "All those odious congratulations."

"It was a matter of convenience. To do with her money. In one sense we're married, in another we're not. She's gone to Germany. I don't know when she'll be back."

However much Sonya wanted to believe him, she couldn't lift the angry scowl from her face.

"That wasn't why you came here, to tell me that," Sonya said, with a glance at Rakhel.

"No," Vitya agreed.

"Well then?"

"A few days ago," Vitya began, "I went to the safe house, the one Anna used to keep. Off the Pokrovka."

"Why?"

"I thought Rakhel might be there. And maybe she'd have a contact address where I could find you."

"Why did you come here? You should have telegraphed."

"I know. That's what I planned. But…"

Sonya eyed Rakhel closely again. Every hint of prettiness had vanished from her face. Her body was skinny and angular. She must have stopped eating. "Is it Committee business that brings you here?" Sonya said. "I certainly hope so."

"Yes, it is," Vitya assured her. "Vital business."

"Perhaps we should wait for Andrey," Sonya said. "I have to warn you, I've taken it somewhat personally, Vitya, this... this tie-up between you and Anna."

"Andrey?"

"He'll be back in an hour."

"You mean...?"

"I'm also a woman, Viktor Pavlovich. Or perhaps you hadn't noticed?"

She watched him digest the news – it surprised him as it surprised everyone in the Movement. It was a reaction Sonya found unflattering.

"Sonya," he said, "you can pick a quarrel with me if you want. I can't stop you. But the reason I came here has nothing to do with Anna."

Quickly Sonya thought through the possibilities – only one made sense. "It's her," she said, with a vicious nod at Rakhel.

"Yes," Vitya agreed.

"They've recruited her."

"Yes. But Sonya, she told me herself. Of her own accord."

"You get rid of one fucking cockroach," Sonya exclaimed, "and the next one crawls out of the woodwork."

The story was quickly told: the MVD with its influx of new money and new people was opening up old cases. The fact that Rakhel and Viktorya Rakovskaya had been in the cells of the Moscow Central Police Office on the same night had been noted at the time but never investigated. The new investigation had meant talking to Rakhel. Her interrogation had started after Christmas and taken a week. Rakhel had kept back as much as she could, but the subtle men who worked on her had trapped her in contradictions to the point where she no longer knew what she'd said or what they believed. They'd questioned her remorselessly about Viktorya Rakovskaya and the Countess Shestakova, especially about the relationship between these two strange women. Rakhel simply didn't know if she'd compromised Anna or not.

"What happened when Vitya came to see you? Is the house watched?" Sonya demanded.

"Yes. But I warned him," Rakhel replied. "Didn't I, Vitya?"

"Of course, you did," Vitya reassured her. Then to Sonya: "After I left, they tailed me, but I shook them off."

"How often do you report to them?" Sonya's voice was so subdued that Rakhel couldn't make out her words. Sonya repeated her question.

"Every week."

"Did they ask you about Vitya after he visited you?"

"Yes."

"What did you tell them?"

"I told them it was the Coalminer. But I didn't know his real name." Rakhel burst into tears of exhaustion and despair.

"Stop that noise," Sonya hissed, her voice sharp with anger. "God knows what damage you've done." She stood up and went to the window, trying to control herself. "This is what comes of working with syphilitic, half-demented whores." She turned to Vitya. "There's a box room. At the end of the corridor. Take her there. Andrey can talk to her later. See if he can get any sense out of her."

When Andrey returned, Sonya broke the news to him. They sat down with Vitya, turning the problem over – how much had Rakhel given away? How far should they cover their tracks? Who should be warned? Andrey spent an hour with Rakhel in the box room, but she was incoherent, and her memory played constant tricks on her.

"If she confused the police like she confused me," Andrey said after he'd left Rakhel, "it'll be ten years before they sort things out."

"Did you lock her in?" Sonya asked. "She's half mad."

"Yes," Andrey sighed. "Poor thing."

Their talk meandered through supposition after supposition till it collapsed well after midnight in silence and frustration.

"And Anna?" Vitya said finally, "We haven't talked about her. She has to be warned."

"Yes," Andrey agreed. "You can attend to that."

"And she'll need new papers," Vitya persisted, "for the journey back to Russia."

"No," Sonya flatly rejected the idea. "You aren't with us anymore. Not like you were. It has to be *no*."

"I *am* with you," Vitya replied quietly. "All evening you've been rejecting me. But I haven't rejected you."

There was a long silence. Sonya and Andrey exchanged glances. Then Andrey said: "There's another plan. A tunnel."

"Is that why Sonya's so angry?" Vitya asked. "She thought I'd refuse to dig it."

"If you had to marry someone, you should have married that cousin of yours," Sonya said crustily.

"I offered. She refused. Where is she now anyway?"

"She did a job for us," Sonya replied, "in Odessa. Popov's old line. Then she disappeared. Took a train to Kiev. Probably she's still there. When really I need her here."

"Kiev?" Vitya asked.

"Who does she know down there?" Andrey asked.

"In Kiev she was with Popov," Vitya replied reluctantly.

"I think she got cold feet. After that girl in Odessa," Sonya said. "You don't know anyone she was friendly with? In Kiev? It's time we got her back."

"There was a gym. She learned a bit of boxing. So she told me."

"That helps," Sonya said. "Let's see what they can find out down there."

"I'll telegraph in the morning," Andrey said. "And then I'll get on to Anna's papers."

# V

Evgenya unlocked the door and gingerly pushed it open. "You?" she exclaimed in astonishment, seeing who was sitting on the floor.

"Evgenya? You here?"

"They said someone was locked in here." Evgenya looked at the haggard woman sitting cross-legged on a thin, flock mattress. It was Rakhel. Not the buxom and more or less blithe Rakhel she'd known in Anna's safe-house, but a sick shadow. She went to Rakhel quickly and sat beside her. So this was why Sonya had dragged her away from Kiev! This was her job!

"Evgenya," Rakhel muttered, blinking in the bright light from the open door. "They said someone was coming. I didn't know it was going to be you."

"Someone was coming?" Evgenya repeated blankly, overwhelmed by the question of what to do now.

"They think I work for the Section."

"Yes."

"And that's your job now, isn't it? Like Popov."

Evgenya had no reply.

"Isn't it?" Rakhel repeated.

"I did it once," Evgenya said quietly, "but it isn't my job. No."

"You killed someone? For Sonya?"

"Yes."

"Who?"

"An Azeri girl."

"What was her name?"

"Elif."

The name seemed to satisfy Rakhel's curiosity.

"What happened?" Evgenya asked cautiously. "I can't imagine…"

Rakhel told her story in gasping little sentences. She had a rag in her hand, red with bloodstains. She wiped her mouth with it each time she coughed. "I told Vitya. I told him myself. I thought maybe I'd given Anna away. I got so confused – who was Viktorya, who was Anna. What they said. What they did. Were they sapphic? How could they be sapphic? They're the same person. I couldn't understand. How can you be sapphic with yourself? I don't understand anything anymore."

"And you told Vitya… all about it?" Evgenya asked, trying to piece the story together. "Why?"

"So he could warn Anna. Just Anna. I don't give a jackdaw's tit for the rest of you. Not even Vitya. He brought me here. To that she-devil."

"Sonya?"

"God damn her."

"Rakhel. He'd never do something like that. Not to hurt you."

"So what anyway? It doesn't matter anymore," Rakhel began to cry. "I'll soon be dead. I've got the sores all over me now. And my nerves are eaten up. With this horrible thing in my chest, eating away at me. Making me cough up my insides all the time."

"Sonya's gone out," Evgenya told her, "and Andrey."

"And you?"

"She said there was someone in this room…"

"Yes," Rakhel agreed. "Me."

"Rakhel! She didn't tell me who it was. Just let me walk in on you. If I'd known…"

"You'd have refused? Don't make me laugh! But it's too late. Take me away from here, Evgenya. Finish me off. I don't care anymore. If it isn't you, it'll be somebody else."

Evgenya put her arm round Rakhel's shoulders and drew her closer. "That's how I've felt for a long time too. Not caring anymore."

"Since… what was her name?"

"Elif."

"Since her?"

"Yes."

"Talk to me, Evgenya. No one's talked to me for days. What did you do after… what was her name?"

"Elif. I was… I was fighting. Prize-fighting. My second fight, I got half killed."

"Fighting? Is that the fighting they do? Naked girls? So men can bet on them?"

"Yes. They roar at you to kill each other. And they bet who

can take most punishment."

"What happened?"

"I won. Somehow or other. Got my purse. Yakub had a boy in another fight – bet a fortune on him. He won too, but… I can't remember the details. After a fight it's all a blur. Anyway, Yakub didn't get his money. It got nasty. Knives and such. I went back to our gym with Yakub. He was in a worse state than I was. I did a few more fights – just with our own girls. No betting. Just decoration. Then Sonya sent for me."

"That's worse than whoring – what you did."

"Hurts more maybe. But it's not so bad. Except the scars."

She was scarred – punches she'd walked into, kicks she'd taken when she should have kept her distance. On the other hand her nose was still straight, and Yakub had cleaned up her cuts with iodine so they'd all healed. But Rakhel – her life had turned into one angry scar that would never heal.

"No one made you do it? Fighting?"

"No."

"Why then?"

"I don't know. Somehow I couldn't get over…"

"That girl… whatever her name was? And him too? The Coalminer?"

"Yes, him," Evgenya agreed quietly. "Him and Elif. He married Anna you know."

The sound of water gurgling through the pipes. A distant shout of anger. Otherwise the oppressive silence of a small, dead room.

"So, tonight it's you and me," Rakhel whispered at last. "You'll walk away, and I won't. Another night it'll be you and… Popov? Where's Popov?"

"Dead. Popov's dead. For a long while now."

"Evgenya. Can I ask you something?"

Evgenya shrugged. What was there left to ask?

"Don't hurt me," Rakhel began to plead. "Please. I've got so weak. I used to be strong enough to take it. You know how I was. And not so long ago."

"No," Evgenya comforted her. "No one's going to hurt you. Ever again."

"And this last year," Rakhel said, with a sudden change of tone, "with Vitya and Anna. And you. It was…" She coughed, the racking cough of the consumptive near the end. No, it was worse, Evgenya saw – the pain spread like fire through her wasted body. Her nerves were burnt, tormented, scarified. Finally she recovered, her face running tears and her yellow eyes streaked with broken veins. She looked at Evgenya, bewildered. "You're still here," she said. "Where's Popov?"

"Let's go to one of those places," Evgenya said, "where you can get opium, morphine… whatever."

"Costs money," Rakhel objected weakly.

"I won my last fight. I told you. Forty roubles." It was more than enough for an overdose – enough to put Rakhel out of her misery.

"Where can we go?"

"I found a room last night. Near the Haymarket. There's plenty of places where they sell…"

"There was one night in my life," Rakhel said, brightening suddenly. "One only, when…"

"The night you found Anna. In the jail."

"Yes. You and me. You put your arm round me. You don't remember." Rakhel's cracked voice had an edge of wonder in it, as though that night had been a miraculous release.

"We could do it again," Evgenya took up the thread. "If you want. It might remind you…"

"Can we?"

"We could go to my room. Change. Make ourselves up. Freeze our backsides off in the streets. Is that what you want?"

"Would you?"

"If it would help you, Rakhel." She held Rakhel close for a second and kissed her forehead. Close to, her skin had a rancid, ugly smell. Evgenya winced. "And there was the 10,000 you saved for them. Don't forget that."

"That was an accident," Rakhel confessed. "I'd stuffed the money in my bag. Didn't know what else to do with it. And Sonya recognised the bag. Sow that she is." The two women laughed suddenly. A fortune slipping through your fingers – that was the way life went.

Three hours later Evgenya lifted Rakhel from a filthy bunk-bed in a cellar near the Haymarket. Rakhel's breathing had stopped half an hour before. When her own narcotic stupour eased, Evgenya carried the dead body to a little park two streets away. She found a seat where the first rays of the morning sun would fall on the bony, painted corpse. She sat on a granite bench nearby. The air was freezing. Through her thin skirt, the cold of the stone gripped her legs, turned her haunches to ice. When she could bear no more, she went back to her room. She lay on the bed, staring at the ceiling, unable to sleep. Rakhel! Rakhel! Why had they made her do such a vile job? Did they think she was fit for nothing but cleaning up their filth? But at least she'd been gentle with Rakhel, kissed her and clung to her as they walked through the streets. They'd drunk brandy together. Retold the story of the one night when Rakhel had been the best of them all.

And now? There was no *now*. Evgenya had eighteen roubles between her and starvation and not much interest in earning more.

# Extract 10

The Trial of the Sixteen in October 1880 was a model of judicial procedure – the government had learned, planned carefully and conducted the trial with absolute decorum. The sixteen accused included three of the most important figures in the Movement: Shiraev, who had been arrested in Moscow a year before with two suitcases of dynamite, Presnyakov and Kviatkovski. The last two were old friends of Andrey Zhelyabov. The evidence against the accused was provided by Grigory Goldenberg; the prosecution's case was unanswerable. The sixteen were allowed to address the court and their speeches were reported. The prosecutors questioned them with a mix of deliberate courtesy and provocation: the sixteen were given enough rope to hang themselves. They followed no clear line and contradicted each other on endless details. They improvised counter-accusations, became mired in irrelevancies, and exploded in fits of petulance. They made a miserable impression, highlighted at every stage by the correctness of the proceedings. In its sentence the court was lenient, another propaganda victory: fourteen were sentenced to hard labour; two, Presnyakov and Kviatkovski, were sentenced to be hanged. We lost sixteen good people, which was bad enough. But worse was our irreparable loss of public esteem. One small sign of this was the fate of the word *terror.* Hitherto we had freely called ourselves *terrorists*; it had much the same ring as *revolutionary. Terror* was simply the first phase of the revolution. Overnight the word became a term of abuse and the exclusive property of the government. That alone might have told us we were following the wrong path. (*Memoir of the People's Will*, Chapter 8.)

# Chapter 11

## I

Evgenya was hungry. Hunger and the sounds of spring drew her out of her cheerless room and into the streets. St Petersburg rang with the sound of shovels scraping cobbles and flagstones. Pioneers and infantrymen from the city barracks heaped carts with rotting ice, grey snow and the debris of winter and then dumped it all into the canals and the Neva. Winter was almost over.

She wandered aimlessly at first, then she went from gym to gym, trying to pick up a few kopeks but without success. After two days of scrounging, a sandwich-board on the Nevsky Prospekt caught her eye – a new venture on a side-street nearby, a gymnasium for women. She found the place. Originally it had been built as a Turkish bath with a Moorish arcade, exotic windows and vivid patches of blue tile. A long decorative banner, battered by the winter weather, advertised its reopening as a *Gymnasium Exclusively for Ladies.* Evgenya stood in the street watching who went in and out. Fashionable women, she saw, one or two of them dropped off by a carriage and four. Grudgingly she was admitted by the woman at the door and escorted to the owner's office. He was a burly middle-aged man, not unlike Yakub, though better spoken and more prosperous. They were quickly at ease with each other. He had a boxing trainer already, he told her. Even so, he felt her arm muscles through her coat and looked surprised. Maybe she could try out as a sparring partner, he suggested. No pay of course – tips only. And on the strict understanding that she didn't hurt anyone. Evgenya agreed without haggling. Keep things straightforward – she knew that from her time with Yakub. The owner showed her round his gymnasium, open for six months already. There was nothing like it anywhere in Russia, he boasted – only in the best spas in Germany. Physical fitness was the fashion now. Most of his customers were foreign, from embassies and trading houses. But it was early days yet – Russian women would catch up in no time. The most popular sport by far was fencing. Fencing and then archery. Exercise groups ran three or four times a day. Shooting certainly – he'd imported the latest air rifles from Japan. And fighting? He'd been unsure at first, but it was working out better than he'd expected. Not prize-fighting like she was used to, of course – real ladies kept their clothes on. They wanted doe-skin gloves and a leather mask to protect their pretty faces, and they insisted on rules like the Marquis of Queensbury's rules for men: two-minute rounds, a count after every knock-down and a ban on kicking. But after their fashion, the ladies fought. Though there was one thing she had to remember – it was his gymnasium. His. She'd have to do exactly what he told her. If she had a will of her own, best not bring it into the gym – best leave it in the locker room with her street-clothes. She agreed and he introduced her to his boxing trainer, Asya. He told the two women to take off their clothes and put on gloves – he wanted to see what Evgenya could do. Asya was a woman of about thirty. Evgenya guessed from her muscles that she was a fearsome hitter and from her scars that she was sensitive as the wall of a public bath. She had the short, thick neck and flattened features of a real fighter. The two women stepped onto the mat and put up their guard. Evgenya tried a few jabs. Asya, she saw, was sluggish from years of beatings. Her guard was slow – she'd take punches rather than dodge them. Even so, the woman counterpunched with a right hook that would knock your head off if it made contact. After a few minutes the owner had seen enough. He was pleased. Evgenya was clean and lithe, he told her as she put on her shift. Quick and neat as well – his customers would like that. Asya was really too tough for them. And Evgenya was a good looker – she was 'a tempting target' he said. That was a good thing, to be tempting. But – seriously – if she planned to whore around, he didn't want anything like that in his gym, not even in the baths. Evgenya told him she just wanted to fight – and beyond that, she wanted to be left alone. And that meant *alone*, she repeated, looking him straight in the eye. They shook hands. Perhaps he caught the smell of hunger on her breath. He offered to lend her five roubles. There was a tavern nearby – the Last Man Standing. If she mentioned his name, she could eat for thirty kopeks, but she should be back by four to start work.

Sparring with the customers was easy work, letting them land an occasional punch, nudging them harmlessly with her soft gloves. With no dangerous punches to parry, she amused herself practicing the weaving, dodging and ducking that Yakub had taught her. After a while she could fight with her guard loose by her hips – quick, neat, invulnerable. The owner was right: the customers liked that. As soon as they got to know her, most of the women asked her if it was true – that real women fighters went naked? You didn't have to, Evgenya told them, but there were advantages: when you were fighting without gloves, your clothes were just something for the other girl to grab hold. For the same reason, you bobbed your hair. And when you were totally naked, the crowd liked it. They went wild cheering and shouting when you hurt the other girl or she hurt you. It got you so worked up, you went fighting mad. "Why don't you go naked here?" the women sometimes asked her, but Evgenya refused – the owner wouldn't like it. Then one of the women asked the owner directly: why shouldn't the pretty sparring girl go naked? He called Evgenya into his office and talked it over with her – some of his customers might get a thrill from fighting with her like that, or from watching. Nakedness was an old tradition. It didn't have much point when you fought in gloves but it was part of the sport – for women anyway. He assumed she had nothing against it – why should she? She might prefer it? Get better tips anyway – if he understood the way of the world. But, he warned her, naked was naked, and whoring was whoring. There was a room in the Last Man Standing if she wanted to play the trollop. Naked or dressed like the Tsarina, Evgenya said, it made no difference to her. Before long, if she took her clothes off, the traditional ten-kopek tip turned into a rouble, two sometimes if she took a few punches.

When Evgenya wasn't sparring, she trained hard, skipping to keep herself agile, working with dumbbells, hammering at the punchbag. Each day she sparred with Asya for a while, toughening herself against the older woman's fists and sharp knees. Asya took care not to damage Evgenya's face and repeated for her the familiar litany of the prize-fighter: a punch in the kidneys can kill you, so never turn your back on the other girl; a head-butt works best against the eyebrow – the blood trickles down nicely into the other girl's eyes; and when you kick, go for the knees – always the knees. There was much more, but nothing Evgenya hadn't heard ten times already.

Women from the big gym began to drift in. At first they watched, but then, liking what they saw, they wanted to learn. In a small way, Evgenya was a success, though the owner still refused to pay her a wage. Asya was paid, Asya was in charge. She left the work and the tips to her young friend. It was a living for both of them.

After work each evening, Evgenya had a drink or two with Asya in the Last Man Standing and then ate at a tavern near her room. In the streets round the Haymarket, nearly every cellar was a tavern of some sort. Her regular place was Gremov's. The customers were mostly late clerks and early night-watchmen. Streetwalkers ate there too, though not on the prowl for customers. It was a quiet place, cheap and orderly. And so the months went by.

One evening, Evgenya found a note pushed under the door of her room. Vitya would be round at ten – would she be there? She'd known they'd find her. Why couldn't they leave her alone? That's what she wanted – surely they knew that. Sonya had another job for her, that was obvious, and she'd sent Vitya to sound her out. Well, Sonya could fuck off. She'd see Vitya and break with them – all of them. Tonight. She found a pencil and wrote on the back of Vitya's note: '*In Gremov's. Corner of Apraxin Lane*'. On a sudden inspiration, she changed out of her street clothes into the skimpy blouse and skirt she'd worn on the night months before, when she'd given Rakhel the overdose. She still had the make-up, put away in a draw-string bag. Carefully in the shard of mirror-glass on the wall, she whitened her cheeks: white face, red mouth, dark shadows round her eyes. The clothes, the make-up, the broken straw hat with its cheap pins: it brought back the sharp pain of that night, and that was what she wanted – to feel that rage again, to refresh her fury at Sonya. And all the rest of them.

She rolled up the note she'd written, pushed it halfway into the keyhole and went out into the street. The cool air, the noise, the way her thin clothes exposed her to the gaze of every passer-by – it belonged to Rakhel. She found a brightly lit window and stood for a moment with her back against it. The light shone through the clothes, turning her body into an naked silhouette. It was a trick the girls sometimes played, the ones who couldn't face another night of starvation. A man spotted her, well dressed and at his leisure. He crossed the street toward her, eying her up and down. To his bewilderment, she told him to go and piss his pants. Anger was building inside her. This was the life Rakhel had dragged herself out of, seeking refuge with the Movement and all its clap-trap about equality and freedom. Rakhel had risked her life for them, brought on her consumption by digging their tunnel. And in the end? They'd shut her up in a box-room with hardly a window and told their murdering Gypsy to take her somewhere and kill her.

Gremov's was busy. She ordered vodka with pepper. Her stomach was too cramped to eat. She sat with her back to the door. When Vitya came, he could go round the tables looking for her – on his hands and knees for all she cared.

She'd already drunk half a beaker of vodka when she caught sight of Vitya sitting at a long, crowded table. She hadn't seen him come in. He was dressed like a working man. His gaze was fixed on her, intently and, as she thought, with the embers of his old affection. She beckoned him with a little nod. He stood up immediately. She was sitting at a small round table with two chairs. The other chair was empty, but he didn't take it.

"Can we walk?" he asked. "Or would you rather stay here?"

She shrugged and stood up. With a gracious little movement she'd seen so often, he bowed her ahead. Her clothes were a mistake – she felt it at once. She tried to walk so that the swing of her backside wouldn't make her seem ridiculous. Ugly and ridiculous. And the awful make-up! Surely she could send him to hell without turning herself into a clown.

In the street Evgenya stopped. "Well?" she said.

"Evgenya Antonovna," he began, "I… I found your note."

"Yes. You found out where I live."

"Yes. A while ago. And where you work."

"So you know I'm not… Vitya, I'm not a streetwalker."

"I know."

"So why am I dressed like one? Do you know that too?"

He hesitated. "It reminded me…" he began, "… of the morning we went to the Central. To get Rakhel. That was how you looked then."

"Yes," Evgenya said. "Exactly, Rakhel." Her firmness vanished. The name of the dead prostitute faded into a sigh of grief.

"Sonya told me…" Vitya said.

"She told you, did she? Well I hope she didn't tell you her usual pack of lies."

He held out his hands hopelessly.

"I blame you, Vitya. It's your fault, what happened to her. You brought her here. You turned her over to Sonya."

"No," Vitya contradicted. "Rakhel saved my life, and she was damn near buried alive doing it. She saved Anna. They promised to help her. I thought…"

Maybe it was true. "Come back to my room," she said. "I can't walk with you dressed like this."

He offered her his arm uncertainly. She hesitated, but then rested her hand in the crook of his elbow, trying to walk like a down-and-out sister rather than a successful predator. The street was still in twilight, the disturbing grey-white night of early midsummer.

"So Sonya didn't send you? Tonight?"

"No. I wanted to talk to you. Something important."

"I've got something important to say too. And I'm going to say it first."

"Whatever you want," he conceded.

"I'm finished with Sonya," Evgenya struck out. "All of them. What she did to me. Telling me *someone* was in that room and letting me find out it was Rakhel. I had no idea. I walked in, and there she was. Sick and terrified. And I was supposed to take her out and… I think it was unspeakably vile."

"Is that what happened?"

"You think I'm lying?"

He stopped suddenly. She looked at his face. He was struggling. She'd never seen him so close to tears. "Vitya," she said, alarmed. "Is everything alright? With Anna? They haven't…"

"No, it's not Anna. It's you," he said. "Let's not quarrel. You're right. I see now what happened. You know, Sonya promised she'd take care of Rakhel. And I believed her – but in a good way. It's horrible. Poor Rakhel. And making you… that was worse. What's happened to Sonya? Has she gone out of her mind?"

They reached the house where Evgenya had her room. It was a huge building with old apartments split into cheap rooms and rooms divided into even cheaper cubby-holes. No one knew exactly who lived there and the police had no reason to check; the house was a refuge for dead-beats and played-out whores – no one who lived there posed a threat to the Empire.

"Come up," Evgenya said. The walls of the stairwell were filthy. Outside each door broken crockery, dead plants and fouled clothing lay in heaps. Someone had let a skillet of oil catch fire – the pot stood on one of the landings, infesting the air with its acrid smell.

"Not much of a place," Evgenya said, unlocking her door. They went in and Evgenya lit a lamp. She glanced around. Everything was in place. The bed was made with a clean coverlet. She tried to live like a soldier, the way Popov had shown her. "Sit down," she said. Vitya sat on the low bed.

Evgenya folded her arms and looked down at him. "I'm going to change," she said. She took off her cheap dress, folded it, and opened the lid of a small trunk to put it away. She glanced at him. He was looking at her with the same intent tenderness she'd seen in Gremov's. She took a shift from the trunk and pulled it over her head. Then she went to the mirror, wiping off her make-up with a towel. She turned round to look at him. He was still watching her intently. For months she'd made a spectacle of herself, been looked at, stared at, but never once with a hint of affection. And now this. She took his hand. What did she expect of him? What did he want of her? On an impulse, she raised his hand to her lips and began to kiss his fingers.

"What was it you wanted?" she asked him. "You said it was important."

"It is."

"Well, tell me then."

## II

Evgenya went to the gym the next day, tired and dreamy. She worked the long hours, playing the slave, but hugging to herself the whole time what Vitya had told her: Anna had bought the Grishin estate and made it over to her. And she'd bought up the mortgages on the Petersburg apartment. Her lawyers had tracked down the old Grishin debts – all of them – and paid them off. Vitya knew little beyond the bare facts, and of that little Evgenya understood perhaps half, but one thing was clear – she was free, though first there was a mountain of paperwork. The first batch of documents about the Yaroslavl estate had been drawn up by Kreuzotter and Beil and sent to Evgenya's old address for her to sign.

And there was more: Anna's hands were improving. She was planning to return in the autumn – and she was expecting a baby. Vitya's baby. Evgenya went over the conversation in her mind time after time as the work-day dragged on. The news of the baby had startled her into dressing and dragging Vitya out into the street again. They'd walked blindly out toward the Vassilyevsky Island.

"So you love her?" Evgenya had asked, a question more painful than fifty blows.

"Of course," the reply had come, "but only in the same way you do."

"She took you away from me. Why should I love her? And now she feels guilty, so she's paying me off. That's the business with the estate."

"Think again," Vitya had corrected her. "Try for the best explanation, rather than the worst. What would it be?"

"It would be… she's giving me my freedom?"

"That's all – nothing else. And she didn't take me away from you. You said absolutely, finally and definitively you didn't want me."

"I may have said it. But how could you believe I meant it? I said it because…" And then: "Men are so stupid."

"Well, Anna had her doubts."

"But she still married you, and she's having your baby."

"Why does the baby make such a difference? You even put your clothes on when I told you about it."

It was true. She'd been surprised that Vitya noticed. "I was going to have a baby," she'd whispered. "It wasn't yours. Of course not. We never… I don't know whose it was. It's gone now. Anna took it away."

"Yes," he'd said gently. "She told me."

"It would have been eight months old now." She'd shuddered. "I count every month… When I have my period, I count how old the baby would have been."

"I should have realised," Vitya had said. "You should have…"

"…told you?" She'd shaken her head and let go of his arm, remembering. "What for? And anyway, Anna must have understood."

"Anna said… after Popov… she said Popov was the last." There'd been no reproach in his voice – maybe he'd understood about Popov too.

"Yes, he was the last," she'd agreed. Then an imp of mischief had danced in her brain. "After him, just frigging. Popov said don't do it because it weakens you. Doctor Anna, on the other hand, says once a week never hurt anyone. You don't know who to believe, do you."

"Once a week! How do you survive?"

She'd pulled back her fist and landed a stone-hard punch on his shoulder.

"Owww!"

She'd enjoyed his unfeigned pain.

"I assume that means I'm forgiven?" he'd said.

"Amazing!" she'd replied. "You're beginning to understand." Perhaps he was.

He'd put his arm round her shoulder and she'd put hers round his waist. They'd walked arm in arm, more at ease than if they'd been lovers. One by one they'd cleared away years of quarrels and misunderstandings. He'd not given up on the Movement, and slowly it had dawned on her: she had no reason to give up either. Back in her cheerless room, only one problem had remained – he'd married Anna.

The tedious hot day in the gym wore toward evening. A

Thursday. Evgenya was waiting for a little group of friends, Austrians and Russians, who took their exercise together twice a week. One of them was a spiteful red-haired woman of about thirty-five, the wife of a diplomat. She was the only one of the friends who boxed. The others came to watch after their exercises in the big gym. The woman was Hungarian, and Evgenya had nicknamed her 'Lieschen' after a character she'd hated in *The Possessed*. Lieschen always paid Evgenya a rouble to go naked when they fought. If Evgenya let her land a few punches, the tip went up another fifty kopeks. After they'd taken off their gloves at the end of a bout earlier that week, Evgenya had been distracted for a second by the owner showing a new customer round his gym. Seeing her chance, Lieschen had hit Evgenya in the stomach with all her strength. Evgenya remembered the woman's gasp of excited pleasure as the mean blow went home. Clutching herself in pain but swallowing her anger, Evgenya had said a punch like that was worth more than a miserable fifty kopeks. She'd got a rouble. That little triumph had given Lieschen other ideas – she'd give Evgenya a hundred roubles, she said, if she'd let herself be tied to the punchbag and take a real beating. Evgenya had refused with the servile excuse that the owner didn't allow such things. But now she had a plan.

Evgenya heard a babble of women's voices approaching, speaking in German and shrieking at each other's jokes. They were coming from the big gym. She took off her exercise shirt immediately. She'd greet them bare-breasted and subservient, a little thrill for them, as she knew. Lieschen was wearing a new exercise outfit in a crude shade of green, trimmed with white lace. Green. White lace. Lieschen in the story – that was the dress she'd worn when the crowd had murdered her.

"Same girl as usual?" Asya asked the woman.

"*Ja, der köstliche Nackedei,*" Lieschen replied. With an imperious nod, she signalled Evgenya to take off her drawers.

Before she did so, Evgenya showed the woman the deep

bruise just below her ribs where the punch had caught her days before. She saw the woman's eyes light up. "You hurt me," Evgenya said calmly, making herself naked.

"*Ja und?*" the woman replied.

Asya bound Lieschen's hands and laced her gloves for her. Evgenya's hands were already bound. Asya tied her gloves in a second.

Instead of stepping onto the mat, Evgenya went to the big punchbag which hung in a corner of the room. "Is it still on?" she asked ingratiatingly. "The hundred roubles?"

"Now?" Lieschen replied. She said something in German to the other women that evidently amused them.

"In a while," Evgenya said, "when you're nice and hot. Hundred roubles, right? You can hit me anywhere but here," she put her hand over her kidneys, "for as long as you want." Lieschen hadn't understood.

"You're sure?" one of the Russian women asked Evgenya doubtfully. "You want me to translate?"

"Please," Evgenya replied. "You going to watch?"

"It's exciting, something like this," the woman replied, "but…," she dropped her voice, "she really wants to hurt you. She's been talking about it."

"Don't worry. It's my job. Getting hurt."

The woman smiled, though still doubtfully, and translated Evgenya's words into German.

"*Ausgezeichnet,*" Lieschen said. Asya offered her the leather mask. It was an ugly thing and not particularly clean. Lieschen refused: "*Ich glaube nicht, dass das Mädchen mich verletzt,*" she boasted, and then in heavily accented Russian: "She wants her hundred roubles." The friends giggled.

"Ready?" Evgenya asked, as though dreading what lay ahead.

Lieschen licked her lips and followed Evgenya onto the big sparring mat. Evgenya offered herself as an easy target time and again, her face, her belly, her breasts. The woman did her best to strike home, but with a grin Evgenya sidestepped and dodged all her blows. Then, as the Hungarian broke a sweat,

Evgenya took over. A few seconds were enough. Viciously she hit Lieschen in the belly. Evgenya felt the blow go home, the unready muscles caving in. The woman folded like a broken doll. As she fell, Evgenya turned her fist as Popov had shown her. With the heel of her hand, she caught Lieschen under her nose, driving the gristle back onto the bone and the bone back into her skull.

Asya shouted, the women screamed. Evgenya ran to the locker room. She'd laid out her clothes ready. She pulled on her blouse and skirt, and ran barefoot into the street with her shoes in her hand. Ten minutes later she was back in her room, no longer exulting in her shabby triumph but sobbing with relief that her long humiliation was over.


# III


Evgenya looked apprehensively across the street at the door with its peeling paintwork and then up at the windows on the third floor. Her home.

The *droshky* dropped them off in the next street and they walked back to the apartment where they'd lived together for four years. The yardkeeper was not in his room. From the cellar they heard the sounds of a coal shovel. They went down. "We're looking for the Grishins," Vitya said to the old man.

Evgenya stayed in the shadows, and the yardkeeper scarcely glanced in their direction as he worked. "Not here," the old man said. "Gone to Voronezh. Months ago."

"Why?"

"The old lady got some disease. Bright's or something, they called it. Anton Antonovich went with her. Ain't paid for their coal, so I cut off their heat. That's the sort of people they are." The old man spat.

"Don't they have a housekeeper?" Vitya asked.

"Maryanka. Yes, but she's gone."

"Gone?"

"She comes here sometimes. Airs the place, I suppose."

Vitya gave him ten kopeks. "Drink that for me," he said.

Vitya still had his latch-key. Inside the apartment, Evgenya stood a long while by the door. Then she went to the icon stand at the end of the hallway. The icon lamp was out. She stared silently at the blackened silver, icons pierced to let the dark faces of the saints stare out. She fell to her knees, closed her eyes, and began to pray as her mother had taught her. She knew only a handful of prayers which, even as a child, she'd not taken seriously. She opened her eyes again. John the Baptist, who she hazily remembered had been beheaded by a girl called Jezebel, was looking at her with celestial disapproval. She closed her eyes again, immersing herself in the smell and the sounds of the ugly apartment.

Letters were arranged in heaps on the piano. Maryanka's work. There were two heavy packets of papers from Kreuzotter and Beil, one addressed to Evgenya and one to her father. There were three notes that Evgenya recognised instantly – notes she'd written to her mother postmarked in Moscow. From Germany Anna had sent a postcard to Evgenya with anonymous greetings in her tortured left-hand script: *'Thinking of you with great love.'* There was nothing else.

Their next visit, on Vitya's insistence, was to Sonya's apartment. If Evgenya wanted to stay in the Movement, she'd have to make her peace with Sonya. A note would be enough if Sonya wasn't there.

As it happened Sonya was in. She was delighted to see Evgenya and showered her with trivial questions. Evgenya answered easily but gave no hint of her new-found independence. Sonya avoided any mention of Elif or Rakhel, though the two dead women might have been taking tea with them, their presence was so palpable. It was an uneasy conversation.

"And how's your family?" Sonya asked. "Have you been to see them?"

"They're in Voronezh," Evgenya told her. "My mother's taking the waters."

"Nothing serious I hope?" Sonya said.

"No. Nothing serious." Some years before, her mother had shown symptoms of Bright's disease. If the sickness took a turn for the worse, the doctor had said, it could be fatal in a few weeks. But there was no reason to tell that to Sonya.

"Will you go to Voronezh? Get out of Petersburg for the summer?"

"I would if I had the money," Evgenya replied lightly.

"Money's an eternal problem of course, except for the idle rich like Vitya."

Evgenya made no reply. The conversation was going nowhere.

Sonya cleared her throat. "I'm glad you came," she said. "I think I may have a job for you in the autumn. A job, but not in Popov's line," she added quickly.

For a second, Evgenya seemed to hear Rakhel's deathly cough from somewhere deep inside in the apartment. "Whatever you want," she said quietly.

"That's what you always say: 'whatever I want'."

"Is that good or bad?" Evgenya asked with a hint of menace.

"Well, perhaps I might want something that went against the grain – something you didn't like the sound of."

Was Sonya taunting her? The words came dangerously close. "Really?" Evgenya said, beginning to scowl. "That's hard to imagine." She was playing with fire. It wouldn't take much to set her at Sonya's throat.

"We're thinking about a workshop to make dynamite," Sonya said, veering away from a fight. "You'd be very useful."

Evgenya nodded. "Sounds alright," she said. And then: "Think about it, Sonya. *Yes ma'am. No ma'am. Whatever you want ma'am.* You can kick a skivvy around as much as you like, but she'll smash your face in come the revolution."

"Not *my* face I hope," Sonya said with a false laugh.

"Who knows?" Evgenya replied. "There's always work for the Popov's of this world." The sensation came back to her with extraordinary vividness – Lieschen's nose crunching under the heel of her hand. She shuddered. It was evil, what she'd done. Nothing in life would persuade her to do such a thing again. Not even to Sonya.

# IV

Sonya had predicted it all along. Andrey had a plan to blow up the Kammeny Bridge and the Tsar along with it, but it all failed and for the cheapest of reasons – Makar Teterka had no alarm clock and arrived late on the critical morning. With brainless bunglers like Teterka and vapid intellectuals like most of the others, all their schemes were doomed. "I'm beginning to understand why they call us nihilists," she rebuked Andrey, "because we achieve absolutely fucking nothing."

"If you can do better, do it," Andrey retorted.

"I intend to," she said shrewdly.

"It had better be good," Andrey replied, preparing himself to listen.

"I think we've been making the same mistake all along," Sonya began. "We plan for a single event – a single chance, like the train. Instead, we need something that's in place all the time. We just wait for the moment when He comes to us."

"He," Andrey repeated. "With a capital letter as usual."

Sonya shrugged. "His Imperial Highness," she said.

"And what sort of moment are you thinking of?"

"A mine under a street where He goes regularly, once or twice a week maybe. The mine is there all the time. One day when He happens to be on top of it…"

"He changes his route all the time."

"He can't. When He goes to the Manège there are only five possible routes back to the Winter Palace. And since He's always in a hurry…"

"… There are only three."

"Exactly."

"It seems obvious now you say it," Andrey said ruefully. "Have you found a good place?"

"No. I start looking tomorrow."

"Shall I come with you?"

"No. I'm going with the Coalminer. He's picking me up at ten."

"He surprised me, the Coalminer. Staying with us after he won the sweepstake. He's a rich man now."

"It hasn't changed him, as far as I can see. And anyway, would you give up? If you married a fortune?"

"No," Andrey replied, "but I'm a peasant. He's a gentleman."

"Vitya says there are lines in life. You have to decide which side of the line you stand on, and then what you're going to do about it.

"What sort of line?"

"Between freedom and tyranny, for example."

"Fine words. Who does he think he is? Danton?"

"No. Nor Robespierre either. But he'll stick with us to the end. You'll see."

"And Countess Anna? The new bride? What's the spring in her clock?"

"I don't know. She's not like the rest of us. She has plans."

"And we don't?" He shrugged. "And that little cousin of his? Hear any more about her?"

"Gypsy? Vitya took her to Voronezh. Her mother had Bright's disease."

"Had?"

"She died last month. Evgenya missed the funeral."

"Where's she from? Petersburg?"

"Her family has an apartment on the Kurskaya, but her father's disappeared to Italy. Apparently Anna's been rather generous to him."

"I'd like to meet your Gypsy. Two brilliant jobs she did – Elif and that Jewish girl."

"She's the best. What a team she'd have made with Popov!"

"Not much in Popov's line any more. There's only fifty of us left, with all the arrests."

"Fifty! More like fifteen."

# V

Sonya met up with Vitya next morning on the Anchikov Bridge and together they explored the streets around the Sadovaya, looking for a cellar to rent. The area was a jumble of shops and cafés, smart apartments and fashionable tailors. Sonya had a shopping basket over her arm. In a dozen cellars in half a dozen streets she bought a few apples or a small piece of cheese. While she pestered the shopman with questions, Vitya looked at walls and floors and stairs guessing the layout of the drains and what might lie between the cellar and the street. Sonya intended no more than a reconnaissance, but in the Malaya Sadovaya, Little Orchard Street, they struck lucky. A cheese-shop was up for rent with stock, furniture and fittings. The location looked hopeful.

"Moving away?" Vitya asked the shopman.

"It's my rheumatism," he replied, "all day long in this hole in the ground. Damp as a dungeon and cold as an orphanage."

"Looking for somewhere sunnier?"

"Already found it, but first I need a tenant for here."

"Is it your place?"

"Lease. Ten years to run still."

"Well, best of luck," Vitya said cheerily.

"Come on," Sonya scolded him, "we can't stand here chatting all day."

At the top of the stairs Sonya stopped and leaned back against the railing. "Put your arms round me," she whispered. "Pretend you love me."

"Nobody loves you, Sonya," he replied, hugging her. "And nobody ever will."

"Not so tight, you imbecile," she said. "I want to get a

better look at the place."

Next day Yuri Bogdanovich and Anka Yakimova, posing as the cheese-monger Kobozev and his wife, agreed to take the shop. They negotiated the rent down to 250 a quarter and paid a hundred to secure the deal.

Sonya's next problem was dynamite. The explosive ingredient in dynamite is nitroglycerine. Nitro is dangerously unstable. To turn it into dynamite, it is mixed with an inert substance such as clay, sawdust, flour, sugar or charcoal – even horse manure will work. It takes a powerful detonation to make dynamite explode – a big electric jolt, a hefty detonating cap, or the explosion of something volatile like mercury fulminate. Nikolai Kibalchich had been manufacturing nitroglycerine for years. It no longer interested him. The 'donkey work', as he called it, began with glycerine. In Petersburg, Kib bought his glycerine from a candle factory by the river for a few kopeks a litre – usually the factory poured its glycerine straight into the Neva. Turning glycerine into nitroglycerine was not difficult, but it was dangerous. First sulphuric acid and nitric acid were mixed in a glass bath, twice as much sulphuric as nitric, both at full concentration. The combination heated up immediately. When the reaction stopped, the glycerine, thick as syrup, was stirred in. After a while, this mixture separated into two layers – the bottom layer was nitroglycerine. The mixture was poured into a vat of cold water to be washed. The nitroglycerine settled to the bottom, any unused acid and glycerine floated. The water was trapped between. The excess acid was poured off and dumped in the cesspit. After several washings in the cold-water vat, the last traces of acid and glycerine disappeared. The pure nitro was thick and oily. The last of the water was sponged from the nitro in another tank, thickly lined with blotting paper. The work was risky – a spill of acid burnt through clothes, skin and bone in seconds; a spill of nitro could detonate all the explosive in the workshop and demolish half the street. Even a moment of inattention with a tiny quantity, could rip a hand from an arm.

Grisha Isaev had lost his left hand that way. He still worked with Kib, though with only one hand he was slow and clumsy.

When Sonya had first asked Kib to set up a new workshop in Petersburg to make dynamite, he'd refused. Then he'd made conditions: an engineering laboratory where he could do the work that interested him, building the detonator. And he'd need an assistant for the donkey work – if it was a good-looking girl who didn't mind spreading, so much the better. Sonya immediately thought of Evgenya, and this was the job she'd offered her when they'd met in June.

Money was short all round – money for a proper engineering lab was out of the question. Of all Sonya's acquaintances, only Vitya had ready cash – she had no idea how much – and he refused to put up the 4,000 roubles Kib demanded. Finally Vitya offered 2,000, and Kib accepted. Sonya's plan required two kinds of detonator – the one for the big mine was easy. The problem with the big mine was not detonation but size: how big must a mine be to kill a man riding over it in an armoured carriage? Nobody knew. If the carriage was merely stopped or half-wrecked, then hand-bombers would have to move in and finish the job. But a small, safe, portable detonator for the hand-bombs? Nobody had such a thing, not even the army. Yet Sonya, as Kib complained bitterly, demanded this miracle of engineering in three months out of a lab that cost 2,000 roubles. It was next to impossible.

Kib found a workshop in Mursinka, a squalid quarter of smithies, foundries and glassworks on the left bank of the Neva, ten miles from the river mouth. In many ways it was the perfect place. The glassworks and potteries needed chemicals, and local dealers asked no questions when Kib bought the baths or the acids he needed. It was the same with tools and sheet metal – industry was booming and suppliers had sprung up in Mursinka by the dozen.

Sonya had always doubted that Evgenya would move into the workshop when the time came, even though she'd agreed without making difficulties. The work was dirty and dangerous.

A half-mad engineer and his crippled helper – they were no company for a girl like the Gypsy. She'd seen nothing of Evgenya since June and communication through Vitya was tenuous. And so, as Sonya took the early horse-tram for Mursinka one September morning, she hardly expected to see Evgenya when it reached the agreed stop. If the girl failed, there would be consequences – and they'd be unpleasant. To her surprise, however, Evgenya was there, dressed like a factory girl in a cheap dress, a shawl and a headscarf. She was carrying an untidy bundle bound with rope. Sonya scanned her tail – no one followed her on to the tram. Even so the two women sat apart for the two-hour journey. That was the plan.

From the tram-stop just outside Mursinka, Sonya led the way down a street of cheap shops and stalls. Kib's workshop was still half a mile away. The screwmaker who'd run it previously had died of cholera just after Christmas, and Kib had rented the place from his widow. The front of the workshop was boarded up and splashed to the eaves with mud, baked hard by the summer sun.

Sonya rapped at the door – the familiar rhythm. The door opened, and Sonya slipped inside, gesturing Evgenya to follow. The place was black with cutting-oil and smelt of harsh acids. Kib was working at a bench. The man who'd opened the door was Grisha Isaev. Sonya knew him from the Hartmann House – he'd been one of her diggers. She didn't like him – he was slow and complained too much. Now he cut a pitiful figure with his hand blown off. His face was ash grey and his eyes watery, with a fleck of pus in each corner.

Kib looked up from his work.

"This is Evgenya," Sonya said flatly. Kib had never seen her before. He was pleased, as Sonya saw immediately, and she certainly fitted one of his requirements – he'd asked for a good-looking girl and she was one. Whether she'd *spread* for him, as he put it, he'd have to find out for himself. In fact Sonya doubted it – Evgenya was not at all the girl she'd been in Odessa. Kib and Evgenya nodded to each other in the offhand manner of the People's Will and muttered "Hello."

"Grisha, show her where to put her bag," Kib said, "I must strike while the iron is hot." He went back to his bench where a gas-torch hissed venomously. Grisha pushed aside a curtain of burlap that concealed a gap in the wall. Behind the curtain was a room little bigger than a cupboard. There was a flock mattress on the floor. Clothing hung from nails.

"Whose things are these?" Sonya demanded.

"Mine," Grisha replied.

"Get rid of them. She'll want this corner to herself."

"Where shall I put them?" Grisha whined.

"Where the fuck you like," Sonya snapped, "and then go out and buy a clean mattress and some whitewash." She turned back to Kib. "My God!" she exclaimed. "You said you'd have things ready!" She took a quick decision. "Evgenya and I will be back in an hour. If the place is still a pigsty, you've lost her."

Kib shut off the gas-tap and the burner fell silent. "I didn't know a girl was coming," he said. "There's my space under the roof. She can have that. If Grisha sleeps on the floor down here, I'll take his cubby-hole. Go out and get some lunch. I'll sort things out."

"Where's the privy?" Sonya demanded.

"Out the back."

Behind the workshop was a yard full of rusted iron roofing and burdocks. The screwmaker had dug an earth closet in the furthest corner and improvised a roof to keep off the rain. A water pump stood outside the workshop door a few yards away. That explains the cholera, Sonya thought, remembering hundreds of similar yards they'd passed in the quarter. "Drink bottled water if you can get," she said to Evgenya, "or *kvass* if you can't. This is a filthy place. I'm sorry."

"It's not for long," Evgenya replied coldly. "Only one thing…"

Sonya was certain that Evgenya wouldn't last a week in Mursinka. "What?" she asked, expecting Evgenya to negotiate a retreat.

"I saw Kib looking at me."

"Oh… yes. I saw it too."

"Tell him I don't fuck around like I used to. And tell him now. So I'm sure he understands."

"And then you'll stay?"

"Yes," Evgenya agreed quietly. "Why not?"

They went back into the workshop. Kib was giving money to Grisha and telling him what to buy.

"Kib," Sonya said, "Evgenya wants me to say something. So listen."

"What?"

"She hasn't come here to fuck around. Only to work. Understand?"

She watched a dozen replies flicker through Kib's mind: obscene, insolent, obsequious, ironic. What he actually said was: "That's her perfect right. Thank you for saying it so clearly."

That was one lesson you learned in the People's Will, Sonya thought – grace in defeat. Maybe Evgenya would change her mind, but probably not. She was such a strange mixture of strength and weakness. As they all were – that was the great puzzle. Would the sum of their strengths ever be enough for victory? Or would the sum of their weaknesses destroy them? "Are you hungry?" she asked Evgenya.

"No," Evgenya replied, "better if Kib explains my work." Her dark eyes hardened: "You don't have to stay."

# VI

Sonya saw nothing more of them for six weeks. Then, in late October, Kib sent her a telegram: *Baby just about to walk. Come Thursday Okhta ferry station at ten. See his first steps.*

Kib had been working for years on what he called a 'hand grenade'. The problem of size and shape he'd solved – a container flat enough to hide under a pea-jacket or a woman's coat but containing enough explosive to do serious damage. Kib had tried a dozen ideas for the detonator, Sonya knew, but all without success.

Sonya took the ferry to the Okhta side with high expectations. Kib was waiting with the other two. They greeted each other with a nod, Kib offhand as always. They began to walk. Kib explained to Sonya where they were going: a marsh where the Artillery School tested its own explosives. They'd been there half a dozen times already. It was a long walk from the ferry – a mile through dockyards and warehouses and another through gardens and forest. When the artillerymen weren't testing, the marsh was deserted. No cattle grazed there for fear of blind grenades. There was an observation mound and a pit that muffled explosions. Sonya asked if the detonator was ready. Nearly, he told her. It was small enough now to fit into the container. There was a lever held in place by a pin. When the pin was pulled out and the lever released, it took five seconds, sometimes more, for the grenade to go off. The idea was completely new. But was it reliable? That was something they'd know by lunchtime. He'd made four grenades. Evgenya had sewn special pockets into her clothes and Grisha's to hide them. Sonya asked who would set off the grenades. Evgenya, he told her. Kib looked at it this way – the Committee could live without her, but not without him, so she took the risks. How did Evgenya feel about that, Sonya wanted to know. Kib shrugged. Evgenya herself had certainly heard the question, but she couldn't be interrupted – she was too busy listening to Grisha explain his idea for an artificial hand.

They tramped for nearly an hour before Sonya saw the first sign of the testing ground – a barrier in the forest painted red and white and a 'No Entry' warning. When the army was there, Kib told her, the barrier was guarded and warning flags were hoisted every half mile along the track. In a few minutes they'd be out of the pinewoods and she'd see for herself.

"And Evgenya sets them off. That's what you said."

"It's a loud bang, but not dangerous," Kib explained. "If a grenade goes off on the ground, all the force goes upward. If you're lying on the ground, you can't get hurt. It gets dangerous when one of them's a blinder. You can't tell if it's a complete dud or just a slow-spender."

"So what do you do?"

"Evgenya knocks them out with her revolver."

"How will the bombers work?"

"That's what we've been practicing. Evgenya's perfected it. Dump the grenade at his feet. You've got a second or two to flatten yourself on the ground. And I mean *flatten*. Right Evgenya?"

"It's worked so far," Evgenya agreed. Sonya scrutinised the girl. Her appearance had changed – and not for the better. Her black hair was greasy and pulled back in a careless knot behind her head. She had no scarf. She was wearing a brown work-dress she must have found in a second-hand market. It looked as though she'd slept in it for a week, and it was stained with food and cutting oil. Her fingers were burnt with chemicals, the nails black and broken. Yet she seemed blithe enough – at least with Kib and Grisha. Kib treated her as a comrade and listened to her opinions, a compliment he paid no one else in the Movement.

They reached the testing ground. Grisha gave his two grenades to Evgenya and trudged to the top of the look-out mound. The artillerymen had built a windbreak of wooden stakes, and Grisha stood in its shelter, scanning the approaching tracks with a pocket telescope. The others went to the pit. Steps had been hacked into the mud by the soldiers and reinforced with wattles. Evgenya climbed down into the pit and stood waiting.

"Which one's His Imperial Majesty?" she asked, looking up at Kib. The pit was littered with the remnants of dummies blown apart by the army.

"What about that big green one?"

She went to a heap of green rags and kicked at them with her foot. "Won't hold together," she said.

"I'll come down."

In a few minutes they'd tied enough rags to a stake to make

a scarecrow tsar. They found an old stake-hole and stood their victim upright. Sonya watched. She saw Kib go over the mechanism with Evgenya one last time and the girl nod in understanding. Then Evgenya slid the grenade into a special pocket in the front of her skirt. The two of them worked well together, the Engineer and the Gypsy. She wondered if, in the meantime, Kib had talked Evgenya into opening her legs for him. She hoped he had. It might teach the girl a lesson. There was a coldness in Evgenya now that fretted Sonya painfully. But no. She could see from the way they handled the grenade – they weren't lovers.

Kib climbed out of the pit. "I give the word," he said to Sonya. "Watch the Gypsy till she starts her run. Then dive and stay down for the bang. Bits of that canister go everywhere."

Sonya watched Evgenya take her place in the pit, ten paces from the ragged green tsar. The girl looked up at Kib.

"Go," he shouted.

Evgenya slipped the grenade from its pocket. She tugged at the pin as Kib had shown her, but it was stiff and her fingers had trouble gripping it. As soon as it was free, she ran.

"Dive," Kib shouted. Sonya felt his arm round her, dragging her down, away from the pit. The crash as the grenade detonated was not as loud as she'd expected. No shock wave hit them as they lay in the tussocky marsh grass, though the ground trembled. Kib sprang to his feet. And Sonya. Evgenya was lying with her face pressed into the earth two feet from the hole where the tsar had stood. She wasn't moving. The pit was full of dust and smoke. The air stank of explosive.

"It's a fearful shock each time," Kib said. "She's only that far from death." He held his hands two feet apart, then narrowed them a few inches. "From up here it doesn't sound much, but down there it's a hell of a bang."

"Is it?" said Sonya apprehensively, wondering why Evgenya still hadn't moved.

"You'll see when you try," Kib told her cheerfully.

"Me? I'm not going to…"

"Of course you are. You can't ask a girl of nineteen to do something you're scared to do yourself."

"She's been practicing."

Evgenya was heaving herself to her feet, shaking her head. "It's so fucking loud, this new one," she shouted up to Kib. "I better plug my ears."

"Let's check out His Imperial Majesty," Kib said.

The tsar had been shattered completely. "How was the pin?" Kib asked.

"Much tighter than it was in the lab. I cut my finger on it." She showed them her bloody hand.

"Hmmm," Kib said. "Not good."

"You could drill a hole in the end of the pin and put a ring in it," Evgenya suggested.

"Yes," Kib agreed. "As long as there's no way the pin can slip out by accident."

"Well," Evgenya said, "if it did, I wouldn't know much about it, would I? Look what it did to him."

They looked at the bundle of dismembered rags and the shattered pole. "If that was Alexander II, the next one can be Alexander III," Kib said. "Right Sonya? The heir is next on the list once we've fixed the father?"

"Why do you need another bomb?" Sonya asked. "You can see the thing works."

"It has to work three times in a row. Four is better."

"And is it really safe, lying next to it? Like Evgenya?"

"The bang won't hurt you," Evgenya said dismissively, "though on the day you might get a bayonet in the back."

"I've asked Kib to let me try too," Sonya said, knowing Kib wouldn't contradict her. "It isn't fair to ask you to do something I'm not ready to do myself."

Evgenya set off the second grenade much as she'd set off the first, but the third was less successful. She dived too early and, stretching for a few more inches, fell heavily on her shoulder. Sonya heard a sharp scream from the pit – the sound made her shudder with fear and her guts go soft. A second after the scream, the grenade exploded in the pit. Sonya lay on the grass quivering in horror: the girl was dead. They'd sent her into the pit to be torn apart by Kib's infernal machine.

But she wasn't dead. Kib was quickly on his feet, cursing Evgenya for her carelessness. "If you've injured yourself," he was shouting, "how the fuck can we finish the tests?"

"He's dead. Dead. Dead," Evgenya was screaming back, pulling the plugs of chewed cloth out of her ears. "And I'll do Alexander V. Shoulder or no fucking shoulder."

"Is she bad?" Sonya asked quietly, crawling forward on her knees and looking into the pit.

"With ten Evgenyas we could blow off every crowned head in Europe," Kib said. "I love her."

"You love nothing but bombs," Sonya retorted.

Kib decided it was too risky for Sonya to detonate the last grenade. She had no experience and the pins were definitely too tight. Sonya, however, insisted on being in the pit with Evgenya. She'd lie on the ground in front of Alexander V, and Evgenya could dive beside her.

Kib climbed out of the pit, leaving the two women together.

"Is your shoulder bad?" Sonya asked.

"Yes, but don't tell Kib. He hates anything like that."

"I'll look at it afterward. Get you some arnica." Sonya tried to keep her voice steady, but she couldn't.

"You're scared," Evgenya observed. "Some people are."

"Yes," Sonya said. "When I heard you scream… I lost control… of myself."

"Thought I could smell something." The two women looked at each other, and Evgenya laughed. "It happens," she shrugged. "Just think about the next step. Forget tomorrow. That's what Popov told me."

"You've got good nerves. Much better than mine," Sonya admitted.

Evgenya shrugged again, distant, immune to compliment.

"What's going on down there?" Kib shouted. "If you want

to hold a meeting, wait till we're back in town."

Evgenya showed Sonya where to lie and told her to press her face hard into the ground. If the grenade didn't explode, she was to lie still. Nothing else. Just lie still. Sonya lay as Evgenya told her, her face pressed into the infernally foul earth. She heard Evgenya and Kib exchanging insults. Then his: "Go when you're ready." She heard Evgenya's running feet, the thud of the grenade at the feet of the ragged tsar, and Evgenya's cry of pain as her shoulder hit the ground again. Then the earth roared and rose up, and Sonya's body took the devastating shock of the explosion.

On the way back through the woods, Kib and Grisha went ahead. Evgenya was slower, exhausted by the tests and by the pain in her shoulder. Sonya walked with her, silent but wanting to show the girl that they were comrades. When they'd first met, it had been Evgenya's boldness that had appealed to her – a handsome young girl, fearless, shameless and ignorant. Reckless too, foolhardy even. Since then, what Evgenya had learned set her apart from the other women Sonya knew. The girl's recklessness had disappeared – she was familiar now with fear in its ugliest shapes. And her deepest fear? Sonya guessed it was fear of her own nature, of her power – and her willingness – to maim and injure and kill. She had the temper of a fiend. Yet she faced danger – real, immediate danger – with the calm of an icon. And pain? To throw herself on an injured shoulder so that Kib could finish his test! There was something inhuman about it. Inhuman – but enviable. Absolutely to be envied. For the second time in her life, Sonya confessed to herself that her feelings for Evgenya were nothing more complicated than jealousy. And now she urgently wanted to get close to the girl. To burn away the coldness between them.

"I heard about your mother," Sonya said timidly. "I'm so sorry."

"We weren't very close," Evgenya replied, "but still it was… I can't describe it."

"My mother's the only person in the world I'm close to," Sonya said, "much closer than Andrey. She knows… what work I do. In a way, she even knows what I am."

"And what are you?" Evgenya asked, with the careless candour of a child.

"If I could say it in words, I wouldn't need a mother to understand me," Sonya smiled. "I know how I use people, and I know it's wrong. I even lied to you. Just now. I didn't ask Kib if I could go into the pit – he told me I had to. But with my mother…"

"You'll be caught some day, Sonya. We all will. Will she come to you then, your mother? The night before they hang you?"

"Yes, she will," Sonya replied, shocked at Evgenya's callousness. "What a cruel question."

"Don't talk to me about cruel!" Evgenya stopped, confronting Sonya in fury. "You should have told me. That was the cruellest thing I could ever imagine."

"Told you?"

"Don't pretend you don't understand."

Sonya did understand. Now, for the first time, she grasped the barrier Evgenya had built against her. "That it was Rakhel? In that room?" she asked.

"I'd have taken her. I'd have helped her with the morphine. That's what I did anyway. Why in the name of God didn't you tell me?"

"I was afraid," Sonya replied simply. "Like I was afraid back there in the pit. You know how to face things… I can't. Not like you."

"'Tighten the knot on my shawl when we say farewell,' Evgenya quoted. "I thought that meant something."

"It did. It does."

"I want that to be true, Sonya."

"It is."

"And with Rakhel, you were afraid… afraid to tell me? Why? You thought I'd back out? Or were you afraid to be there when I saw… how sick she was?" Evgenya fell silent – she'd understood correctly. Then: "Why do feelings scare you so much, Sonya?"

Sonya made no reply. She knew Evgenya was softening. In her *heart*, she might have said, using the words of the poem, except Sonya knew that the heart was simply a pump.

"Will you look at my shoulder now?" Evgenya asked her. "So we'll know what to buy back in Petersburg."

# VII

Anna had taken Dunyasha, the maid from Evgenya's estate, to Wiesbaden, but no other servants. She had decided to stay in the *Vier Jahreszeiten* rather than set up an apartment with a cook, a footman, housemaids and all the rest of it. The *Jahreszeiten* was in the middle of the town, opposite the opera house and the Kurpark, and only a few steps from Professor Arnson's clinic in the Taunus Strasse. Even in a good hotel, a woman staying on her own is the subject of enquiries and explanations, which the presence of a companion, in particular of a male companion, does much to prevent. Despite Anna's cold looks and austere manner, a stream of would-be acquaintances left cards on her, accosted her in the park, or presented themselves at her table in the dining room. Everyone seemed to know her name, to have heard of her recent marriage, and to be interested in her plans for the next few weeks. If there was anything she needed, she only had to ask. A seat at the opera, a coach-ride to Schlangenbad, advice on choosing a *masseuse* – any problem, no matter how trivial, the Russians of Wiesbaden were ready to resolve for her. She retreated into haughtiness, but it made no difference. On the contrary, it enhanced her reputation as a 'real lady,' or so she gathered from Dunyasha's gossip.

Anna's hands improved immediately the shock therapy began. Nerves, it seemed, could be reactivated and connections re-established. As a neurologist, Anna found the process fascinating. She struck up a friendship with Dr Arnson that soon occupied a welcome part of her day. He was an ugly, pompous man who had never married, but he was passionate about two things in life: the regeneration of nerves and the music of Wagner. He offered her a seat in his box at the opera. Most of the Wiesbaden productions were cheaply staged trivia, but the first Wagner performance of the season, *Tannhäuser*, moved her profoundly. She had seen the opera before, but somehow she'd missed the tragedy of the rebel devoured by the revolution he stirs up and cannot control. This time, from the first subdued E-major chords of the overture, she was swept away. She wept. Arnson saw her tears as proof of the healing power of music. It was clear to him, he told her after she'd attended her third performance of *Tannhäuser*, that more than just her hands needed healing. He, however, approached the human organism through the nervous system, not through the mind. With her hands he could help her. As to the rest, he had no more idea than his cook.

Each day Anna wrote a few lines to Petersburg. Holding a pen in her cramped left hand was painful, sometimes excruciating, but she wrote affectionately, sometimes wistful, always hopeful. At the end of each week she sent it all to Vitya – rarely more than a single page – *poste restante*. He wrote to her with equal affection and a refreshing indelicacy. She was his wife, though *wife* was a word neither of them used. And he wanted her. Quite unexpectedly. She knew she aroused him, deliberately aroused him, with words, more than with caresses. And not with words of love. She'd never doubted the real object of his passion – Evgenya, his cousin. Not Evgenya as she was now – that was Anna's decisive insight – but rather Evgenya as she'd been when he'd first seen her. Evgenya was his cousin, though living *en famille* she'd been as close as a sister. At fourteen she'd been a child. Child and sister – *taboo* for two reasons. Knowing this, Anna stimulated his mind with fantasies where his own imagination refused to go. With words tender and harsh, sometimes obscene but mostly euphemistic, she brought into the open things he remembered but had shut out. Evgenya was untouchable – for years he'd honoured that prohibition – at times imperfectly and always against the cry of his real being. Now, veil by veil, Anna lovingly exposed his passion, put it into words and faced it with him. The intensity of her language implied, in a way, that she shared it. In her wisdom, Anna freed him to love his cousin. She knew that her own body was a surrogate, eager perhaps and responsive – but a surrogate. For her it was enough. In fact it was far more than she'd anticipated. And now? The slip of a girl her husband had loved no longer existed. He'd offered to marry the stranger who'd replaced her, but the stranger had refused – insincerely refused, Anna guessed, but a *no* was a *no*. And so Anna had married him, not for the sake of happiness, though, oddly perhaps, happiness had been the result. She understood too that this promiscuous love affair with her own husband had contributed a great deal to her recovery. Despite her hands, he wanted her, he found her beautiful. In his letters he told her so in the language of a mining engineer, identifying contours and conjunctions that might have been better left to a poet. But no, she decided finally, Vitya's way was best: unfeigned, unpolished and obsessive. No wonder Evgenya loved him.

In the less explicit parts of his letters, Vitya resurrected Tobik from their first excursion to the Drentelns and gave him a companion, Lyuba. The dogs, Anna quickly understood, were Andrey Zhelyabov and Sonya – from their canine adventures, she unravelled much of what was happening to the Movement in Russia.

Though she enjoyed remembering her weeks with Vitya, Anna's mind was hostage to the future. As soon as she was certain that she was pregnant, she had herself examined by a Ukrainian professor, a gynaecologist. He was taking the waters in Wiesbaden with his wife and staying, like Anna herself, in the *Vier Jahreszeiten*. Alexey Alexeyevich saw no reason why the baby shouldn't be healthy – Anna was somewhat too skinny, and she should take care to eat well. Her breasts were, to use his word, 'opulent'. He assumed she'd use a wet-nurse. If not, she might find herself 'somewhat less shapely' afterward. And she was, of course, over thirty which was late for a first child. On the other hand, thirty wasn't forty – with luck there should be no complications. After the examination, Anna sent Vitya an immediate note, blurred with shameless tears.

At about this time, it became obvious to her and to Arnson that the improvement to her hands would go no further. She could function: eat, bath, attend to her personal needs, write a little. A glove maker in the Wilhelm Strasse made her special gloves that she could take on and off without help. She couldn't tie knots or fasten tight buttons, but together with a dressmaker she invented hooks and buckles at least for her simple clothes. For a walk in the Kurpark or a *grande toilette* for the opera of course, Dunyasha dressed her, and a *coiffeuse* came in to fix her hair.

With Arnson's treatment finished, Anna had no reason to stay in Germany. Unfortunately, as long as her passport showed her as Anna Petrovna Shestakova, returning to Russia was impossible – whatever Rakhel had or had not told the police, Anna would be picked up at the border for certain. Vitya had told her in the usual cryptic way that he was arranging new papers for her to cross the border back into Russia. How and when the papers would arrive, he didn't know. Anna waited. She pressed him a little – whatever happened, she wrote, her baby would not be born in Germany.

Early in July, a shabby young woman of about twenty-five approached Anna as she walked aimlessly though the Kurpark with Dunyasha. Anna was well used to the flicker of eyes across her face, seeking recognition or acknowledgement. She gave neither.

"*Entschuldigen Sie*," the woman said with a strong Russian accent.

Anna glanced at her icily.

"Lyuba sent me." Lyuba was Tobik's canine friend – Sonya.

Anna allowed herself to smile, as though a beggar had asked for alms at an opportune moment. "You have something for me?"

"Yes," the woman replied.

"Dunyasha! Give her fifty *pfennigs*. She looks hungry."

Fussily Dunyasha gave the woman the coin and took from her a small package – the long-awaited papers.

"Where are you staying?" Anna asked coldly.

"Hotel St Petersburg. In the Museum Strasse."

Anna nodded. "Come Dunyasha," she said, and they passed on toward the English church.

That afternoon, Dunyasha was sent to the Petersburg Hotel. She waited in the lobby until she spotted the stranger from the Kurpark. She took her back to the *Vier Jahreszeiten*, where Anna learned from the gossip of her new friend that the Jewish prostitute Rakhel had been executed and that someone called the Gypsy had been the executioner. Rakhel dead – Evgenya following in the steps of the monstrous Popov. The news chilled Anna, and she sent the stranger packing before she revealed more horrors.

Her new papers meant that Anna could return immediately to Russia. When she told Dunyasha to begin packing, however, the old woman fell into embarrassed silence. The truth emerged slowly. Anna had been generous to Dunyasha. During the months they'd been together, Dunyasha had accumulated a sum of money, a pittance by Anna's standards, but enough to make Dunyasha attractive to one of the waiters at the *Vier Jahreszeiten*, a Lett who planned to open a tavern in the Rhein Strasse. The Lett had offered to marry her, Dunyasha explained, if Anna had no objections.

Anna had objections and they were serious – she couldn't travel without a maid, and for the journey to Petersburg she couldn't take on a maid she didn't know and didn't trust. Dunyasha shrugged – she liked the Lett, she liked the idea of the tavern and servants hadn't been serfs for twenty years. But if Her Honour insisted... Anna did not insist. She asked

Dunyasha how much she'd saved, and doubled it. The word *serf* had been well chosen. Like many maids, Dunyasha had come to understand her mistress better than her mistress understood herself.

The news of Rakhel's death, the thought of an exhausting trip and now the loss of Dunyasha all poisoned Anna's mood. Sitting gloomily at dinner, she saw Alexey Alexeyevich enter the dining room with his wife on his arm. He smiled at her with distant intimacy, walking the same tightrope that every gynaecologist must walk who has recently examined a society lady. His wife, however, tugged at his arm – she wanted to be introduced to the celebrated heiress who was, as she'd gathered from her husband, one of his patients. Anna always disliked gossip with nobodies, but it was impossible to refuse – she did her best to smile at the approaching couple, though she knew she looked glum and distant.

"Anything wrong?" the professor asked.

"My maid's given notice," Anna remarked. She smiled up at the woman. "This must be your excellent wife."

Introductions were made.

"How long are you staying here?" the professor's wife asked. "I'm sure there are maids to be found."

"In a few days I'm going back to Russia," Anna replied. "It's always difficult to find a woman who suits." Of the three subjects women generally talked about – clothes, children, and problems with servants – Anna resorted to the last two only in desperation.

"Then…" The professor looked at his wife. "Perhaps Anna Petrovna could travel with us?" He turned back to Anna: "My wife has a maid, of course, and we have a man for the luggage."

So it was, as she wrote to Vitya, that Anna began her journey back to Russia in mid-October 'in the best possible company for a pregnant woman.' She was just beginning her seventh month. Good as the company might be, she nevertheless parted from it unexpectedly in Warsaw, when a note in Anna's clumsy and easily faked writing was delivered to the professor's hotel room: *Going no further. Thank you for your help.* With that, Anna disappeared into the custody of the MVD.

# Extract 11

In the autumn of 1880, the People's Will gathered its strength for a last desperate attack on Alexander II. The end was near – that was obvious to all of us. The arrests through the summer of 1880 cost us many old campaigners. Others deserted – emigrated, attached themselves to different causes, went into hiding. Why were there no recruits to fill the gaps?

Radical politics was still the fashion among educated young people. However, the *frisson* of risking everything for one's principles could be achieved more or less painlessly by attending a debating circle or a reading group. We did find recruits, but many of them were girls, disturbed, violent and attracted by the role played by women in the People's Will. Vera Zasulich, Sofya Perovskaya – those were their idols. The girls that we recruited, and their rather less fanatical boyfriends, made poor conspirators: they lacked a sense of time, an instinct for obedience, or the least talent for self-concealment. As a terrorist organisation, the People's Will was close to the end.

Our final plan, when you look at it today, betrays a mixture of conspiratorial genius and political despair. Sofya Perovskaya found a cellar shop for rent on the Malaya Sadovaya. It was well sited. The shop door was at the foot of a staircase that led down from the sidewalk, well out of the yardkeeper's view. When the

Tsar went from the Winter Palace to the parade ground, as he did several times a week, his carriage often passed the door. A tunnel from the cellar to the middle of the street would be seven yards long – no more. It was the perfect location for a mine. The mine would smash the carriage then bombers would move in: fifteen bombers were planned at one stage. One by one the bombers would force their way through the crowd and hurl – each of them – a grenade at the Tsar's feet. In the ever-increasing chaos, one of them would kill him. That, as I recall it, was the plan. (*Memoir of the People's Will*, Chapter 11.)

# Chapter 12

## I

Evgenya was to bear the bad news – the workshop had run out of money, and Kib had no more credit with the acid suppliers or anyone else. On 26th October, he sent Evgenya into Petersburg to talk to Sonya. The last horse-tram left Mursinka at six in the evening, and it was ten before Evgenya arrived at the cheese-shop on the Malaya Sadovaya. Sonya wasn't there, but Vitya and Vadim, Sonya's only recruit during the last few months, were still busy. Each night they boarded up the entrance to the foul-smelling tunnel.

"How much money does Kib need?" Vitya asked her. "To finish?"

Vadim was working at the boards slowly and quietly, listening to their conversation.

"500," Evgenya shrugged. "So he says."

"300 then. When will everything be ready?"

"Middle of December. But I'll have the nitro done in a week – if Kib gets the acid. After that I don't have a job."

"Walk with me," Vitya said urgently, lowering his voice. Then louder: "I have to go to the *poste restante*."

Evgenya wasn't sure what he meant – the *poste restante* wasn't open on Sunday evening. She sensed Vadim becoming suddenly more intent.

By the time they reached the street, Evgenya had guessed the problem. "Anna?" she asked.

"She's on her way to Kiev. I've had no proper word from her for two weeks. Just a postcard from Berlin. I don't know what's going on."

Evgenya glanced behind them. Vadim was leaving the shop, following them it seemed.

Vitya told her about the telegram he'd received from Wiesbaden on 12th: *Your package ships to Kiev tomorrow via Warsaw. Final destination Drushkino.* Anna had an estate in Drushkino, Vitya explained, near his own place. Anna planned to bring a doctor from Kiev and have her baby there.

"Why?"

Vitya hesitated. "Sentimental reasons," he hinted, looking at her uncertainly. She understood the look. It was many months now since she'd told him about her own baby – the aborted child, she knew, weighed almost as heavily with him as with her.

They hurried through the empty streets toward the main post office on the Poshtamtskaya. Vadim still trailed them. As they walked, Vitya told her all he knew about Anna's last days in Wiesbaden.

"Would Kib spare you for a day or two if I gave him the whole 500?" he suggested. "You could go to Kiev. Find this Alexey Alexeyevich. See what you can find out."

"Why can't you go? At least the professor will know who you are."

"The tunnel's turning into a disaster," he told her, "nothing but quarrels. I can't leave now. And the cheese-shop… anyone can see it's not a shop at all. No stock. Nothing. You were there just now. What did you think?"

"I think… I think Anna's right. Even if this latest mine works, there's nothing planned for afterwards. We're…"

"… like a gang of foolish virgins."

"No oil in our lamps," she agreed. "But Kib always says: 'We blow up the building. Someone else can decide what goes in its place'."

"Is that enough? For you?"

"No," Evgenya said. "I've been thinking over what Anna showed us. All those guns. She's right, isn't she?"

"That's one reason we have to find her," Vitya agreed. "You and me."

They reached the *poste restante* with a little show of frustration that they'd forgotten it was closed. They made quick arrangements for the next day and parted company. Vadim followed Vitya. Evgenya went back to the cheese-shop and slept there overnight. Next morning she bought clothes and a second-class ticket for the journey to Kiev, while Vitya took the money to Kib in Mursinka.

In Kiev, Evgenya hunted for a professor of gynaecology named Alexey Alexeyevich. There was only one. He showed her the note Anna had sent to his room in Warsaw – he knew no more and there had been no time to make enquiries. He let her make a copy of the note. He knew about the postcard from Berlin – the Victory Column. Anna had asked him to buy the stamp and post the card for her. Yes, Anna had seemed nervous at the border. No, she'd said nothing about a change of plan. Yes, for a woman seven months pregnant, she'd held up well under the strains of the journey.

On 4th November when Evgenya got back to St Petersburg with her meagre budget of news, she found anger and disarray. Presnyakov and Kviatkovski, who'd been sentenced to death after the summer round-up of revolutionaries, had been hanged that morning. That may have been the reason Sonya was so furious about Evgenya going to Kiev "without permission." Vitya argued back that he'd given Kib 500 roubles "without permission" and that if Sonya complained about the one thing, she ought to complain about both. The tunnellers took sides vociferously. They were weary and frustrated. Work on the tunnel was stalled because they'd hit a main sewer between the cheese-shop and the street. Some blamed Vitya for bad planning. Others retorted that nobody, not even the City Council, knew where the sewers ran, or had collapsed, under the city.

Indirectly Evgenya's return triggered yet another quarrel. With nothing to be learned in Kiev, Vitya demanded that the Committee find out if Anna had been arrested. Sonya angrily reminded him that the last time they'd helped Anna, it had cost them the Hangman. She wasn't prepared for more sacrifices on behalf of someone who'd given up the *Narodnaya Volya* to have a baby. In a fit of temper she called it a 'fucking baby', which did nothing to conciliate Vitya.

It took Andrey many hours to calm them down. The Committee would find out what it could from the Ferret. And Vitya would find a way round the main sewer.

The sewer problem was a huge wooden pipe that ran under the street. The top of the pipe was too near the surface to risk going over it, and the underside sat in swamp water. The sewage pipe had never been watertight. It stank of every pollution, sickness and rotten thing in the city. For fear of typhoid, no one wanted to work in the tunnel, and the cheese-shop reeked of sewage.

After Andrey had brokered the peace, Vitya bought a heavy saw from a tool maker and sections of wooden pipe big enough to crawl through from a cooper's yard. It took a night and a day of sawing, cutting and heaving pipe under Stygian conditions before the sewer was bridged and the ends of the new cross-pipe were sealed with mortar and window-putty. Now that they were working again, no one shirked the nauseating duty – hatchets were buried, though not deep. Tunnelling could start again.

Mikhailov and the Ferret met many times before there was fresh news of Anna. At first all the Ferret could find was an old file on Anna Shestakova and a new one on Viktorya Rakovskaya. The last entry in Anna's file dated back to March – it was permission for her to travel to Wiesbaden. At a slightly later date, in Viktorya's file, he found the muddled information Rakhel had given her interrogators and a note 'Cross-check Shestakova.' Not until mid-December, when Anna was moved from Warsaw, did the Ferret see the new, secret, file that had been opened on her. Anna, it appeared, had not crossed into the Russian Empire at the Polish-German border under the name in her forged papers, but as Anna, Countess Shestakova. Before the train reached Warsaw, an order for her detention had been issued, an 'administrative order', which meant that no reason for arrest was required, and none had been given. The police had arrested her in her hotel in Warsaw. She'd offered no resistance. The arresting officer had ordered the prisoner to write a note to Professor N, her travelling companion. A medical inspection had shown that she was pregnant and therefore unfit, according to prison guidelines, to travel. A stillborn, premature baby had been delivered in the prison hospital in Warsaw. After that Anna had been moved to the Schlusselburg.

The Schlusselburg Fortress was like no other in the Empire. It was built on the banks of Lake Ladoga, thirty miles east of Petersburg, fifty miles by river steamer. Only dangerous prisoners were kept there, nearly all of them in isolation. The most famous was Sergey Nechaev, lingering there half alive, seven years into a sentence for murder. No one had ever escaped from the Schlusselburg, and few survived the dropsy, the hepatitis and the dysentery which flourished in the filthy cells. Of those who survived, many were insane when they were released. It was here they'd sent Anna.

## II

Evgenya hurried toward Sazikov's. The horse-tram from Mursinka had derailed three times, and she was late. The note had come from Vitya through Grisha: *one slide*. The brevity, the ambiguity, were a warning – from now on she'd have to be as wary of the Committee as she was of the police.

There was no ice-slide outside Sazikov's until January, but she was sure Vitya would be at the site at one o'clock. It was nearly three, dusk already, foggy and cold. He was still there, dressed in the coat he'd worn when he'd lived with her family – he must have gone back to the apartment on the Kurskaya. He saw her. They passed each other without a sign and then continued, walking in opposite directions, checking each other for a tail. She headed for the gym where she'd worked in the summer, knowing he would follow.

She stopped on the Anichkov Bridge, lounging against the balustrade. She glanced at Vitya as he approached. He looked tired and dispirited. She smiled, but he made no response.

He stood next to her, gazing down at the cat-ice on the Fontanka Canal. "They've taken her to the Schlusselburg," he said.

"And the baby?"

"Stillborn. In prison."

She heard the tremor in his voice. She took his hand – there was no strength left in him. Anna's dead baby was his child too. The shaft of grief that pierced him, pierced Evgenya just as painfully. She took him in her arms, there on the bridge, and held him to her. Perhaps he'd take from her the strength he needed. He embraced her softly, and she felt the sobs that racked him. Defiantly she choked back her own pain – for the next few moments she'd have to think for them both. She led him away from the bridge and past the handsome old gym where she'd worked, heading for the Last Man Standing. She'd been there often with Asya, and she'd been happy to see the last of the place. There was a shabby room at the back that could be rented by the half-hour. The prostitutes who worked under the Moorish arcade often used it. Evgenya nodded familiarly to the woman behind the bar, gave her fifty kopeks and pulled aside the curtain that screened the room. There was a mattress on the brick floor and a wooden chair. Otherwise the room was empty. She led Vitya by the hand and made him sit on the chair.

The bar woman put her head round the curtain: "If he wants a clean sheet, Genya..."

"Rouble extra. I know," Evgenya replied. "Not sure he can raise it tonight – see what I can do though."

"Nice-looking," the woman cackled. "F'you need any help."

"I'll call you," Evgenya said, kneeling between Vitya's legs.

As soon as the woman had gone, Evgenya sat on mattress. "Sorry about this," she said, "but I had to get you off the street."

Vitya shook his head. "You're a miracle," he said and sat down lethargically on the mattress beside her.

"Tell me what happened," she whispered, putting her arms round him, trying to give him strength.

He told her what he knew. "Sonya says Anna will talk now – and she knows enough to destroy everything. They're scared as crayfish in a cauldron."

"Anna won't talk," Evgenya replied staunchly. "She'd bite her tongue out first."

"Let her talk," Vitya said. "They're worthless. The whole pack of them put together. If talk will save her…"

"She can't. It's not in her."

"But what are we going to do?" Vitya began to moan. "The Schlusselburg. How can they take her there after she just lost a baby?"

"Vitya. I'm going to say something. About the baby. It may help, or it may make it worse."

He nodded.

"We talked about this, me and Anna. When she took my baby away. Rather than let a baby be born in prison…"

He touched her hand. "I thought of that too. You think she decided?…"

"Yes."

The curtain twitched. They looked up. The woman's head peeped in. "All alright?" she asked.

Evgenya stood up and went to the curtain. She whispered something to the woman who disappeared with a cackle.

"Vitya," Evgenya began on a new tack, "you're her husband. Doesn't that give you some rights? To ask where she is?"

"You think I should talk to Kreuzotter?" he said hopelessly.

"Why not?"

"He's on the side of the estate. Not Anna's. Not mine. Just the money."

"He'll do his best for her."

"For her, no. If she's a criminal all her money is forfeit to the Tsar, even the entailed parts."

"But you married her. Doesn't that change anything?"

"There's only one way for Kreuzotter to protect the estate – if Anna's uncle proves she was totally insane when she married me. Then he inherits. Anna explained it to me. I can't remember the details. But Kreuzotter doesn't have much choice, that's the line he'll take."

"Then another lawyer."

"I thought about that too. Maybe Fanarin?"

"Yes. He's famous. Will you go to Fanarin? Tomorrow? Vitya, we have to do something." She sat down again beside him on the mattress.

"You know," Vitya said, "in all of this, you're the only one who's on her side. Apart from me."

"Then we can't lose," she replied. "Can we, Cousin?" She took his hand. "As long as you buck up a bit."

She felt him squeeze her hand. "But you know what scares me most?" he said.

"Sonya? Andrey?"

"Yes. They want her dead. Now."

"Then…" Evgenya reflected. "Listen, Vitya, we'd better part company. Play-act a bit. I hate you. You hate me. You want Anna free. I agree with Sonya – I want her dead."

"Yes," Vitya saw the point immediately. "You go with Sonya. Me against her. So we've quarrelled again. And what about this time?"

"About Anna. What else? She stole you from me, and now you've come whining round me for help. You evil bastard."

"Exactly," Vitya said. "Not only credible, but more or less true."

"No," Evgenya replied. "I'm helping Anna, because…" She fell silent, a long declaratory silence which brought her closer to Vitya than she'd ever been before. He needed her. He needed her because, in a way and for a while, she was the stronger and more resourceful.

"If we play that game with Sonya, we'll still need to stay in touch," Vitya said at length, submitting the question to her judgement.

Evgenya glanced round the cheerless room. "Here?"

He followed her glance. "Horrible place. And that nosey woman, she knew your name."

"I used to come here after work. Drinking with Asya. She wanted me to come in here – so we could frig each other."

"Did you?"

"None of your business."

"But did you?"

"No – not even with the clean sheet."

Vitya punched her on the shoulder. "You're hopeless," he said.

"So," Evgenya picked up. "Let's use our nosey friend – Pulcheria she's called – as our letterbox. We can leave notes with her and come by every day or two to collect. You come about this time. I'll come earlier – so we don't meet by accident."

"And emergencies?" Vitya asked. "I'll be mostly in the cheese-shop. You go there, and if either of us gives a signal, we meet here as soon as possible afterward."

"What signal?" she asked. "Maybe we say a word… something quite normal? How about *cheese*?"

Vitya hugged her. "You're so crafty," he said, "you should join the Movement."

# III

Evgenya read Vitya's first note with surprise. It had taken him four days to see the great Fanarin. The visit lasted ten minutes and produced only an appointment for the following Monday. Fanarin had asked him to bring along a relative of his wife's, preferably female. A petition, if one were appropriate, could then come from the family and not from the 'inconsolable husband'. Fanarin's words apparently. Evgenya was now a cousin of Anna's by marriage – she'd have to make her excuses to Sonya and go to the meeting.

Fanarin's study was austere and underheated. The advocate waved them to sit down, completing notes on his previous client with a scratching, busy pen. He listened to the details of Vitya's story with a professional frown. When Vitya was finished, he asked to see a notarised copy of his marriage certificate, and Vitya laid it on the wide desk, inlaid with simple green leather. The advocate nodded shrewdly as he studied the names on the paper.

"And the property?" he asked. "It was a complicated probate when her father died – you still hear it talked about. She was awarded absolute possession as I recall."

Vitya nodded: "Yes she was."

"And was there a renunciation? When you married? Or a transfer?"

"Renunciation," Vitya replied. "I have no rights. She even kept her own name."

"That's Kreuzotter for you," the lawyer agreed. "Keep everything in the family. But a monthly…?"

"… 10,000."

"Handsome," the lawyer commented, making a note. "It means you can probably afford my fee." He laughed agreeably – the most important issue had evidently been resolved. "Now," he continued, his face suddenly grave, "your wife's a prisoner, you say?"

"As far as I know."

"Do you have reason to be certain? Or reason to doubt?"

"Reason to be certain," Vitya said.

"I imagine the charge, if one is ever made, would be political?"

"I assume so," Vitya replied.

"She is, of course, innocent."

Evgenya stared at the advocate's blotched, unhealthy skin, amazed at his callous detachment and at the nimble accuracy of his mind.

"Please answer," Fanarin said. "If I am to act for you, I must have an assurance that your wife is innocent."

"If I don't know the charge," Vitya said, "how can I say if she's innocent?"

"You have reason to believe she's being held in the Schlusselburg, you told me."

"Yes."

"Then the charge will probably be treason, conspiracy to overthrow the state, conspiracy to murder a member of the government, or something equally serious. Can I assume she's innocent?"

Vitya said nothing.

The lawyer sat back on his chair and gazed at the fine stucco cornice. "Can I assume she would *plead* innocent if she were charged?"

"You can act on that assumption," Vitya said.

"Excellent my dear fellow," said the advocate, making a quick note. "Now – you wish me to act in the matter of the detention, while Kreuzotter and Beil continue to act for the property? Shall we act together or separately?"

"Separately."

"Yes," Fanarin agreed. "The quicker your wife can be separated from the property, the safer it is from confiscation."

"Confiscation? By the government? But she has to be guilty of something before they confiscate, doesn't she?"

"A quick trial and a long appeal afterward. Confiscate first, ask questions later. That's how they'll seize the Shestakov millions."

"Oh," Vitya said.

"Oh, indeed. And a related question – if an attempt were made to prove your wife insane, what direction do you imagine it might take?"

"I don't think she's mad."

"No, no. For once you miss the point of my question," Fanarin objected reproachfully. "What might be said in support of an application for a certificate of insanity?"

"She's the sanest person I know," Evgenya chipped in.

"Ah!" Fanarin exclaimed. "How touching! Touching and valuable." He made a note. "And how exactly are you related to Anna Petrovna?"

"I'm a cousin of Viktor Pavlovich. So I'm her cousin too."

Fanarin looked disappointed. "Your name?"

She told him and he made a note. "Distant," the lawyer said, "but... still perhaps usable." He put a question mark against Evgenya's name. "And the insanity petition? I would imagine her uncle is preparing to make one."

"She waited all those years and finally picked on me to marry," Vitya replied. "I believe that's held against her. And she withdrew somewhat from society to pursue agriculture. She has... liberal opinions on most matters."

"All regrettable perhaps, from a certain perspective, but all falling short of insanity. Did she, perhaps, indulge in opium smoking or excessive drinking? Was she sexually deviant, for example with animals or children? Did she have an inclination for members of her own sex? Did she seek gratification through whipping? Or other extreme forms of self-denial? Was she a religious fanatic? Was she a member of any extreme revolutionary organisation? And if so, is there the possibility that any of this could be proved?"

Evgenya's mind went back to the apartment on the Pokrovka and to the police who'd questioned her. Alcohol and morphine, she'd admitted on Anna's behalf. A taste for girls, she'd denied, though not forcefully. If it was all in Anna's file...

"Nothing like that," Vitya said. "Nothing that isn't perfectly common in her social class."

"Fortunately for her social class, it's not facing dispossession on the grounds of insanity. At least, not yet."

"Not yet," Vitya repeated. "You think the time will come?"

"If it does," Fanarin remarked, "I hope I shall be acting for the prosecution and not for the defence." He paused for Vitya to answer his questions about Anna's sanity more fully – hearing nothing more, he moved on.

"Now, the petition as to whereabouts. We can't go for *habeas corpus* because officially we have not been informed that Anna Petrovna is in custody, and we cannot reveal the source of our information. Is that correct?"

Evgenya was startled again at how little they had to explain to Fanarin – he saw straight through everybody and everything.

"Correct," Vitya agreed. "But I didn't know we had *habeas corpus* in Russia."

"In the English form no, but we have our equivalent. After all, Russia is a civilised country. What Kreuzotter and Beil would call in their native German, a *Rechtsstaat*." Fanarin was warming to the discussion now – he sat back in his chair ready to deliver a lecture on comparative law to the young man with 10,000 a month sitting captive in front of him.

"*Recht*... whatever? Is that the petition?" Evgenya asked naively. She saw Vitya nod – they should be talking about the petition.

"Ah yes, the petition," Fanarin said leaning forward again. "Ideally we must keep Viktor Pavlovich's name out of it as long as possible. A petition to the Ministry of Justice to reveal Anna Petrovna's whereabouts, if known to them, can be made by any relative. Evgenya Antonovna? Might we use your name?"

"If it helps get her back," Evgenya replied, "anything."


## II


Sonya eyed Vitya doubtfully. "Where were you?" she demanded.

"I told you. At the lawyer's. It took longer than I thought."

"And what did he tell you?"

"Nothing new."

"I doubt you'd tell *me* if she'd sprouted wings and flown to America."

"Sonya! You think she'd be better off dead. You've said so often enough. What Fanarin told me is neither here nor there."

"And where's the Gypsy?"

"How should I know?"

"She disappears at the same time you do. It makes me nervous."

"I didn't disappear. I went to Fanarin's. If Vadim knew his job, he'd have told you."

"You think I had Vadim tail you?"

"Sonya! For fuck's sake! When I left here, he was following me. When I got to Fanarin's, he'd lost me. If you didn't send him, who did?"

"He didn't lose you. You shook him off. Why?"

Frolenko crawled out of the tunnel. "You two at it again?" he said. "Vitya, get changed, can you? We've hit something and we don't know what it is."

"What sort of thing?"

"Masonry."

"Be with you," Vitya said, and went into the Kobozev's bedroom to change into his tunnelling clothes.

"Ease up on him," Frolenko said when Vitya was gone. "We can't finish without him."

"I know," Sonya groaned, "but ever since we lost the Guardian, I just can't…"

Three weeks before, the Guardian had been arrested – a stupid affair. The Committee had written a pamphlet promising vengeance for Presnyakov and Kviatkovski, who'd been hanged a few weeks earlier. The pamphlet was to have photographs. For photographs they needed prints and these had to be made in a print-shop. The print-maker had recognised the faces of the two executed men and alerted the police. When the Guardian had collected the prints, the MVD had picked him up. As easy as that. Terminal incompetence. And the Guardian knew more about the *Narodnaya Volya* than anyone else. Would he talk? Maybe, maybe not. Just before his arrest, the Guardian had warned her not to trust Vitya – Vitya's loyalties were split between the Movement and Anna. There was a chance that he'd make a deal with the Ministry to buy Anna's freedom. She'd defended Vitya fiercely, but, to her despair, the seed of doubt was sown. If she couldn't trust Vitya, then who? Andrey? Impossible. He hardly ever came to their apartment any more. Where was he? What was he doing? Off with some girl somewhere. How she hated it all! The only thing that had gone right was the dynamite. The Gypsy had finished it and moved out of the workshop. She'd made enough dynamite to blow the Winter Palace into the Baltic.

"Any idea who's taking over security?" Frolenko asked casually.

"Andrey thinks Trigony could do it," she said. "They're old friends."

"Milord? The fancy lawyer?"

"I don't know," Sonya moaned. "Who else have we got?"

Vitya came out of the bedroom just as Evgenya came down the stairs into the cheese-shop. A quick look of mutual reproach and they turned their backs on each other. Vitya disappeared into the tunnel without another word.

"Headache better?" Sonya asked unsympathetically.

"No," Evgenya replied. "Worse."

"Lie down then."

"Where? I've just been chucked out of my new room. Have to be gone by tonight."

"Why?"

"Madame thinks she caught Monsieur eying me up."

"Was he?"

"I certainly hope so."

"That's the problem with respectable rooms. What'll you do now?"

"Move in with you and Andrey, I suppose," Evgenya shrugged. If she had to cosy up to Sonya, what better way than to move in with her.

"Andrey doesn't come home any more. Not to sleep anyway."

"Then just with you." Evgenya shrugged again, even more offhand.

Was the girl serious? The idea of her moving in struck Sonya as a tidy solution to several problems, among which paying back Andrey for his desertion was not the least attractive.

"That's settled then," Sonya decided unceremoniously. She took her house-key from her pocket and gave it to Evgenya. "Go and get your bag. Go to the apartment and let yourself in. I'll be back later. Lie down for a while and try to get rid of your headache."

Evgenya took the key. "I'm not sleeping in *that* room," she said.

"No," Sonya agreed. "Of course not." The shadow of Rakhel still lay dark between them. "You can sleep on the sofa. Or..." she hesitated, "with me if you like. The bed's big enough."

"You don't snore?"

Sonya smiled: "Not as far as I know."

Evgenya stretched out her arms and hugged Sonya to her, kissing her forehead playfully. "You be back at ten," she said. "I'll make a gypsy stew." Sonya gave her the key of the apartment and she was gone.

For a while Sonya stood motionless in the dank cellar. Without the least forethought, she'd spawned a revolution. From tonight she was sharing her home, her food, even her bed, with a wanton, a slut who'd slept with half the men in the Movement. With an apostle of the appalling Popov. She raised her hand to wipe Evgenya's kiss from her forhead. But... but if there'd be stew on the table and someone near her through the night...

Vitya, Frolenko and the three other diggers emerged from the tunnel. "It's the roadbed," Vitya said. "Building rubble. We have to change tools."

"Wonderful," Sonya said cheerfully. "Something to be happy about."

She saw the men look at her, some with relief, some with incredulity. "How long now?" she asked, still inexplicably merry.

"It'll be slow," Vitya said. "Some of the masonry is big. We'll never get it out."

"You'll think of something," Sonya said with a smile. "You always do."

"We'll try," Vitya assured her. "But there's something else. We have to get the dynamite over here. In case the Guardian…"

"You're right," Sonya agreed. "If they find out who he is, they'll rip him apart. He may give them the workshop to save the tunnel."

Vitya nodded. "At best."

"Let's move the dynamite, then," she said.

When Sonya arrived home some hours later, Evgenya opened the door dressed in a respectable day-dress of grey merino. Her hair was bundled into a knot and her work-roughened hands were scrubbed painfully clean. The apartment smelt of cooking.

"I don't want you here as a glorified housemaid," Sonya snapped immediately, taking off her heavy, dreary shawl.

"I'm here as your friend, Sofya Luovna. Let's make a rule. No harsh words inside that door. You're going to fall apart unless you learn to calm down."

"Are you telling me how to live?"

"Of course I am. You don't know, so someone has to tell you."

"That was something even Andrey…" Sonya was indignant but at the same time on the verge of collapsing into Evgenya's arms in tears.

"He was here, Andrey. About an hour ago. I told him I'd moved in."

"Did he make a pass at you?"

"Yes. He always does. Some men are like that."

"Will he be back?"

"He didn't say. He just told me to look after you. 'Without her, we're nothing.' That's what he said. And I agree. Now come and eat."

Evgenya had tidied up the small apartment. The dining table was clear of papers and dirty clothes. Supper was laid for two. Sonya ate hungrily. "Who taught you to cook?" she asked.

"Popov," Evgenya replied.

"Popov could cook?"

"He was a chef at one time. On the Volga. One of the big steamers."

Sonya shook her head. "I didn't like him," she said. "But, as you see, I know nothing about him."

"So why am I here? Because you *like* me? Or why?"

"I do like you, Gypsy. You know that."

"As long as I do what I'm told."

Sonya tutted. "In the past, maybe. But now you're telling me what to do."

"Only because you want me to."

"Do I? You know so much about me?"

"I know you have your doubts."

"What about?"

"What happens next?"

"You mean about putting so much dynamite in one place?"

Evgenya laughed. "No!" she exclaimed. "About you and me. Sleeping together."

"That *is* a problem of too much dynamite in one place," Sonya began to laugh too.

"No. Kib always says: 'The dynamite isn't the problem. The problem is the detonator.'"

"That's a problem you solved years ago," Sonya said, a little ruefully.

"You not?"

"No. Never."

"Well," Evgenya said. "When we've done the washing up,

we might dabble a little with percussion caps. If they don't work at first, we can turn up the heat. I'll show you."

# V

Sonya slowly brought the threads together. Trigony arrived in St Petersburg on 30th December and took over security. Excavation of the tunnel was slow. Vitya insisted that they took no risks – if this attempt failed, there might never be another. The dynamite was packed in cheese-barrels and stored in their only dry cellar. Over Christmas, Kib had finished the grenades and closed down the workshop in Mursinka. Evgenya began to train the hand-bombers with dummy grenades. The pit beyond the Okhta crossing was deep in snow and they'd leave too many footprints, so she found a place in the Lesna Forest.

Sonya wanted everything in place by the end of January – the clock was ticking and the Guardian wouldn't hold out forever. Even if he did, too many people knew about the cheese-shop. Sooner or later someone would turn informer. Minimise contacts, send no messages, shut down the printing press, stay off the streets. Apart from the cheese-shop, the *Narodnaya Volya* drew in its horns completely. As soon as the trap was set, they'd have nothing to do but wait – one day the Tsar would walk into it.

From the beginning, Sonya found her *ménage à deux* with Evgenya surprisingly comfortable. The Gypsy could turn away sharp words with an even-tempered joke, she converted the chaotic apartment into a barrack-room, but she never dropped a hint of this new-found intimacy in front of the others. All this met Sonya's inclinations exactly. Their closeness remained strictly within the confines of Sonya's apartment. There was nothing in it of passion, and little of overt affection. It was more a collision of overcharged minds and bodies, desperate for release. As days passed into weeks, Sonya began to experience a pattern of tension and relief that she realised was close to addiction. But each repetition brought a new access of strength and energy. Her plans took on a sharper edge, her decisions were more readily accepted. She could smile now at a mistake which before would have brought down fire and brimstone. She mended fences with Vitya, though she still had him followed. Even with Andrey things improved – she stopped nagging him about his infidelities, and they became comrades again. She seldom discussed with Evgenya the strange new bond they'd formed. Once, however, when Evgenya was throwing out a hoard of powders and tonics she'd found in the bedroom, Sonya came close to an explanation: "Throw them out? Of course you can. They're for my nerves. But now I've got you…" Evgenya hadn't taken this as a compliment. She'd shrugged her shoulders in her matter of fact way and made some indecent reply about spending oneself for the Movement. Sonya often recalled Kib's remark out on the marsh: "With ten Evgenyas we could blow off every crowned head in Europe." In a way it was true. Yet in every relationship between addict and drug, there is ambiguity. If Evgenya had a fault, it was that she adapted herself to Sonya's needs too perfectly. If Evgenya had made demands, insisted on some sacrifice from Sonya, or let her violent temper fly, perhaps Sonya would have surrendered to her Gypsy completely.

On 25th January Sonya visited the *poste restante* on her way home from the cheese-shop. She showed the elderly official the identity papers the Guardian had set up for the *poste*: Agafya Yermolinskaya. Sonya expected to find nothing – all communication but the most urgent was frozen. To her surprise, the old man behind the grille handed her a telegram. It was from Polya Fomina in Moscow, more or less the only member of the *Narodnaya Volya* still active there: *Should the box be 24x37x11 or 26x12x14? Please confirm.*

Back at the apartment, Evgenya decoded the numbers in a few seconds: *SMFREE.* The Snowman had been released. Sonya was startled. She watched Evgenya's reaction shrewdly.

During two months of intimacy nothing had been said about Vitya's suspect wife. Anna's name, like Rakhel's or Elif's, was never spoken. From years of conspiracy, Sonya knew that silence was more significant than carefully chosen words. Evgenya's forehead wrinkled: "'Snowman free'," she read again. "How odd."

"Yes it is," Sonya agreed.

"And why release her in Moscow? She was in prison here. In the Schlusselburg."

"Very strange."

"You think she made a deal with them?" Evgenya asked.

"We should ask her, shouldn't we? But first we have to find her."

For a moment, as she tested Evgenya with awkward questions, the charming Gypsy vanished. Instead Sonya saw the white scars on Evgenya's nose and forehead, and the damaged skin on her chin – she was a fighter, a killer. She looked at the acid burns on Evgenya's hands from the workshop, at her broken fingernails. So many injuries, so many imperfections. Was a treacherous intimacy with Anna one of them? Sonya did her best to prompt words from Evgenya that might indicate betrayal: 'Let me find her' or 'I'll find her for you'. But Evgenya took the opposite line: "Tell Trigony, he'll know how to find her. But... keep it from Vitya. For as long as you can."

"Why not tell Vitya?" Sonya probed. "Anna's free. He can't make a deal now – it's too late."

"Maybe he made a deal already. He can be a treacherous bastard when it suits him."

"Treacherous to us – but not to Anna?"

"She made him rich. He wouldn't want to be poor again, would he now?"

Sonya weighed the words carefully. They were bitter enough – Evgenya had good reason to hate Vitya and he, presumably, to hate her. The message was clear. On the other hand, if Evgenya and Vitya were still on the same side – in

340

effect, on Anna's side – Evgenya would have to play exactly the card she'd just played. Was the girl clever enough for that? "Vitya hasn't made a deal," Sonya said, "he's been tailed for weeks. The only thing he does apart from work and sleep is visit a tavern called the Last Man Standing. Some prostitute he's taken a shine to."

"That goes flat against your rules," Evgenya broke out. "'Drop all contact with strangers.' I think he should be…"

"Disciplined?" Sonya prompted.

"Yes. Disciplined," It was a strong reaction and spoken with venom – it seemed Evgenya really was smarting over her lost lover.

"He's not the issue," Sonya said. "What should we do about Anna?"

"Find her. Bring her here. Question her like we did Reinstein. All of us together. If we agree she's guilty…"

"Yes?"

"Find out what she told them and then…" Evgenya grimaced and made the gesture of cutting her throat with her finger.

"You'd do it?"

"Not on my own. I'd want Trigony there at least. And you. Anna's tough as hell."

"But in principle you'd do a Reinstein on her?"

"If we all agreed. Or she confessed."

"And Vitya?"

"Keep him out of it. Completely. Send him to Yalta. Anything."

"You really hate her, don't you?" Sonya asked, her doubts fading.

"Popov showed me how to break collarbones," Evgenya said quietly, "and with luck I'll break hers before she goes in the ice-hole."

# VI

Anna, from the start of her interrogation, had fallen back on the time-honoured plaint of the political prisoner: "I admit nothing. I deny nothing." How often had she repeated the doom-laden words in the last three months – sobbing them, screaming them, spitting them out in anger and contempt? And that was all they'd got out of her beyond her name and the address of her estate in Rostov. She was sure. There were long gaps in her memory, especially after her little girl was born dead, but she was sure she'd told them nothing. And today they'd set her free. Free to do what? To lead them to the very people whose existence she'd refused to confirm or deny with such desperation. She couldn't see through a prison wall, but she could see through that.

She lay on her bed in the Dresden Hotel, her arms clutched against her belly, trying to ward off the devastating cramps that racked her, often for ten minutes at a time. Shock after the stillbirth, bad food and prison fever had weakened her savagely. The strength that remained to her was not enough to act – only to refuse. She'd go nowhere, send no telegrams, write no letters. She'd lead them nowhere at all. Just lie on her bed. She'd had newspapers sent up to her room, but she'd taken in no more than the date – 25th January, 1881.

A knock on the door. She was too weak to make her "Come in" audible. Perhaps it was the doctor already – one of them at least. If only he could take away the cramps.

Professor Couderc held the Chair of Internal Medicine at Moscow University. He was followed into Anna's spacious bedroom by Professor Lavrov from gynaecology, Professor Baltsev from pharmacology, and two nurses. When the Governor of Moscow Prison had spoken to her the day before, he'd promised her the best care that money could buy – her money of course. He'd kept his word – the Tsarina herself had no better doctors. And her money was still hers – that she'd also been promised.

It was bliss, to surrender her body into the hands of clever men whose only concern was her recovery. She listened to the respectful hum of their voices. The medical jargon, the names of exotic drugs, and the occasional "wrongful arrest" or "serious mistake by the police." When the long examination was over, Professor Couderc sat beside her bed and gave their opinion – the fever was gone, but it had left her very weak. With diet and exercise she would soon recover. The stillbirth had been badly handled. She knew she'd lost a great deal of blood and she wasn't suprised when Couderc told her she'd lost tissue too, enough to make her infertile. She was acutely anaemic but iron would cope with that. The cramps had no physical etiology. Rest, diet, exercise and the company of congenial friends might quickly cure them. Music too, if she was so inclined. Medication would, of course, reduce the frequency of the cramps and relieve the symptoms. The nurses would look after her unless she preferred the attention of her personal servants. And by way of a peroration – he, Professor Couderc of Moscow University, believed that she'd been shamefully treated. In his opinion, the matter should be brought to the attention of His Imperial Majesty.

The white lace-edged sheets, the neat, sober nurses, the rich broth and sweet, sustaining wine – it all soothed her sorely tried spirit. And now she began to plan. For a while she should disappear, far away – America. She'd go to America. She had money hidden in accounts all over the world. If they really had left her control of her fortune, she should sell her Russian securities now and move the cash. As much as she could. But how could she get to America? St Petersburg, Liverpool, New York. It wouldn't be easy.

After the visit next morning by Professor Couderc, Anna got out of bed. All her luggage from Warsaw was in her room. A chambermaid from the hotel helped her unpack. Dunyasha had a special way of folding lace, Anna remembered, with all the edges pointing inward. None of the lace was folded that way now. She opened her travelling bag. It had contained gold, and the gold was there still. She grimaced – they'd killed her baby, but they hadn't taken her gold. Along with her passport as Anna Shestakova, she found the forgery – Natalya Grigoryevna Shukhova, governess. She shivered – it was a name her interrogators had thrown at her time after time: "Who is Shukhova? Where is she?" She groaned – how stupid she'd been at the border! She went over it again, forcing herself to remember new details, regenerating her unwilling and broken memory. She'd expected to get off the train with the other passengers and file through the border post to show her papers. That was how it had been in April on her trip to Germany. That's how it always was at a border. But there had been rain, a torrential downpour, hammering on the roof of the train for hours. Alexey Alexeyevich's wife – she fought for the woman's name, but it was lost – had fallen asleep. She remembered her own struggle to stay awake. The train was hours late. Nobody knew where they were or when they'd arrive at the border. She remembered repeating in her mind her new name – Natalya Grigoryevna. She remembered the syllables clattering to the rhythm of the wheels. She'd nodded off and awoken again in blank horror – railway police were opening the travelling bag on the seat beside her. She remembered Alexey Alexeyevich explaining and apologising twenty times over: because of the storm, the first-class passengers had stayed on the train, she'd been asleep, so he'd shown the guards where she kept her papers. What could she have done – the guard already had her passport in his hand? Anna, Countess Shestakova.

With the help of a pretty, young lady's-maid from the hotel, Anna bathed and dressed. She enjoyed it, the pampering and her quick, harsh anger at the least mistake. If the maid had been her own, she'd have pinched her black and blue. As it was, she gave the girl a five-rouble tip and told her she was stupid as a bedbug. One more hard-pressed girl, she reflected, who'd be happy to slit the throat of her tormentor come the revolution. Once she was dressed, a *coiffeuse* and a manicurist occupied another hour.

Anna's purpose in getting dressed was to visit Oppenheimer's bank which was on the opposite side of the Tverskaya and where she had an account which Kreuzotter knew nothing about. She told the nurse on duty to put on her cloak and to follow five paces behind her in case she needed help. In the bank she signed an order to liquidate 530,000 roubles in securities and to transfer the money to an account to be opened immediately with Oppenheimer's branch in New York. Turning the rest of her fortune into cash would take weeks, and she'd need Kreuzotter's help. She waited while clerks consulted ledgers and made notes. She waited while a long telegram was encoded and sent to New York, then waited for confirmation from New York that the new account had been opened. It took five weary hours.

Back in the lobby of the hotel, she saw an oddly familiar face. For a moment she couldn't place it. Then part of the name came back – Polya. Polina... she'd seen her in the forest in Lesna eighteen months before. She knew from Vitya's cryptic letters in the summer that the *Narodnaya Volya* had more or less abandoned Moscow. That meant Polina was probably in Moscow on her own. And now she was hanging around the Dresden Hotel. Things were becoming clearer.

Anna sat down on one of the big sofas in the lobby, beckoning the nurse to sit next to her. If the *Narodnaya Volya* knew she was in Moscow, it confirmed something she'd suspected ever since her release – the Ministry, the MVD, had tipped off the Committee. No one on the Committee knew she'd kept her mouth shut through months of questioning, cost what it might. If she was released, Sonya and the rest would think she'd done a deal: facts for freedom. And they'd liquidate her, just as Popov had drowned Reinstein and Evgenya had drowned Elif.

More pieces of the puzzle fell quickly into place. Another six months in the Schlusselburg and she'd have been dead or insane. So they'd released her. They knew she'd never willingly lead them to the Committee, so they'd decided to tip off the Committee and let the Committee find her. The Committee would sniff after her, and the Ministry would sniff after the Committee.

But surely, she thought, even a second-rate mind like Sonya's would see the trap – stay away from Anna, she's bait, she's rat-poison. On the other hand, a lot would depend on *how* the Committee had been tipped off. Who could deliver the message so that the poison was, at least for a while, invisible? Then she spotted the ruse and saw why the MVD had transferred her from the Schlusselburg to Moscow. Polina was the key. In Moscow, Polina was more or less on her own. Probably the MVD had sent Polina a note in Anna's easily imitated, left-handed scrawl. Then, confronted with Anna's release, Polina would need instructions. She'd telegraph St Petersburg, in code for sure, and the roll-up could begin.

She glanced across the lobby at Polina and scanned the faces nearby for a likely tail. There were several. She herself had a tail – probably it was the nurse. No, *certainly* it was the nurse, though there might be others. There was nothing to be gained by delay. She turned to the nurse: "You see that woman over there," she said, "in the frightful shawl, sitting by the column? Please ask her to come and talk to me."

The nurse stood up, crossed the lobby and summoned Polina. Polina protested, bewildered and horrified, but the nurse was insistent. A moment later Polina was trembling next to Anna on the sofa.

"Please will you stand over there, out of earshot," Anna said to the nurse. "I have something confidential to say to this young lady."

"If you're sure you're strong enough, ma'am."

Anna's eyes flashed, despite her weakness. The nurse had seen a display of Anna's temper in the bedroom and evidently had no wish to risk a scene in the lobby.

"That was stupid…" Polina began.

"Hold your tongue," Anna broke in. "We're both being followed so it makes no difference if we talk. Now, just answer. Have you telegraphed Petersburg?"

"Yes."

"Fool."

346

Polina's face crumpled toward tears.

"Did you receive a note in my handwriting?"

"Yes."

"I wrote nothing, because unlike you, Polina, I'm not mentally defective. Whatever the note said, how could you be stupid enough to believe I wrote it?"

"How could I know?"

"For Christ's sake! Why do you think they let me out? So some novice like you would get to work and give us all away. Next question – did Petersburg reply?"

"Not yet."

"So you decided to watch me anyway?"

"Yes."

"When Petersburg replies, they'll tell you to make contact with me."

"How do you know?"

"And they'll tell you to take me to Petersburg."

"I don't understand."

"Pitiful!" Anna exclaimed. "How pitiful you all are."

"What are you going to do?"

"Exactly what Petersburg wants. You'll be here on 28th, in this lobby, ready to travel, at eight in the morning. As soon as you hear from Petersburg, telegraph that we're on the way."

"Anna Petrovna!" The girl had gone the colour of cottage cheese.

"They're rolling us up, Polina." Anna craned her neck quickly to look behind the sofa. A bellboy was trimming a dying palm. "Come here young man," she demanded. He glanced at her. "Did you hear everything? Or should I say it for you again more slowly."

At the time of the lawsuit with her uncle, Anna had become familiar with half a dozen reporters who'd covered her story. One of them, a young woman who'd worked at that time for the *Moskovskie Vedomosti,* now ran a daily column under the name of *Spyglass.* Anna sent her a telegram asking her to visit the Dresden Hotel next afternoon. Nervous excitement had sustained Anna through the last hectic hours. As it drained away, she lost all animation. The lady's-maid undressed her, and the nurse put her to bed. As Anna fell into grateful lethargy, she heard the nurse whisper: "I really am a nurse, ma'am. Only they asked me to tell them..." And that was all.

Next afternoon the reporter was quickly briefed: Anna, Countess Shestakova, had damaged her hands while riding to wolfhounds. In Germany she'd received electric therapy which had partly cured her. As a well-known public benefactor, the Countess wished to bring this new treatment to Russia. She intended to open a clinic and was at the moment deciding between the claims of Moscow and St Petersburg. On 28th January she'd be going to St Petersburg to discuss the matter with a number of eminent physicians and the Deputy Minister of Public Health, her old friend Vladimir Grigorievich.

"And," she asked Spyglass, "can someone from your paper meet me at the station in Petersburg on Wednesday? I think you'll be surprised when you hear how much money I'm going to spend."

# VII

Evgenya had already encoded the telegram to Polina in Moscow as a price list for pewter spoons. *'Bring SM here now. Urgent.'* Trigony would have to agree the telegram before it went. Finding him would give Evgenya a chance to find Vitya as well. She had to talk to him.

"Trigony?" Andrey told her in the cellar of the cheese shop. "He's gone. He always eats somewhere. Maybe Vitya knows."

Vitya was kneeling with his back to them, sharpening the teeth of a saw.

Evgenya grimaced quickly at Andrey. "Eating in the same place twice is against orders," she said. "Milord's supposed to be in charge of security."

"Specifically the order says: 'Everyone except Milord must eat at a different place each day.'" Andrey joked. He gave her a cheeky smile. "How's Sonya? You're wasted on a girl like her, you know."

"Sonya's fine. We stay in and eat bread and cheese, but not from this shop, thank God."

"This is the only cheese-shop in Russia that doesn't actually sell cheese," Vitya observed without turning round. He'd understood the code-word and repeated it.

Ten minutes later Evgenya was in the Last Man Standing. Vitya would take longer. First he'd have to lose Vadim or whoever was tailing him. She ordered a samovar and two glasses. Pulcheria, the woman behind the bar, set it up and brought it with a grin. "Another session with your handsome friend?" she asked.

"No. Just talk."

"You don't need the room then?"

"Maybe later."

Evgenya waited, sipping tea. The tavern was cold and almost empty. Finally she heard feet scuttling down the stairs. Vitya.

She poured him a glass of tea. "Like some bread and cheese?" she asked.

He shook his head and sat down: "Something important?"

"Yes," she agreed, "Anna is out."

"Out!" he exclaimed.

"No reason given. Everyone thinks she made a deal."

"Presumably they let her go to see who she'd contact."

"She's not stupid. She won't make contact."

"Where is she?"

"In Moscow. The message came from the Moscow Section?"

"That's Polina. There's no one else there."

"Sonya wants Polina to bring her here. So they can…" She made a gesture of cutting her own throat.

"You? Again?"

"Probably. Sonya trusts me. And who else is bitch enough… to do a Reinstein on her?" She glanced at Vitya. He'd understood her words exactly – there was no way Anna would follow Reinstein.

"If Polina sent us the telegram, it means she's been tipped off," Vitya said, "by the MVD. They're watching Anna. And they're watching Polina too, hoping she'll lead them to Sonya and the others."

"Polina's telegram was addressed to Agafya Yermolinskaya, as always," Evgenya said.

"And Sonya picked it up?"

"Yes."

"Then probably they're tailing Sonya already."

"Probably they are, but they'll think it's someone called Agafya."

"Yes," Vitya agreed.

"So Sonya has to vanish," Evgenya concluded, her head buzzing with so many layers of who might know what about whom.

"Yes, she has to vanish," Vitya agreed again. "At least if we still want the cheese-shop to work."

"Do we?" Evgenya asked. She heard an edge of control in her voice that took her by surprise – Vitya's answer to the question was important, but, she realised, it wasn't as important as her own. It was a new experience.

"The mine has to work," he replied. "It's our last chance."

"And if it comes to a choice?" Evgenya asked. "Does Anna come first? Or the mine?"

She watched him struggle between two imperative loyalties. "Anna first," he said. "What do you think?"

"Yes, Anna first," Evgenya agreed slowly. "Not the mine."

Footsteps scuffed down the stairs. A girl and a man. Pulcheria looked up and indicated the curtained room. The girl nodded. "Pay first," Pulcheria said, eyeing the man doubtfully. The man paid, and the couple disappeared behind the curtain.

"You know…" Evgenya said thoughtfully. "We've got it all wrong, haven't we? We talk about freedom. I've read our pamphlets. At first I thought I didn't understand them. But now… I don't think they mean anything. Nothing at all. People like Sonya and Milord – they're tyrants. And we have to plot and scheme against them just to stay alive. What would a government of Sonyas be like? Absolutely awful."

"You've been living with her for weeks. You don't sound any closer."

"I'm her medication, Vitya. Take twice before sleeping. Excellent for overwrought nerves and upset digestion. Just so she can bully and wheedle you all next day. Just so she can have the satisfaction of butchering the Tsar. She'd change places with him to-fucking-morrow if she had the chance."

"Yes, probably she would," Vitya agreed. "But Sonya won't survive. None of them will, and they know it. There are so many sane people out there, Evgenya. When the Tsar's gone and this whole rotten system…"

"In a hundred years maybe," Evgenya said bitterly. "Not in our lifetime."

Pulcheria sidled up to them from the bar. "Sure you don't want to?" she asked, nodding toward to curtained room. "After them two's finished. Such a waste of time, talking."

"Piss off," Evgenya told her with easy brutality.

When Pulcheria was back at her bar, they looked at Sonya's telegram to Polina. A pricelist for pewter spoons looked innocent enough. But the MVD in Moscow, the VD as they called it for short, would pick up everything addressed to Polina. In fact, the VD in Petersburg would be watching out for anything sent *to* Polina, so sending her a telegram would be more or less suicide. Best let Milord send it – after all, he was in charge of security.

They drank tea, arguing, planning. What would happen next? Polina would get the telegram. She'd contact Anna and bring her to Petersburg. If Anna had any sense, she wouldn't come. She was safer doing nothing in Moscow with the VD watching her day and night. But if she did come to Petersburg? If Sonya and Trigony really wanted to get hold of her without giving themselves away, they'd have to snatch her – make her vanish under the eyes of the VD. That wouldn't be easy. Unless...

Unless that was what the VD wanted – for Anna to be snatched so they could sniff out her trail and unearth the *Narodnaya Volya*.

Or another *if* – maybe Anna's release had nothing to do with the *Narodnaya Volya*. What if Fanarin's petition had worked? Maybe Anna was being released for the most unRussian of reasons – they had nothing against her. They agreed that next day Evgenya should go to Fanarin on the off-chance that the wheels of the law had been grinding in Anna's favour.

Evgenya watched her cousin leave the Last Man Standing with a shudder of longing. Nothing was left of his old way toward her – no condescension, no reproach, no cousinly distance. Through all their urgent talk, they'd exchanged smiles of understanding, the sort of smile a prisoner might exchange with his wife during a prison visit – tender but agonisingly separate. He'd kissed her three times on parting. If he disappeared that night and she never saw him again, she knew from the tenderness of that last kiss that he knew exactly who she was, that he loved her, and that nothing in life would ever change his love.

Although Evgenya had no appointment with Fanarin next morning, she was not kept waiting. He saw her in a small, plain room, explaining that he'd abandoned another client for a moment or two to talk to her. The Shestakov fortune had not lost its eloquence.

"And how can I be of service to you?" Fanarin enquired.

"Perhaps you already have," Evgenya replied. "I... we... Viktor Pavlovich thinks his wife has been released."

"Indeed," said Fanarin.

Evgenya nodded. "Do you know anything about it?"

"My dear Evgenya Antonovna, we have not applied for her release," Fanarin said, "only for a statement of her whereabouts."

"Have they told you anything?"

"Very little," said Fanarin.

"You mean nothing?"

"Not quite as bad as that," Fanarin objected with a smile. "We've learned how important she is – since they refuse to admit her arrest."

"That's no great comfort."

Fanarin nodded agreement. "They seldom release people," he remarked, "but if Anna Petrovna has been released, it is either under the provisions of Paragraph 2012 of the Code of Criminal Procedure, which requires the release of persons against whom no case will be made... or as bait." He grimaced. "The second alternative seems the more likely."

They exchanged a long look, Evgenya could see that the lawyer's mind had understood in a few seconds what she and Vitya had unravelled with great difficulty the night before.

"Viktor Pavlovich wondered..." Evgenya began doubtfully.

"...Whether I would write him a letter," Fanarin nodded, "a letter stating the paragraph number and an expectation that his wife will be released under its provisions." He was already writing on a sheet of notepaper with a heading of chastely imperial grandeur. Evgenya watched. The lawyer wrote without hesitation, signed with a flourish, folded, sealed and addressed the letter. "I won't play games with you." He changed his tone abruptly as he handed her the letter. "Tell your people it's a Paragraph 2012, and get her out of the country as soon as you can. Understand?" He made her a quick bow, rang a silver bell on his desk and disappeared through a padded leather door.

Why were there no Fanarins in the *Narodnaya Volya*? Evgenya asked herself bitterly as her sleigh swished to a halt in the Nevsky Prospekt. Milord was a lawyer, but beside Fanarin's quick intelligence, Milord looked paltry and self-indulgent.

Andrey Zhelyabov? Kib? Mikhailov the Guardian? They were dedicated men, they'd die for the cause without hesitation, but none of them could think straight. Even Sonya… She'd argued half the night with Sonya, trying to convince her that Polina's telegram was the bait in a police trap. But Sonya had refused to listen.

Evgenya paid the driver, jumped out of the sleigh and cut her way through the traffic to Mellier's book-shop. It was a good place to check her tail – she was clean.

It was a ten-minute walk to the cheese-shop. She folded the letter from Fanarin into the newspaper she'd bought, hoping to find a way to pass it to Vitya. A headline on the back page of the newspaper caught her eye: 'Shestakova'. Below the headline was a picture of Anna taken years before. She scanned the text – Anna would arrive in St Petersburg in two days time with, it seemed, not only half the VD watching her but a press escort as well.

She hurried down the steps into the cheese-shop. It smelled faintly of milk curds and rennet – the Kobozevs must have bought new stock.

"Smells better today," she said to Anka, who sat behind the counter waiting for the customers who never came.

"They're all in the cellar," the cheese-monger said. "Sonya's asking where you are."

As she entered the cellar, she caught Sonya's raised eyebrow of enquiry and nodded to show she had her explanation ready.

Vitya shot an impatient glance in her direction – a silly fly-by-night who interrupted important discussions. They could all see his contempt for her. "I'm telling them how to tamp the tunnel," he said. "It doesn't concern you."

Evgenya waited while Vitya finished his explanation of how the tunnel should be filled with mud and masonry to prevent the explosion blowing back. It would be a huge explosion, and he wanted all of it to go upward, not outward.

When he'd finished, Evgenya cornered Sonya immediately. "Two things about Anna," she said. "I thought she might have sent a telegram to my old address in the Kurskaya, so I checked. Nothing. And this…" She held the newspaper up to the light with the story about Anna folded outward.

Sonya read the article twice. "That's so fucking clever," she said. "She's got everybody watching everybody. But she won't get away. Trigony's got a plan to snatch her. It involves you, so you'd better talk to him." She paused. "And you'd better show this to Vitya."

"Why? He can buy his own newspaper."

"Don't argue all the time," Sonya said. "Just do it."

Vitya had gone with a lantern into the dry cellar where the dynamite was kept. Evgenya followed him. "Coalminer," she said with a jeer in her voice, "something in the paper about your *wife*."

She passed him the paper, allowing the letter to poke out an inch or two and making sure he saw it. With her back to the door she mouthed the words: "From Fanarin. What you wanted."

Vitya's eyes flashed in warning – Sonya was approaching from behind.

"Gypsy," Sonya said. "I told Milord you'd see him this morning. You'd better go now."

Mischa Trigony's plan, as he outlined it to Evgenya, was not complicated. Anna would leave her hotel and enter a closed sledge. The sledge would naturally be followed by the VD. In the sledge would be a change of clothes – some peasant garb probably. There was an awkward corner on a street near the Navy Hospital. The road ahead would be blocked by a cart coming the other way. Anna's sledge would be forced to stop. She'd slip out of it and the corner would screen her from the VD behind. There was a covered market that sold leather coats and hides. She'd enter the market and then exit through the back way. An open sleigh would be waiting.

"And why should Anna do any of this?" Evgenya asked. "Right now the VD are protecting her, and we're the threat. There's no way she'll get into any sledge of ours or get out of it when we tell her."

"You'll be in the sledge. We believe she still trusts you."

"Maybe she does? But why should she get dressed, leave her room, and go downstairs to a sledge. She won't."

"She will if she thinks it's your plan and your sledge."

"And why should she think that?"

"She's travelling with Polina. They're staying in the same hotel. We'll get a message to her through Polina. A message from you."

"A message she thinks is from me? How are you going to work that?" The answer was obvious, but Evgenya wanted more time to think. If Trigony planned to snatch Anna from the VD, maybe a second snatch would get her away from Trigony.

"Part of the message could only come from you. Something only the two of you know about. As I said, you'll be in the sledge when it picks her up. You'll help her through the leather market. Keep her calm."

"It could work," Evgenya said, "then we'd have her, wouldn't we."

"Evgenya Antonovna," he addressed her pompously, "you did an excellent job for me with Elif. It rebuilt my trust in you which your earlier behaviour…"

"Mischa," Evgenya broke in. "I came to see you because Sonya sent me. Personally I think you're a snot-nosed little shit. If you say the word *trust* again, I'll feed your balls to the crabs. Understand?"

"Do you know what?" Trigony began to laugh, a self-satisfied gurgle. "Popov once said something very similar to me. And look where he is now."

# Extract 12

I have never been able to explain the popularity of Chernyshevsky's pompous and implausible novel, *What is to Be Done?* It does contain, however, one thought-provoking prophecy which I quote now from memory: 'Men will take second place to women intellectually as soon as the reign of brute force is over.' In the People's Will, I think we saw that happening. In the villages, in the factories, the reign of brute force is still very much with us. But when it comes to terrorism, a woman can shoot as straight, can mix dynamite as scientifically, or hang at the end of a rope with the same finality as a man. Many a woman in her early twenties, it seems to me, has the same intellectual energy, the drive, the instinct to dominate and conquer as a man first acquires in his thirties. But what outlet does a young woman have for this surge of energy? For many, home, children, drudgery in factories or fields is all they can expect. But during the 1870's a number of exceptional women found their way into the Movement and discovered what was, perhaps, the first free and equal society in the world. Clearly they were not all Sofya Perovskayas: ardent, dedicated and puritanical. For some, sexual liberty turned quickly into *libertinage*. For others, exposure to violence developed in them a strain of brutality that in most women is severely suppressed. For all of them, indeed for our men as well, placing themselves above the traditional moral law, in particular above the commandment 'Thou shalt not kill', led to insoluble ethical conflicts.

To end on the gallows or on a filthy bunk in a filthy cell is not a fate to be envied, but I never heard one of our women express envy of her sisters who lived in comfortable homes with comfortable families and suffered the restrictions inherent in such comfort. Never once.

Looking at Russia today, I do not see that our women have made great strides forward during my quarter-century of incarceration. Peasant women are still slaves, little girls still prostitute themselves on every street corner in our cities, our workshops teem with ever more women working eighteen hours a day in unspeakable conditions. And the rich? Of them I know only what I see in the newspapers. But the opportunities for frivolity, vanity, waste and stupidity seem now to outnumber by far those available in the 1870's. Have we then achieved nothing? Maybe one thing, and one thing only. Perhaps we have shown that equality between the sexes is more than just a dream. For a year or two we pioneered successfully in the heart of Russia a way of life that may one day become normal everywhere. If we did, then our revolution was not entirely without meaning. (*Memoir of the People's Will*, Chapter 14.)

# Chapter 13

## I

Anna was still a jump ahead. Reporters from three newspapers had met her at the station. She'd installed herself and Polina at the Hotel de l'Europe, though Polina was far away in an attic room. The improvised meeting with Vladimir Grigorievich at the Ministry of Public Health had gone well. Next day it was announced in several newspapers that the Countess Shestakova was selling three estates to pay for the new clinic. Kreuzotter and Beil were summoned and given the necessary instructions in front of Vladimir Grigorievich and his superior. A little later, but still in the safety of the Ministry, Anna gave Kreuzotter instructions about liquidating all her remaining Russian securities, though she doubted he would carry them out – her uncle was pressing him hard.

Scheming, acting the role of a sane and healthy public benefactor, watching constantly for a way to escape – it took her last reserves of strength, but at the same time it strengthened her. Only when she was alone in her bedroom with the nurse guarding the door did she throw aside the mask, weeping with fear and loneliness on her exquisite lace-trimmed sheets.

She heard the nurse tap at her door. Then silence for thirty seconds. The two women had reached an understanding. The nurse would report to the MVD exactly and in detail everything she saw and heard, but she wouldn't break in on

Anna, and in a crisis she'd give Anna ten minutes to get away. It was an expensive understanding, but it had held so far.

The nurse ushered Polina into the room. Polina was carrying a copy of Aksakov's *Childhood Years*. Folded into the book as a bookmark and plainly visible was a flyer, a price list from Sazikov, the silversmith. The book had been carefully examined twice, once by the policeman dressed as a page who sat in the elegant curtained lobby of Anna's suite, and once by the nurse. The flyer had been unfolded and held up to the light. It was innocent.

"Close the door," Anna ordered.

"I'm sorry ma'am. I have to leave it open," the nurse replied in a loud voice, silently closing the door.

Anna sighed – fifty roubles a day was a small price to pay for a closed door. She looked at Polina. "So, here comes Baba Yaga to bite off my head," she said.

"I don't know," said Polina. "Can we talk? Safely?"

"Polina, my dear, you can do nothing safely. Your days are numbered. When I go, you go. Don't forget it."

Polina was trembling. "This was pushed under my door," she said, handing Anna the flyer. "I think it was pushed under everyone's door."

"I saw it too," Anna replied. "What are you telling me? It's code?" It must be code, or Polina wouldn't have brought it to her.

"I had nothing else to do in my room, so I started on it."

"That's clever. That's actually clever," Anna said. "I wondered how they'd get a message to you."

With the help of the start-word and Aksakov's *Childhood Years*, the two women decoded Milord's plan. Halfway through was a puzzling fragment: *Tyomka's front teeth*.

Polina didn't understand and wanted to re-run the code.

"No," Anna told her. "I see what it means."

"What then?"

"Can you imagine any reason I'd get into that sledge?"

"To get away from the VD? To escape."

"They think I betrayed them. They want to kill me."

"But you *didn't*. I've been watching you. You'd never betray anyone. Never. I'd trust you with my life."

"Do you mean that, Polina?"

Polina's own strength was at an end. She sat on Anna's bed in a flood of tears. "They were on to me even before I sent that stupid telegram to Sonya. I'm dead, aren't I? Nobody cares what happens to me."

"I have friends as well as enemies," Anna told her. "This message comes from a friend."

"Tyomka?"

"No, not Tyomka." She paused. "But it's true what you said, Polina. They won't help you. You've got a fat file with the MVD, and Sonya hasn't given you new papers. You're dead."

"Anna. Help me," the girl sobbed.

"You don't think I'm in trouble enough of my own? Unless, of course..." It might be useful – someone else in her corner, even someone as clumsy as Polina.

"Unless what?" Polina's sobs stopped with a jerk.

"If one person can get into a sledge, two can. But you'll have to promise."

"What? Anything."

"Stay by me. Do what I tell you or what the other girl in the sledge tells you. The Gypsy."

"Yes," Polina said, taking Anna's gloved hand and kissing it. "Yes."

"The sledge will be outside the hotel at ten. That's what the message says. So tonight... be ready."

That evening just before ten, Anna was standing with Polina and the nurse in the lobby of the Hotel de l'Europe. The concierge had been told to alert the carriage porter. Even through the enormous double doors of the hotel, they heard the distant shout: "Covered sledge for the Countess Shestakova."

"Put your arm in mine," Anna said, "and get into the sledge first."

The concierge returned a few minutes later – the sledge

was waiting.

"With style now," Anna encouraged her young friend. "The eyes of the MVD are on you."

In the forecourt of the hotel, falling snow sparkled brilliantly in the white glare of the new gas lamps. The carriage porter, as magnificently dressed as a deputy minister, opened the door of the sledge and folded down the low step for the ladies.

Anna steered Polina ahead of her. Nobody was expecting Polina. In the momentary confusion, Anna could check that Evgenya really was in the sledge. If she wasn't, there was still time enough to back off.

A male voice: "Who are you?"

"She's coming with me," Anna said. "Let her in." She peered into the sledge. Evgenya was there.

"Nobody said nothing about…" Another man with a Georgian accent.

"Well, I'm saying. Now make room."

It was a tight fit, five people in a sledge with four seats, but the step was folded up and the door closed. The driver clicked his tongue and cracked his whip for the horses to move.

Enough light from outside filtered through the windows of the covered sledge for Anna to see the faces of the two men opposite. One she remembered from the execution of Reinstein – a Georgian who'd been with Popov. The other man she'd never seen before.

"Who said you could bring *her*?" the unknown man began querulously.

"Hold your tongue, Vadim," Evgenya snapped. "I give the orders. I ask the questions."

The word *bitch* hung in the air, but Evgenya let it go.

The sledge slipped into the light evening traffic. Even by the dingy yellow street lights, Anna could see the scowl on Vadim's face. She was sitting crushed between Polina and Evgenya on a padded bench intended for two. She glanced at Evgenya.

"Who *is* she?" Evgenya asked, in a tone even more

menacing than Vadim's.

Anna said nothing – if Evgenya was against her, she was finished.

"I asked you a fucking question," Evgenya growled. "Answer it."

"She's the fool who telegraphed Sofya Luovna. Her name is Polina. You know her better than I do, I should imagine."

"A piece of expendable shit," Evgenya said. "Vadim, listen. When I tell you, open the door and kick her out. Let the VD pick her up. They've got an army following us." There was a small oval window in the back of the sledge. Evgenya turned to look through it, pushing Anna aside. In the jostling, Anna felt a hand clutch her arm and squeeze her three times.

"I wouldn't kick her out if I were you," Anna said, when Evgenya was sitting in her corner again.

"None of your business." Evgenya's tone was as remorseless as before, but now Anna knew what it meant.

"If you kick her out," Anna said, "she knows the plan and she'll tell it. Why can't any of you think straight? They'll stop the sledge immediately, and you'll all finish up in jail."

"You included," said Vadim, who had only partly followed her argument.

"No, not me. I asked the hotel for a covered sledge at ten so I could see the Deputy Minister of Health. It's not my fault if it contains a gang of brainless revolutionaries."

In reply Evgenya let fly a vicious insult and then ordered Anna to change into the peasant clothes.

"No," Anna refused flatly. "I'm safer with the VD than I am with you. Why should I do anything you say?"

"Two choices," Evgenya replied. "You change quietly and let Polina help you, or these gentlemen will lend a hand. You decide."

With a show of ill-will, Anna changed clothes. Whatever Evgenya told her to do, she'd do it. And Evgenya, it seemed, wanted her to put on a show of resistance to impress the men. Unless, of course, Evgenya was playing a horribly subtle game.

For almost an hour the sledge twisted and turned among alleys and back-streets. Anna lost her bearings and glimpsed no familiar landmarks out of the windows. She had no idea in which part of the city the blocked street might be.

Evgenya checked the back window again. "Two *troikas*," she said, "six VD in each. Where we stop, the street is narrow. We go out of the *left* door in this order: Stepka, Anna, me, Vadim. Polina last. We must all be out before any of those twelve men make the corner. Our driver will back the sledge so it blocks the street completely. No way to squeeze by – none at all. There's a leather market. Stepka goes first. We go through the market as fast as we can. Outside the back entrance there's an open sleigh. Three seats, so it'll be a crush for five. We're nearly there."

Stepka grabbed the door handle, ready to spring out. The sledge slowed for the difficult corner. With a vicious grind, the runner grazed the wall to the right. The driver shouted, the whip cracked. The sledge staggered a few more yards and stopped. Stepka grabbed Anna's arm and burst out of the sledge like a mad bull. Evgenya followed instantly. The leather market was a long hall of stalls and kiosks. Anna, half dragged, half stumbling, collided with a stall of leather aprons and jackets. She cried out. She felt the Georgian's grip tighten, wrenching her forward. Then a crack, a revolver shot, and the grip loosened. Anna fell to the ground. The Georgian span away, blood spurting from his face. Above her she saw Evgenya, a revolver in her hand, turning now, taking careful aim. Another shot. Market women screamed. A man, it was Vadim, crashed into a pile of skins, bellowing in pain.

"Get up," Evgenya screamed, pulling Anna to her feet. They ran together, Evgenya grasping her wrist, out of the leather market and across the street, up a short, cobbled alley. Someone was following them. A corner. Another street. And then a sleigh. They tumbled into it – it was little more than a basket of bast on runners. The sleigh jerked forward as its runners cracked out

of the ice. Behind them they heard a scream. "Wait!" It was
Polina.

"Wait for her," Anna gasped.

But it was too late. Behind Polina a man ran out of the alley
and into the street. Then another. It was a difficult shot. Anna
covered her ears with her hands and hid her face. Three shots.
Then Anna felt Evgenya sink into the basket beside her. The
sleigh sped away – three good horses with little weight behind
them.

"You killed her," Anna said.

"The VD would have got her otherwise." Anna heard
Evgenya's voice, drained of energy, empty of triumph. "I knew
her, Anna, and she knew me. From years back. I broke her
glasses. She knows who I really am. Like Reinstein knew you.
If the VD got her…"

"She was finished anyway," Anna said. "The VD knew
exactly who to tip off in Moscow."

The two women adjusted to the discomfort of the basket
as best they could, their arms round each other, Anna's
exhausted head cradled on Evgenya's shoulder.

"Who's driving us?" Anna asked as the sleigh hissed into
familiar streets near the Nevsky Prospekt.

"Your husband," Evgenya replied. "Who else?"


## II


Sonya had the morning paper in her hand. She flashed the
headline at Evgenya: '3 Dead in Market Gunfight'. "What the
fuck happened, Gypsy?" she said.

"Let me see." Evgenya snatched the paper and scanned the
story.

"Two unidentified men dead," Sonya said, "and one
unidentified woman. I thought the woman was you." Her
voice was flat.

"Well, aren't you pleased?" Evgenya exclaimed. "At least

you don't have to change your medication."

Sonya was standing at the curtains looking down into the street. No loungers, no parked sledges or sleighs, nobody walking up and down with nothing to do and nowhere to go. Of course she was pleased to see the Gypsy again. But what could she say? Everything she'd struggled for since she was a child was being swept away. Evgenya's gallows humour was no consolation. "Was it Anna?"

"No. It was Polina."

Sonya shook her head. "Polina," she repeated painfully. "You know, we're finished. We really are."

"Finished?" Evgenya questioned. "Why? Vadim and Stepka hardly matter, and Polina – she was lost anyway."

"They've arrested the Ferret," Sonya said with a flash of anger.

"Oh no." Evgenya crushed the newspaper between her hands. "How? That's terrible."

"That fucking Milord, changed the way we get our information. 'We can't afford Maria and a complete safe-house just to talk to the Ferret.'" She mimicked Milord's upper-class lisp.

"He's a mistake," Evgenya said, "we have to get rid of him. He fucked up last night too."

"Tell me," Sonya asked wearily.

"The VD were close behind us, as we knew, but what we didn't know, they were ahead of us as well. When we tried to get through the leather-market, they were waiting for us. Stepka panicked and pulled a gun. Vadim did what he could, covered me and Anna. We made a bolt for it. There was a lot of shooting. More or less what it says in the paper. Somehow I missed our sleigh, so we headed into the alleyways. Polina was behind us. I heard her cry out and some shots. What was she doing there anyway? What was Milord up to?"

Sonya reflected on the story. It meant there was a leak in Milord's organisation, the handful of newcomers who worked for him. And it meant a confrontation with Evgenya.

"If Anna got away, where exactly is she now?" she asked quietly.

"Sonya…"

"Exactly where, Evgenya. I want to know." Sonya heard the raw tone of resignation in her own words – if the girl refused to tell her, what could she do?

"From what I understand," Evgenya said slowly, "Anna told them nothing."

"Possibly," Sonya agreed.

"But it isn't important to Milord whether she talked or not. He…"

"… Wants her head on a platter."

"Why?"

"To show he's as good as the Guardian. Mikhailov had a knack of finding Reinsteins. And Milord wants a Reinstein of his own. He'll want one even more now the Ferret's gone. A success to balance his failure."

"Whether Anna talked or not?"

"Disgusting as that sounds, it's possible."

"Bastard," Evgenya said. "Her hands are ruined, her baby's dead, God knows what they did to her in the Schlusselburg – she won't even talk about it. And he wants his Reinstein! If she'd squealed, we'd have been in jail weeks ago. All of us."

"Evgenya…"

"He's not having her. I'll blow his brains out first."

Sonya said nothing – if Evgenya was threatening to murder Milord, she might well do it. "Does Vitya know?" she asked at length. "Where she is?"

"No."

"This fuck-up last night?" It was a sudden idea, but it explained a great deal. "You didn't set it up with Vitya, did you?"

"Why should you think that?"

"Did you?"

"No."

Sonya looked out of the window again, certain Evgenya

was lying – though really it made no difference any more. "I never understood how it was between the three of you," she said. "You and Anna and Vitya. Sometimes I'm sure you hate her. But sometimes, like now, I wonder if you…" Sonya hesitated. She wanted to say *love*, but the word might sound like an accusation: *you love her but you don't love me*.

"We're cousins, all three of us," Evgenya said. "Leave it at that."

Yes, Sonya thought, leave it at that. "And you'll stay with me? Till He's dead?"

"Him? Romanov? The only man in your life, Sonya?" Evgenya shrugged her shoulders. "Yes, I'll stay. But not in this place. It's not safe anymore."

Sonya watched a nursemaid wheel a baby up the street. Hadn't she seen her once already? "Listen," she said, "you can keep Anna. Tell Milord she's dead. The unidentified corpse in the skirmish. Just stay with me, Evgenya. Please."

"Stay with you?" Evgenya asked.

The nursemaid vanished round the next corner. "You've been pretending, Gypsy. All these weeks," Sonya said shrewdly. "But I haven't…" She glanced at the girl. Evgenya was scanning the newspaper again, hiding her face. There was a long silence.

"You joke about my medication," Sonya continued at last. "Once I think I even explained it to you like that. But…" Her voice dropped to a painful whisper. "… you're more like the blood in my veins." The nursemaid appeared again, strolling in the same direction as before – she'd circled the block. "Come and take a look," Sonya said, "the Nursery Section of the Imperial Chancellery seems to be watching us."

She felt Evgenya's arm round her waist. The two women watched the maid walk on and turn the corner. "She walks like a jailer," Evgenya said.

"Time to clear out," Sonya agreed, putting her own arm round Evgenya.

"You know somewhere? To go?" Evgenya asked.

"I've got a cellar. Only Vera knows about it. My final bolt-hole."

"You want me to go there?" Evgenya's voice was still hesitant.

"Yes. You can trust me, Evgenya."

Evgenya shook her head. "*I* can trust *you*. What's so odd is that *you* trust me."

The two women embraced. Sonya sensed in Evgenya's touch an unfathomable mix of hesitation and yielding. A treaty had been sealed between them, but Sonya was painfully uncertain as to its terms.

Sonya's cellar was in a tenement building near one of Guchkov's huge textile mills. A horse-tram ran from the factory into the city as far as the Nevsky Prospekt. The journey took half an hour. Each evening, Evgenya disappeared for four or five hours. Sonya guessed that she went to see Anna, and that Anna was hiding in the old Grishin apartment on the Kurskaya. Probably Vitya was there too, but warily Sonya asked no questions. For Sonya the hours of waiting were tedious and edgy. Each night she was sure it would happen – the Gypsy would fail her. Then, just as loneliness and longing were about to overwhelm her, the thrill of quick footsteps on the brick stairs and the creak of the unlocked door: Evgenya.

Work on the mine was almost finished. The dynamite was stacked under the road, the tunnel was ready for tamping and the cheese-shop was almost clear of mud and timber. Boards were cut and whitewashed for the cellar wall at the head of the tunnel. Each night they were nailed into position. When it was ready, the cellar would stand a casual inspection – maybe even a search. The Kobozevs had stocked the cheese-shop and it attracted a few customers each day.

Sonya's cheese-shop plan depended on a well-known habit of the Tsar. Every Sunday morning during the winter he reviewed one of his regiments in a huge hall called the Manège. He was often at the Manège during the week, but the times were too erratic to allow a plan of attack. The

Sunday review always ended at one o'clock. Afterward, the Tsar rode back to the Winter Palace, stopping off sometimes to visit one of his imperial brothers and sisters. The route from the Manège to the Winter Palace was not announced in advance, but at least once a month it ran past Number 4 Malaya Sadovaya, where the Kobozevs had their cheese-shop.

Every Sunday the streets in the quarter were thickly patrolled by mounted police and watched by a horde of agents and loungers in plain clothes. The Tsar rode in an armoured carriage, iron-clad and bullet-proof – a detailed description had been published in the *Moskovskie Vedomosti*. The armour meant that the cheese-shop mine had to be huge – Kib reckoned the carriage would fly a hundred feet in the air if they got the timing right. *If.* The timing wasn't easy. They wouldn't know whether the Tsar's carriage was coming down their street until it took a turning about 200 yards from the mine. That meant a first signal. Another signaller would wait at the corner. A third would stand in the Malaya Sadovaya with the mine in full view. That would be Sonya. The carriage went at a stiff gallop. When it was fifty feet from the mine, she'd give a signal to the cheese-shop, and Frolenko would detonate the mine.

Would it work? If the mine went up a second too late it would kill some of the escort, but the carriage would escape. Better too early than too late. An early explosion would stop the carriage – but possibly no more. If the carriage simply came to a standstill, then the bombers would move in. The bombs were ready, stored in Milord's rooms. Evgenya had trained her bombers well in advance, but here events overtook Sonya's planning – one by one the trained bombers disappeared. The new police under the MVD were efficient and menacing. Arrests multiplied. Fearful and despairing, half the bombers deserted the *Narodnaya Volya*. The rest gave up for a different reason. They saw hope in the reforms announced by Loris-Melikov, the new Prime Minister –

democracy and a constitutional monarchy, though the official language was more veiled. Trapped between hope and despair, the bombers, the printers, the messengers and the propagandists melted away. Andrey found new bombers, four raw youngsters hungry for excitement. They were loyal to him but doubtful revolutionaries and hopeless conspirators. They scoffed at Evgenya – they'd take orders from Andrey or nobody. So Andrey was training them to use the grenades, and, with less success, to show a proper revolutionary respect for women.

It was a nervous time. They waited, suspicious of each other, anxious about leaks, and afraid of every stranger they saw twice in the same street.

On the last Sunday in February they met at the cheese-shop early in the morning, took up their positions in the icy streets, and went through the motions of assassination, refining their procedures and watching for signs of new police tactics.

That evening five of them ate supper in a quiet *traktyr* near the Finland Station. Though the table was covered in snacks, they ate without appetite and spoke in little more than whispers. They chose a big table by the window, watching the street, ready to scatter at the first hint of danger. Every twenty minutes a police patrol, two men in uniform with smoothbores slung over their shoulders, trudged past their window or along the sidewalk opposite. Tensely they watched one of the patrols stop a young peasant with a heavy bundle over his shoulder. The boy unhitched his load and dumped it on the icy pavement. Scrap metal: rusty iron and a few strips of copper. The patrolmen kicked among the pieces, looking for anything suspicious.

"Make good shrapnel," Kib said. "They think they can control everything, but they can't."

"Yes they can," Evgenya contradicted him. "They're in control of every street corner, and it makes me wonder – what comes next?"

"Next?" Sonya repeated. "For us, nothing comes next. I told you before – they round us up and hang us." She spoke harshly, as she often spoke to Evgenya in front of the others – everyone had known for weeks that she and the Gypsy had some sort of understanding, but secrecy had become Sonya's second nature. She found a subtle pleasure in hardening her voice and poisoning her look.

"He's in trouble," Vitya said still looking out of the window. "No papers."

"What Evgenya means is this," Kib hissed, ignoring the fate of the peasant. "Why are we so utterly, despicably and hopelessly ill-prepared on the propaganda side? We printed a few dozen pamphlets declaring the revolution has started. But there's no one to give them out. Does anyone even know where they are?"

He looked around the group. He was right – the pamphlets were as good as lost. "It's pathetic. We should have a huge organisation in place, cells everywhere, all waiting for the signal. We should have half the army on our side. We need guns, money, presses – everything."

"And we have nothing," Andrey agreed nervously. "But that's what we always said, ever since Lesna – we'll kill him. Then comes the power vacuum. Others will fill it. Not us." Sonya looked at him anxiously. His voice had become erratic, sometimes overbearingly loud, sometimes inaudible. He was close to the end of his strength, unable to sleep, quarrelsome and often careless. His only resource was brutal hard work – it soothed his mind and calmed his nerves – but the time for hard work was almost over.

"What 'others'?" Kib objected. "Who are you talking about?"

"But we all agree?" Andrey insisted. "When Alexander goes, the tyranny is over? Finished? Right?" He looked round the table.

Sonya hoped that Kib would concede the point – Andrey was close to an outburst.

Kib shook his head. "We give the signal, and the revolution begins? Who gives a damn about signals? The workers? The army? The fucking peasants? Who? This isn't a revolution. It's an assassination. That and nothing else. The Tsar is dead! Long live the Tsar!"

"No," Evgenya broke in, "what I meant was this. Our theory is that revolution automatically follows when we kill him. But what if Kib is right? What comes next could be worse than what we have now. By far."

"But…" Andrey growled.

"Andrey! Let me finish." There was command in Evgenya's voice. Sonya heard it with surprise and glanced at Andrey to see what he'd make of it. "Even if we knew for sure that nothing would come of it," Evgenya continued, "should we still go ahead and… execute him? That's what I wonder."

"Exactly," Andrey agreed throwing his arms in the air. "You hit the nail on the head."

"*Should* we go ahead?" Sonya asked, suddenly unsure. "Who doubts the answer?" Was Andrey backing out? Kib? Evgenya? Was it possible?

"Maybe I can put it another way," Andrey confronted Sonya directly. "Why does *He* always have a capital letter in your mind?"

Andrey had said the same thing before, but he'd never asked her why. What was happening? He'd agreed with her in the past and now he wasn't so sure? She needed words. Urgently. "The Little Father," she began, "that's what the peasants call him. That's enough, isn't it? Just the name?" Sonya seldom made speeches, but she leaned forward now, her knuckles on the table, glaring at the ring of familiar faces. "Little Father. Well, He lives like a father, He thinks like a father, He acts like a father. The Little Father of this whole swamp of despair we live in." She glanced at Evgenya. A theme sprang to mind that they'd wrangled about time and again. "Just take one thing," she said earnestly, "the way women get beaten.[2] Every peasant wife from one end of Russia to the other gets beaten, whipped, thrashed, tormented. Some of them to death. And it's the husband's perfect right – his uncontested legal right – to strip his wife, tie her legs together so she can't run away, and flay the skin off her body with a rope. As often as he wants. Imagine it. Living with a drunken madman and being his slave. Millions of women out there. And the Little Father lets it happen." She felt anger bubbling inside her. The Furies that pursued her were closing in on her brain. "They talk about reform. But not reform of the most barbaric thing anyone can imagine. I can't do much, but if I kill Him, I'll have done something. He could stop the beatings, and a hundred other filthy things, and He does nothing. Like my father. Like all the great and glorious fathers in this fucking Empire. I wish I could put them in one carriage and blow them all to hell." She saw a waiter approaching, craning his neck to catch what she was saying. She felt Evgenya's warning hand on her shoulder, intimate but commanding. For an instant there was pleasure in yielding to Evgenya's control, yet a second later

[2]  It is not easy for the modern reader to comprehend how all-pervasive physical maltreatment of peasant women was in nineteenth-century Russia. This is how Dostoevsky describes it: *'Have you ever seen how a peasant beats his wife? I have. He begins with a rope or a strap. Peasant life is devoid of aesthetic pleasures – music, theatres, magazines; naturally this gap has to be filled somehow. Tying up his wife or thrusting her legs into the opening of a floorboard, our good little peasant would begin, probably, methodically, cold-bloodedly, even sleepily, with measured blows, without listening to her screams and entreaties. Or rather he does listen – and listens with delight: or what pleasure would there be in beating her? The blows rain down faster and faster, harder and harder, countless blows. He begins to get excited and finds it to his taste. The animal cries of his tortured victim go to his head like vodka… Finally she grows quiet; she stops shrieking and only groans, her breath catching violently. And now the blows come even faster and more furiously. Suddenly he throws away the strap; like a madman he grabs a stick or branch, anything, and breaks it on her back with three final terrifying blows. Enough! He stops, sits down at the table, heaves a sigh, and has another drink.'* The translation is from Orlando Figes, *Natasha's Dance*, Chapter 4.

she jerked her shoulder away with unpretended spite.

Vitya had been watching her intently, not smiling, but following her words closely. "Sonya speaks for me," he said gravely. "My own father isn't a bad man. He stops the bailiff flogging our peasants. He gives out grain in hard winters. But he's ruined the estate. No school, no doctor, no proper roofing on the huts, no road. Half our girls finish up in Chernigov before they're thirteen. And like Sonya says, the men beat their wives. Beat them and beat them. My father – he can see what's happening, but he does nothing to stop it. We owe… our families owe an appalling debt to… to… all these people. What's the word we use in our pamphlets? *Bloodsuckers.* Well, it's true. We *are* bloodsuckers. All of us, except you Andrey. And if we destroy the Little Father, even if they catch us and hang us – maybe we'll pay back a bit of what we owe…"

Andrey shook his head. "They'll hang me too," he said, "next to Sonya if I'm lucky. She's…" He grasped for words to express his emotion but found none. "You know what I mean."

"Next Sunday then," Sonya said, calmed by what Vitya had said and by Andrey's strange words. Andrey was the only man she'd ever loved. She loved him still. But she had nothing in her of the mistress. And he – nothing of the lover. They'd tried and failed. But she was desperately sorry for him now – his enormous strength ebbing away, his vitality sapped. "This week, lie as low as we can," she said. "Stay away from the shop unless there's good reason to go there. If we fail with this mine, there won't be another chance. Ever."

## III

Evgenya waited with Vitya while the others left the *traktyr* one by one. Vitya paid the bill and left a good tip for the waiter. In the cold street outside, Evgenya teased him about it. "You're so stupid," she said, "we never go to the same restaurant twice so why leave a tip at all. And if we're trying to spread revolution, why make people happy? You should want him angry enough to cut your throat." She laughed.

"You lived on tips all those months," he said, "and in the end you broke that woman's nose. Tips humiliate people, make them into vicious, revengeful little beasts."

"So you think I'm a vicious, revengeful little beast?"

"Can you deny it?"

She turned away, suddenly serious. "I've done a lot of things I won't do again," she said. "You're right... I'm a piece of shit."

They were walking arm in arm, and she felt his grip tighten round her waist, holding her closer. In her turn she drew him nearer, knowing that he too stood in dire need of comfort.

"I'm worried," he said, with sudden new emphasis.

"About Anna?"

"Yes. She keeps saying she'd be better off dead, so she won't come between us anymore."

"She's had an awful time, Vitya. Be patient with her."

They came to the *droshky* stand outside the Finland Station. Vitya signalled the first *droshky* in the line. The driver climbed down from his box and took the padded blanket off his horse. The horse woke up and shook itself. The frozen leather straps and iron fittings of the harness rattled together. Vitya handed his cousin into the *droshky*, and the driver gave them a blanket full of holes to put over their knees.

The driver cracked his whip, and the horse struggled to break the runners out of the ice. The *droshky* had no bells. "Where to?" the driver croaked.

"Head for Semyonovsky Square."

The *droshky* ran smoothly. Evgenya put her arm round Vitya, partly for warmth and partly because the prospect of the ride in the dull little sledge filled her with unexpected happiness.

"You don't think she'll do anything silly?" Vitya asked.

"No. She's getting stronger, all those walks she's been taking. She won't let herself go now."

"You've helped a lot, you know. Coming to see her every day. Why don't you stay with us? After all, it's your apartment, and nothing will happen now till next Sunday."

"No," Evgenya said. "You stay with her. I should get back for Sonya."

"Sonya," he repeated. "You made a deal with her, didn't you?"

"A while back. She gave us Anna, and I promised…"

"But now?"

"Now it's different. She knows Anna said nothing. It wasn't so obvious at first."

"So why do you keep going back to her? There's no point."

Ever since they'd rescued Anna, Evgenya had been grateful for her nightly excuse: 'I should get back to Sonya.' How could she spend the night in the old apartment with Vitya and still be separated from him? Not that Anna tried to keep them apart – quite the opposite. But it was impossible. Impossible! And Sonya? She simply sat on one of their comfortless wooden chairs reading till Evgenya returned, however late it might be. But really – why did she keep going back? What bound her to Sonya? She hardly knew. In fact she wasn't sure that she even *liked* Sonya. But the way Sonya looked up from her book, the way she sprang to her feet, her hard kisses of welcome, brutal almost… Insistent. Demanding response. And afterward? There was no pattern, nothing that always happened, but often enough Sonya exhausted her, spent her to the point of annihilation, arousing in her a passionate craving for another moment of death in life. And she aroused the same craving in Sonya. It excited her unbearably, the way Sonya's mind, her nerves, her body caved in time after time, astonished by ecstasy. That was what dragged Evgenya home each night to the cellar by the cotton mill – to annihilate and be annihilated. But she could hardly explain this to Vitya. Instead she said simply: "I promised."

"Well, a promise is a promise," he shrugged, not convinced but willing to let the subject drop.

Evgenya pulled the driver's ancient blanket over their legs and nestled against Vitya. He put his arm round her and they fell silent. Even her mind went still. For a moment she had no regrets and no anticipations. The world was reduced to the creaking of the harness, the thud of hooves, the swish of runners on packed ice, and Vitya beside her.

He directed the driver from the Semyonovsky Square to the Borovaya, one street away from Evgenya's old home. They paid off the *droshky* and walked the last few hundred yards. No one was following them, and the house was not being watched. Even so, something was wrong. The apartment was in darkness.

"Carry on walking," Vitya told her, "circle the block. I'll go up. If I light the two candles, you can come up too. If there are no candles in five minutes, go straight back to Sonya. And make sure you aren't tailed."

She began to protest, but he pushed her ahead and started across the street. To make a scene would attract attention, so she walked on. In a pocket sewn into her skirt she was carrying her revolver. She stopped at the street corner. From there she could watch the apartment. If she saw Vitya again in the doorway – Vitya with a police escort – she'd snatch him. She knelt on one knee as though tying her boot. She fumbled under her skirt and unbuttoned the heavy pocket. She stood up again clutching her revolver now inside the breast of her coat. It would be risky, but at least they'd have a chance. She watched the doorway intent as a mother watching a fever-crisis in her baby. Then she saw light in the window where the candles burnt. She walked back down the street. Two candles, one above the other. But the police might easily know that signal. How could she be sure that Vitya had set the candles himself? She crossed the street, hurried past the yardkeeper's door and up the stairs. At the familiar doorway she put her ear to the panel. Silence. She tapped at the door: *Na-rod-na-ya-Vol-ya*. The police probably knew that signal too – after all they had three-quarters of the Movement in jail. She stood back, the revolver cocked, ready to open fire.

The door cracked open. Vitya.

"Police?" she asked, seeing the fear in his eyes.

"No," he said. "She's gone." He had a note in his hand, and he held it out to her.

Evgenya pushed past him into the apartment and closed the door. He gave her the letter.

*My darling Vitya: I have gone. You belong to Evgenya. I love you both so dearly. I'm weak and useless. Something inside me is terribly injured. You have a right to be happy – both of you. How can I inflict myself on you? I can't tell you how much I love you, Vitya. You and our poor little baby who was never born. I shall get stronger but never strong enough to fight beside you again. Think of me kindly, my darling. Remember me when I was the Snowman and we were happy – in our own strange way. The hunting lodge has been made over to you. Kreuzotter agreed you should have it, but nothing else. Everything I do now, is done out of love for you. And for Evgenya. Love each other. Five years from today I will be officially dead, and the two of you can get married. That is my dearest wish. Think of me on your wedding day. Don't try to find me – it will be impossible. Anna.*

"We must find her," Vitya said.

"When did you leave the house this morning?" Evgenya asked.

"Six."

"Fourteen hours ago. Thirty trains a day leave Petersburg. Ships too. She has a whole apartment full of disguises. Near the Haymarket."

"What about papers?"

"She's done a deal with Kreuzotter. He could easily get papers for her." Evgenya tried to keep her voice level and calm.

"Then…"

"Then nothing." Her voice rose to a cry of pain. Anna was gone. They'd loved her, but somehow their love had failed. Anna hadn't understood how precious she was to them. And she was gone. In her pain Evgenya sank to the floor, beating her hands against the boards. "Come back," she sobbed. "Anna, don't leave us."

Vitya was kneeling beside her. She felt the touch of his hand on her shoulder. She looked at his face – it was streaming with tears. He tried to say something, but he was choked with crippling emotion.

They clung together, kneeling in the hallway beneath the gaze of the silent icons. Then they sat for a while at the old dining table, silent, grieving. Finally Vitya said: "Will you go back to Sonya tonight?"

"Yes," Evgenya replied. "Yes. Where else?" She burst into tears again. "Anna – she wanted to bring us together, but somehow she's come between us again."

"No she hasn't," Vitya said very quietly. "Don't think of her like that."

"I love you, Vitya," she said. "Whatever I've become since we sat at this table years ago, it makes no difference. I loved you then, and I love you now."

He was looking at her across the table. She held his gaze, knowing how he must see her now – not with the love of a clever young student for a pretty child. Now he could see her as she was: her weakness, her strength, the evil she'd done that had changed forever the look in her eyes. The look – she'd seen it herself in the mirror and it frightened her. Would he tell her, she wondered, in this moment of grief and deprivation that he loved her? Whatever he said, it would be the solemn truth – just as she'd spoken truth to him.

"I didn't love you then," he said. "I thought I did, but I didn't have the least idea who you were. And now…" He fell silent.

"Yes?" she whispered.

"Now you're a woman. You have blood on your hands, as we'll both have, if this business comes off next Sunday. How can we talk about love – with Anna gone and murder in our hearts? And in a minute you'll go back to Sonya, and share your bed with another woman."

"Yes," she whispered again, "with Sonya."

"And you still want me to say I love you?"

She looked across the table, but the word *yes* wouldn't form.

He waited. "Then… just as you are, Evgenya, yes – I love you."

## IV

Sonya was startled when Evgenya jumped out of bed at the first blast of the factory siren – in half an hour the morning shift would begin. "Where are you going?" she asked, the heaviness of night blurring her voice.

"I've got something to see to," Evgenya replied, already shivering in the icy air. Sonya heard her light the lamp and then crack the cat-ice on the water-bucket. She heard water pouring into the basin on the wash-stand.

Sonya propped herself on her elbows. Evgenya was washing already, though she'd not done her exercises. "What's going on?" Sonya asked.

"I have to go out."

"Where?"

"You really want to know?" Evgenya's teeth chattered as she spoke. She was sponging down her body with the icy water.

"Is it about Anna?"

"Yes. She's gone. We have to find her, or try anyway."

"Vitya?"

"Yes. The two of us."

"Tell me what's happened," Sonya said. "If I can help…"

By the time the second siren sounded – fifteen minutes before the shift began – both women were in the street dressed like the factory girls who had just begun to crawl from their frozen crevices and trudge toward the mill-gate.

Sonya knew the city well. All that day she helped Evgenya find every station and jetty in St Petersburg. They showed the uninterested guards and platform-masters a picture of Anna and asked if they'd seen her the day before. The picture was a clipping from the article by Spyglass – Anna in peasant dress beside one of her harvesters. No one remembered her. Sonya knew two apartments where Anna had friends, but no one had seen her.

At dusk they met Vitya in the Last Man Standing. Sonya saw him bridle with anger as he caught sight of her, but she saw too how quickly Evgenya calmed him: 'Sonya's been a great help – we can't do without her.' They exchanged news. Vitya had spoken to Kreuzotter that morning and to Fanarin that afternoon. Kreuzotter had handed him the deeds of 'a small estate', though Vitya didn't mention where it was. Vitya's allowance would be paid for the last time at the end of April. Kreuzotter had answered all his questions with much the same words: he was not at liberty to disclose confidential information about his client. Since no future communication was necessary, Kreuzotter had bidden Vitya an icy and final good-day. Fanarin had been more helpful. He'd been following the story about the new clinic in the newspapers. Through a banking acquaintance he'd heard that much of the unentailed part of the Shestakov fortune had been liquidated. Naturally Fanarin had *not* asked for details, but these days, he believed, the United States was a popular destination for excess liquidity.

It had been a useful hint. Accordingly, after his talk with Fanarin, Vitya had visited Thomas Cook, the travel agent. If Anna had gone to America, many routes were apparently open to her. Three liners left St Petersburg every Sunday, one bound for Hamburg, one for Bremen, and one for Liverpool. From those great ports, dozens of ships left each week for every part of the United States.

Sonya suggested that she and Evgenya should try again next day with Anna's picture at the big hotels near the harbour. Vitya could visit the offices of the shipping lines and look over the manifests of the three ships that had sailed the day before.

Late the following afternoon the three of them met again in the Last Man Standing. Sonya and Evgenya had learned nothing, and Vitya had not found a single name on the manifests that hinted at Anna. Worse, all the women passengers had been travelling with large parties or at least with a male companion. They ate a cheerless supper and then Sonya excused herself – she wanted to go to the cheese-shop to check that everything was still in order. She'd meet Evgenya at eleven at the tram-stop – they could ride back to the cellar on the same tram. Evgenya suggested they meet at nine; now that Anna was gone, she explained with a hint of shyness, she had no reason to go to the Kurskaya that evening.

Sonya made her way from the tavern to the cheese-shop feeling strangely exuberant. For two days she'd tramped the cold streets looking for traces of someone she had no interest in finding. But only a few moments ago in the scruffy tavern, Evgenya had said they should meet not at eleven but at nine. And now – surely now – Evgenya had *every* reason to go back to the Kurskaya, and to stay there. But apparently not. As she walked, Sonya's footsteps fell into the rhythm of Polonsky's gypsy poem. She even tied a knot in the two ends of her shawl but then untied it again, chiding her own silliness – yes, Evgenya was a nice girl, but for heaven's sake!

From the street the cheese-shop looked exactly as normal, but what she heard in the next few minutes shattered Sonya's mood completely. Anka was on her own and very frightened – she couldn't stop trembling. Milord had sent them a message – he was being tailed and he couldn't shake his tail clean for more than twenty minutes. There must be a hundred people watching him. And worse – Andrey often visited Milord in the evening. Andrey! He had to be warned. Everyone from the cheese-shop was looking for Andrey far and wide – that's why Anka was on her own. If they couldn't warn Andrey, the police might pick him up along with Milord that evening.

Milord! Sonya was blind with fury. Milord in charge of security! He couldn't hold a Kremlin against a herd of syphilitic sheep! Evgenya had said she'd shoot him. She should have gone ahead and done it.

Though her own spirit was in turmoil, Sonya's first task was to calm Anka. Then she'd have to find Andrey. It was Tuesday: five more days to get through somehow or other.

"Annushka," she said quietly. "Don't worry too much about Milord. He exaggerates sometimes, and he's very jumpy at the moment. He won't come here if he knows he's being followed. But you did right to look for Andrey. Good, you've done well. Close up the shop now." She put her arms round the distraught woman, calming and soothing her.

Andrey had planned to work a few hours each day, finishing off the tunnel and the mine. Sonya went into the cellar to see that he'd left everything as it should be. The wall where the tunnel started was completely boarded with whitewashed planks. Andrey had daubed the heads of the nails with fresh whitewash so that the new hammer blows wouldn't show. He was thorough, but even so in the corner of the cellar she spotted muddy work clothes splashed with whitewash. He'd been so careful, yet so destructively careless. Perhaps she should take him in hand for the next few days – on Sunday at the *traktyr* he'd seemed at the end of his rope. She picked up the clothes and wrapped them in newspaper – she'd dump them in a dirty corner somewhere outside.

She found Andrey in a railwayman's tavern behind the Moscow Station. They'd often gone there during the slack months of summer. Sonya was still dressed like a mill-girl. No one glanced at her as she slipped onto the bench where Andrey was eating a solitary supper.

"All alone?" she asked him. "Don't need a girl by any chance?"

"Don't have the fifty kopeks," he replied, "otherwise I might."

She told him about Milord.

"Maybe it's true," he said, "but he's losing his nerve. With the Ferret gone and Countess Anna whisked away from under his nose. You don't know what happened to her, do you?"

"No."

There was a long silence. "Five more days," he said at last.

He took a deep draught of black beer and fell silent. He seemed to be gathering courage. "You wouldn't think…?"

"What wouldn't I think? You want me to move in with you or something?"

"Just till Sunday. I'm going mad. I can't sleep." He looked at her pathetically.

"Oddly," she said. "That's what I was going to suggest." She took a swig of beer from his mug. "Where are you living now?"

"The old place. It's clean – I don't know why you two moved out."

"Mistake maybe. We thought they were watching it."

"Will you come?"

"Just have to tell the Gypsy, that's all."

She met Evgenya at the tram-stop at nine. For a few moments they ignored each other, checking the street and the passers-by. Then Sonya moved closer, close enough to talk.

"Andrey wants me to move in with him again," she said. "I think I have to. He's not in good shape."

"Where?" Evgenya asked.

"The old place."

"It's not safe," Evgenya argued.

"Andrey says it is."

"No problem then."

"See you on Sunday."

"Yes, Sunday."

They waited, listening for the sound of the approaching tram, the iron-shod thunder of the tram-horses. The tram drew up and stopped.

"Bye then," Sonya said.

"Bye."

Evgenya jostled her way onto the crowded tram. A bell rang, the driver smacked the reins against the backs of his horses, and Sonya watched the tram disappear into the green-yellow fog of the February night. Her eyes began to itch in the cold air, and she rubbed her coat-sleeve across them. She was not crying – she was definitely not crying.

Three days later, on Friday afternoon, Andrey announced that it was all nonsense about Milord. More than once he'd tracked Milord through the streets – no one was following him. No one at all. Sonya was unconvinced. Even so, when Andrey said he was going to visit Milord – they had a lot to discuss – she raised no objection. She went with him in a cab, dropping him off at the public library in the Bolshaya Sadovaya at about six o'clock. When he didn't come home, she went to bed assuming he'd spend the night with Milord.

At ten the next morning, Saturday, he still hadn't returned. She stood by the window looking down into the familiar street. If the police were watching the apartment, they were making an unusually subtle job of it. Then a naval uniform and a familiar figure – Nikolai Sukhanov. In a hurry. It could only be bad news. She ran to the door of the apartment and opened it, hearing Sukhanov's footsteps climb the stairs two at a time. She whisked him into the apartment and closed the door behind him.

"It's Andrey, isn't it?" Her voice was gone. The words scarcely formed.

"Last night. At seven. Andrey and Milord. Both."

He poured out the story. The police were waiting in ambush in an empty apartment next to Milord's. Andrey had tried to escape. He'd pulled a gun, but the police had been too many and too quick for him.

"What now?" Sonya asked, her head reeling, her breathing tight and painful.

"Vera's called a meeting. In her apartment. At three."

"Vera? Called a meeting?"

"I looked for you. I didn't know you'd moved back here, so I went to her."

"You looked for me out at Guchkov's mill?"

"Yes, she told me it was a secret."

"Was a girl there? The Gypsy? Evgenya."

"Yes."

"You told her about the meeting."

"Yes."

"And the Coalminer?"

"No one knows where he is."

Sonya told him the address on the Kurskaya and he hurried away.

Sonya stood for a moment, waiting for her head to clear. Andrey! She glanced round the apartment – chaotic, disorganised as the man himself. She'd better prepare for the worst. When she'd left with Evgenya, they'd purged the apartment completely. But meanwhile Andrey had hidden a code-book and some letters under the floorboards. Suspicious tools were lying about too and some labels from the cheese-shop. She retrieved the papers and burnt them. She'd attend to the tools later. She locked the door and hurried away to Vera's. What had happened? Where were they holding Andrey? How could they find him? They'd sprung Anna from the warehouse, and now they had to spring Andrey. *Had to*. It was even more important than the mine next morning. It was the only thing that mattered.

At Vera's apartment, two more blows struck home. "Have you heard?" Vera hissed as she opened the door. "The cheese-shop's been raided. And we've lost the bombs."

Vera's apartment was already crowded. From the hubbub Sonya put together the stories. That morning General Mrovinski of the Corps of Engineers had inspected the cheese-shop 'for sanitary reasons.' The General had asked about the boarded up wall, about the large heap of coke, about the unusual quantity of straw. His police escort had formed up in the street ready to tear the place apart. Luckily Anka's cat had rubbed itself against the General's polished boots, and Anka had entertained the General with the cat's life history. And that was all – the General had bowed politely and left. Obviously there had been rumours about the shop, but just as obviously, the MVD was still in the dark.

With the mine still intact, the lost bombs had to be replaced immediately. They were hidden in Milord's apartment, well hidden apparently. After his arrest, the police had searched the whole building and found nothing. The building was sealed now – undoubtedly it would be searched again.

"So," Sonya announced. No one could have heard Sonya's thin voice over the urgent and noisy conversations, but the room fell suddenly silent. "Kib, Sukhanov, Vitya, Evgenya – four bombs by the morning. Can you?"

"Yes," Kib said.

"Dynamite? Detonators?"

"Plenty of dynamite. Only four detonators," Kib reported.

"Why only four?" Sonya asked, the chill of authority steadying her voice.

"The rest are hidden at Milord's. On his orders."

Sonya bit back the insult that sprung to her lips.

"If you want four bombs, we only need four detonators," Kib said with a shrug.

"Isaev," Sonya snapped, ignoring what Kib had said, "go to the cheese-shop now and arm the mine. Will you need help?"

"Evgenya," he said simply.

Sonya nodded agreement. "Everyone else back home," she said. "Burn everything. If tomorrow fails, it's the end. The round-up will begin – and the fewer papers they find, the better our chance of surviving. Specially legals like Evgenya and Vitya. But…" She knew how sorely they needed encouragement. "But why should we fail?" she said quietly. "We have the mine. We have the bombers. I'll take over Andrey's job. The hard part is over. A battery, two wires touching, and He's dead." It wasn't much, but it was the best she could do.

Next morning only two grenades were ready: slender and discus-shaped with neatly soldered seams. Two more had been improvised out of kerosene cans wrapped in newspaper. Time had run out.

Between ten o'clock and eleven, Sonya walked the street with each of Andrey's new bombers, showing them one by one where to stand and pointing out the cheese-shop. None of them had heard about the mine before. She told Vitya to scout the streets for any sign that the police knew their plans. She wasn't sure how long Andrey and Milord would hold out under interrogation: Andrey was physically shattered and for Milord she had nothing but contempt. At eleven-thirty they gathered in the arcade of the Gostinny Dvor, in a corner where two walls met. They were well hidden among the Sunday crowd: seven people, meeting by chance, exchanging gossip, nothing unusual.

Sonya now explained the mine in detail to the new bombers. "The explosion will be huge," she said in her weak, broken voice. "It's the signal. The coach won't get more than a few yards. There may be a crater in the road, and the coach may be in it. There's a good chance He'll be dead already. You start to move in, slowly. Keep about ten yards apart from each other. Kotik first, then Timofey, Emilianov, Rysakov. I'll be opposite the coach. I'll make Kotik a sign; if I know He's dead, I'll shake my head and you all disappear. If I nod, Kotik goes in, and then you all go in, one after the next, till it's over."

"If anyone's too scared, say now," Evgenya broke in. She looked round the group. "Kotik?"

Kotik was the weak link – they all knew that. He was short and skinny with black curly hair. Sonya had silently christened him the Ballerina. She saw his face crumple with shame and his mouth open ready to say the disgraceful words: *Yes Evgenya, do it for me.*

"Kotik?" Evgenya repeated.

Sonya shuddered. Unless the mine did its job better than Kib expected, Kotik's next words would be Evgenya's death sentence – if the bomb didn't kill her, the escort would hack her to death on the spot. Or if they took her prisoner – that would be worse even.

Kotik nodded, trembling.

"Come with me then," Evgenya said coldly. "I'll take care of your package."

"Go. All of you," Sonya said, biting back the words that might have saved Evgenya. With the Gypsy as first bomber, His last hour had struck.

Three of the men scuttled off. Kotik turned away and hid his face against the wall. Evgenya and Vitya stood motionless, staring at each other like bewildered children.

"Go," Sonya repeated. They ignored her.

Then quickly Evgenya took both of Vitya's hands in hers and kissed him on the lips. "Goodbye Vitya," she said, turned her back on him and walked away.

## V

Evgenya left the Gostinny Dvor and joined the Sunday crowd loitering along the Prospekt. Without looking round, she knew that Kotik was following her. She turned right toward the Moscow Station. There was a maze of alleyways nearby where Kotik could pass on his package. A few yards down the Prospekt, she felt a hand grip her elbow. For a second she pulled away in panic, but it was only Kotik.

"Evgenya," he said. "I'll do it. You… I lost…"

"You're new to this," she said evenly. "I used to get scared too. Nothing to be ashamed of."

"I'm sorry," he said.

She shrugged. "What for? Now go back to Sonya and tell her what you've decided. And tell her – I'll go back to my original job."

"You'll do your original job," Kotik repeated and disappeared back toward the Gostinny Dvor.

The original plan was for Evgenya to mingle with the crowd outside the Manège. As soon as the Tsar arrived, she was to report to Sonya. If the parade was cancelled or if the Tsar arrived on horseback, they'd have to vanish immediately. If a miracle happened and the cheese-shop survived another week, they could try again the next Sunday.

The Archduke Michael's Manège was a covered riding school big enough to exercise a regiment. Outside the high, closed gates, a line of soldiers was drawn up, standing at ease but perfectly motionless. Sappers, Evgenya recognised – the uniforms of the household regiments were in the Guardian's handbook. She joined the small crowd that had gathered on the other side of the street, waiting to cheer the Tsar. The neighbourhood clocks struck a quarter to twelve. A moment later the crowd began to murmur. Evgenya heard the unmistakable clatter of cavalry approaching. Cossacks. The sergeant of the guard called his men to attention, and the crowd burst into cheers as the Tsar appeared – a black coach with a hand waving at the closed window. It was Evgenya's first glimpse of the Tsar: a man's face, bearded, not particularly imposing. At once the whole thing seemed impossibly easy.

Sonya was waiting for her now on the Fontanka Bridge. She hurried away with her news. As she approached the bridge, she saw Sonya lounging with Vitya against the balustrade – a Sunday couple like so many, with nowhere to go.

A barefoot girl dressed in rags was selling snowdrops on the bridge. Evgenya bought a bunch, gave the girl two kopeks, and then stood at the balustrade a few feet from Sonya. Carefully she began to pick the head off each flower and drop it onto the ice below. "He arrived," Evgenya said quietly. "In the carriage."

"Good," Sonya replied. Then she repeated the word with a passionate gasp of relief: "Good." What Evgenya heard was: 'You're safe, my Gypsy. I was ready to sacrifice you and I still am, but it was taken out of my hands. I love you.' Then Sonya's familiar level tones: "You know what to do now."

"Yes." Evgenya had picked her flowers to pieces. She threw the stems onto the ice.

Evgenya, it was planned, would go back to the Manège. If the Tsar was going to drive over the mine, he'd turn right out of the Manège as soon as the parade was over. If he turned left, his route would be along the Catherine Canal, and their prey would have slipped through their fingers, probably forever. Evgenya simply had to watch for the left turn that would cancel everything and report it back to Sonya.

Well before the parade ended, Evgenya was back at the Manège. Three of the Tsar's guard had formed up outside the gateway on tough Cossack horses. Mounted police ambled on the icy cobbles. The crowd was thicker now and gathered on both sides of the street. Evgenya pushed along the wall of the Manège almost to the gateway. Her way was blocked at last by a burly, well-fed man, dressed in a shabby overcoat and a broken hat – VD for sure. A few moments later, the huge wooden doors of the Manège rattled as the bolts shot back. One door opened a crack, letting the sounds of the parade spill into the street: shouted commands, stamping feet, and then, at last, the cry repeated three times over: "Long live the Tsar."

The doors opened wide. The mounted police took their positions on either side of the street. As soon as they knew which route the Tsar would take, they'd go ahead, stopping the traffic, clearing the street. The three Cossacks turned their horses and trotted back into the building – almost for sure the little procession would form up inside, then spill out to the street at a trot as Evgenya knew from the parades she'd watched earlier. As the Cossacks disappeared, the crowd swirled quickly in front of the open gates, blocking the way. Evgenya held firm, her back against the wall. The man in the shabby overcoat eyed the crowd professionally. Two sections of infantrymen with fixed bayonets emerged from the Manège at the double, forcing the crowd back. Shouts rang from inside the building, and the thud of hooves on sawdust. In seconds now Evgenya would know – left to the palace or right to the mine.

The first of the escort emerged, wheeling right. The Cossack on the leading horse waved his whip to the mounted police – go right. The Tsar's black coach trundled onto the filthy ice. A cheer from the crowd. Then, suddenly, the coachman heaved on the reins, the brakeman wrenched at the brake lever, and the coach slithered to a stop. The escort pulled up instantly and took positions round the coach. An adjutant in the uniform of the Sappers jumped from his sledge and ran to the Tsar's window. The window dropped. The Tsar was twenty paces from where Evgenya was standing. Her gun was in her pocket. A quick draw, a second to take aim – it was all she needed. But she had no right to act alone – a mistake would destroy all their plans. It was one of Sonya's constant themes – discipline, not heroics.

"A dangerous place to stop, Your Imperial Highness." A parade ground voice.

"… change of plan…" Evgenya heard. "… the Archduke's Palace. Half an hour…" The Tsar: querulous, human, vulnerable.

"Yes, Your Imperial Highness." The officer saluted and ran back to his sledge shouting orders. The window closed. The procession turned left.

The crowd dispersed. Evgenya moved quickly through the streets. She'd tell Sonya, and they'd call it off. Somehow they'd survive another week.

As she neared the cheese-shop, she glimpsed Vitya ahead in the crowd. He'd seen her too. He dawdled until she was a few paces away, then turned casually and walked for a few seconds behind her.

"He went left," she said. "Go back to the Kurskaya."

"Evgenya…"

"I'll be there in an hour," she said, "I can't stand it on my own anymore."

She met Sonya opposite the cheese-shop. "He went left," she repeated.

"Then it's finished," Sonya said with a little cry.

"Sonya!"

"Go," Sonya gasped, "go with Vitya, to Chernigov. We're dead here."

"Are we?" She put her arm round Sonya's waist, leading her away from the cheese-shop and toward the waiting bombers. "Surely there's *something* we can do."

"Improvise? After all these months of planning?" Sonya whispered. They drew level with Kotik.

"Follow at a distance," Evgenya said to him.

"It's useless," Sonya said in a frozen whimper.

"Listen," Evgenya urged her, remembering, imagining. "I heard where he's going – to the Archduke's Palace. After that he'll go back along the Catherine Canal. He has to."

"Maybe he will – but…" Sonya agreed.

"No buts – it's our last chance. We don't have another week. Today or never. Think now. We could spread out along the embankment. The first one throws a grenade under the carriage. That stops it. After that it's like we planned with the mine. The next one goes in and so on. You'll be there. I'll be there. We've got revolvers."

"But a grenade isn't enough," Sonya objected, but suddenly alert. "A grenade won't stop a carriage."

They passed Timofey and Evgenya told him to follow.

"Grenades are all we've got," she said to Sonya.

Sonya looked at her gravely. "It's suicide with so many police about. For nothing."

"You think there's no chance at all?"

They ignored Emilianov as they passed him, but he saw he had to follow.

"There's a chance," Sonya said. "There's always a chance."

"Then why are we waiting? A last chance – a small chance. What else do you want?"

"Evgenya," Sonya gasped, "thank God I've still got you."

Rysakov saw them coming and turned with the others to follow. Sonya led them to a deserted place – a boarded up fountain in a little garden next to the Foundling Hospital. There she explained the new plan to them. The bombers would be stationed along the Catherine Embankment fifty yards apart. Evgenya was to stand on the steps of the Book

Society. She knew the place. She'd sometimes borrowed books there for her mother. If she stood by the big notice board, she could keep watch on the whole embankment. If all else failed, a pistol shot might still be enough.

Evgenya found her place. It was Sunday and the Book Society was closed. A clock struck the quarter. On the notice board outside the library was a blurred picture of a woman's face with the words 'Sofya Luovna Perovskaya' and 'Wanted' in bold letters. She scanned the other notices: opening times, the address of the nearest hospital, a proclamation about the prevention of cholera, and a small, badly printed flyer for a piano recital: Balakirev, Cui, Mussorgsky. The pianist was Oleg Kryukov. There was no picture of him – just the name. A name from the other side of the great divide in her life, half-forgotten, meaningless.

Hoof-beats on the ice. Mounted policemen clearing the street ahead of the Tsar. Horses, sledges, handcarts – everything pulled into the kerb and stopped.

Evgenya stared at Oleg's name on the poster again. Her right hand began to tremble, out of control. The street fell silent with expectation. She forced her trembling hand into her pocket. The feel of the gun calmed her nerves. She looked along the embankment – everyone was in place.

More hoof-beats. The first of the Cossacks turned the distant corner, trotting. Slower than she'd expected. More Cossacks. She saw the black coach again, more than 200 yards away, coming toward her. Timofey was at the corner. Nothing. Silence. Failure. Rysakov was next.

The explosion, when it came, was far away and hopelessly feeble, but the street was instantly in uproar. One of the Tsar's coach-horses reared. As its hooves hit the ground again, it bolted, panicking the others. The coachman stood up on his box, whipping the horses forward. The coach was down at one corner. One wheel was smashed – nothing more. A few more seconds and the Tsar would be off the embankment and in safety.

Evgenya screamed. For a second she was down again,

naked, half-dead and grovelling on the canvas. The Arab girl with her broken nose and her tattooes was swaggering away certain of victory but all the while exposing her back to a deadly head-butt. Evgenya's fingers tightened on the gun in her pocket. If she shot the leading horse, maybe... Then, suddenly, she saw the coachman crash back on his bench, dragging at the reins with all his strength. The horses slipped and struggled on the ice. The wheels locked. The coach slithered to a stop seventy yards from where Evgenya was standing. The escort, taken by surprise, overshot the coach. For a moment, the Tsar was sitting unguarded in the middle of the street. Then the door of the coach swung open. A colonel of the guard, his hand on the hilt of his sword, stepped on to the ice. He turned and held out his hand. The Tsar was leaving the coach.

"Kotik," Evgenya said softly to herself. "Now!" She started to run down the street, toward the coach. In the confusion she could get within inches of the Tsar and shoot him point-blank.

The Cossacks were galloping back now, stampeding their way through the mob. They reached the coach, its door open, the Tsar gone. The commander shouted an order, and the horsemen formed up, senselessly protecting the empty, black vehicle. Meanwhile the Tsar was striding rapidly away, back to where Rysakov's bomb had exploded.

Evgenya fought her way through the crowd, some struggling to escape, some to follow the Tsar.

The Tsar stopped. Evgenya couldn't see him, but the place was marked by the white plume of the colonel's helmet. There were no houses on this stretch of the embankment, only the low wall of the Archduke's garden with a fence running along the top. Evgenya pushed her way to the wall and climbed onto it – from there she could see everything. Rysakov was a prisoner. Two men in plain clothes held him with his arms twisted behind his back. The Tsar was talking to the three of them. The crowd blocked the street completely.

Then the Tsar moved again. If he went back to the coach,

Evgenya would be just a few inches from him. She saw the Colonel's plume turn anxiously in every direction. They weren't going back to the coach but further up the embankment. "Somebody. One of you!" Evgenya cried aloud, jumping down from the wall. Punching and pushing, she forced her way nearer the Tsar.

The blast of Kotik's bomb, even though she'd expected it, was shattering: a short, sharp thunderclap of dynamite. The crowd reeled back, screaming, turning, fleeing. Evgenya pressed herself back against the fence, letting the mob spill past her. A few seconds and she was free. Twenty yards away, the Tsar was lying on the ice, his legs blown to shreds. And there were other bodies. Kotik writhing on the ground and screeching. Children. A woman staggering toward her, clasping with one bloody hand a shattered stump where her arm had been. Evgenya's hand went to her pocket. Her finger checked that the safety catch of her revolver was on.

It was finished.

# VI

Evgenya was already in the Semyonovsky Square at four in the morning. It was 3rd April, 1881, a month after the assassination. A dozen men were working by lamplight, finishing work on the scaffold. Around the square, spectators were gathered already, waiting for the hanging. Sonya had been caught along with Kibalchich and a dozen others. At first Evgenya followed the story in the newspapers each day – the mourning for the dead Tsar, the uncompromising proclamations of Alexander III, his son. She read the reports of the trial but fleetingly: Andrey's rhetoric, Rysakov's sobbing repentance, Sonya's quiet dignity.

As dawn broke she saw the huge cross-beam of the gallows with six ropes hanging from hooks. On one of them Sonya would strangle to death before ten o'clock that morning. She turned away, sick with a fever that hadn't left her for many days.

She crossed the square slowly, her legs weak and aching, close to collapse.

She saw a man, standing alone, staring at the scaffold. His back was to her, but she knew instantly who he was – Vitya. For two weeks they'd stayed together in the old apartment on the Kurskaya. Together but impossibly apart. Anna, Sonya, her dead mother, her vanished father, the icons in the hallway, and one ghostly memory after the other heaped themselves into a barrier they could not cross. Love? Yes, there was love. And because she loved him, she'd moved back to the cellar near the cotton mill, feverish and despairing. He'd told her he'd go back to Chernigov. She'd said she'd join him there when she was ready. When and if. She'd made no promises.

Vitya hadn't seen her. She didn't stop but walked past him. Ten steps, twenty steps. Then she turned, irresolute. "Vitya," she said so quietly she could hardly hear the word herself. At that moment he turned and looked in her direction, shaking his head, distraught and puzzled. Then he recognised her.

"They're going to hang Sonya," she said quietly.

He couldn't hear her. She held her arms out to him. He hesitated, looked back for a second at the gallows, and ran to her.

Together they left the square.

# Extract 13

I was arrested together with Nikolai Kibalchich on 14th March, two weeks after the execution of Alexander II. Kibalchich was identified; I was not. For this reason, he was tried along with Andrey Zhelyabov, Sofya Perovskaya and the others, and he was hanged with them. My trial came later. I was sentenced to imprisonment and served my term in the Schlusselburg, twenty-five years all but a few months. Twenty-five years is a long time, most of it spent in solitary reflection.

Since my release, there has been another attempt at revolution, the ill-fated days of 1905. That revolution failed, but not for the reasons we failed. Ours was a revolution based on the idealism of youth and on boundless energy. We had no programme beyond: 'Level the ground, and others will come and raise the building.' We believed that the destruction of Alexander II would level the ground at one blow. It did not. His son, Alexander III, led a regime more repressive than anything his father could have imagined. The police were no longer instruments of the regime but its masters.

Outside Russia, the death of one despot encouraged other despots, great and small, to look to their own safety. And others in harsh straits, as we were, turned to terror to gain a political end – in Ireland, in Germany, even in America. Six months after the execution of Tsar Alexander, James Garfield, President of the United States, was assassinated. I don't know the circumstances of that assassination, but almost the last act of the People's Will was to denounce political murder in a country such as the United States. I have the pamphlet, given me by a friend of the old days: 'The free will of the nation decides not only its laws but who should rule… Violence can be used only in answer to violence.' So they wrote in 1881. Perhaps the situation in America is not as we imagine it, but the danger is apparent. Terror has an attraction for the young and the unemancipated of any age. Its logic appears irrefutable; action always seems superior to argument, deeds to words. But it is not so. If the People's Will led others to follow its example in circumstances less desperate, then the People's Will did evil.

As to the Movement itself, it was destroyed, not so much by the arrests and the hangings that annihilated our leaders, but far more by the inadequacy of our ideals. We saw, everyone saw, that a passionate will to do right cannot survive the need to act. Action demands choices, choices from a handful of alternatives none of which, perhaps, is right in itself. And in the end, when endless compromise has hedged us about with evil, there *is* no right, only variations of wrong, one of which we are forced to choose…

I loved and admired many of those who died for the cause in 1881. As far as I know, only one of the original group survived: Vera Figner. Unfortunately she was no organiser and no judge of character; it was not in her to revive the Movement. Flawed people – they were all deeply flawed. But who is free of such flaws? In a sane and fair world, they might have achieved good things in their different ways, and their weaknesses would have passed uncommented. But none of them died cursing, none of them died as I have seen men and women meet their end, tormented and insane in the Schlusselburg. I have heard how Sofya Perovskaya died on the public scaffold, with dignity and at peace with herself. After all that has happened, I can only wish myself such a death.[3] (*Memoir of the People's Will*, Chapter 18.)

---

[3]   Mikhail Fedorovich Frolenko, if he is indeed the author of this memoir, died during the Second World War at the age of ninety-four. Under pressure from Stalin he joined the Communist Party in 1936 at the age of eighty-eight.